Every Good and Perfect Gift

Every Good and Perfect Gift

BRENDA JERNIGAN

Harmony Books
New York

Published by Harmony Books, New York, New York.
Member of the Crown Publishing Group.

Random House, Inc. New York, Toronto, London, Sydney, Auckland
www.randomhouse.com

Printed in the United States of America

Design by Lynne Amft

Library of Congress Cataloging-in-Publication Data
Jernigan, Brenda.
Every good and perfect gift : a novel / by Brenda Jernigan.
1. Women mystics—Fiction. 2. Women healers—Fiction.
3. Southern States—Fiction. I. Title.
PS3560.E69 E84 2001
813'.54—dc21 00-054134

ISBN 0-609-60790-1

10 9 8 7 6 5 4 3 2 1
First Edition

For my mother and my father,

Jean Hawley Jernigan

and

Raymond Elbert Jernigan

Grace and love defined.

ACKNOWLEDGMENTS

Montaigne said, "It is not the arrival, but the journey that matters." My journey with this book owes much to many people.

To people who gave me the opportunity to work and write: Stephanie Fanjul, Dean Debnam, Jim Tompkins, Jerry Smith, and John Spain. I thank you for your flexibility.

To people who worked with me and sometimes around me and always encouraged: John Fanella, Tonya Loggains, Latrelle Dechene, Jana Fransen, and Brian Geis. I thank you for your dedication.

To people who read and helped me grow as a writer: Schelli Barbaro Whitehouse, Bonny Harrison, Marlyn Brock, Jeri Board, Bill Stroupe, and Melanie Gundrum. I thank you for your insight.

To people whose friendship sustained and cajoled: Leigh Ann Biddix, Kami Spangenberg, Nancy Foushee, Teri Holbrook, and Rosie Bowers. I thank you for being there always.

For telling me their stories, I thank Louetta Pascal Morris, a preacher and so much more; Noah and Westa Barefoot; and Lola Hardison Jernigan, my grandmother. I thank you for your inspiration.

A special thanks for listening to me, giving good advice, and allowing me the space to whine to Lee Smith. I thank you for keeping me straight.

For getting me back to the book: Craig Lesley, the Rupert Hughes Writing Award, and the Maui Writer's conference—mahalo. I thank you for your encouragement.

Thanks to my family: Raymond, Jean, Becky, Doug, Cynthia, Nathan, and Jacob Jernigan, and Michael and Amanda Hardee.

And thanks especially to my two children, Benjamin and Katherine Chesson, who are amazing always. I thank you for your love.

To my editor, Shaye Areheart, who is so special and worked so hard for this book, thank you for your spirit and your eye. Thank you to Vivian Fong, Shaye's assistant, for invaluable help through the process and the incredible professionals at Harmony who made publishing a joy.

To my agent, Mary Ann Naples, for being a steady hand, a dedicated professional, and a friend. Thank you for believing in me.

"We are put on earth for a little space

that we may learn to bear the beams of love."

—WILLIAM BLAKE

Every Good
and
Perfect Gift

CHAPTER

1

As I sat in Sunday school with my crinoline pricking my skin like a holly bush, God revealed Herself to me as a woman. I was ten. The combination of the hard wooden chair, the crinoline about to draw blood, and Mr. Paul Lovingood telling the story of Jonah and the whale for at least the fortieth time in my years of church attendance caused my eyes to stray from the picture placed before us: Jonah in the cavernous belly of a whale.

I looked around the ring of Sunday-school faithful, wondering if Granny would allow me to sit with Annie Hudson during service later. Mr. Lovingood shook his head to emphasize a point of particular wickedness, and I thought how much the shape of his head reminded me of a cantaloupe. Off to the side, a circle of light drew my attention. Coming in through the window, the light looked like it was so thick you could touch it, sunbeams that had weight. Beyond the window lay fields of tobacco yellowing in the sun and the farmhouse, still and white, where my mama and my granny and I lived.

In the light hovering by the window was a woman. She was dressed like Mary in the Christmas program, only the top piece of her outfit that covered her dark hair, the one that we made out of a linen dresser cloth for our Mary, that top piece shone with every color of the rainbow and yet it was white. I cannot say how I knew She was God.

She spoke. "Feed my sheep."

The light became brighter and brighter until I thought She would surely burn up in its intensity. Love poured up around me and in me like the milk going down my throat when it came warm from the cow. The light encircled me, thick and heavy as the pile of quilts I used for cover in the front bedroom. Under those quilts, I imagined myself back in my mama's womb. The sounds of the house were muffled in that hollow warm spot I carved out in the bed.

That's how the light made me feel.

I suppose I said, "Pardon?" then because all my classmates said Mr. Lovingood repeated something to me about the evils of Nineveh right before I slid away.

Next I remember, Mr. Paul Lovingood was bent over me, wiping the sweat rolling under his chin with his handkerchief, his good Sunday one that had his initials on it, and yelling my name.

"Maggie. Maggie. Can you hear me, Maggie?"

Right over his shoulder I saw the faces of my fellow Sunday-school pilgrims wearing a mixture of concern for my limp body and relief at having been rescued from hearing about Jonah one more time. Will Atkinson predicted there would be a run on fainting now that it was known that a faint was capable of grinding the forward progress of a Sunday-school lesson to a halt.

As sure as the cool concrete beneath my head, I knew the woman of the light was God.

"Mr. Lovingood, I saw Her. I saw God. He's a woman."

Mr. Lovingood wiped a stray drop of sweat. "Will, run fetch Miss Naomi. Maggie's hit her head and got a concussion."

The other faces behind his shoulder drew back. Afraid, I suppose, of catching it from me. Mr. Lovingood held up two fingers. "How many fingers am I holding up, Maggie?"

"Two. She talked to me, you know, standing right off the left side of your head."

A high-pitched giggle, the same kind Miss Sally Owens made

every time an eligible bachelor was within three feet of her, came from behind Mr. Lovingood's shoulder. I was sure it had to be one of the Matthews twins; Granny called them a couple of Mexican jumping beans. Mr. Lovingood turned his head; the spot with no hair shined at me. The giggle stopped and feet shuffled.

"Maggie needs air. You children, go to the sanctuary and sit quietly. I'll be there shortly."

I pushed down the light blue skirt of my flounced dress and started to sit up. "I feel fine. Better than ever. I'm sure God talking to me direct and everything is what caused the blood to leave my head."

Mr. Lovingood shrieked, "Lie down! You mustn't move until Miss Naomi has a chance to look at you." As Granny would say, he was terrible worked up now, and the sweat rolled off his face so fast, his handkerchief was hard pressed to keep up with it. I put my head back down. He turned to the group behind him. "Be of some use, James Williams; go find something to put under her head. I thought I told you children to go to the sanctuary." Out of the corner of my eye, I saw black patent-leather shoes capped with anklets and neatly pressed pants' legs shuffle into one line and move for the door. And still Mr. Lovingood watched me as if I might sprout two heads. I almost wished I could at that moment, only so as to see the look on his face. Granny would say that's the Lily in me coming out. Make no mistake, whenever there was a devilish thought in me, they all attributed it to my mama, who I sometimes thought must have come out of the Cape Fear River fully formed, like one of those ancient pagan goddesses. That she was my granny's flesh and blood was as strange to me as if Abraham and Isaac, the two yard dogs my granny kept, were to take wing and start flying.

Maybe that's what started me thinking about God. If the devil could be a woman, then surely God could be the same. I suppose I'd been thinking on that for a time in the way you do some things. Ideas buzz around your head and never stay still long enough to really take form, and then something happens and they sting you. My crinoline that day was the idea of God being a woman stinging me.

"Lord have mercy, what have you done now?" Granny's voice preceded her black oxfords into the room. The ankles atop the black oxfords were thick and sturdy. A lot of women around Canaan had ankles like young dogwood trees; Granny had ankles like stately oaks.

Mr. Lovingood stood up. "Miss Naomi, I think she got too hot and fainted away. Must have hit her head on the floor; she seems confused."

Her head appeared above me, the hair pulled straight back from her face and gathered at her neck in a bun. At night when she brushed and plaited her hair, it fell past her waist in a wave of black with streaks of gray that grew wider every year. "Maggie, do you know who I am?"

"Yes, Granny."

"Do you know where you are?"

"In the Canaan Free Will Church, Canaan, North Carolina."

Granny eyed Mr. Lovingood suspiciously. "She seems all right to me, but I'll take her on home and let Lily watch her whilst I come back for service."

Mr. Lovingood coughed and jerked his head in the direction of the door. Granny didn't get the hint or chose to ignore it.

From down below, I could half see and the rest guess that Granny looked down her nose at him, a habit usually reserved for Mama, farmhands, and occasionally me when I strayed from the straight and narrow. I worked hard not to be a recipient of that gaze; it was most always followed by a weeping-willow switch on my behind. Granny felt that she and Granddaddy Eli had been too easy on Mama, which resulted in her lack of character, and if I was going to have anything in this world, I was surely going to have character.

"Granny—"

"Hush, child, I'm talking with Mr. Lovingood."

"Granny, I saw God."

Mr. Lovingood mumbled something into his handkerchief. Granny knelt beside me and started feeling my head for knots. Over her shoulder, I could see Will Atkinson by the door. He was standing back so Granny and Mr. Lovingood couldn't see him.

"Granny, God is a woman."

Her grip on my head loosened. "Nonsense. I might expect that of some heathen child, but not from a young woman who has seven perfect attendance pins on her dress."

Convinced I had suffered no head injuries, Granny stood and looked Mr. Lovingood in the eye. "Ten-year-old foolishness."

I felt the name Lily pass between them. And I got angry. My mama was not exactly like I would have asked God to make her, but there were plenty worse and Granny and Mr. Lovingood knew it.

Mr. Lovingood began to gather up his Bible and lesson materials. "Well, Miss Naomi, I'll be getting on to the sanctuary to find my class."

I jumped up from my concrete sickbed and stomped my foot.

"I did see Her. She was over Mr. Lovingood's left shoulder and She talked to me the same as I'm talking to you."

Granny looked down her nose at me. "I've got a weeping-willow switch that will talk to you after service if you don't hold your tongue."

My mouth opened, but instead of my voice there was a cry of pain. We looked around us for the source of the noise. Will Atkinson had closed the door on his finger trying to move out of the way before Mr. Lovingood found him out of place. By the time we got to him, the finger was slightly swelled and bent. Granny examined the finger the way she had my head. She turned it this way and that, which caused Will's face to turn red, connecting his many small freckles into one big one.

The feeling of warmth that had flooded through me earlier returned. With it came a voice as clear as my granny's: "Take the hand and pray for it."

I looked behind me, but only the empty seats of the Sunday-school room were there. Granny and Mr. Lovingood didn't pay any mind to me or the Voice. Granny continued her examination of the finger. "I don't know as what you shouldn't have your mama take you to see Dr. Kincaid with this finger. You can't ever tell, it might need setting."

"Granny, let's pray for it." I reached out my hands and took Will's hand between them. He wrinkled his nose when I touched the finger. Granny and Mr. Lovingood looked surprised. Mr. Lovingood turned to Granny and then back to me. "I don't suppose it could hurt."

They bowed their heads. "God, our Mother and our Father, restore to us the faith of our childhoods. . . ." I could hear Granny and Mr. Lovingood's prayers beginning to move up from their bellies and out of their mouths, adding harmony to my own. "Take the pain from Will's finger and use his hands to glorify your name." The warmth that filled my body moved up and into my hand and through to Will's finger like electric current. I opened my eyes, but the room dropped from my sight; only Will's hand remained, surrounded by the light. "Heal his finger according to your promise—'where two or three are gathered in my name, there am I in the midst of them.' Amen."

The warmth left and I felt weak. My muscles ached like I had gotten out of the bed after a week of the fever and tried to take my first step.

Will looked at me as I dropped his hand. Where his face had been red moments before, now there was no color, to the point where you couldn't see his freckles at all. He stretched out his hand, his bent finger straightened. "It don't hurt anymore."

"Doesn't," Mr. Lovingood corrected him. Granny reached up and took Will's hand. I walked back to my chair to gather up my Bible and the black patent-leather pocketbook Mama bought me for Easter.

"Granny, fainting tired me and I'm going to walk on back to the house. I can't sit through service today."

Granny acknowledged I had spoken with a nod of her head, and Mr. Lovingood offered to drive me home. The house sat so close to church that Granny and I often walked, but I gladly accepted Mr. Lovingood's offer of a ride.

During the short ride home, we were silent. As I stepped from the car, Mr. Lovingood tipped his hat. "I hope your head gets to feeling better. Maybe I'll see about bringing a fan next Sunday. Keep the room a little cooler."

"Thank you. And thank you for the ride," I said as I shut the car door.

At home, the screen door was unhooked and Mama lounged on one end of the couch, reading a *True Detective* magazine.

"I got too hot at church and I'm going to lay down."

"Why, Magdalena, you have no color. Do you want some water?"

"No, ma'am. I'll be okay."

I said nothing of my vision, knowing that if I told her, Mama would find my revelation a fascinating thing and want to talk about it for hours. I stripped off my clothes and put on my cotton summer gown, white with hand-crocheted lace, which was a hand-me-down from my cousin Norma. When the side of my face met the feather ticking, I slept. Neither Mama nor Granny woke me for dinner. It was close to suppertime before I got out of the bed. I heard them talking, but when I opened the bedroom door, they quit and both were busily reading by the time I walked into the kitchen. Granny read the Bible and Mama read her magazine.

Over a supper of cold fried chicken, peas, and new potatoes, Granny told me that Will's finger had completely healed by the time the church service was over. He told everybody that I did it.

I bit a new potato and felt it give beneath my teeth.

"Of course you didn't," sniffed Granny, and she was right.

It was that Woman in the light. Her presence brought comfort and healing that Sunday morning.

CHAPTER 2

From beneath the tablecloth fashioned from one of Aunt Willowdean's sheets, I looked out on the dangerous territory of Uncle Peter's back porch. Backed up to the wall of the house, the table provided a perfect hiding place to spy on those gathered for the cornhusking. The rough boards beneath me sloped gently toward the outer wall of the enclosed porch; the table above me held food for the evening meal. Through the pop-out windows of the porch flowed the cool air of the September evening. The tablecloth blocked the comfort of the breeze from me, but not the stinging words of my aunts.

I inched back toward the wall one muscle at a time and found myself torn, as always, between the mysterious and the practical. Should I be Mata Hari or Miriam tonight?

On the one hand, Mata Hari's adventures in gay Paree had been detailed in a story Mama read me. She liked Mata Hari so much because of her name. Mata Hari wasn't her given name, Mama said; she had been born with some dull Dutch name. However, being a spy required a special name, so that dull Dutch name became Mata Hari, Hindu for "eye of the dawn."

Miriam, on the other hand, was not nearly so exotic sitting in the bulrushes keeping an eye on her brother, Moses. But Miriam spied for a righteous cause, for the Lord and for her mama. Had

Miriam thought her mama was odd to send her on such a crazy errand? Or did she accept the joys and burdens that come from having a different sort of mama?

Underneath the table, I wrapped my arms around the rough denim of my overalls and brought my legs up close to me. As the denim pulled tight, the clasps of my overall bib dug into my chest, forcing me to ease sideways to keep the sharp edges from pushing into my flesh. Not three feet from me, a pair of legs moved up beside the table. Above my head, a butter knife clanked against the glass of a pie plate. I held my breath. A good spy never tipped the enemy to her presence. The legs moved closer. If I reached out my own leg, I could touch my toe to them. My heart beat a rhythm like one of Benny Goodman's swing tunes.

The legs retreated from the side of the serving table. Elephant's knees, I thought, with the skin thick and folded over itself. I pushed my hands into the side pockets of my overalls, searching for something I might use as a decoder ring, an essential tool for any modern spy. I came up empty in the last possible pocket about the time Aunt Vernie started talking.

"I need me one more taste of this blueberry cobbler before I start on that corn again."

Aunt Vernie was my granny's oldest sister. With a noise like a circus elephant she settled in a seat not five feet from my hideout, her legs encased in support hose and her feet in sturdy black shoes. Aunt Vernie's legs dwarfed the legs next to hers. Those legs and feet with their brown oxfords that pinched into a point belonged to Aunt Willowdean, Uncle Peter's wife. Aunt Vernie finished her dessert and the two aunts shucked corn, plopping silkless ears into big metal bowls and tossing the green husks into brown Piggly Wiggly bags.

"You don't know why these things happen in a family," Aunt Vernie said. "I always said Eli and Naomi were cut from the same bolt of cloth."

Dark, stiff, and constricting fabric it must have been, to hear my mama tell of growing up with Granny Naomi and Granddaddy

Eli. They used to give her the itch as bad as the blue wool Sunday dress she wore in the winter.

From the time I nestled in her womb, I felt the ocean of difference that separated Mama from everyone else in the Parker family. My mama, Lilah, nee Lily, reveled in her difference. I, on the other hand, longed for sameness. It wasn't that I wanted to be like everyone else; it was more that I didn't want to stick out for my faults like a wormy ear of corn. Life with Mama was an adventure, always something new and different to talk about. There were times when life with Mama felt like Christmas every day. Indeed, the thought is better than the reality.

At ten years of age my mama declared herself to be Lilah. Mama thought her own name was too plain to suit her. If Granny insisted on naming her for a flower, at least it could have been an exotic or expensive one, Mama said. Orchid, for instance.

Granny looked down her nose and replied, "I named you for the lilies of the field. 'Consider how the lilies grow. They do not labor or spin. Yet I tell you, not even Solomon in all his glory was arrayed like one of these.' " Then Granny snorted. "I don't know what was so wrong with the name. It's in the Bible."

Though everyone around Canaan soon called her Lilah, my granny continued to call her Lily. That never changed even after Mama ran away at sixteen and married my daddy, Butch Davidson.

My birth seemed a miracle in itself. My mama lost two babies in three years and the doctors in Raleigh told her it was no use thinking about children. Mama was a victim of a tipped uterus, they said. It must have righted itself because two years later I was born. Mama took one look at me and called me Magdalena.

Granny said, "Magdalena. What kind of a name is that for a baby? Magdalena! Hasn't anybody round here ever been named Magdalena."

My mama smiled and said, "I don't know what's so wrong with that name. It's in the Bible." *Magdalene* is the name in the Bible, but Mama never was a stickler for details.

Granny wasn't to be outdone on two names, so she started calling me Maggie and that's what everybody in Canaan mostly called me except my mama. I think folks felt sort of guilty over the Lily/Lilah issue and a name like Magdalena stuck in the throats of most everybody around. They just could not get it to come out of their mouths. The older I got, the greater my gratitude for Granny's choice. A name like Magdalena stood out above the crowd like Clyde Elliot's oldest boy, Clyde Jr., who had to duck his head to fit through the doorways at the church.

"Folks said they never saw two people of the same mind all the time like Naomi and Eli were." Aunt Vernie lowered her voice to a whisper and I could picture her leaning over to Aunt Willowdean. "It was almost unnatural."

I placed my hand carefully on the rough boards of the porch, trying to avoid splinters as I scooted further back.

It was unnatural. Opposites attract. We learned all about the pull of opposites in science, did little experiments with magnets and such. That being the case with the magnets, I do not know what could have possibly attracted my granny and granddaddy to each other.

From my hideout beneath the table, I saw Aunt Vernie's feet inch toward Aunt Willowdean.

"When Peter was born you could see the resemblance immediately, but then Lilah was born and, well, it makes you wonder."

Aunt Vernie shifted the hem of her flowered housedress over the top of her support hose.

The way I figure it, every gene my granny and granddaddy had of the opposite nature pulled together to form my mama; Mendel could have used her instead of those peas to prove his theory.

Aunt Vernie was right about Uncle Peter. All the like genes my grandparents had went to him. Five years older than my mama, Uncle Peter preached the hellfire and damnation of God every chance he got. He preached over in Johnston County at New Bethel Free Will Church and farmed tobacco during the week to make his living. Mama used to tell me, "Your uncle Peter's problem is he stopped with the Old Testament."

Aunt Vernie continued on, her words compassionate, her voice the voice of the crowd when they shouted, "Give us Barabbas."

"Then that thing happened with poor little Maggie last summer. Naomi has never said as much, but I've been told the child said she saw God. Said God looked like a woman. Have you ever heard of such? Naomi should have put her foot down with Lilah years ago. Of course, I've always said bad blood will out, and I've never known any of Butch Davidson's people that were worth the effort God wasted on making them."

The hot fire of anger started in my stomach. I pulled my legs closer to me. Who was Aunt Vernie to say how God's time should be used? My tears formed of their own accord and I realized that my teeth clenched a piece of my tongue, holding it as tight as I wanted to hold my parents when people judged them so harshly.

Aunt Willowdean crossed her ankles. "You're right about that. Butch is a lost cause. Peter prays for Lilah every night and for Maggie. He says that sometimes when he is standing next to Lilah he can smell the smoke of Hades itself. It's so sad. . . ."

I curled my head as close to my knees as possible. If I curled myself up tight like a roly-poly does when it's prodded with a twig, maybe I could shield myself from Aunt Willowdean's words.

"And of course, the Bible says the sins of the fathers will be visited on their children."

Part of me wanted to jump from my hiding place and demand to know what she would have done if *she* had seen the revelation. Tell the most loving, powerful being she had ever seen, "I'm sorry, you're not God. If you were, Peter would have told me to expect you?" Or "Hold on, I'll go get Peter and bring him on back so you can talk to him?"

Besides, hadn't everyone told me from the cradle to seek out the Lord? But now that the Lord had put in an appearance, they were all buzzing like hornets over it. In the year since that time, I had not seen God again, not that I would have told any of them if I had.

And then the Voice spoke. It was so plain underneath that table that I lifted my head, sure I'd been found out. "Remember, I have promised to preserve thee from all evil."

Bathed in the warmth of the Voice, I rested. Time stilled. No evil could reach beneath the table cover; no words could wound me. In my mind I could see the two aunts, their mouths set in thin lines. And further over, my mama sat in her Doris Day pants, stripping the green husk from an ear of corn and laughing with Mrs. Martha Elliot, Clyde's wife. Mama's golden red hair shone, her mouth moved this way and that, and her laughter filled up the space on the porch. In that moment, I no longer wished for sameness. Instead I felt sorry for my two aunts. My tears were no longer tears for me, but tears for them.

The urge to sneeze overwhelmed me. I pinched my nose, but a small sniff escaped. The metal bowl of shucked corn clanged a warning as the brown oxfords bore down on the table. A hand flipped the tablecloth and I blinked when the light hit my eyes.

"Who is that?" Aunt Vernie asked as I scooted out from under the table.

"It's Maggie," Aunt Willowdean replied, pointing out the obvious.

Aunt Vernie shook an ear of corn in my direction. Silks flew into the air around her. "Child, you are old enough to know better than to sneak around. Make yourself useful and go get me some more corn. These ears are all wormy."

The warmth of the Voice stayed with me awhile, as it had in Sunday school the previous summer, but I refused to share it with my aunts. A spy revealed nothing to her enemies. The rest of the evening I sat next to Aunt Vernie, listening to her remind me of a child's place. By comparison, Mata Hari got it fast and easy. They shot her.

I told no one except Mama what happened when the Voice came. The story of Will's finger still sprang quick to some people's minds. It produced more questions than anything else. Most of the time, these questions aimed more to trick me than to help them understand what happened. A whole group of folks felt like Aunt Vernie did—that my imagination had been working overtime. Most of them took that as confirmation of the fact that I was the daughter of Lilah Parker Davidson, a woman known for flights of fancy and crazy notions.

I told Mama about the Voice I'd heard at the cornhusking.

"And it was a woman's voice?"

"Yes, ma'am."

"Magdalena, I'm fascinated. This whole notion that God's a woman." Mama puffed on a cigarette and attempted to blow a smoke ring as she spoke. She recently had taken up smoking, thinking it added a certain air to her persona. "Well"—she waved her cigarette—"it's just fascinating."

I waved my hand back at her to push the smoke over in her direction. "Granny is not gonna be happy when she sees you smoking. And believe you me, you wouldn't be so *fascinated* if you were the one people kept staring at in the Open Air Market."

Mama ground her cigarette into the blue melmac ashtray. "Don't try to change the subject. I've been thinking of giving it up anyway, but not because of your granny. Now really, Magdalena, why do you suppose God came to you that way? Why not in the burning bush like Moses, or the dove on your shoulder like Jesus at his baptism?"

"I don't know, Mama. One thing I think about is that I've always had that problem with the Easter situation."

Every year at Easter, I experienced the resurrection of my thoughts on the words of St. Luke. I could never get past the disciples' reaction to news of the resurrection. There was poor Mary Magdalene and the other women, giving the disciples the best news of their lives, and they couldn't believe her and the others. *And their words seemed to them as idle tales, and they believed them not.*

What did a bunch of women know anyway? And while the disciples rushed off to *do,* Mary Magdalene stood there and wept. So it was to the women that the angels appeared, and then next Jesus came to her. Not to those men, for they were already organizing, already locking themselves in the Upper Room, already picturing *Oral Roberts' Hour of Power.*

Mama never hesitated when I asked her why this was so. "Some people can only go at things one way. Rigid habits and rigid thoughts. Things must be done in a certain way, and they don't even know why they are doing them that way. God is pretty big, Magdalena. So there must be hundreds of ways to approach Him. The problem is He is too big for some people. They're afraid if they start imagining Him and thinking in new ways, they'll lose themselves. Fly apart. Go crazy. So maybe that's why God chose Mary; He knew she could take it. 'And be not conformed to this world: but be ye transformed by the renewing of your mind, that ye may prove what is that good, and acceptable, and perfect will of God.' "

Granny thought differently. "Pshaw," she said, "you can think yourself right into a corner if you try hard enough."

"Oh, that's right," Mama said, taking the ashtray over and dumping its contents into the trash can, "the Easter situation." That answer seemed to satisfy her. "I think I might have read something about the psychology of that once in the *Reader's Digest.*"

She continued. "Well, as much as I hate to say it, for all practical purposes, we might want to keep this to ourselves."

"Mama, who in the world do you think I'd talk to about this? Best I can tell, the sin-entered-the-world-as-a-woman crowd wouldn't think much of the idea."

"That's true," Mama said, opening the side door and waving her hand to dispel the cloud of blue haze that hung over the couch like a thundercloud. "Still, I wouldn't mind seeing your uncle Peter's face. . . ."

"No." I slapped the edge of the chair. "Mama, I mean it! You cannot tell a soul. Do you hear me? Not a soul." My breath came in little short spurts. "It'd be worse than when Mrs. Sue Spell came out of the bathroom with the back of her dress tucked in her girdle. All my private parts exposed."

"Magdalena." Mama cocked her head at me like Abraham did when he heard a shrill noise. All big eyes and innocence.

"Mama." I stared at her without a twitch or a blink. She had to know how serious I was. Mama's plans often missed any thoughts of abiding effects.

"Oh, okay." She shrugged and walked to the sink, holding the blue ashtray under the tap to rinse the last remnants of the ashes down the drain.

"Hand on the Bible? No crossed fingers?" I asked. I needed her promise as much as I needed air to breathe.

"Yes and no," she said as she held the ashtray above her and squinted to see any trace of ashes left inside.

I longed for the Woman of the light and for that peace. I tried bargaining with God, promising to be good until well past eternity. I tried pleading, with no success. For a while, when I thought I felt the Spirit moving, I would look around fast, hoping to catch a glimpse of Her over my shoulder. None of these things brought Her to me again. She did not return when I wanted Her to, but in Her own time.

CHAPTER 3

The spot appeared on my cousin Norma's dress when I was fourteen. As big around as a grapefruit, it stood out black against the plaid fabric of her dress. No one else saw it, like we were in one of those three-dimensional movies and I was the only one who got a pair of the special glasses.

It happened at New Bethel on Homecoming Sunday. Granny insisted that we go to Homecoming services there every year. Uncle Peter's sermons held nothing for me. I studied the white-washed walls for patterns and made up little ditties to tell Mama when I got home. (Her favorite was when I ended the first line of the chorus to "Love Lifted Me" by singing "Put me down!")

Uncle Peter and Aunt Willowdean had one girl and three boys: Norma, James, Adam, and Eli. James could spit a watermelon seed across the sow's pen, while Eli was as sour as a ball of penny candy. Norma had a bit of spunk, but on the whole they were a milquetoast lot, the sort of children teachers sat between the troublemakers.

Uncle Peter's heavy hand pulverized their personalities into pieces no bigger than chicken feed. Their greatest source of joy in life came in taunting me that my parentage was nothing less than a pact with the devil.

On Homecoming Sunday, dinner on the grounds followed the

worship service, and then an afternoon service of singing, so joyful that even Uncle Peter could not destroy it.

After the last amen sounded in church that morning, we walked out into the October sunshine. Only the colored leaves above us kept the temperature from convincing us it was early summer. On the rolls of wire mesh strung between large oak trees was a feast as colorful and ample as the fall leaves.

Uncle Peter blessed the food with a booming voice. If you stood next to Uncle Peter when he prayed, you could feel the breeze from his hands as they gestured wildly while he petitioned God. When I was younger, I played a game to see how close I could stand and still dodge his hands as he flung them this way and that. It was my opinion that if God's eye was even on the sparrow, then flagging him down to get his attention shouldn't be necessary.

Mindful of my manners and Granny's strict orders, I occupied the end of the serving line, thinking how good it would feel to get out of my scratchy skirt and into some blue jeans when I got home. When it came to clothes, I was much more like my granny than my mama. Mama wore a dress like it was an extension of her flesh. Granny wore one out of duty to the occasion. However, around the farm, she could be found in pants and work shirts. If anyone mentioned that the Bible prohibited women from wearing men's pants, they were quickly told, "And that's so. That's why I'm very careful to wear women's pants."

The serving line moved slowly. A couple of boys sat over at one of the tables in the churchyard. I had noticed one of them earlier looking at me as we came out of church. Unlike most boys around my age, he was taller than me. He had wavy brown hair that he'd tried to style like Gary Cooper. Mr. Almost–Gary Cooper smiled at me when he caught me looking at him. Embarrassed, I spun around, but not before he nudged his friend and gestured toward me.

I stared hard at the back of the woman's head in front of me in the dinner line. Her hair piled high up off the top of her head made me wonder if she had to use a crochet hook to scratch her scalp when it itched. While I stared, she turned around and smiled.

I tried to act like I was studying something on the front of the church and not her hair.

"My goodness, it's Maggie. You're just about a full-grown woman now."

She pretended to search behind me, straining her neck first this way and then that. "Now, where is your mama? I don't believe I see her."

"Mama's not feeling well today." A long curly hair protruded from the woman's chin, and I worked hard not to stare at it. "It broke her heart not to be here, but she had a terrible headache."

Mama's attendance at worship came and went like the seasons. Thoughts of listening to Uncle Peter preach brought on a headache big enough to ensure her absence from New Bethel.

"I'm sure sorry to hear that. You tell her Mrs. Autry was asking about her. Didn't she have the headache last year, too?"

My eyes kept coming back to that chin hair like your tongue does to a kernel of corn stuck in between your teeth. "Yes, ma'am, I believe she did have a headache last year. You know"—I lowered my voice—"she has female problems."

"And so young." Mrs. Autry wore a look of genuine distress but asked no further questions. The Homecoming dinner line was not the place to discuss "female problems." Of course, Mama didn't have any, but it certainly made quick work of the discussion on attendance.

As penance for my fib, I carried Mrs. Autry's tea to her table for her and then settled myself on the side concrete steps warmed by the sun. From my perch I could observe unnoticed the families where the mamas and daddies sat together like matched sets of cream and sugar bowls. I longed to bounce down the road in the backseat of a Rambler with a daddy at the wheel and a mama laughing at his jokes, to have a brother or sister to pinch or fuss with in the backseat. Somehow that all seemed like the perfect thing.

The breeze carried my napkin off my lap to the bottom of the step. I picked it up and walked over to the dessert table. Aunt Vernie's eight-layer red velvet cake formed the centerpiece. The other pies and cakes radiated out from it like spokes on a wheel. From among the seven-minute frostings and fluffy meringues, I chose with great deliberation.

No sooner had I tucked my skirt underneath me on the steps again than here came Mr. Almost–Gary Cooper.

"Say, aren't you Preacher Parker's niece?"

"Who wants to know?"

"President Truman. He's waiting in a car down the street to meet you." He grinned.

"In that case, tell him yes, I'm Preacher Parker's niece, but I didn't get the secret code for the A-bomb that he needed."

He laughed. "Maggie, ain't it? I recognize you on account of that red hair. I'm Russell. Russell Spellman."

"It is Maggie. Maggie Davidson. Nice to meet you." There was another fib. I didn't care if I ever met him. I'd promised myself long ago that I would not make my mama's mistake. No marriage at sixteen for me. No Mr. Almost–Gary Coopers were going to get in the way of my schooling and leave me to depend on others for the rest of my life. My mama seemed perfectly able to stake her independence on the one hand, but to use the other hand to reach for whatever she needed from you. Somehow this never created the unhappiness in her that it did in me.

"No need for you to sit in those front pews with all them old people this afternoon. You oughta come back and sit with us."

Before I could tell him no, up flounced Norma. At fifteen, Norma was the youngest of Uncle Peter's children.

"Maggie, does Granny know you're over here flirting with the boys? I'm gonna tell." Norma would have told on herself if it got her daddy's attention. Neglect is an awful thing. My daddy did it from a distance, but my uncle Peter did it close up.

"Be my guest, and while you're there, tell her you had your eyes open the whole time your daddy was praying."

Russell laughed.

"At least my daddy prays. And at least my daddy's here. Yours couldn't be bothered to show up for your birthday party. He's too busy with the other heathens and their unspeakable abominations." Norma flicked her limp blond hair over her shoulder.

" 'Unspeakable Abomination' would have been a perfect title for your daddy's sermon. What's that on your dress?"

Norma glanced down. "Where?"

"Right there," I pointed at a spot over on the right side of her dress, just below her waist.

"You are such a fibber, Maggie Davidson," she said. "There is nothing on my dress." Her voice became breathy and soft. "Russell, you can see anything. Do you see a spot on my dress?" That was what always happened when boys were around; perfectly normal girls started saying the silliest things. Girls who were slow to start with were struck dumb entirely, and no one seemed to notice.

Norma held the front of her dress for us to inspect. Her fingers covered part of the spot. I pointed between them, touching the dress and her stomach beneath it. I couldn't feel anything on the fabric. She squealed, dropping the dress. "Don't touch my stomach. You faker, you know my stomach hurts. Somebody must have told."

"I didn't mean to hurt you. Nobody told me anything about your stomach. You sure you don't see that black spot?"

Norma held her side, bending slightly as she talked. "I mean it, Maggie. Quit trying to trick me. I'm telling Granny if you don't stop."

Russell began to walk away, shaking his head. He turned and said, "You never answered my question."

"No, I'll sit with my granny, thank you."

Norma called after him, "I'll sit with you."

He didn't seem to hear and walked on. I felt a twinge of superiority. No boy sought Norma's company even though she desperately wanted someone to. What Norma didn't know was that two years earlier my daddy did show up for my twelfth birthday party, but he came a day late because he couldn't remember which day I was born and then he was so drunk that my mama, who forgave him everything, wouldn't speak to him. Mr. Neb, who worked for Granny, tried to convince him to get back in his borrowed truck and go on his way, but that didn't sit well with Daddy and he took a swing at Mr. Neb. Drunk as he was, he just looped around in a circle like he was getting ready to pin the tail on the donkey. That's when Granny brought out the gun where he could see it and suggested that he leave the property. Mama sat on the steps behind her and cried. That's what a sweet-talking man had done for my mama and me.

Norma turned on me. "You've always got to act like you know something the rest of us don't, Miss High and Mighty. Well, we'll see how high and mighty you are when your daddy gets shot by some woman's husband."

I turned, but she continued. "And your mama thinks she is so beautiful, putting on airs, writing poetry, and wearing makeup. Well, she must not be all that special; she can't hang on to your no-account daddy."

In the face of such hatefulness, it was only right that I get mad, but anger directed at my cousin was wasted; she hated herself much more than I could ever hate her.

I picked up my plate and walked past her to help gather up Granny's serving dishes. I searched among the now-ravaged dishes for familiar bowls, pots, and pie plates. It looked like some late arrival to the dessert table had used their tongue to clean out Granny's chocolate meringue pie plate. I threw the dishes in the boot of the Oldsmobile. Later, when we raced along the bumpy back roads, they would rattle and bang like the Angel of Death's chorus. I thumped the boot lid closed the way I would have liked to thump Norma on the head.

Several hours into the afternoon sing, the Ladies' Trio began the first verse of "If I Could Hear My Mother Pray Again." I stretched my feet out under the pew in front of me and glanced behind me at the back of the church.

Norma staggered from a back pew toward the door clutching her stomach, the spot on her dress wadded in her hand. The trio sang on, but I couldn't sit still. In one motion I got up and turned, walking in small quick steps down the side aisle and out the same door as Norma. Once outside, it took me a moment to track the sound of her retching. She stood over to one side of the churchyard barely past a line of parked cars.

When I reached her, she moaned, her knees folding under her. The vomiting began again and Norma gasped for air between her stomach's spasms.

James came through the line of cars.

"James, go get your mama and Granny. Norma's sick."

He turned and ran back toward the church.

I knelt down and put my arm around Norma. Her skin burned my hand even through the cloth of her dress. The heat of her skin frightened me. I knew she needed my calm, not my fear. I talked in my mama's voice, the voice she used for all-night bouts with the stomach virus. "It's okay, you're okay. Dear Jesus, please help Norma."

Norma's dress had caught on one side. I pulled it back down to cover her slip. The black spot had disappeared. In its place a bright red spot glowed. A chill moved through me despite the heat from Norma's body.

Behind me, I heard Granny and Aunt Willowdean talking as they came through the line of cars.

"Norma. Oh, Norma, honey." Aunt Willowdean dropped down beside Norma on the other side. "Oh, she's burning up."

I rose to give Granny room to kneel beside Norma. "Norma, are you hurting?" Granny asked.

Norma nodded.

"Where do you hurt, Norma? Point to it for Granny." Norma pointed to the glowing spot on the right side of her dress.

Aunt Willowdean moaned and rubbed her hand up and down Norma's back.

"Willowdean, we need to get her some attention. Maggie, bring the car around here as close as you can. James, go with her and get one of my dishcloths out of the boot. Wet it to lay across Norma's forehead."

Aunt Willowdean moaned as if she were the one with the belly-ache. As James and I went across the churchyard, I heard Granny say, "Willowdean, straighten up now. Do you want to get Peter to go with us?" A pause and then, "Willowdean, answer me."

I pulled the car around, frightened for Norma. Praying quietly, I was torn between whether I should say nothing or tell Granny about the spot on Norma's dress. How would I explain it if I did?

Aunt Willowdean went off to tell Uncle Peter, while James helped us get Norma in the car. Her retching had subsided, but I pulled Granny's chicken-and-pastry pot out of the trunk for her to use if need be.

"Maggie, you get in back with Norma and let her put her head in your lap. She doesn't need her mama crying all over her now."

"Peter's staying," Aunt Willowdean said, stepping from behind a Studebaker and wringing her hands. "He wants to finish the service and to lead prayers for Norma."

Granny raised her eyebrows at the news and then instructed James to put his mama in the truck. "James, go the fastest way you know to the doctor. I'll keep up with you."

I wiped Norma's head with the damp dishcloth. She moaned every once in a while, but for the most part, she lay so still I feared she had died. In a way, her fever was a relief. As long as she was warm, I knew she was alive.

"Please, God, please, don't let her die," I prayed silently as we drove.

The sun streamed in the back window of the car, reflecting off the pastry pot with such intensity that it forced me to close my eyes. When I opened them, She was there. As intense and as loving as the first time I saw Her. All the time since then fell away and my heart became the heart of a young child, open and trusting.

Her presence swaddled me in love and quiet ecstasy. Like a spillway in the spring rains, my soul overflowed with joy. I felt so small and yet so much bigger than the world, so full of flight I could soar, and yet so firmly planted in Her presence.

"Pray for Norma."

I blinked and the words came again. "Pray for Norma."

I placed my hand on Norma's side and prayed. "Dear God, dear Jesus, please help Norma. Heal her. Whatever weakens her, take it from her. In your time, in your way. Amen."

I felt the warmth from my hand move down into Norma's side. I saw her in my mind as she stood in the churchyard a few hours earlier. The warmth left me and I opened my eyes. The light was gone.

Granny echoed my amen but otherwise spoke little, concentrating on keeping up with James, who had taken her at her word and sped along the back road, slinging gravel at every curve. The dishes from Homecoming clattered with each bump.

The vinyl of the seat rubbed my legs, reminding me of the firmness I'd felt moments earlier when I wasn't aware of the seat at all.

After my prayer, Norma felt a bit cooler, but the intensity of the circle on her dress never faded. Did that mean my prayer would not be answered? I felt secretly chastised for every less-than-Christian thought that I had harbored toward my cousin and prayed with increased fervor. Once I thought I heard the word "Peace," but when I looked up, no one was there.

The doctor examined Norma from over the front seat of the car and wasted no time in pronouncing a ruptured appendix. He grabbed his hat and kissed his wife and then rode in the front seat of the Oldsmobile to Good Hope Hospital in Erwin, jumping from the car before it completely stopped at the emergency room door.

He shouted orders to the staff and two large orderlies whisked Norma away. Two nurses closed ranks behind them and followed. Granny explained to Aunt Willowdean what the doctor had said in the car, leaving out the part where he whispered to Granny that a ruptured appendix poisoned the system and he could not predict whether Norma would live or die.

The waiting room was empty except for the four of us. James and I pooled our change to buy everybody a Coca-Cola out of the machine. Glass clanked every time James pulled the black lever and the machine spewed out a bottle.

"Your mama seems real upset."

"I reckon so. Norma's been complaining off and on for a couple of days. Daddy rubbed turpentine on her stomach yesterday. Eased the pain some. He told Mama to give her an aspirin this morning when she complained and she'd be fine. Mama tried to say that maybe she needed a doctor. Daddy said no."

The surgery lasted half the time the doctor estimated. When he came to us sitting there with Coca-Colas in our hands, he pulled his surgical mask down and allowed himself a half smile.

"She's a mighty sick young lady, but she's going to make it. Ninety-nine percent of the infection seemed contained in an area right around the ruptured organ. A pocket of tissue kept the pus from her system."

A collective "ThankyouJesus" went through the group.

"I've seen my share of appendicitis, but I've never seen another appendix with that kind of pocket present. This one's a miracle. As much as I'd like to say I had anything to do with it, I can't."

"So does that mean you won't be sending a bill for your services?" Granny's mouth turned up at the corners.

"Mrs. Parker, you know me better than that." The doctor's smile grew bigger. "I'll stay around for a few hours. I need to make rounds anyway. We've got her on penicillin. Other than that, she needs rest."

Aunt Willowdean sat wiping her eyes and sniffing.

Granny looked at her and looked back at the doctor. "Willowdean, don't you have any questions?"

Aunt Willowdean shook her head.

Granny drew a loud breath. "How long will you keep her?"

"If she does well, it might be as little as five to seven days."

"Well, Willowdean, that's good news, isn't it?"

Aunt Willowdean looked at her hands. "It is. I'm sure Peter will have some questions when he gets here." She sobbed.

"Just have him ask one of the nurses to find me." The doctor put his hand on Aunt Willowdean's shoulder. "Really, Mrs. Parker, Norma is going to be fine. The nurses will let you know when you can see her."

The doctor left and Granny turned to Aunt Willowdean.

"Willowdean, you need to calm yourself down before you go in there. The way you are right now, you'll scare the poor child to death. James, go see if one of the nurses can find an aspirin for your mama. Willowdean, do you hear what I'm saying?"

I longed for sleep and found a chair apart from the others where I tried to rest. My effort was in vain. Shortly, Uncle Peter arrived with the other boys and the waiting area filled with church members. After Norma woke up, Uncle Peter and Aunt Willowdean went in to see her.

Then I went in with Granny, mentioning what James had told me about the turpentine and aspirin as she and I walked down the hallway alone. She shook her head as I talked.

The hospital room smelled of medicine and bleach. Norma lay swallowed up by white sheets stiff with starch. Her face matched the color of the bed sheets, and the edge of her green hospital gown above the sheet provided the only color in the room. Even her blond hair seemed to have the color sucked out by the pillow.

Granny inspected the room while I stood by the bed. When I put my hand on her arm, Norma attempted a smile as she faded in and out of her ether sleep. Satisfied at last with the room's condition, Granny came and stood on the other side of the bed.

Norma opened her eyes. "Maggie, I felt it when you prayed for me. The light. I knew I was coming back then."

Granny stroked Norma's head. "None of that now. You need your rest. If you need anything and we're not around, you tell the nurses to call me." I'd rarely seen her so tender.

As we were leaving the waiting area for home, Uncle Peter lifted up his hand and turned to those around him. "This, friends, is what happens when the righteous pray."

Granny looked down her nose in his direction. "Can't even appreciate it when the Lord saves him from himself. Wait right here, Maggie."

She took Uncle Peter outside, and before the discussion ended arms waved in all directions.

I slept on the way home, waking about a mile from the house. When I stirred, Granny looked over at me.

"What Norma said back there? Was it the same as with Will's finger?" she asked.

"Pretty much, yes, ma'am."

"I don't suppose it is ours to question, then. The Lord works in mysterious ways, His mighty wonders to perform." She paused. "He was a he, wasn't He?"

"Actually, no, ma'am. It was the same, a She. I saw the light when we were in the car on the way to the doctor's house. I guess that's when Norma saw it. You didn't see it, did you, Granny?"

We pulled into the drive at the house. "Lordy, no. I was too busy keeping up with James and trying to keep this automobile from slinging itself into a ditch."

I sighed.

"Don't worry about it, Maggie. I'll study on it and pray about it, and worst comes to worst, we'll just wait on God to explain it to us."

Granny didn't mention it again, though Norma told Mama about it when Mama visited her at the hospital the next day. Norma tried to tell Aunt Willowdean and Uncle Peter about the light, but Uncle Peter refused to listen and did not return to the hospital after that. He sent Aunt Willowdean and James to pick up Norma when the time came.

I told no one else. I was not interested in answering questions nor in being held up for ridicule. The days became months, and then years, and God did not show Herself to me again. I convinced myself that God's appearance was only possible in the sweetness of childhood, in the time when possibilities were without end.

CHAPTER 4

"Did you come to hear the Holy Word preached as you never did before? Say Amen." Brother Mike thumped down his Bible onto the music stand he used to direct the crowd. As the front man for Brother Oscar's Traveling Tabernacle, Brother Mike was charged with inciting the masses into shouting glory and dancing in the Lord.

"Amen!" the crowd roared, pounding the wooden benches beneath them for emphasis. Already the women fanned themselves against the stiff humidity of the September night.

"Have you put away the ways of the heathen? Are you going to heaven? That's what Brother Oscar is about, my friends. Glory. Glory. Glory!" It seemed that Brother Mike's reedy frame contorted into a showcase of letters better than the cheerleaders did on Friday night at a Salemburg High football game.

G, L, O, R, where was the Y?

Norma banged my leg.

"Quit rolling your head around. You want him to think you've got the Spirit?" she hissed.

"Glory," the crowd shouted.

"Well, I'm not the one who is here to impress John Herring." I nudged Norma back. Ever since her appendectomy five years earlier, Norma spent more and more time at our house. According to Mama, she was working Uncle Peter out of her system. I could almost like her.

Brother Mike danced around the platform. In front of him sat a quartet of two men and two women. The women wore powder-blue dresses and the men wore blue seersucker suits.

"Hasn't God been good to you? Don't you want the heathen to know how good God is? The unsaved are out there on the wide road to perdition."

"Preach it," a member of the quartet shouted.

"How can we get those heathens off that road and onto Jesus' interstate? Brother Oscar, that's how. You cannot know the number of wounded and broken souls that Brother Oscar has led to the Lord.

"Friends, the Communists are all around us, threatening our homes and our families. When you least expect it, the godless will be upon us. Someone must stand up to them. That someone is Brother Oscar."

"Amen."

I imagined Brother Oscar, a squat Statue of Liberty guarding the United States, reaching up to grab the *Sputnik* from space, then staring down Khrushchev and sending him back to Russia. Those around me shouting *Amen* seemed not to understand that they were more likely to lose all they had to bad weather than to Mr. Khrushchev and his band of heathens. When they lost it all, Brother Oscar would not be there for them.

"He cannot do it alone, friends. He cannot. He needs your support. He needs your prayers. He needs your money. It takes money to keep the Word of God rolling along the highways. This tent and piano don't just up and move theirselves. These beautiful appointments for the worship service don't take wings and fly. No, sir."

Every year the wooden benches and platform of the tabernacle received a fresh coat of paint. By the time the tabernacle reached Canaan, cracks revealed hints of last year's color, threatening to break out from underneath. Brother Oscar was like that as well, I thought. Every now and then his preacher shell would crack and you could see what was underneath, sort of murky and dark.

Brother Mike turned and picked up two buckets. "I'm going to ask members of the quartet to pass these offering plates. Give as God has so freely given to you."

"If those are Brother Mike's offering plates, I'd hate to see what he calls a bucket," I whispered to Norma.

A slight nod of Brother Mike's Brylcreemed head and the piano player began pounding out "Bringing in the Sheaves." We sang as the quartet passed the buckets up and down the rows, their feet moving noiselessly on the carpet of sawdust throughout the tent.

Beside me Norma pouted. "His cousin and his sisters are here. Where do you think he is?"

Norma's religious fervor was in direct proportion to her certainty that John Herring and his family would be at the tent meeting. She had been flirting all summer with him when they met at various 4-H functions. At twenty, she held a part-time job at the drugstore in Fuquay-Varina and helped Uncle Peter and her brothers out on the farm. I, on the other hand, was in my second year at Pineland, an academy and junior college for women in Salemburg. My studies were part of my plan to make sure I could make my own way in the world.

I shrugged. "You know how it is this time of year. He could still be at one of the tobacco barns."

"Let's stop by the Tastee-Freez on our way home. Maybe he'll be there."

The clinking of change sounded around us. Norma and I passed the bucket over to the waiting quartet member at the end of our bench. He paused a moment to smile at Norma, which caused her to hold on to his arm with one hand while she dug change out of the bottom of her pocketbook with the other. She tossed it into the bucket, returning his smile.

"He saw you coming," I whispered. Norma wrinkled her nose at me.

People around us began to jump and shout in time to the music. The piano player rolled right into "When We All Get to Heaven." On the last line of the chorus, Brother Mike shook his tambourine. "Shout the victory, friends. Shout the victory." He jumped from the platform, shook the tambourine, and skittered across the top of the sawdust like a Jesus bug on the water.

I noticed the two male members of the quartet take the buckets around the platform, going by Brother Oscar's chair so he could survey their contents. Brother Oscar walked to the edge of the platform and said something to Brother Mike as we sang, "Just one glimpse of Him in glory will the toils of life repay."

As the song's last notes sounded, Brother Mike motioned to a member of the quartet, a young blond girl whose outfit clung to her with no material to spare.

"Friends," Brother Mike intoned solemnly, "I can see that some of you don't understand how critical Brother Oscar's ministry is to sinners who are down in the depths of human debasement. Sister Louise is gonna come on up here and tell you about what a difference God has made in her life and how without Brother Oscar's ministry she might still be a part of abominations so awful we cannot even speak of them on this stage."

Sister Louise began the story of her life of degradation. Several men around us leaned further forward in their seats, trying with all their might to imagine what unspeakable things this sinner-turned-saint had been party to.

With the toe of my saddle oxford I pushed the sawdust in front of me, writing my initials over and over again. Sister Louise finished. The piano player began another song.

"Don't worry, friends. If the spirit has convicted you because you didn't give enough, we will be taking up a collection when Brother Oscar has finished tonight's message from God."

Even with the sides of the tent rolled up to allow fresh air through, I found the atmosphere under the patched brown canvas suffocating. When I was younger it was fun to watch Brother Oscar stomp around his platform, but now I could see people like the woman across the row. She wore shoes that looked like they'd been resoled many times and yet she put paper money into the bucket. Most likely it was her grocery money. Beside her sat a little girl with a limp arm. They waited, no doubt, for Brother Oscar's healing prayers. I walked toward the back, hoping for a breeze other than the one created by jumping bodies and opened mouths.

Across the fields, I saw orange tongues lapping up the side of Mr. Clyde Elliot's tobacco barn. I screamed, but my voice blended in with the others. Norma stood with her hands across her chest and shook her head at me.

I grabbed her arms. "Norma, it's on fire. Mr. Clyde's barn—"

"What?" she shouted at me, trying to be heard above the victory shouts of the saints around us. They had to stop.

I turned from Norma and ran forward screaming, "Fire!" Brother Oscar came toward me, his hair shining in the lights under the tent, raising his arms to restrain me.

"No," I shouted at him, "no." I stamped my foot. "Not me," I shouted, "Mr. Clyde's barn, his tobacco." Brother Oscar looked around for some of his faithful to take me away, possessed as I was by demons. Prayers for demon possession were later in the program. And still people around me shouted and danced and the sister playing the piano continued with a pace that would have been the envy of any of those rock and rollers, Jerry Lee Lewis or Elvis or their like. Two quartet members had grabbed my elbows to escort me to the rear of the tent, when the back row, acting almost as one person, realized that there was a fire across the next field and started to move out of the tent and run toward the flaming barn.

The men dropped my arms. The practicality of country life dictated that a real fire take precedence over a possible demon possession. The crowd began to move out of the tent until even the sister at the piano quit playing, in mid-song, to go and see exactly what was the problem.

The soft gray earth gave under our shoes as we ran toward the barn. Mr. Clyde came across the field. Even in the distance his movement looked frenzied. His arms and legs flailed independent of each other. It was a wonder that they propelled him forward in a direct line. He approached the outer edge of the group.

"I just went to get Martha at the mill. I thought the fire was low enough. It wasn't that long."

He grabbed his tobacco sticks from under the tin overhang of the barn. As he threw the sticks to the side, smoke escaped the ends and joined the haze around us. Women cried for him to stop while the acrid smell of the smoke filled our noses. The smoke caused us to snort and shake our heads like mules ready to get to the barn after a day of plowing.

My feet stayed anchored to the earth as though the gray soil was mud. I felt torn between helping him and screaming for him to quit. Several of the men stepped forward both to help him and restrain him. Several others shepherded the crowd back. The buildup of gas from the burning tobacco could be dangerous.

"It's gonna explode," someone shouted.

The barn seemed to groan loudly and then one wall blew apart. Bits of hot tarpaper and wood flew around us. Flaming boards fell across Mr. Clyde's back. His mouth flew open in protest as he dropped down to his knees and rolled across the ground.

I put my hands up to shield my face. Norma turned away. Women screamed and children cried. The crowd moved back, the light of the flames flitting across their contorted faces.

Mrs. Elliot dispatched the oldest Elliot boy, Clyde Jr., for the doctor. She sent Ben, the second oldest, to the house for a bucket of water and some baking soda.

Several men dragged Mr. Clyde out of harm's way. Someone else stretched a shirt on the ground for him to lie across. The flames continued their climb toward the heavens. The heat pushed the crowd back further, and smoke thickened the air while the barn fast acquired the look of a giant flaming match head stuck in the soil. The smell of the tobacco reminded us that we watched new shoes for the Elliot children, grocery staples, and next fall's school clothes go to nothing but flaming cinders before our eyes.

The smell of charred flesh nudged us to remember that all those things could be replaced, but a life could not.

"GEEsus," Brother Oscar began a loud and mournful prayer. It was that whiny, singsong variety that I believed got on God's nerves. If God struck down a few of the whiners, I felt certain simpler straightforward petitions would follow.

Brother Oscar fell to one knee, lifting his arms toward heaven. The wall of flame created a dramatic backdrop to his pose.

I stood toward the back of the crowd, overwhelmed by the sadness of it all. That such hardworking people like the Elliots had to suffer seemed so unfair. Then, as if this was my burning bush, God appeared at the center of the flames as magnificent as the first time I had seen Her nine years earlier. The feeling of warmth went throughout my body and the words She spoke were the same: "Feed my sheep."

Like dry grass quenched with the first spring rain, my soul felt alive. There was no separateness anymore, only the oneness of the womb's dark water.

Such love as I had never felt went through me, and I thought that I might lift right up off that gray soil and fly away. It had that much power and that much terror. Who could be worthy of such love? Tears formed in my eyes. "Not me," I said.

The light intensified and the words came from it: "You are chosen. Blessed alone among the many, you will have a healing touch for body and soul. Troubles will be revealed to you, that I may heal my children's souls. Go and pray for the wounded."

The cool breath of God fanned me like immense wings. "But Brother Oscar is already praying. My prayer cannot be better than his," I protested to God as Moses had done centuries before in the hot desert of the Sinai.

"Go and pray for the wounded."

As Granny so often said, I could not do otherwise. The Voice of the fire demanded obedience.

I walked forward, stepping gingerly to try and stay on top of the soil. Brother Oscar went full tilt now, his voice frantically running circles around all the reasons the Lord should heal Mr. Clyde's back as if Brother Oscar could contain the power of God and twist the will of the Almighty like a piece of strawberry licorice.

Mrs. Elliot took the water that Ben brought and gently wet the skin on Mr. Clyde's back. She shook the baking soda box. White powder floated down and caked onto the red skin that boiled up angry on Mr. Clyde's back. When she tried to spread the powder out, pieces of black skin stuck to her hand. Mr. Clyde screamed. Norma turned away, her hand clasped over her mouth.

"Oh dear Lord, his skin's a-peeling off." The woman with the resoled shoes rocked back and forth in the gray soil, clasping her child to her.

My feet moved forward, powered by the force of the love within me. I knelt beside Mr. Clyde and reached for his hand. I heard several in the crowd behind me gasp. Mr. Clyde let me hold his hand, even placing it palm down in my palm. Later I would think to be surprised about this, but when he did it, it seemed as natural as him saying, "Come see us," every time he left our house.

When I placed my other hand on his shoulder above the ridge of red skin, I felt the heat. It was not the heat of Mr. Clyde's skin, not the heat of the fire—the air around me was cool—but the heat of the vision, moving like a river current down my arm into my hand. The smell of burning flesh faded, replaced by the light, sweet smell of a Peace rose.

His skin grew cool beneath my touch.

"Oh God, you have said, 'I AM that I AM.' We can never know your mysteries or your ways, but we ask that you visit your healing upon us now in this hour of need and sadness."

Brother Oscar quit praying.

"There is none that can heal but you. Amen."

I don't know that Brother Oscar felt his edge slip away or what, but he smoothed his greased hair back and got very busy. He and Brother Mike herded the crowd back toward the Traveling Tabernacle, which sat out of harm's way.

I sat back on my heels. "I'm not going back, Norma," I said.

"Great. So much for the Tastee-Freez."

Norma turned her back on me and clopped across the field in a manner that suggested I had just made her best beau throw her over for me. The quartet member who smiled at her earlier put his hand on her shoulder as they neared the tent.

Mr. Clyde's back went from red to pink. He seemed grateful for the relief, but looked past me to the still-burning barn, and a pain that could not be fixed filled his eyes.

"I'm so sorry about your tobacco," was all I could think to say. It didn't relieve the "if onlys" in his eyes. If only he had sent one of the boys to watch the barn, if only he had left the fire a little lower. Mama termed these regrets "if onlys." She had no use for them.

The cool air that had sheltered me evaporated and I felt the heat of the flames. My body ached. I wanted to stretch out across that gray dirt and sleep.

Mrs. Elliot motioned to Ben. "Maggie, you look like you're all done in. Ben, go on over to the house with Maggie and take her home."

I stood up and told her, "Don't bother with that, someone else will carry me."

"Nonsense," she insisted. "I'd never be able to look Naomi or Lilah in the face if anything happened to you."

We made our way through the crowd. Despite the shepherding of Brother Oscar and Brother Mike, many in the group had not returned to the tent. They did what neighbors so often do in the country: They stayed to offer assistance, and if no assistance was possible, then they offered their presence as a way of bolstering the suffering party.

Ben Elliot and I rode back to my house in his daddy's pickup truck. We smelled of smoke and sweat. Exhausted, I spent much of the ride dazed, trying to convince myself that I wasn't scared and that I wasn't angry with God. I didn't want to spend my time dealing with the likes of Brother Oscar. Why now? It was crazy. It didn't make sense. I had plans—plans that weren't going well. Hadn't

Norma stomped off in a huff? The memory of raised eyebrows in the crowd stayed with me. What about knowing the troubles of many? I'd always tried to help people the best I could.

"Ben, did you see anything unusual in the fire tonight?"

"Like what?" He turned his head slightly.

"Oh, nothing. I guess I spent too much time out in the field today."

He laughed ruefully. "I didn't see anything but a lot of hard work going up in smoke. Wasn't it about this time of year when you thought you saw God during Mr. Lovingood's Sunday-school lesson?"

When I didn't answer, he continued. "You sure did take a lot of ribbing for that at school. Course, Will Atkinson swore out that you fixed his finger."

I'd learned very quickly that fall of my tenth year that visions were not the stuff of everyday conversation. "Will always was one to exaggerate."

After that we rode in silence. At the house, Mama sat listening to the radio and Granny worked at the table, reading through some papers necessary to deal with crop allotment. Their noses wrinkled at our smell. All their activities were forgotten with the mention of the fire. After the dark of the car, the light of the kitchen seemed bright. I squinted as I told Granny and Mama about the fire, feeling its heat again on my face as I talked.

Before I finished, I could see my granny starting to make a list of the things that needed to be done to help the Elliots. Clyde had enough boys to work his piece of land so he could supervise the farm for my granny, and she, in turn, treated him more like a son than a tenant. When Granddaddy Eli died, she didn't sell or give the farm over to one of his brothers like everyone thought she would. While she didn't believe in "toting the pocketbook," once Granddaddy Eli was dead, she did so out of default and her extreme dislike for his kin. Granddaddy Eli's older brothers were involved with that Sanford fellow in Shiloh, Maine, the one who got everybody to give all they had to the Lord. Then when they were starving, he told them if they only trusted God, they would have plenty to eat like he did. When the whole Shiloh situation fell apart, the uncles came back home to live, but Granny never trusted them with matters of money. They would likely give it all away and then wonder why they starved. Granny looked at me sternly whenever we had these discussions and said, "The Lord helps those what helps themselves."

I tried to get Ben Elliot to leave without letting on about my prayer. I knew soon enough it would get back to the house, but I wanted sleep, not questions. Ben squirmed throughout my story until he finally found an opening large enough to get his news through.

"Maggie prayed for my daddy's back and it went right to healing before our eyes."

I shrugged as Granny looked at me and Mama showed new interest in the night's events. "I felt led to pray. That's all."

Though Granny clucked her tongue at me, she could not argue with the Lord's moving.

"Yeah, but that slick-haired evangelist wasn't making no progress at it. That's a fact."

I slipped from the room as Ben answered questions. In my room, I left my clothes where they fell as I shed them. The last thing I remember, the cotton sheets smelling of my mother's sachet closed around me, pushing back the odor of the smoke.

I woke the next morning startled by the sun in my eyes. Granny never allowed me to sleep late on a Saturday, what with chores to do and tobacco in full swing. I helped Mr. Neb with much of the farm routine while everyone else harvested the tobacco.

The kitchen was empty. Tessie, the Negro woman who usually helped with cooking and such, was off visiting relatives in Clinton for the weekend. Tessie and Mr. Neb were married, but he did not go with her to Clinton. Like Mama going to hear Uncle Peter preach, Mr. Neb never lacked for a reason to not go visit Tessie's family.

I lifted an inverted plate in the middle of the table to find the remnants of breakfast. The yellow of the eggs faded against the bright yellow oilskin tablecloth. Along with the eggs, there were pieces of fatback, salty and crisp, and cold biscuits. I heard Mama in the yard talking to someone. Out the window over the sink I saw Mama wave to the occupants of a blue Studebaker I didn't recognize. The passengers waved back as the engine started and they backed out of the yard in a cloud of dust.

Mama came in, the screen door banging behind her, and seeing me, squealed and put her arms around my neck.

"That makes the fourth carload of folks who have come by this morning."

I pulled the butter plate from the Frigidaire and sat down with a biscuit. "They lose their way?" I spread butter and then grape preserves across the bumpy white inside of the biscuit.

Mama sat down and leaned on her elbows, looking at me like I had arrived from Santa Claus that morning with a big bow around my neck. "Clyde's back is completely healed."

I broke the biscuit in two and grape preserves dripped down onto my hand. "Even Mrs. Rachel Newsome can talk the fire out of you. That's no big deal. I can't believe they came all the way out here to tell you that."

"No, silly, they were looking for you. Word has gotten around. Dr. Kincaid couldn't even find any damaged skin on Clyde's back."

I licked the spot of sticky preserves off my hand and made a face. "It wasn't me, Mama."

"I know that and so does everyone else. Clyde getting healed was not the only thing that happened last night."

I chewed the broken biscuit. Mama looked like she did when she came twirling out of the bedroom in a new dress.

"Brother Oscar went on back to his tent, and when he realized how many had stayed at the barn, he became very upset."

"That's simple enough. He hadn't gotten all the collection he wanted yet. The fire robbed him of the chance to rob others."

She put her hand on my arm. "True enough. But he went to preaching about you. 'How could a mere girl think she was fit to get up among the saints of God who were assembled there and pray?' They say he said girls like you were why this nation was going to the Communists, and they better start practicing calling one another comrade instead of brother."

I felt a lump of biscuit in my stomach, and despite the preserves and butter, the biscuit in my mouth had gone dry.

In Mama's excitement she jiggled the table. "Then a spark from that tobacco barn floated over while he was in the midst of this tirade about you, and before anything could be done, the tent caught fire and burned up completely. They only barely saved the piano."

CHAPTER 5

From the moment that spark touched the fabric of the tent, our lives were never the same. People rode by the house in various combinations on Sunday afternoons. Young and old in a blue New Yorker, two fat ones and a thin one in a black DeSoto, a man and woman and five children hanging out the back of a green Oldsmobile, all driving by the house in a slow parade with windows rolled down until later when it became cold and then with faces placed flat against the steamy window glass. About every fifth or sixth car produced a camera and snapped pictures for those back home, bedridden and infirm. Abraham and Isaac had to be locked in the potato house every Sunday afternoon or they flat wore themselves out running after cars and barking.

Mama welcomed our newfound celebrity with varying degrees of enthusiasm. One day it was a miracle; the next, the mere unstoppable progression of women who deserved the world's attention. Mama referred to the carloads of people as "well-wishers." Granny, on the other hand, was not so gracious.

"I guess these people sit around after dinner on Sunday and say to one another, 'What shall we do this afternoon? Certainly not study the Holy Word to see how we need to be living our lives. Oh no, let's ride on over to Sampson County and make life miserable for those three women trying to scratch out a living on the land.

Let's kick up enough dust that neither they nor their animals will be able to breathe, and generally ruin as much as we can by driving through.' "

Without hardly pausing for breath, she added, "And let's us forget our manners entirely and stare like white-trash Republicans or Yankees raised us every one."

Amidst the whirlwind of scrutiny, we tried hard to maintain a normal routine. I continued in my classes at Pineland. My studies were my refuge.

More and more our house had become Norma's refuge. Often she came by on Sunday afternoon to talk of movie stars, and boys, and to let us know who wore falsies at the drugstore where she worked. Uncle Peter's telephone was a party line, so Norma was forced to send news of her flirtations with John Herring by mail during the week. In early October, we received a short letter from Norma—at long last, she had a date with John Herring. Would Mama do her hair for the occasion?

The following Saturday afternoon, Norma arrived at our house with her pink bag of hair curlers in one hand and a movie magazine in the other. Mama often did Norma's hair for church on Sunday. After Mama rolled her hair, Norma would sit under the big bonnet dryer, reading her *Photoplay.* Then she would share the latest from Hollywood while Mama sprayed and styled, flipping Norma's bangs over her eyes so she looked like a starlet getting ready to kiss her first leading man.

For this routine, we moved Mama's vanity bench to the sitting area next to the kitchen. That Saturday, Norma sat in the middle of the bench like a queen on a throne, her royal robe made of a towel clipped around her shoulders with an aluminum hair clip. A crown of pink curlers would soon replace her wet blond hair.

Mama walked in wearing a gauzy white shirtwaist dress. It reached the floor by a series of tiers, each accented with lace. Her red hair was swept away from her face in a Gibson girl style. She looked beautiful.

My red-gold hair was one of the few characteristics bequeathed to me by my mama. My hair was my most glorious feature, whereas with Mama it was one of the many notable things that made up her stunning good looks. The color wrapped around her in dainty waves that she eventually styled under, like Rosemary Clooney, making her look more like my sister than my mama. My hair, thick and curly, could never be counted on to go in the right direction, or any particular direction, for that matter.

"Aunt Lilah, what in the world are you wearing?" Norma's head tilted for a better view.

"This dress belonged to your great-grandmother. Isn't it wonderful?"

Norma nodded her head, closing her mouth in the process.

"As soon as we're done," Mama continued, "I'm going to take the Bible and go sit on the front porch."

Mama found the front-porch glider a perfect place to strike a pose for our weekend tourists.

"Sometimes we'll get a few 'well-wishers' on Saturday afternoon. I hate for them to take home a picture of a white farmhouse with an empty front porch."

Norma clutched at the towel around her neck. "People can't see in here, can they?"

Mama glanced at the kitchen window. "My heavens, no. Maggie told me your delicious news. And don't you worry. By the time we're done with your hair, John Herring will think you belong in the movies."

Mama had almost finished rolling up all of Norma's wet hair when Granny's truck pulled into the side yard. We heard her walk to the front yard, and presently there was the sound of the front screen door opening and closing. Granny came into the sitting room.

"Well, hello there, Norma. Maggie tells me that you're stepping out with one of the Herring boys. There's a fine family for you. Just plain good people."

Norma tried to nod her head, but Mama had a piece of her hair pulled tight, wrapping it around a roller.

Granny went right on, never expecting anyone to disagree with her assessment of the Herring family. "You will not believe what they are telling for the truth down at the Feed and Seed in Salemburg. Some woman from Clinton has come over here and pulled off a piece of one of my hydrangeas. Gone all over telling everybody that she stuck it in her bathwater and it cured her eczema. Have you ever? I looked out there on my way in and, dog my cats, if there isn't a big stem missing off one side of my smallest blue bush. Craziest thing I ever heard of."

"Mama, people don't all think the way we do," my mama said as she stuck the last plastic pick in Norma's hair.

Granny looked down her nose. "No, they don't. There's some that believes there's a man in the moon."

Norma and I laughed.

Granny looked at Mama's dress. "You're not planning to sit on that porch all afternoon, are you?"

Mama smiled. "Now, what could be wrong with studying the Scriptures for a few hours?"

"Aunt Lilah, you are too much." Norma laughed.

Granny nodded. "Now, there's a statement I could agree with. I'm going out and check on my collards. If you need any edification of those Scriptures, just holler." And she was gone.

By the time Norma left a few hours later, her hairstyle would have rivaled Connie Francis's latest. My own hair fought successfully to escape its ponytail. No matter. Instead of a movie, I planned to get ahead in the reading for my courses at Pineland, hardly the most exciting thing for a young woman of nineteen. It would be nice to go out and not worry about who saw you and who didn't and, by the way, could you come over here and meet my cousin Ed? He's got the shingles and we need you to snap up a little miracle while you're here. On the other hand, the thought of having to spend my evening thinking of enough interesting things to say to

John Herring or smiling a certain way at him all night long didn't appeal much to me either. I didn't wish so much for what I didn't have, but more I wished for less of what I did have.

That had always been my way, even during the camp meeting week we attended every year in Falcon. Granny would rent a room over in the dormitory and we would spend the week in services and prayer. From up on our third-floor balcony, Falcon extended out before us, a jewel of rich green fields. After supper every evening, groups of boys and girls would promenade around and around the tabernacle. Gradually many would pair off to walk with a like-minded saint of the opposite sex.

I was never one for promenading with anyone but girls, and would walk with a group until they paired off with boys and I was left to walk alone, or Granny called me in for the night. Until I was nineteen, boys would ask me to walk with them and be refused. I had no interest. Each time I said no, I walked a little taller. These were only boys, regular boys whose interests were limited to farming and breeding and such. Some had more interest in breeding than anything else. No, I was not going to make the same mistake as my mama. And so I would refuse. After I was nineteen, no one asked anymore.

Mama adored camp meeting in Falcon. She could scandalize large groups of people without ever leaving the county. It was a chance to be out of the woods and away from the farm, providing inspiration for much of her poetry. The visiting evangelists would often read a piece of hers from the pulpit, having no idea of the "example of her life," as Granny called it.

Within two weeks, Granny's hydrangea bush disappeared completely. One poor soul even came at night and dug up the roots. I can't imagine what that did to their bathwater.

The yard around us might have been spirited away piece by piece, except that Granny, the two oldest Elliot boys, and Mr. Neb kept watch with shotguns at night. The boys and Mr. Neb politely asked people to move on about their business and not come back on the property at night. When Granny caught someone, she'd flip on the porch light and yell, "If you've come to get you a healing souvenir, you better pray to the dear Lord that you find one that will take care of the hole I'm gonna shoot into you if you touch one thing on this property."

No one ever took her up on it.

Wherever I went, attention followed. It would have been nice to enjoy all the notice paid me like my mama did, but I couldn't. I still carried that vision with me, and it made me restless. Nervous, too. For I never knew when God might appear again. Would I be able to do what the Lord asked of me? On the practical side, I could never leave the house, not even to run to the Open Air Market for Oxydol, without Mama inspecting my appearance.

My life changed as well when the Traveling Tabernacle became a pile of ash and a sooty piano. With the exception of Norma, who embarked on a steady courtship with John Herring, people treated me like they would the preacher. They became mindful of their language and seemed afraid to express strong emotion around me. This soon had them avoiding me altogether, for nobody can stand to stay on their preacher-in-the-house behavior but for so long at a time.

My personal history sprouted new details. For instance, Tessie told everyone who would listen that I had been born with a caul over my face, an event whose significance was passed on to her by a transplanted mountain woman. The woman had interpreted Tessie's dream from the night before my birth, a dream of a baby being born with the skin over her face, the sign of a special person.

"Sure enough, that baby was Maggie," Tessie said, with a look that dared anyone to doubt her. This was Tessie's contribution to my myth.

The story of Will Atkinson's finger got rehashed all over again. Even adults nodded to me as if I was somebody important but unapproachable. On the one hand, I was treated like someone with the stoutest reputation in town; on the other hand, I received the same welcome reserved for folks with strong body odor.

I wanted to run after them and shout, "I'm the same as I always was. Don't be afraid."

For once, Granny and Mama agreed that if I acted normally, people would come around eventually. I did my best. When I wasn't doing my chores or attending classes, I studied and read more than I had in all my nineteen years. I searched the Scriptures, devoured all the books at the school library, and practically memorized Granny's medical reference book, looking for the cause of my apparitions, to no avail.

When Granny was not around, Mama asked me over and over again to tell her about my vision at Mr. Clyde's. I don't understand why this is happening, I told her. Her words of comfort were, "Magdalena, if faith were only believing in what we can see or know, then it would not be faith. Faith isn't understanding; don't confuse the two. Too many people do."

"But still, Mama, why?"

With a shrug of her shoulders Mama said, "Magdalena, if we could explain all the whys of God, then there wouldn't be a God. God is as little a mystery as why chickens have wings but can't fly and as big a mystery as why your uncle Peter says all the right words, but the concept of love escapes him as completely as if he were an alien from outer space."

One evening in the spring, Granny and I went to check on a field one of the Elliot boys had plowed for us. As we rode along, she questioned me about Mr. Clyde's back.

"It was God again, Granny. She was there just like when I prayed over Will Atkinson's finger."

"You still hold out that He's a woman? I'd have thought you'd have grown out of that notion by now."

"No, ma'am. I mean yes, ma'am, She is a woman. She's more beautiful than anything you can imagine."

"Maggie, ain't no such of a thing." Granny banged the steering wheel with her hand for emphasis. "God is not a woman. Just because your mama is a mind to chase after crazy notions doesn't mean you have to follow right behind."

"Mama never told me God was a woman."

"I'm not saying she did, but there are entirely too many possibilities in your mama's life. The Bible is God's Holy Word, and when they write about God in the Bible, they say 'He' and that's final."

"Then you think I'm crazy."

Granny's tone softened a little. "No, honey, I don't think you're crazy. And I'm not saying you're not having a vision. Your great-granny used to know things sometimes ahead of the rest of us. The Lord does move in mysterious ways."

"So you don't think I'm making it up?"

"Never said that. I've seen you raised up to be an honest young woman. No need for you to be untruthful. Walking around saying God's a woman isn't the best way to get attention. You're smart enough to know that. Maybe it's an angel talking to you. I don't know, but I do know that there is not one thing you can say to convince me that God is a woman. And I do know that you'd best keep the details of these visions between you and the dear Lord. Not everyone knows you like your mama and I do."

"I made Mama promise she wouldn't tell," I said.

"I reckon that's the best we can do, then."

That settled it for Granny. However the Lord decided to appear to me was between God and me, but unless the Almighty was planning to send angels to work the farm, there was no time to sit around arguing the finer points of my visions. Crops still waited to be planted.

I received the Word of Knowledge about many who came and sought me out at Canaan Free Will Church. I knew their troubles as soon as I looked in their eyes. The sanctuary became a mass of people on Sundays that spilled into the churchyard and down the road. We found offerings in our car and on the porch at the house. Folks laid in wait for Granny to leave so that they could put their gifts on the front porch without putting themselves at risk of the widely known shotgun.

Mama ran interference at the front door, talking with people about their troubles and being so sympathetic that many felt their burdens lift without even speaking to me. The gentle suggestion Mama gave to each involved seeing me in church on Sundays or on Wednesdays. On campus at Pineland, I avoided the public areas and sometimes Mama picked up my lessons for me to do at home. And so we made it through that first year.

The following September, Granny received an emergency summons from the Hobbs family, the tenants on the very edge of the back forty. Mr. Reginald Hobbs was suffering with his heart. Could Granny please come see if she thought anything could be done?

Timmy, the oldest of the Hobbses' children, shuffled his feet on the kitchen floor; their bareness was a testament to the last days of Indian summer. "If it wouldn't be too much trouble, Mama thought Maggie might come along. In case she was of a mind to pray for Daddy."

"That or go get the doctor," Granny agreed.

I put the last supper dish in the drainer and we set off for the Hobbses', the three of us in the front seat of the pickup with Timmy now riding in the truck bed. My legs had grown longer than Mama's by then, but I still sat in the middle with my feet resting on the black hump in the floor and my legs folded up around me.

Mostly what you saw when you entered the Hobbses' house was children. The Hobbses had thirteen of them. One a year like clockwork since their marriage. Somewhere along the line Mrs. Hobbs lost three babies, bringing it up to sixteen years of marriage.

They never went to church at all since they didn't have the right clothes. Mrs. Hobbs explained this to Mama when she came to see her as a Home Demonstration Agent to help update Mrs. Hobbs's methods of canning. Mama certainly sympathized with the excuse, but it went nowhere with Granny.

"The Lord looked upon Adam and Eve when they had no clothes on. He is certainly not going to be bothered with a little faded material."

Mrs. Hobbs stood in the doorway twisting a dishrag around and around in her hand. Mr. Hobbs lay stretched out across the bed in the front bedroom stiff as a mummy. The Hobbses called Granny not so much for her medical knowledge as for money to fund the doctor's bill. For Granny, that was all part of being an owner. She kept the same tenants for years since most owners were known for being tight and considered the tenants' troubles as none of their own.

Granny questioned Mr. Hobbs thoroughly. Location of pain? Length of pain? How many days in pain? Was it a burning or a pricking?

Mr. Hobbs mostly grunted in reply. Meantime, Mama carried on a conversation with Mrs. Hobbs about the coming season and the latest baby who was attached like a monkey to Mrs. Hobbs's hip.

Mrs. Hobbs's only attempt at decoration was a brass plate Mama had brought her back from a convention when she worked with the Home Demonstration Club. Shiny dark lines ran through it, forming a picture of a horse and buggy going over a bridge bordered by flowering cherry trees. I stepped closer to look at a detail in the shiny surface. The circle of light started in the center and widened to take in the entire plate. She spoke to me from the light: "My Son said inasmuch as you have done it unto the least of these. Here is a soul in torment. Help him."

She faded, though the warmth stayed with me. I wanted to ask Her questions, but She was gone. I turned to Mr. Hobbs, whom Granny still questioned. An angel above his shoulder spoke clearly. I repeated the words as the angel spoke them to me.

"The fortune-teller is powerless over you, except for the power you give her. She binds you up with sickness not because of a curse, but because you believe in her power. Pray for your spirit's release. Your body is fine."

Mr. Hobbs sat up on the bed like one of those bodies in a Frankenstein movie. Mrs. Hobbs started to cry.

"How did you know? How did you know? Lord, they said she could see things, but I didn't hardly believe it."

Granny folded her arms and looked at me. "I'll be talking with you later." Then she turned to Mrs. Hobbs. "What happened?"

"Reginald's been feeling poorly ever since that fortune-teller come through about a week ago. She took one look at him and could see that he had a curse on him. Said it was something awful. She said she'd be of a mind to take it off."

Granny looked first at one Hobbs and then another and then back again. "Upon my soul, you have not paid a fortune-teller for this?"

Mrs. Hobbs smiled at her in relief. "No'm, we done spent all our tobacco money. We didn't have no cash money left to give her. I couldn't hardly think who would've worked the roots on Reginald. I asked why would a body trouble with Reginald—he don't do anybody no harm. But she wasn't telling—it was cash money or nothing. I just played along like maybe we had some money, trying to see if she would slip and tell us."

Granny blew at Mrs. Hobbs like she was a candle on a birthday cake, causing her proud smile to momentarily fade.

"What else did she tell you?"

Mrs. Hobbs went into a long explanation of how the woman was going to cast a spell to cure the deadly rash that she noticed on the baby's face. But that was before she realized they had no money. All the Hobbses chimed in on the last of the story, pleased to reveal that the baby's rash had been nothing more than a dark red candy that the knee-baby, Parker, had given her earlier. Upon that revelation, the fortune-teller turned her sights on Mr. Hobbs.

"That's what I'm telling you," said Granny. "The woman doesn't know a rash from candy. Imagine if you had given your money to that woman. Now, aren't you glad the Lord looked after you with your empty pockets?"

Mrs. Hobbs nodded her agreement with Granny's insight. "That's so true, Mrs. Parker. She told us such terrible things for free, I couldn't have stood what we'd have found out if we'd had the money to pay her."

Mama gazed out the door at some unknown point on the horizon; her mouth twitched at the corners.

Mr. Hobbs came up off the bed like Lazarus. He shrugged his shoulders as if to shake off the last of the curse from which he believed I freed him. The Hobbses weren't much for reasoning things out, but they worked hard, and before we finished arranging ourselves back in the truck, Mr. Hobbs had his sons on out about their chores.

CHAPTER
6

There were no clouds in the sky, and the sweat trickled down, caught by my bra and slip, warm against my skin. The stiff slip that Mama insisted I wear, so that my dress stood out at just the right angle, itched as bad as a case of poison ivy.

Mama brushed some tiny piece of lint off my dress. It was a navy dress with cap sleeves and navy bows down the front of the bodice. The full skirt stood away from me, supported by the slip as uncomfortable as any ancient mystic's hair shirt. If I complained, Mama only shrugged and told me that beauty came with a price.

"I don't know what made you decide on navy today, Magdalena. It picks up everything but men."

"Lily! It's the Lord's day and we are going to church. The way you're carrying on, you'd think Maggie was some teenager off to her first lemonade social."

I nodded my head in agreement with Granny. Mama's lint picking made me feel like some sort of monkey at the zoo getting cleaned by its mama.

Granny piloted the car through the crowd. All it took to create the carnival we faced was one newspaper reporter from Raleigh, noticing that the most spectacular (as he termed it) healings occurred on the third Sunday of the month. This third Sunday in October found Canaan so full of people that the crowd lined the route from Granny's house to the church as if it were the Fayetteville Christmas parade.

"I'm sure I would want to do ever thing I could if someone in my family was afflicted, but I swanee, a good portion of these people have got to be thrill-seekers and such." Granny sniffed. "Belong back in their home churches doing something constructive for the Lord."

Mama's voice came from beside me in the backseat. "Sometimes, Mama, people need to do something for their souls. Sometimes people need something more than their home church."

This from the woman who still brushed at the lint on my dress as if it were radioactive. Satisfied at last with my dress, Mama waved and smiled as we drove along, like a beauty queen sitting on top of a parade float. Occasionally she leaned across to wave out the window on my side of the car. She wore a dark green paisley dress with a string of pearls that looped twice around her neck and then were knotted on the end.

Outside the door of the church stood Mr. Atkinson and Will. They tried to let as many people in as the concrete building could hold, while at the same time making sure that all the members present found a seat. I got out of the car and moved toward the door.

When he thought I couldn't hear, Mr. Atkinson remarked, "Don't seem right for folks who come to church regular like to not even have a place to sit on Sunday because outsiders think they are going to get to see a carnival act."

A carnival act. I looked across the people pressing forward and prayed for something, anything. They pressed harder, a girl with a limp leg in a yellow shirtwaist dress supported by an elderly woman and man, his overall bib stained with chewing tobacco. Jostled by those behind them, a young couple pushed forward on the other side, the wife with dark circles under her eyes and a body rounded by impending motherhood, the husband slumped under his love of alcohol like it was a yoke across his neck. I wasn't who these people thought. It wasn't right. I didn't even want to be who these people thought I was.

Around me I heard comments.

"She's taller than I thought she'd be."

"One of them's wearing makeup."

"Doesn't she have the most rich-looking hair?"

"My Milton says he's sure she's a fake."

I closed my eyes. I wanted to open them and say, *Your Milton's exactly right. I am a fake.* Then this circus would be all over. Eventually people would forget and leave me alone.

The church door loomed in front of me; the flaking white paint seemed unfamiliar, even sinister. I wanted nothing more than home. As I turned to go back down the walk, I opened my eyes and there he stood. A boy, leaning on a crutch, smiling up at me with no hesitation. In that moment, I knew his pain and I knew his hope. They swallowed my need just like that whale swallowed Jonah.

She floated beside him and the brightness of Her blotted out everyone else. Where moments before there was a crowd, now only he stood.

I moved forward. People stepped back. Mama told me later it was the Red Sea parting before Moses. I took his small hand, muscled from the use of the crutch.

"Do you know that God loves you?"

He nodded yes.

"Do you have faith that with God all things are possible?"

He nodded again.

I took his hand and prayed, "God, it is not our will, but yours which we seek. Guide us to know the way that we may serve you and show your face to the world through our love." My arm tingled with heat. "Heal this leg, for this soul is already at peace with you. Amen."

The boy smiled and in his face was the glory of God. He pushed his crutch aside. He leaned on me and we walked a few feet. He let go of my arm and continued along, taking shaky steps like a newborn calf. The radiance of God smiled upon me and the still, small

Voice said, "Well done." I fell to my knees, praying to have the peace of the child.

But it was not to be.

Hands grabbed at me. People cried, "Me," "My son," "My daughter." As the radiance of God faded, I found myself among the seekers, pressed from all sides. The light faded; the day turned dark.

I tried to stand and fainted.

When I woke up, Mama was sitting in the rocking chair beside the bed, reading *True Detective* magazine and patting my hand. Once Mama felt certain that I was in no danger of going out again, she told me all about how the clouds had come from nowhere. Then she wiped my face with a cool washcloth. Once the clouds came up, Mama said, people saw Jesus in them right above my head when I held the boy's hand and walked with him. After I fainted, there had been reports of spontaneous healings and speaking in tongues.

Several men in the church had brought Mama and me home, and Mr. Paul Lovingood carried me in the house for Mama. Granny remained behind for service more out of principle than anything else. Will Atkinson slipped away early to check on me and tell Mama all the things she missed after we left.

The local newspaper published pictures of the cloud formations. Then the Raleigh papers printed them and so on. The boy was besieged by reporters and ministers unhappy about missing money from members of their congregations who flocked toward the Canaan Free Will Baptist Church on Sunday. The ministers and reporters wanted medical records proving he had infantile paralysis. They wanted a doctor's certificate of healing. It was provided. The boy, a child of ten, posed holding his crutches horizontally, and the picture met the same fate as the cloud pictures.

In the days that followed I thought often of skipping rocks. It was one of the only things my daddy had ever taught me to do. He showed me how to pick out a smooth flat one and throw it just right, low and straight above the water, so that it jumped and skimmed the surface before it finally could not defy gravity any longer and fell beneath the surface. Before Daddy left the last time, I could get a rock to skip two or three times every now and then. Daddy could skip them four or five times every time. I felt like one of those rocks hovering above the water, sure that any minute I was going down for the last time.

The chain of events surrounding the publication of the boy's picture grew like the circles in a pond when you throw a rock straight in. They kept getting wider and wider, going further and further, taking in more and more.

CHAPTER

7

They say grass is always greener on the other side of the fence. Granny said, "Greed is like a tapeworm. It eats you from the inside out and one day there won't be nothing left of you but a shell." Granny's experience with this was firsthand. Her daddy had bought more and more land after the war until he had nothing but land and his reputation for greed throughout the lower Cape Fear region. He lost it all in the Hoover years. Two weeks after the sheriff showed up at the door to deliver the writ claiming his land, my great-granddaddy shot himself while he was on a drunk in Wilmington.

"You see, my daddy had nothing to sustain him but what he owned, nothing on his inside." Granny thumped her hand against her chest. "Nothing. Not faith, not a love for his family, no reason to live. He spent his whole life getting and never once figured out the giving."

It was the closest I ever came to telling my granny that I loved her.

God can use greed to good purpose.

By this time in my life I generally observed that when people didn't want to do their own dirty work, they formed a committee.

Canaan had a few standing committees such as the Fourth of July and the Civil Defense Committees, although the latter was disbanded after no one would agree to dig a communal bomb shelter on their land. The business district wasn't much more than a post office, a service station, and a drugstore. If you needed other things, you went to Lawton, Berryville, or Clinton. But Canaan did have a mayor.

Canaan's mayor was Butte Norris, a tall, serious man. Your first thought when you saw him was that his professional calling must be undertaker. Actually, he farmed and owned the service station in town, which Harmon, his son-in-law, managed.

When Butte came up the walk that February evening followed by an informal mayor's committee, he looked like he had come to fetch a body. Despite it being a Tuesday, he wore his Sunday suit. With him were the mayors of Lawton and Berryville dressed likewise. They moved more natural in their suits, whereas Butte's looked like he'd picked up somebody else's clothes by mistake and hadn't taken the time to adjust them.

Granny and I arranged ourselves in kitchen chairs between the front-room couch and company chair that the men occupied after much protest. Mama stayed in the kitchen. Butte had requested a meeting with Granny and myself, adding as an afterthought that it would be fine for my mama to attend. She declined with a quick shake of her head, but she came and offered coffee and pie all around. There were no takers. She winked at me as she came by and rolled her eyes. Meetings of this nature held no interest for a free spirit such as herself. It suddenly made me realize just how much of the responsibility Granny had shouldered for us all those years.

The mayors of Lawton and Berryville shared the couch. The Lawton mayor, Neely Lipscomb, had hair like Porter Wagoner, the country singer. He smoothed it up in a curl like an ocean wave and then laid it down like a helmet on his head. Hair wasn't the only thing Porter and the mayor had in common. Years later when Porter started *The Porter Wagoner Show,* I thought how much those sequined suits he wore reminded me of Neely Lipscomb, all flashy and fake.

The preliminaries over, Butte hurried on to the reason for the meeting. "Miss Naomi, Maggie." He nodded as if meeting us on the street. "We've come to talk with you about something that could prove beneficial to us all—"

The Lawton mayor interrupted, "A great benefit, *particularly* to your family."

Interrupting was the mark of a demi-breed in Granny's mind. I saw her start to look down her nose at Mr. Neely Lipscomb. He, unaware of the ill winds that began to circle around him, continued, "We all know about *Life* magazine planning to visit you and all. Certainly, when that article gets released, there will be even more publicity. Now, it is quite evident that God is blessing you with his gifts. And we know, being the kind of neighbors you are and all, that you want to share his blessings with the community."

Granny's eyes never moved off him. "Well, Mr. Lipscomb, I'm sure you know that we've always tried to be generous with our neighbors." She leaned forward in her chair. "As far as who the Lord chooses to heal, if that's what you're after, that is certainly not up to any of us."

It relieved me that she gestured around the room and not to me.

"Certainly not. But there are other ways to share blessings. We have several hot springs outside of Canaan in the county. Now, if Maggie here were to start using a little of that spring water as she is laying on the healing hands . . ." He paused and pointed first at Granny and then at me. "Well, you can imagine that people would be wanting some, and naturally"—he had a way of dragging out the word *naturally* that made it sound most unnatural—"filling that kind of need could mean economic miracles, if I may use that word, for us all."

"Absolutely." The Berryville mayor, Reese Moore, spoke up as if he were shouting amen or hallelujah during preaching while seconding this point. I noticed Butte making the slightest movement, as he inclined his body toward the door. I believe he saw Granny looking down her nose and was readying himself for a hasty retreat.

The other two men had no such insight into Granny's temperament and so continued along the route of self-destruction, heartily agreeing with each other on points such as prosperity, "what's good for Sampson County is good for the country," and so on. Neely Lipscomb had a broad smile. I thought of what Mr. Neb would say: "He looked just like a jackass eating briars; his lips be all turned up to keep the thistles from sticking to them." The thought made me smile. The two mayors took this as a sign of encouragement.

Butte twitched noticeably now—I hoped he would try to save himself and leave these two to sink on their own, mired in the hog pen they were happily making for themselves. By the time Granny opened her mouth, Butte hovered a full inch off his chair.

"You know, I once heard there was nothing so becoming to a fool as a shut mouth. And I'd have to say that this is all the confirmation I need of that."

I heard Mama drop something in the next room. Her love of drama would have had her listening with one ear to the living-room conversation, and Granny's word choice would have shocked her as much as it did me. We both knew how my granny felt about the scriptural admonishment to call no man a fool.

The men sat like schoolboys getting a scolding, eyes blinking and hands stuck in their pockets. Granny never moved from her seat, but her voice towered over them, pushing them deeper down in their chairs.

"Maggie's gifts are that very thing—gifts from the Almighty. And to think that she would tempt the Lord's anger with such foolishness as this, well, that beats all I've ever heard." Granny paused for breath. There wasn't so much as the sound of a gulp in the room. The men held their breath the same as if they were swimming underwater. "It's the likes of you that makes the poor poorer still. Lining your pockets with what's important to you. The Bible says, 'Where your treasure is there will your heart be also.' "

Now the men began to choke and sputter like swimmers coming up for air and getting water instead. Granny turned to Butte. "I never thought I'd see the day you let somebody talk you into such as this. Sodom and Gomorrah right here, that's what it is."

Butte wrung his hands. The other two men took this as an opportunity to make for the door. The Lawton mayor turned back with the foolishness of Lot's wife.

"Not cooperating with the community might cause some poor feelings about your granddaughter."

Granny's rage was dense around us. I fully expected we'd be placing this man, a statue of salt, out by the stream for the deer to lick.

"A choice between the bad side of the community and eternal damnation don't seem like much of a choice to me at all."

Butte moved toward the door, apologizing all the way. His anxiety worked his mouth into a funny little smile. Even in his haste, he still stuck his head around the door frame and said good night to my mama.

The next day, Butte stopped by to offer his apologies and a promise to make restitution for his error. Whatever and whenever he could assist us, we only needed to let him know. He knew how defenseless three women could be alone together.

CHAPTER 8

Canaan Free Will Church was split on the issue of the healings. Part of the congregation saw them as a natural outgrowth of their faith, and part of the congregation saw them as the work of Lucifer. A prophet is scorned in his own land, Jesus said, and there were those who took it upon themselves to prove that Canaan was certainly Biblical on that point.

Our preacher, Luther Liles, a practical man who had been proclaiming the Word of God, winning souls to Jesus, and overseeing the sanctification of the saints at Canaan Free Will Church since I was an infant, rejoiced in the windfall. A former football player for Salemburg High School, he ended every service, winter or summer, with his shirt soaked through, like he'd been baptized right there in the pulpit. Preacher Liles (who ran a body shop during the week) prayed with me through every service until we had invocated over the last pilgrim faithful. The extra money from the Sunday-morning collections over the previous year financed an addition to our cement block church building. It was almost complete by the time the *Life* magazine reporter and photographer arrived. As a result of their visit, an article of a page and a half with several photographs appeared in the magazine.

They had us pose in front of the house. I looked like a startled deer while Mama managed to smile, and Granny scowled despite the photographer's best attempt to get her to do otherwise. (Granny would perk up later when the *Life* article referred to her as a sturdy country woman of great faith.) The March 1960 edition carried Jack Kennedy and Hubert Humphrey campaigning on the cover and Granny, Mama, and myself on the inside—right after an editorial on a California murder trial.

The reporter mentioned how convenient it would be if Jesus would oblige us by appearing in the clouds again so that the photographer could get a professional shot of him. At that suggestion Granny began to look down her nose. I took the reporter down to the church to save him from himself. He tried one more time to get me to pose praying over a man on crutches; I refused.

"Do you get the feeling people laugh at you when you talk about seeing God?" he asked me.

"I imagine people will always laugh at something. For instance, look at Noah. Can you imagine Noah had to look around this dry desert country and tell everybody, 'I'm going to build a boat big enough to carry two of every creature God put on this earth because there is going to be a real bad flood'? What do you suppose folks said to him? What do you suppose folks said about him when he wasn't around? Likely it wasn't any big compliments."

"If these healings turn out to be genuine, what do you make of that?"

"It's not me. I don't know how She picked me, and I don't know when She'll move on."

"Did you say 'She'?"

The blood rose in my face. "Oh no, it must be my accent's confusing you." I tried my most winsome smile.

"Yeah, I guess so." He looked at my flushed face and frowned.

"We've been out in the sun too long, and you must not be used to it being this warm in New York. How about some tea?" I turned slightly and tried to breathe like there wasn't a thing wrong. The sun must have gotten to *me*. I'd guarded my vision of God very carefully since I was ten. The idea of having it photo-spread across *Life* magazine filled me with dread.

The reporter's questions never slowed.

With the *Life* magazine article the floodgates were opened. There followed a string of newspaper, radio, and television reporters, some of whom printed and broadcast less than complimentary things.

One man from the Raleigh paper implied something sinister and off-color about my mama. Granny drew the line. The next time the reporter came round, she stood him down out on the edge of the yard. Echoing the sentiments of A. A. Allen, she said, "I don't doubt you think you know all of what's going on around here. Your eyes are so close together you can see through a keyhole with both of them at the same time, but you are no longer welcome on this property."

I had to sneak around my own life; on occasion, Mr. Neb would hide me in the back of the truck and take me up the road a ways so that I could get out into some wide-open space and walk a bit without having to assume the manners of a Hollywood star or a Russian spy. There were two places that I was in the habit of going. One was an old tobacco barn out behind a grove of pecan trees that my granddaddy Eli had planted forty years earlier. The other place was over near a creek that ran along the edge of both our land and Mr. G. T. Spell's. Mr. G.T., who was head of the deacons at the Canaan Free Will Church, often waved at me as I tromped across the field to the creek.

From the time I was old enough to go out of sight of the house, the creek had fascinated me. I played in it when I was small, watching the water make its way through the rocks. As I got older I rolled up the legs of my jeans and waded in. The water cooled me against the first hint of summer, and the rocks poked into the bottom of my soft skin, my feet having not yet developed their summer shell. In the early spring the wisteria and forsythia bloomed, dusting a yellow coating on any water that remained still long enough. Then the black-eyed Susans appeared, growing all the way up to the edge of Mr. G.T.'s fields. Bluebirds abounded and every year they surprised me, as I forgot through the long winter how awfully bright and delicate they were, blue against blue.

In the midst of the healing storm that April, I stowed away with Abraham and Isaac in the back of Mr. Neb's truck on a run he was making to the Open Air Market. He carried us out of sight of the house and pulled over. I hopped out and opened the tailgate for Abraham and Isaac, who jumped down beside me.

Mr. Neb looked behind us at the empty road. "Looks like you sitting pretty now."

I walked up and leaned in the cab. "Sure am. Thanks a bunch."

"Be careful," he said, and pulled the truck back onto the road. I watched as it melted into the horizon.

I whistled to the dogs and we made our way down through the cleared field that would be planted with cotton seeds as soon as we went a week without rain. The dogs stopped here and there to lift a leg and mark their territory.

We walked about a mile before we came to the creek bank, where the grass grew almost to my knees. If I'd been so inclined, I could have spread my arms and legs and made an angel like Mama taught me to do in the winter of '50 when it snowed as deep as my knees. I settled into the grass while Abraham and Isaac followed scents around the creek's edge before they lay down beside me in the grass to bask in the spring sun. The breeze moved the golden hair on Isaac's back.

As I patted his neck, I assured him, "No potato house now. We're free. No one's burdens to bear now."

I pulled my knees up and looked above me at the budding oak leaves that pushed out the last brown hangers-on from winter. The hint of green to come revealed itself in small bits that swayed and danced in some exotic island hula.

I closed my eyes and listened to the water as it wove its way through the rocks in the creek bed. The sun burned through my eyelids, blocking out all shapes and leaving only a formless bright blob in front of me.

The dogs growled low in their throats as the grass behind me rustled. I opened my eyes, but they were full of the sun's brightness. The dogs growled again, but stopped short after we all heard a clicking sound. Their tails began to thump the ground.

I brought my hand to my eyes. The man who stood before me smiled. He clicked his tongue again and the dogs' tails began to thump faster.

"Hey, Magpie. I'm home."

The bristles of his unshaven face pricked my skin in a hundred places as he leaned down and hugged me.

"I guess you and your mama have been kind of wondering where I've been."

I could feel my mama's heart breaking all the way back home. "No, Daddy, you quit wondering after about three or four years." I used my words like Granny used her shotgun. "You quit wondering and just go on because that's what you've got to do."

Even the ravages of alcohol, the deep lines around his eyes, and the two-day growth of beard could not hide how handsome my daddy was. He sat down beside me. The sweet-and-sour smell of day-old whiskey encircled us.

"Reckon your mama will be surprised?" Isaac put his head down under Daddy's hand to be petted.

"Reckon." *Please, Lord, let Mama still be gone when we get there. Don't make her go through this again.*

"She looks good, real good. That red hair just as purty as the first day I laid eyes on her."

"Mama's not home. When did you see Mama?" I wanted to slap him and I wanted to hug him. What right did he have to talk of my mama? It occurred to me that all this time when I thought Granny was being so mean, she was just trying to help my mama build a summer shell around her heart.

He rubbed Isaac behind the ears and I could see him forming a lie, as good as I could see him scratching that spot that made Isaac lift his leg to scratch back.

I knew.

"Somebody showed you that picture, didn't they?" I looked him straight in the eye.

He looked away. "What picture are you talking about, Magpie?"

"You know the picture I'm talking about. The one that was in *Life* magazine."

"Now thatcha mention it, someone did send me that picture general delivery in Biscoe. I was out making a run, so it was pretty near three weeks before I saw it. I've been planning to come see you just as soon as my luck turned, but seems like the only turn it ever takes is for the worse." He looked back at me and shrugged.

My daddy's luck had always turned for the worse.

"I've been doing a lot of work for a man over in Robeson County. Going from Pembroke to Rockingham and then sometimes over into Charlotte. They shut him down last week. I'm lucky I talked my way out of it. I didn't have any idea I was hauling bootleg. Man takes advantage of you like that, what can you do?"

"I don't know, Daddy. You might try looking in the back of the truck."

"Shoot, sugar, I trusted the man. Say, did I tell you I've been down to Darlington to the races a few times?" He shook his head. "Anyway, there I am inches away from going to jail and you're over here getting famous on me."

"Daddy, why are you here?" I picked a brown leaf from the grass and began to fold it. It was so brittle it crumpled in my hand.

"What do you mean, why am I here? I'm here to see my little girl and my wife." He put his arm around me and squeezed my shoulder.

"Daddy, I'm not a little girl." I let the pieces of brittle leaf fall from my hand.

"No, sir, you're not. I can see that. I bet the boys won't leave you alone."

I ignored him. "Have you been to the house? How did you find me?"

"Mr. Neb told me where to find you. I ran into him up at the Open Air Market."

"You coming back to the house?" I stood and began to pick the blades of grass from my jeans. I wanted to be finished with this; my heart had no summer shell.

"Hold on now. I wanted to talk to you. Just us." He stood beside me.

"Okay."

"Listen, Maggie, I've got a chance to buy me a wrecker. If I could get this truck, I could make steady money. Make something of myself."

I had known this was coming from the moment I'd figured out who he was against the brightness of the sun. I'd prayed it wouldn't be so, but that hadn't changed it.

The tears stung my eyes. "Daddy, I don't have any money."

"Who-wee, all these people and your picture in a fancy magazine and you don't have no money." Isaac pushed his head back under Daddy's hand, but Daddy pushed him away.

"No, Daddy, no money." He looked disappointed, and even though I didn't want to, I felt sorry for him. "Why don't you come on back to the house and we'll talk to Granny about it?"

"Magpie, I can't be doing that. I've got to be getting on back. I've got responsibilities. You tell your mama I said hey and tell her to write me."

He rubbed his bearded skin against my face again and he was gone, a dark shadow walking toward the highway.

That night Mama floated into my room on the cloud of her blue peignoir set. She looked so soft and delicate that it surprised me when the mattress sank under her weight.

"Mr. Neb tells me your daddy was at the Open Air Market today looking for you."

"Yes, ma'am, he found me down by the creek near Mr. G.T.'s."

She pushed my hair back off my forehead. "What did he want?"

"Oh, nothing really. He said to tell you hi. I think you can write to him general delivery at Biscoe, if you're of a mind to do it." I fiddled with the lace on my nightgown. "You know Daddy."

"Yes, I do. Did he ask you for money?" Mama took my hands in hers.

"He did. I told him I didn't have any to give him. Why is he like that, Mama?"

"Sweetie, if I knew the answer to that, we'd be living over in Chapel Hill, and I'd be teaching some sort of class at the university. All I know is alcohol is wrapped around your daddy as tight as kudzu. You have to promise never to give him any money."

She closed her eyes and put her hands down on the bed as if we were on a ship that lurched and she needed to steady herself. "And the saddest part is that he won't ever be able to show you how much I know he really loves you. Every hope and dream and bit of love your daddy has is down in the bottom of a pint liquor jar."

It was then that I realized she was crying, and I reached up with a corner of the bedsheet and dried her tears. "Don't worry, Mama. It'll be all right." The bonds of love and pain all seemed mixed together in a circle without end.

"I know, honey. I don't worry that I chose so bad for me. I've learned to make the best of it. But I hate with all my heart that I did so badly by you. You deserve so much more."

"It's okay, Mama." I kissed her on the cheek. "I love you."

"I love you," she said, and held me to her before she floated out in a swirl of blue, dabbing at her eyes and humming "Blues in the Night."

In all the hullabaloo of the next few weeks, the sadness that wrapped itself around my heart hardly seemed to matter.

Shortly after the article appeared, I started handing out cards for service. Preacher Liles brought up the suggestion at the encouragement of the deacon board. Otherwise, the bodies that pressed forward to be first in line crushed other people under them. The bodies pressed me, too, but even more the spirits that cried out to mine from behind shining eyes, flat eyes, eyes that would not meet mine for fear that they would see no answer for themselves there. Any Sunday morning you could find folks camped on the church grounds, sometimes on pallets of quilts, sometimes on a stretcher, sometimes stretched across the seats of their automobiles, all of them trying to get a card for the service. Looking out over the sea of hopes and hopelessness, I did not know who God would grant healing to here on earth and who God would heal by taking them home to heaven.

Services went on until I exhausted myself, hardly able to walk from one person to the next. Then I called on Granny, Preacher Liles, and the church elders to come and pray with me. Sometimes God provided healing, sometimes God did not. The mystery of God was not to be contained in a cinder-block church in Canaan, North Carolina. The services ended later and later. I struggled home to bed but was unable to sleep, though my body screamed for rest. And still someone would bring a child racked with fever to be prayed over. My most restless nights came when my prayers got no results. It forced me to look into the eyes of a young mother who placed into my hands her most precious life. "I'm getting nowhere. Best get a doctor."

The eyes looked back at me brimming with tears. "He's already said he cain't do him no good."

Then I cried out to God, "What am I to pray for? That a mama could give up the life of her child before it hardly begins, that she could release her flesh and blood and not hold it against you? What, I ask you, what?"

I knew in that instant that all mamas must give up their babies, if not to the grave, then to Butch Davidson or the bottle or the cross. But it's always easier to give up the babies of history than to give up the one of flesh and blood that lies breathing in your arms. It is the giving up before you're ready, the losing the child before you'd been able to make it a home outside your heart, that makes it so very hard. What you do with the giving up, that is life.

The mama turned from me into the comforting arms of the child's daddy. She moved with a dignity that would have been the envy of queens. "Let's us go on home, then, for I'll want to rock him on the porch."

With her went a piece of my soul.

The morning after that baby died, I made my way to the old tobacco barn behind the pecan trees. Normally, I sat on an old ladder-back chair that's final resting place was in the eaves of the barn. That morning I couldn't stay in the chair. Light streamed in from the open slats at the top of the barn, falling down around me in golden pillars as I paced the barn.

"What's the point? Why make me go through this? I don't want to do this anymore. Why did you give me this if you're going to make it so hard? That mama deserved more. I know you move in mysterious ways. I'm tired of mysterious ways. Do you hear me? Tired." I was almost hoping one of those beams of light would turn to lightning and I would be gone, never to look at another mama's tormented face again.

Then She was there in the golden light above me. For the first time it hurt my eyes to look, and I turned my face. But relief was in my body, my heart, my bones. Weak-kneed, I sank back down on the chair.

Sitting on the chair, feeling its rough wood against my legs, I cried. The Voice filled the barn, it filled me.

"Rest, just rest."

Through my tears I shouted, "How can I rest? I know it's You, You know it's You, but what does everyone else know? They want so much I haven't got. Now people come to see if the healing is real or isn't it. They want doctor's certificates and pieces of paper to frame for their walls. I'm a real person, too, not a phenomenon like that reporter said. I feel like Pinocchio. Like I'm spending my life waiting for someone to make me real."

Then I heard my granny's voice: "Be careful what you pray for, you just might get it." I turned to see if She was there. When I turned back, the light had faded.

CHAPTER 9

One soul drowns in the water another one swims through. Even as I came out of the Sunday-school room past the altar in the sanctuary, I noticed the stranger sitting in the last pew. June sunlight lit the pew around him. He had a look about him that made him easy to notice. Even from a distance his clothes looked different. The navy blazer he wore acted as a beacon, calling you to notice him in a congregation where most men never wore a jacket and tolerated ties like they did their mothers-in-law.

The windows of the sanctuary were open, trying to invite a breeze to blow out some of the warm June air. The breeze wasn't stirring, but the bees took up the invitation to join the fellowship. The big red flowers on Miss Hazel Harris's dress enticed them into the thick of us. I found a seat in our usual pew, where I was joined by Granny. Mama came in from Sunday school and stopped still as a deer that had picked up a human scent. She gazed steadily on the back pew until Granny coughed to get her attention and then glared at her until she sat down.

The Matthews Funeral home fans, with their pictures of Jesus' baptism in the river Jordan, beat time to the first hymn, "Heaven Is a Wonderful Place." The feet beneath the pews followed the same rhythm as the fans, *chit-chat, chit-chat*. Occasionally a fan shooed a wayward fly or became a shield to ward off an insistent bee.

I turned slightly as we sang so I could see the man in the back pew. Out of the corner of my eye, I watched as he held the hymnal and joined those around him in song. I lifted my hand and smoothed pieces of my hair that I knew hung loose from my topknot. The back of my dress clung to my legs. I pulled it loose, wishing I'd worn the green dress that Mama thought complemented my coloring. And then I chided myself for such a foolish thought.

Down on the end of the pew, Mama smiled and turned ever so slightly toward the back pew. I studied the words in the hymnal before me. We sang the amen and bowed for prayer.

The crowds seeking "the church of the healer" had thinned. This was first by necessity; the arrival of summer drew many of the local people into the fields. Second, the mayor of Lawton had set up a tent meeting on the edge of town with a preacher and healer that promised wealth beyond your dreams. He'd gotten him some billboards out on the interstate to try and pull in the unsuspecting as they passed through on their way to visit a long-lost aunt in Kissimmee, Florida. Still, many came to Canaan to be prayed over and the service lasted until well after noon.

Despite my fatigue from the service, I found myself glancing around, hoping for another glimpse of the stranger. I turned to speak to Mama, and he stood in front of me.

"I want to introduce myself. I'm Alex. Alex Barrons."

Sweat coated my palms. "I'm Maggie. Maggie Davidson."

"Yes, I know. I saw your picture in *Life* magazine."

My stomach felt as if I'd gotten up on Christmas morning and found a lump of coal in my stocking. He wasn't interested in me; he was interested in the girl in the magazine, the one who worked wonders.

"What do you want from me?"

My directness seemed to surprise him. "Well. Well, I was wondering if I might talk with you."

Now I was surprised, surprised at how much this pleased me. "I don't mind."

"I'm a seminary student at Princeton University. I'm doing a summer project as part of my thesis work on modern-day mystics and visions. I'm very interested in your visions and what you think they mean."

There was an edge to his smile that made me uncomfortable. I felt a twinge of regret that he'd voiced the interest that I already knew he had, an interest in visions and in girls who heal, not in me.

"If you want the doctor's certificates and the photographs, I'm sure they are all on file at the Clinton newspaper office. I don't really have anything to say."

Mama's hands gripped my shoulder from behind. "I'm Lilah Davidson, Magdalena's mother. She's completely forgotten her manners." She smiled at Alex. "We'd love to invite you home for dinner."

Alex returned her smile. "Thank you, I'd be delighted to accept. What time this evening?"

Mama laughed. "If you wait until evening, we'll be finished. Dinner should be ready in about thirty minutes."

When Alex looked a bit confused by this, she quickly added, "You're more than welcome to come on home with us now. We're just down the road." Mama smiled and used her hands to turn Alex in the direction of the house.

"See you there, then." Alex returned her smile as he walked toward a small green car parked under a large oak tree in the churchyard. Behind the wheel of the gray Oldsmobile, Granny pushed the gas pedal lightly, revving the engine. Mama and I waved to Alex and got into the car.

At the house, while Granny made biscuits, Mama entertained Alex with stories. His deep laugh struck a pitch not often heard in our home. When Alex went off to wash his hands, Granny dusted the flour from her hands and spoke tersely to Mama. "Lily, quit looking at that boy like he's a prize at the state fair."

Alex returned, and I smiled at him, almost sitting on Mama's hat where she'd tossed it on the couch after church. The house, as familiar as the mole on my back, suddenly felt unknown to me. I noticed that the chair Granny sat in could really use some new upholstery, and the picture over the couch hung crooked.

Mama asked, "Maggie, would you please put the drinks to the table?"

I stood and said, "Alex, what would you like to drink? We have tea and Pepsi or water if you'd like."

"Tea would be fine." Alex returned my smile.

The ice crackled as I poured the tea over it. Granny pulled the biscuits from the oven and Mama inspected the plates on the table like she was in a commercial on television for dishwashing liquid. Finding an offending speck on one of the plates, she whisked it into the sink and pulled another from the glass-front china cabinet. I put the glass of tea at the place between my mama's and my granny's, holding on to it for a second to feel the coolness against my hand.

"There you are," I said, and then I turned back to pour tea for Mama and Granny.

"Magdalena, you know that chair wobbles." Mama took Alex's glass and moved it to the plate beside mine.

"Alex, would you return thanks for us?" Granny asked as she put the last bowl on the table. The field peas steamed her glasses, so she took them off and wiped them on her apron before she untied it and hung it back on the hook beside the Frigidaire. Nothing in her face suggested, as Alex helped her with her chair, the true nature of her request. It was a wolf in sheep's clothing, a test disguised as an honor. Alex hesitated only a moment after our heads were bowed.

"For the many blessings we have received, we thank you. For the gift of life, we thank you. We ask that you bless this food to our bodies and our bodies to thy use. Amen."

He didn't mention Jesus by name, which wouldn't set well with Granny, but at least he hadn't whined.

"What sort of seminary is it that you go to?" Granny asked, settling her napkin on her lap. She had provided for her guest and now she was ready for him to provide answers.

"The seminary at Princeton University."

"What church is Princeton part of?" Granny eyed Alex as she passed him the mashed potatoes.

Alex accepted the bowl from her. "It isn't really part of the church, but it is affiliated with the Presbyterians."

"I read something just the other day about denominations," Mama said. "Now, how did that go? A Methodist is a Baptist who wears shoes, a Presbyterian is a Methodist who has gone to college, and an Episcopalian is a Presbyterian who lives off his investments." Mama laughed. "What would you say to that, Alexander?" Mama refused to shorten such a stately name as Alexander.

And in the way that only Mama could, she soon had Alex talking about his family, his school, and *his* beliefs. You would have thought he was Mama's summer project.

"Not much to tell really. My mother died when I was quite young. My father's mother came and lived with us. My father remarried and we went off to boarding school, my brother and I. There's a family brokerage firm. My older brother has a great head for business, and so he works with my father in the firm."

"Sounds practical," Granny noted as she passed a platter of fried chicken to Alex.

Alex continued. "I never much liked business, and when I finished my undergraduate degree at Princeton, I was at loose ends. I felt a seminary degree might be interesting."

" 'Might be interesting.' Is that how the Lord calls you to preach in the Presbyterian Church?" Granny asked.

Alex laughed. "No, ma'am, I'm not a candidate for the ministry. I'd like to teach one day. Social action in the church, that sort of thing. I think the church in this country is at a crossroads. Our churches should be leading the civil rights marches."

Granny thumped down her glass of tea. "I don't see it myself. Sitting on a stool just to show you can, what does it prove? How are you living every day? That's what God would ask you. Are you practicing the Golden Rule? Or are you cheating people or working them to death in the cotton mills? Besides, I imagine if you looked around long enough, you might find a few projects you could work on up north of the Mason-Dixon Line."

"I think my father would agree with part of that sentiment. He agrees with the president of Sun Oil, John Howard Pew. Mr. Pew is also the president of the United Presbyterian Foundation that raises funds for the church. Pew said recently that businessmen like my father would be more willing to give their money if the church would stick to its own holy business and keep its ecclesiastical nose out of social issues. He threw in the word *Communist* just to see if anyone was listening. There was quite a to-do at this year's General Assembly in Cleveland. The church's leading publication, *Presbyterian Life,* printed an editorial that basically said, 'Thanks for all you do, but this smacks of spiritual blackmail, and by the way, the Presbyterian Church in the USA is not for sale.' " Alex shrugged. "Needless to say, my father was most unhappy. He likes control. He wants to control everything."

"May just be a man with a little common sense, that's all," Granny said.

Mama smiled at Alex, willing away Granny's words. "Not to change the subject, but have you ever actually seen a protest march, Alexander?"

Changing the subject was exactly what Mama intended to do.

"We've had them at Princeton. The nonviolent movement's catching on. Soon there will be no stopping it. Several of the guys at seminary are working down south of here this summer."

"And instead of doing that, you came all the way here, just to study our Magdalena." Mama spoke as if he were a Greek runner dragging himself that last mile to tell of the battle news before he collapsed and died.

Alex talked to Mama but smiled at me. "I'd read a few things about your daughter. Then when I saw that picture in *Life* magazine, I knew I wanted to come and talk to her myself."

"Might be interesting, like getting a preaching degree would be interesting," Granny said.

Alex laughed; a hint of color came to his face. And some secret thing passed between Mama and Granny that I did not know.

"I have a good friend, Rex Morgan, at the seminary in Wake Forest. I'd planned to spend some time with him as well," he said, his face returning to its normal shade. "Do you know anywhere around here I can stay? I'm at a hotel in Fayetteville, but I'd rather be closer so I have more time for my research."

"I understand just what you mean," Granny said. I held my breath for a moment, sure that Mama was going to suggest Alex stay with us, but she didn't. Instead she began to offer suggestions of people who took roomers.

The next day, Alex rented a room over with the Lovingoods. Mrs. Lovingood, Ellen, was Butte Norris's sister. Ellen had an unmarried niece, Annie Ruth, who was about my age, and after Alex's arrival Ellen began having her to supper quite a bit, according to what Mama heard at the Salemburg Grill one afternoon a week or so later. She wasted no time in making it her business to set Alex at our table for meals, a regular fixture like the salt and pepper shakers.

At those meals, everything seemed more of itself. The yellow in the tablecloth seemed brighter, the corn on the cob tasted sweeter. Still my appetite fell off, and I would realize someone had asked a question and I didn't know what they'd asked, never mind how to answer.

Afterward Alex would sit and talk to me with his pad in hand, asking about all sorts of things. The clear blue of his eyes reminded me of the water at White Lake. Mama and I rode the glass-bottom boat there once, but we never told Granny about it. There was mixed bathing at White Lake, men and women swimming together. As Free Will Church members, we didn't believe in that. The only bathing suit I owned was a make-do one that my mama made me, and I used it only when we went swimming down at the farm pond, sometimes taking Norma along.

I never remember talking so much in my whole life as I did with Alex. My mind went back over these conversations until I wore a path in them, a path that became as familiar as the one that led to the old tobacco barn.

Granny would not tolerate a slacker. If Alex was going to stay around long enough not to be considered company, then he would be expected to pitch in with the work. So we talked as we rode to check on the newly planted tobacco crop, and we talked when we cleaned out the potato house and so forth. A few days later, while in the midst of a discussion on whether Jesus' first miracle was a scriptural blessing to drink wine (being a good Free Will Baptist, I explained to Alex that wine for Jesus was like Pepsi-Cola was to us), I told him about God being a woman. I don't know why I told him, I just did. It might have been that I had a glimmer of what was to be and I wanted to confess and get all my weird tics out of the way. If Alex wanted to run for cover, my confession would surely push him there.

He squinted at me for a minute. "I don't remember anything about that in the *Life* article," he said.

"That's because I didn't tell them," I said.

"Why did you tell me?" he asked.

I shrugged. "Because I trust you. Besides, you're a Presbyterian, you probably believe a lot stranger things than that."

He laughed. "You sure know how to make a guy feel special."

"Seriously, I don't tell that to anyone. Granny and Mama know, but we don't talk about it much. I told some other people about it when I was ten, but since then I've never said another word about it outside the house. Promise you won't say anything?"

"I won't." Alex smiled.

"I'm serious."

Alex held his hand to mine. "I'm serious, too. Would you like to cut our fingers and swear together?"

"No." I took my hand away and looked at the ground. He was making fun of me.

Alex pulled my chin up. "I'm not kidding. I won't say a word. There are plenty of other things to talk about."

Questions were constant between us.

"Why you?" he asked one day as we staked tomato plants.

"Why not, Mama says."

"Well, why doesn't She appear to other people?"

"I think She does, but I think it is very hard for the honest person to say they've seen God. On the other hand, I think it is very easy for the dishonest person to say they've seen God."

Alex laughed. "Good point. But doesn't that put you on the side of the dishonest?"

"I think in my case the first time I saw Her I was so little that it didn't occur to me not to tell people. As I became older and it happened again, I realized how much easier my life would be if I'd never said anything."

"But then we wouldn't have met." Alex took the ax from me and used the blunt end to hammer the stake into the ground.

"That's true, but you would have just found another mystic to study for the summer."

"Not one like you." He held out his hand. I hesitated. "A stake, I need a tomato stake."

"Of course." I reached behind me and took a stake from the pile. Then I got busy cutting twine to tie the plants to the stakes.

A few hours later, Alex was off to the Lovingoods', the green MG he drove bumping down the road.

"Too bad with all the money his family's got they couldn't buy him a decent car," Granny remarked after the sound of the MG died away into the night.

My mama sighed. "Oh Mama, that is the car of a true adventurer."

It was a pleasant surprise for me every day that Alex returned, for I expected that any time we would hear from Butte's sister that Alex had packed up and moved on, having heard all of my story he wanted to know. Then I'd hear the MG pull into the yard, then the sound of his feet on the porch, and all over again I would tell myself that I didn't care, one way or the other, if he ever came back.

People who came to seek a healing interrupted our evening

visits on a regular basis. These were not people who had read of my visions in *Life* magazine or even the newspaper. These were local families who considered putting a little intercessory prayer on an illness the same as one would consider putting a Band-Aid on a cut.

One evening in late June, Mr. Mac Johnson, who farmed over near Varina Springs, arrived at dusk. Granny greeted him on the front porch. Alex, Mama, and I were in the front room working on a jigsaw puzzle of a covered bridge.

"I hate to trouble you like this, Miss Naomi, but my Faye is mighty sick. She asked me to see if Maggie could come and pray for her."

"You didn't leave her there alone, did you?" Granny asked. The front-room drapes were open and we could see Granny and Mac outlined in the sheers by the last rays of the sun.

"No, ma'am, several from the church is with her." Mac rubbed his eyebrow like it was his lucky rabbit's foot.

"You still living by Varina Springs?" Granny pointed in that direction as she spoke. I stood up beside the coffee table and stretched, knowing that I needed to go, but dreading to leave the puzzle undone and exchange the light banter of the front room for the heavy expectations of Faye's sickroom.

"Yes, ma'am, right off Highway 202 up from Turlington's Crossroads."

"Well, you go on back. Maggie will be right on." Granny turned as she called to me. "Maggie, you need to go up to Varina Springs. Mac Johnson's wife is bad off. You can drive the truck."

I sighed big enough for Alex to hear, but not so loud as to offend Mr. Mac.

"I'll take her over," Alex volunteered, standing beside me.

Maybe it wouldn't be such a bad trip after all, I thought. The idea of riding over with Alex was much more appealing than riding with Granny or Mama.

"She'll be on in a few minutes, Mac," Granny shouted at Mr.

Mac as he started his truck. He nodded and waved as the three of us joined Granny on the front porch.

"What a wonderful idea, Alex," Mama said.

"You might better take the truck. The noise from that car will most likely scare Faye right on over to Jordan." Granny started in the house.

"I want to ride in the MG." Even to myself, I sounded like a spoiled child. Alex winked at me.

"I promise, Miss Naomi, I'll turn off the motor and coast in if that'll relieve your mind."

"It'll take a lot more than that to ease my mind at this point. Give my best to Faye." Granny let the screen slam behind her for emphasis.

Mama winked as she turned to follow Granny in the house. "We'll save the puzzle for another night."

Shortly thereafter, the MG bumped along until we reached the paved road, and then its speed surprised me. Alex drove like he thought, fast and a little dangerously. He smiled at me.

"When we come back, we'll ride with the top down."

At the Johnsons', the bedroom was filled with people praying and beseeching the Lord to send his healing power. Faye Johnson lay in the bed propped up by pillows, a quilt pulled up to her chest. She looked pale and weak. The prayer group opened a space for me to get to the bedside. Alex stayed at the door.

I spoke to Faye, and when I touched her, I could feel her let go. Whatever it was, she released her burden. I knew my prayer was simply a benediction to the prayer of Faye's heart. Sometimes we don't need a bright and shining light or the tongues of angels to shout out loud; sometimes all we need is the touch of another pilgrim to loose grace upon us. Even so I prayed, asking God to send healing and to restore order in Faye. As I prayed, with my hand on Faye's arm, I could feel her unclench.

"Where two or three are gathered in my name, there I am in the midst of them. Amen." I lifted my head.

Faye lifted a hand into the air. "Praise God, I'm healed."

There was a general shout of approval from the prayer group. Faye hugged me and thanked me for coming. As I turned to go, my eyes met Alex's. He stared with such intensity that I thought I might melt away. I reached for the wooden bedstead to steady myself.

Faye threw back the bed covers and started to get up. Mac pushed through the group while he rubbed his eyebrow with one hand and tried to use the other to hold Faye at bay like a lion tamer uses his chair.

"Faye, honey, you're weak. You rest on awhile." He patted the bed, looking to the prayer group for support.

Faye swung her legs over the side of the bed, gathering her pink chenille robe around her.

"Mac Johnson, the Lord has healed me. I felt the power go right through my body. If you think I'm going to lay in this bed and lose my healing, you're wrong."

Mac grinned. The crisis of Faye's illness behind them, the prayer group turned their attention to Alex, eyeing him like he was a peach fallen from the tree. They searched for that bruise that must be hidden from view. I pleaded that Granny needed me back home, and we were able to get on out with short good-byes.

On the way home we talked about Alex's trip to Wake Forest the next day. He was going to visit Rex Morgan at the seminary. I talked loudly, trying to be heard above the roar of the car, and I hoped that my raised voice would chase away my disappointment. What kind of day would it be with no visit to look forward to? Already the day ahead seemed as flat as a cake you'd slammed the oven door on, the promise of the full layers pressed into the bottom of the cake pans. I closed my eyes against the thought.

Alex stopped at Turlington's store and bought us each a Coca-Cola. I drank mine while he rolled the top down on the MG. The Coke bottle felt cool against the ever-increasing humidity of the June night.

When the top was all neatly rolled away, we leaned against the car, finishing our drinks, draining the sweet dark liquid from the bottles.

"How would you explain what just happened back there to a person who has no faith?" he asked.

"What would *you* say? You are the one going to school to study religion, not me." I smiled.

"I'm serious, Maggie. You know there are plenty of people that would say that this is all psychosomatic, that the sickness and the healing is all in these people's minds."

"Do you think that?"

"Well"—Alex traced a circle in the dirt with his shoe—"you know it's not an easy thing to believe in. History is full of kooks and charlatans that prey on people in their worst times. They use God's name to mask their own evil."

"And I know that's true," I replied. "It's not just history that's full of it. We've got churches full of people whose sole ambition in life is to put God in their pocket and pull Her out every time they want somebody to act a certain way. It's a wonder that God survives all we put Her through. But who are we to judge other people's healings, Alex? As for faith, you believe in these things or you don't. But everyone has faith. We have faith in something, whether it's God or ourselves or Rock Hudson at the movies. Nobody could live without faith."

He took the bottle from my hand, walked over and put it in the return rack inside the store, waving to Huey Turlington in the process. Huey came to the door and sent his greetings to my family. Huey never married, and I think he's always been a little sweet on my mama and a little afraid of my granny.

Lightning streaked the distant sky. I watched Alex come toward me, his body blocking much of the light from the store. He opened my door and I turned to face him. "What do you believe in?"

"That's a good question. There are days I'm not sure."

We rode in silence for a bit. The wind pushed back the humid air so we could breathe. Finally Alex spoke.

"There are days when I wish that I had your faith. It seems so simple and easy."

"What makes you think it is so easy? Because I didn't go to college to study it? Would that make it complicated?"

"No, that's not what I meant."

The thunder boomed above us and lightning cut open the dark sky close by. Alex laughed. "You want to stop and put the top up or try and outrun the storm?"

"We won't melt. Don't stop."

We were a hundred feet from the driveway when the rain started. Alex squeezed the MG under the shed in a space by the tractor. We ran for the house, stopping on the porch to shake the water off.

Alex reached over and pushed the hair back from my face. "You didn't melt, but maybe you smudged a bit."

The rain poured off the porch roof long into the night.

CHAPTER 10

In Sampson County they say that you can tell a girl's age by counting the blue rings on her legs, rings that she gets every berry season from picking huckleberries. The next morning, I put my plastic pails out by the back steps and went back into the house to get a rubber band to pull the hair up off my neck. By late June, the humidity hangs almost as heavy as the huckleberries in eastern North Carolina.

Back outside I bent at the waist and flipped my hair over my head, gathering stray pieces into the rubber band. A pair of white Converse high-tops appeared on the ground in front of me. I brought my head up and lost my balance. Alex's hand reached out to steady me.

"Hey, better watch that, you could get hurt."

My hand went to the old blue jeans I'd put on to keep the brambles off my legs and then tried to straighten the worn shirt of my granddaddy's that I'd grabbed to wear out into the woods. "I must look a mess," I said. "I thought you were in Wake Forest."

"Changed my mind."

Tessie stuck her head out the door. "Morning, Mr. Barrons."

Alex had given up trying to get her to call him Alex. After one long discussion on the subject, he asked her when was she going to call him by his first name. "When pigs fly" was her response.

"Maggie, if you go on and get berries, I'll make pies for tomorrow's dinner. You want Neb to go with you?"

"No, Tessie, he's got his own work to get done this morning. I'll get the berries." I smirked at Tessie. She knew good and well that Mr. Neb was not going huckleberrying with me and, furthermore, she knew that I could pick plenty of berries on my own.

Alex grabbed up a bucket. "I'm ready. Lead me to the garden, Eve. So that we may pick the fruit together." He bent forward with a flourish.

Tessie chuckled. "Mr. Barrons, they teach you funny at that school. But they sure done you no favors when it comes to real sense." She pointed to his shirt. "Come on in this house and get you a shirt. You're gonna ruin them clothes out huckleberrying."

Alex changed his shirt and we set out across the field to the woods. These woods were one of the reasons my mama married my daddy. She told me this once when I, fit to be tied because I had no one to take to the Father/Daughter 4-H banquet, asked her why she chose Butch Davidson.

"The woods," she said. "I married him to get out of the woods. When I was growing up all I could see were trees. Everywhere I looked—trees. I wanted to get away from them, go to town. Live in a nice house and have the smells of town all around me. Get out of these woods and go somewhere exciting where people valued things for their beauty, not their usefulness."

As Alex and I walked further, the dense trees blocked the sun's radiance and brought a measure of relief from the summer heat. We walked deep into the woods until we came upon the thicket of bushes in a clearing. The sun lit the clearing with a clear fine light as we settled our buckets in front of us. Alex reached into a huckleberry bush thick with dark green leaves.

"Did I tell you that snakes love huckleberry bushes?" I asked.

"No." He jerked his hand back from the bush with such force that I expected to see a snake attached to it.

I laughed.

He folded his arms and tried to look down his nose at me like Granny did.

I shook my head. "Don't think you can make me feel one bit bad about doing that. You had it coming. Besides, you really do need to watch for snakes." We picked berries quietly for a while, letting the sound from the woods echo through us like an ancient tribal language.

After my bucket was half full, I turned to Alex. "I've been thinking about last night when we were coming back from Faye Johnson's."

"What about it?" he asked as he tossed a hard green berry into the woods.

"You limit yourself." I looked at him out of the corner of my eye as I continued to pick the dark blue berries.

"How's that?" He eyed me with suspicion.

"Well, you've been to a football game?" I wiped my hands on my blue jeans and pushed back a piece of hair that had fallen onto my forehead.

Alex stopped picking and turned to me. He nodded.

"For instance, the one between Princeton and Yale? I bet that's a pretty exciting game to watch." I pulled four or five berries and dropped them in the bucket.

He nodded again. "Well, sure. It can be."

I stopped picking. "Okay. So do some people yell and scream, get all excited?"

"Yes." In the woods behind us a blue jay screeched and another bird answered.

"I bet some of them even dance and shout." I waved my hands in the air.

Alex began to smile. "Yes."

"Now, you don't find that strange?" I sat down on the ground, Indian-style, and searched the bottom of the bush for berries.

"No, not really." He sat down beside me and his smile grew wider.

"But if someone decides to get a little emotional with their religion—then they're odd." (I said the word *odd* with the same tone as Granny said the word *Yankee.*)

"Maggie, there's a difference." Alex popped a huckleberry into his mouth.

"There is?" I pulled a dark berry from the bush and ate it.

"Yes, there is." Alex shifted on the ground.

"Oh, I think I see it now." I tapped my finger on my forehead. "In one case, you have people excited to be in the presence of the God so omnipotent that the Israelites wouldn't even call him by name, so great was His power, and in the other case, it's all about a brown piece of leather full of air."

Alex rubbed his forehead, adding a streak of blue to several already there. He began to take on the look of an Indian in war paint at the Saturday matinee. "Come on, Maggie. It's a game, a sport." He added, "I think they should have let me study another year before they turned you loose on me."

"You analyze. Faye Johnson feels. Who's right? Who's wrong?" I brushed my shirtsleeve across my face, wiping a mixture of blue and sweat with it.

"Maybe I should have gotten my Ph.D. first. Maggie, I'm not saying there's anything wrong with feeling. But what if you're a thinker, what then?" Alex reached over and touched my face.

"I suppose you do the best with what you're given." I turned back and started picking, trying to hold the sensation of his touch on my forehead.

"Too bad my father doesn't feel that way," Alex said.

"What do you mean?"

"I'm getting letters from him every day. He's ready for me to finish and get on with my life. He's always thought of my graduate degree as one more way of wasting time until I get into some real work."

"And real work is—what?" I asked.

"The family firm, of course. Stockbroker."

"But I thought your brother ran the firm," I said.

"He doesn't run it yet, but he will one day. But that's not enough for Dad. I'm not going to be some useless academic if he gets his way. And trust me, he's used to getting his way."

"But what about how you feel? Don't you tell him?" I tried to picture Alex's father in my mind, adding pounds to Alex's frame and imagining a bald and wrinkled head.

"Yes, but he's not much of a listener. And then there's money." Alex broke a small stem off the huckleberry bush.

"Money . . ."

"Every discussion we have on my life ends with my father reminding me that the only way I'll see any of the family money is if my life is suitable." Alex stripped the leaves off the stem. "Suitable means doing what he wants."

"Is money that important to you? Would you give up what you love?" I didn't understand.

"Well, it's not that money's so important." Alex shrugged. "But not having it kind of is."

"Won't you make enough money if you teach?" *How could you not?* I thought. Because I'd been raised so close to the land, money was just a different system of bartering for me. No one lived a frivolous life at our house, but I never felt that I wanted for anything, either. Maybe I just wanted less than most people.

Alex looked away. "Not the kind of money that my family has."

My shoulders felt tight and I found myself counting every berry as I threw it in the bucket. Alex and I had long and heated discussions on God, but this was different. This subject, money, seemed like the fable of the blind men each touching a different part of the elephant and thinking they knew how to describe it.

After an hour or so our buckets threatened to overflow with round blue-black berries. I led the way through the trees on the narrow path carved out by many summers of berry pickers.

"Stop," Alex yelled. I half turned toward him.

"Snake," he whispered, and tried to point with one of the buckets in his hands.

I turned back. "That won't work."

Buckets clattered and two arms wrapped around me. They jerked me backward, taking my foot out of the snake's striking distance.

Alex folded me to him and we fought for balance like a pair in a three-legged race. Frightened by the commotion and flying berries, the snake slithered into the underbrush.

Steady at last, I turned to Alex. "Sorry. Next time I'll believe you."

He didn't answer. Instead he kissed me. His lips tasted of sweet huckleberries.

After a moment I stepped back. This couldn't happen. "At college, don't they discourage you from kissing your summer projects?"

"Maggie—"

Despite all the talking we'd done over the last three weeks, I didn't want to talk about the kiss. I didn't want to be told things I could not believe. Hadn't my mama believed everything my daddy told her?

"We better get these huckleberries up and get on back to the house. Tessie will be waiting."

"We should talk." Alex's hands were righting buckets and scooping berries, but he kept looking at me.

"I can't right now. Maybe this evening. I need time to think. Watch out now, you're getting twigs in those berries."

He stood and pulled me back toward him. "I seem to remember a young woman who just explained to me the evils of thinking and not feeling."

"Oh, I'm feeling, all right. Total confusion."

In fact there couldn't have been more confusion at the Tower of Babel than there was in my head at that moment. He couldn't love me. He belonged to a world of stockbrokers, debutantes, men in tuxedos, and women in puffy pink chiffon dresses; a world of cathedrals, preachers in flowing robes like the prophets, and churches awash in the stilted nuances of the Social Register. I belonged to the world of farmers, men in overalls, and women in dresses made from Simplicity patterns; a world of cinder-block sanctuaries, preachers in white bucks, and churches awash in the emotion of the next world. Hadn't he just finished telling me that the right amount of money was as central to his life as sunlight was to the crops we grew each summer?

I pulled away and fled toward home.

CHAPTER 11

Jealousy. Jealousy, plain and simple. I wish I could claim some loftier reason, some higher-minded ideal that caused me to kiss Alex Barrons, but I can't. I wish I could say that I'd decided to overcome my fear, to quit worrying over repeating my mama's past of being loved and left, and to take a chance on love. But the truth is—it was jealousy.

The Monday after our huckleberrying experience, I came upon Alex and Annie Ruth Norris in the Salemburg Grill. Miss Patsy Crumpler, old maid aunt of the Crumplers who owned the Grill, stood behind the cash register and nodded to me as she made change for a boy who held a hot dog in one hand. Miss Patsy knew everything that was going on in the county and then some. Her knowledge came soaking into her skin from days spent at the green-flecked counter of the Salemburg Grill, and her face wore a thousand tales etched in its creases.

The jukebox played "Heartbreak Hotel" and Miss Patsy's nephew, Monroe, sang along from behind the grill, trying to twitch his hips when he thought his aunt wasn't looking.

When I saw Alex and Annie Ruth sitting there, every bit of me that I'd packed in fine clear lines all my twenty years started coming out in every direction. That person I'd built on a rock-solid foundation of Scripture became a pile of ashes in the flame of jealousy. I breathed in the smell of french fries and hoped that the familiar scent would mold me back together, that the smell of frying potatoes would bind around me like twine.

Annie Ruth waved real big at me like I couldn't see her and Alex sitting there in the booth. Then she crossed her legs, bouncing her foot up and down so I'd notice her new saddle oxfords.

Alex jumped up. "Hey, Maggie, what are you doing here? Sit down, sit down." He leaned over and patted the booth seat.

"No thanks. I promised Granny I'd pick up her order from Sears Roebuck and come right home," I said evenly.

I'd gone to pick up a pair of shoes and a new set of Craftsman wrenches from the store in Fayetteville.

Alex shifted from one foot to the other, as if they'd suddenly developed blisters and he was trying not to weigh too heavy on them. "I called, but your granny said you were gone for the afternoon. Then Annie Ruth came by the house and suggested we come get an orangeade. You ever had an orangeade here?"

I laughed. "I believe so."

Annie Ruth reached out and grabbed Alex's hand with the air of one who plants a flag on freshly claimed territory. "Now, Maggie, Alex wouldn't have known that." She dropped his hand and turned her fingers to me. The scent of Ambush cologne wafted my way. "Have I shown you the new black onyx ring I got for my birthday?"

Alex continued to look at me.

"Yes, I believe you have. Anyway, I'll talk to you later. Good to see you, Annie Ruth." I smiled and waved at them as I walked toward the counter.

"My, my, Maggie, I don't hardly ever see you," Miss Patsy said, wiping her hands on a dish towel hung behind the counter.

"The summer is just flying by. Are you doing all right, Miss Patsy?" I asked.

"Fair, I guess. Can't complain. Wouldn't do me no good if I did," she answered, and laughed with good-natured understanding at the thought.

"May I have an orangeade to go?"

"Sure thing. How's everybody at your house doing?"

"Fine, thank you," I answered as she turned away and began to cleave oranges, her knife lopping them in half as cleanly as a guillotine.

I studied the letters painted on the front window while Miss Patsy turned the crank on the stainless-steel squeezer, pulverizing the orange halves and sending juice into the cup below. Even though I watched Miss Patsy, I kept an ear to what was happening in the booth behind me. Annie Ruth tittered as Alex talked. How could that possibly interest him? It made me mad that I even cared enough to think about it. I pressed my hands against the cool countertop, trying to soak up its firm indifference like Miss Patsy did gossip.

She finished with the oranges. "Bobby Owens was in here the other day. You know, he just had him some lung X rays redone last week. Doctor couldn't find a thing. There'd been a spot before, but I just think that Avery boy that runs the X-ray machine at the hospital probably got his thumb in the way. Didn't you pray with him a few weeks ago?" Miss Patsy didn't pause for my answer. "I know Bobby was relieved, seeing as I heard the other day that he and Lucille are expecting a change-of-life baby." She stirred the sugar and juice into a cup of crushed ice. "Bobby said he thought it was gonna be a record tobacco crop this year. What's your granny think?"

"You know Granny. She doesn't like to count on anything until that last leaf's been sold. But it looks like a good year."

Miss Patsy patted my hand as she slid the orange and white paper cup across the counter. Then she leaned over and raised her eyebrows in the direction of the booth where Annie Ruth and Alex sat. "I never like to see a girl throw herself at a boy. It's so common," she whispered. " 'Act like a lady and you'll be treated like a lady' is my motto."

"Good to see you, Miss Patsy." I ignored the opportunity for a little gossip. As I walked outside, I sipped the sweet pale liquid.

"Maggie." Alex came up behind me as I reached the car.

"You'd better get on back in there. Annie Ruth might die of loneliness," I said. "Maybe you could get her to go huckleberrying."

Alex laughed. "I don't think so. She's nice enough. Most concerned with how much money a professor makes." He paused. "If I didn't know better, I'd say you're jealous."

"Well, know better. I am not jealous." I reached for the car door handle.

"Hey, wait," Alex called as I opened the door and got in. The wrenches rattled as I threw my pocketbook onto the brown paper package on the seat. He tapped on the glass and I rolled down the window.

"You know, this wasn't my idea." Alex leaned in the window. "Come on, Maggie. How about I come by later and we go get some ice cream?"

I started the car. "My goodness, all those sweets in one day. You'll have a stomachache."

"Don't be like that." Alex smiled. "I promise no kisses if you'll go with me."

I looked across the empty street and then at Alex. The sun had kissed his skin a golden brown in the weeks since his arrival in Canaan.

"What fun would that be?" I leaned forward and kissed him on the lips.

He banged his head on the roof of the car.

"See you soon," I said, and drove off, leaving him to stare after me and rub his head like he'd never known it was on top of his shoulders before.

That evening Mama insisted I get my bath early. She wanted to roll my hair and I refused. Instead I sat on the couch and caught up on my summer reading for school, trying to concentrate on the Wife of Bath's story in *The Canterbury Tales* while my hair dried. Granny sat at the desk filling out forms for the Farmer's Bureau, and Mama worked a needlepoint project for the Home Demonstration Club, humming "Que Sera, Sera."

The Wife of Bath's words kept slipping from my mind. Instead of reading her story, I found myself tracing the pattern of the plaid in the couch and wondering how she had survived five husbands. It didn't look like I would survive one summer with a seminary student.

I thought Alex would phone, but he didn't. In my mind, I pictured him and Annie Ruth swapping intimate tales and inane jokes across the booth at the Grill. I wished vile and petty things on Annie Ruth, things such as the top flying off the ketchup bottle and red sauce spattering down the front of her blouse.

My deep satisfaction at kissing Alex now wavered on the edge of woe. Why had I done that? All these years when I thought I was above having a boyfriend, maybe I knew in my heart that I'd be awful at it. Obviously, Alex wasn't as impressed by my kiss as I thought.

Someone knocked on the front screen door. I looked up, but Granny and Mama acted like they hadn't heard. Mama continued to hum. The rapping came again. I popped my book closed.

"I'll get it."

Alex stood with one hand behind his back, smiling at me. He wore a navy sports jacket, khaki pants, white shirt and a tie.

I felt better about my kiss. At least it must have meant something to him. "We don't usually require coat and tie to sing along with Mitch," I said as I pushed the screen door open.

Alex stood where he was and brought a bouquet of yellow roses from behind his back. Baby's breath was sprinkled throughout the roses like delicate lace. I couldn't seem to breathe, and yet the tender smell of roses surrounded me.

"I was wondering, Magdalena, if you would do me the honor of dining with me at Butler's Family Restaurant this evening."

I caught my breath. "Is this on the syllabus for the summer course on mystics?"

Alex laughed and stepped inside. "No, ma'am. This is independent study."

The green tissue rattled when I took the flowers. A thorn pricked my finger through the tissue, but it seemed like the finger didn't really belong to me, so there was no need to cry out. I brushed at my jeans with my free hand. "Well, I'll need a minute to change."

"I've got time. Plenty of time," Alex said, catching my hand and squeezing it. Again I felt like a pile of ashes that a slight wind could have floated away.

Mama came up behind me. "Don't you worry about a thing, Magdalena. I'll get those flowers in some water, and your granny and I will entertain Alex."

"That's what worries me, Mama."

In my room, I found several dresses laid out across the bed. Evidently everyone had known my plans for the evening except for me. I ignored the dresses on the bed and picked a white dress with navy polka dots out of the wooden wardrobe. In my hurry, I forgot to undo the navy belt. When I slipped the dress over my head, it sat on top of my shoulders until I reached up and unfastened the belt clasp. The dress loosened and I pushed my arms through the sleeves. Sucking on the finger I'd pricked on the roses, I wedged on my navy shoes with my free hand.

I put my hair up. I took it down. I put in a ribbon. I took out the ribbon. And without so much as a "How about that," I'd entered a world where simple decisions took longer than reading the begats in Genesis.

"Magdalena, do you need some help in there?" Mama knocked at the door.

I tied the ribbon for the second time. "No, Mama, I'm fine."

"We're in the front room whenever you get ready." The front room—the front room was for company. Alex wasn't company.

At last I called a truce between ribbon in, ribbon out and hair up, hair down. I turned my back on the mirror and went to find Alex. When I walked into the front room, he stood. "You look beautiful."

"Not bad," Granny said. She smoothed her dress, and for the first time that I could remember, words didn't seem to come easily to her.

"You look gorgeous." Mama hugged me. Then she stepped back, tapping her lip with her finger like she was Sherlock Holmes about to announce the murderer. "I liked the green print dress better."

"Mama."

Tessie appeared from the kitchen, stood in the door as if she was listening for something, and then, after a moment, wiped at her eyes. "I can't believe you're so growed up."

"Tessie, what are you doing here?" I asked. Tessie and Mr. Neb had left right after I returned from Fayetteville.

"I forgot the pot of beans I snapped for supper. Neb just ran me by to pick them up." She gestured toward the kitchen, but the pot of beans story was suspect.

Mama fiddled with the ribbon in my hair and handed me a scarf. "You'll need this or by the time you get to Butler's, you'll look like a bird nested in your hair."

"Thanks, Mama." I saw the yellow roses on the whatnot shelf behind her. I'd never imagined in all my life, particularly the last few months, that a man would bring flowers for me. For me, and not as a tribute to God's goodness through me. Or that Mama, Granny, Tessie, and I would stand around the front room like other families must and talk of pleasant nothingness.

A stem of baby's breath had fallen out onto the table. I picked it up and pushed it back into the vase. Alex took my hand. "We'd better go."

Mama, Granny, and Tessie followed us onto the porch. Mama hugged us both. "Wait, wait." She pulled at the ribbon again.

"Mama, the scarf's going to mess it up anyway. I'll fix it when we get there."

"Okay," she sighed, and kissed me on the cheek one more time.

"Don't be too late," Granny called as we walked to the car.

"Enjoy yourselves," Mama said. "You're the perfect couple, Tony Curtis and Janet Leigh."

Granny turned to Mama. "Lily, quit talking nonsense."

"Mama, it's not nonsense, it's—"

Her words were lost as Alex cranked the MG. Turning the rearview mirror toward me, I tied the scarf under my chin.

"Hey, how do you expect me to drive?" Alex turned the mirror back.

"With two hands on the wheel, if you don't mind."

Alex backed into the road. Tessie waved, while Mama and Granny continued their discussion. I waved, and then they were gone from my sight. I shifted in the seat so I could turn and see them still standing there, Mama and Granny waving their hands at each other, Tessie with her hand in the air.

"How long do you think they'll stand there and argue?" I asked Alex as I turned back around.

"Until your granny figures out there is something better she can do or Tessie tells your mama that it's almost time for *Sing Along with Mitch*."

The evening air carried our laughter out across the tobacco fields around us. We practiced kissing once on the way to the restaurant, nearly landing the MG in the ditch right up from McGee's Crossroads.

Alex reached over to hold my hand. "Two hands on the wheel, Mr. Barrons," I said, "or we really will end up in somebody's tobacco field."

Butler's Restaurant sat on the edge of Fayetteville. The low building had a neon sign out front that read BUTLER'S FAMILY RESTAURANT in glowing scripted red. Then printed underneath in white letters it said, HOME OF THE CHARBROILED STEAK.

I untied my scarf as we got out of the car. "I bet you've never had cuisine like this."

Alex studied the sign and smiled. "Maybe once in Brooklyn. I'm not sure."

Inside, an older gentleman, whose hair sprouted on either side of his bald spot like earmuffs that weren't long enough to reach his ears, pointed us toward an empty table. "Y'all go right on back there. I've got to go get you some menus. I've told these girls and told these girls to bring them on up front, but they don't pay me no mind."

We made our way through the crowded restaurant to the two empty chairs. Alex's hands brushed my shoulders as he helped me with my chair. The gentleman returned and slapped two plastic-coated menus down in front of us. "Enjoy yourselves. JoAnn will be right with you."

In a moment a petite woman, her blond hair teased in a bouffant style, put two red plastic glasses of water in front of us. "Hey, how are y'all doing tonight?" She hesitated a second and then wiped her hand on her white uniform as she spoke. "Say, aren't you that girl that heals people?"

Before I could say anything, Alex smiled and said, "You know what? People tell her that all the time. She must look exactly like that girl."

"She does best I can tell." She turned to Alex but continued to watch me out of the corner of her eye. I studied the menu with the eye of an archaeologist, staring intently like I was trying to figure out what ancient civilization had produced it.

"You're not from around here, are you?" she asked Alex as she flipped the order pad closed.

"No, I'm not. It's pretty perceptive of you to pick up on that," Alex said.

"Don't much get by me. That's what my husband tells me anyway. Says, 'JoAnn, there ain't much that gets by you.' " She stuck her order pad down in the pocket of her white dress. "You want me to bring you some tea while you look over your menus?"

"That will be fine."

I fanned myself with my menu as she disappeared into the kitchen. "Alex, you told her a story."

"Did not. I never said you weren't you, and you do look exactly like you." He picked up a menu. "I'm not interested in sharing you with the world tonight."

I'd thought many times what a boring thing it would be to have to giggle and say aren't-you-so-amazing things to a man on a date, but this was just Alex, and I could be exactly who I was. I soon forgot the debate that had raged only minutes earlier over ribbon or no ribbon, hair up or hair down.

When we finished eating, Alex covered my hands with his. "Maggie, this summer has been the happiest time of my life, especially the last few weeks." He waited for me to second his opinion.

I couldn't disagree, but I argued all the same. "It's Mama and Granny. You said yourself how much you missed growing up without your mama." We stared at each other. If everyone in the restaurant suddenly dropped dead and fell out of their seats, we wouldn't have noticed.

"Don't try to psychoanalyze me, Maggie Davidson." Alex smiled. "I've been a goner since I looked in your eyes that first Sunday. Then I watched you speak to people. I watched your compassion. Like Faye Johnson—whether you brought her healing or not, you brought her comfort. You allowed her to let God take the best in her and get her up out of the bed."

I felt like a child who'd been spinning around and around in the yard; my head couldn't catch up with my stomach.

"But even if you had just stood in the churchyard and smiled at me, I would be crazy about you, Maggie. I don't care if God heals everyone you touch; I don't care if God heals no one you touch."

I closed my eyes and tried to imagine that here was a man who saw past Jesus in the clouds, who saw me standing there. I could barely think it, let alone believe it.

I squeezed his hand. "Alex, I think a lot of you, but if you had gotten off a flying saucer six weeks ago, you couldn't be any less foreign to me and to Sampson County. All my life I've wanted different, but maybe we're too different. We can't ignore that. Best I can tell, my mama and daddy fell in love and then tried to work out the details of being different." Even as I spoke those words, I hoped Alex would try to show me the error of my thinking.

JoAnn stopped by to refill our tea glasses. "Can I get you folks something else tonight?"

Alex looked at me. "We're fine. Thank you."

"Be right back with that check, then," JoAnn said, and smiled.

Alex waited for her to leave before he spoke. "Maggie, I don't want to know what you think of me; I want to know what you feel for me. Kiss me and then talk to me about your mama and daddy. I'm trying to tell you that I came here a guy who knew exactly where he was going, a guy on an intellectual quest with the answers predetermined, and I ended up on a journey of my heart. Kiss me and then say that we can't work out the details."

The intensity of his eyes made me blink. I had to move this conversation back to the center of the road. We'd veered sharply into the land of feelings I couldn't explain. Ask me about *the Almighty,* the great *I AM,* just don't ask me about men, promises made in the moonlight, and ribbons in my hair.

"I will not be kissing you in the middle of Butler's Restaurant. Even if I was inclined to do such a thing, don't think that word of your fast college boy ways and obvious negative influence wouldn't reach home faster than we would."

He winked and brushed my lips with his.

"We'd better be going," I said.

"Good night, folks." JoAnn waved as we made our way out. As we walked to the MG, the medley of plates being cleared and the tinkling of the silverware faded. Looking at the sky, I recited:

> *"Star light, star bright,*
> *First star I see tonight.*
> *Wish I may, wish I might,*
> *Have the wish I wish tonight."*

"And what did you wish for?" Alex asked, standing behind me with his hands on my shoulders.

"I'll never tell." *That the night would never end, that I could love him without worrying, that God would richly bless us.* Us: Would we become an us?

"I have ways of getting you to talk. Fast college boy ways." He kissed my neck.

I laughed and pulled away. "We'll see."

The noise of the night was lost in the clatter of the MG's engine. Alex waited until I tied my scarf before putting the car in gear. While the white lines on the road flashed by us, we held hands and shifted gears together until about two miles after McGee's Crossroads. Not far from where we almost ran into the ditch earlier, we passed a truck on the side of the road. The MG's headlights illuminated a bent figure standing next to it.

"Looks like trouble," Alex said as we passed. He slowed and circled the MG around in the road to go back for another look. We pulled onto the shoulder of the road. I moved my hand so Alex could work the stick shift and the clutch to slow the MG down, but our heads bobbed as we stopped behind a dirty green pickup. Several spots of paint were rubbed off the back like it had suffered a case of the mange. The tailgate read ORD, the letter F having met the same fate as the paint. In the bed of the truck were four Negro children all leaning over the side, talking to an older woman who was studying a flat tire. When the MG's lights flashed on her, she straightened and took her hands from her hips to shade her eyes. In one hand she held a handkerchief, luminous against her dark skin.

Alex cut the engine. "Need some help?"

"Praise Jesus, we do," the woman answered as she fanned her handkerchief against the stiff heat. The children began to jump up and down. "It's my son's truck and I don't have no idea about how to get that tire changed."

A small boy leaned out of the truck bed. "I told you, Granny, you've got to jack it up."

"And Granny told you, Leonard, I don't have any idea where the jack is." The woman shook her head at the boy.

Alex walked up to the side of the truck bed. "Leonard, is it? Well, Leonard, we've got to get the dead weight out of the back of this truck."

"I'm the oldest," Leonard said as he raised his arms and Alex swung him to the ground. "They my cousins." He pointed to the other three children, who lined up for a turn. Alex swung them one at a time to the ground, circling each child through the air until they squealed with delight.

He threw me the keys. "Maggie, would you pull the MG closer so we can use the lights?"

"Sure." I eased the car into gear and bumped closer to the truck so that the headlights shone on the collapsed tire.

Alex took off his suit coat and tie and rolled up his sleeves. Looking at him, I realized how very different he was from the men I knew—a man not afraid of his head or his hands. But what about his heart? Could I really believe what he told me? And what had I told him? All night I'd been reciting the answers of my life to him like they were a catechism. Did he believe me?

CHAPTER 12

Alex folded his jacket and handed it and his tie to me before he crawled under the truck. The children bent until their heads almost touched the ground to see what magic he was working beneath the old truck. I stroked the coat with one hand. I had become the magician's assistant.

The smell of pines was heavy around us, and the night filled with the scat song of the crickets and the bass of the frogs. I took the jacket and tie to the car.

"Oh."

"Look at that."

I turned as the crowd cheered Alex, who produced a jack from under the truck. The crickets echoed their pleasure.

"I told you we needed us a jack, Granny," Leonard said. The other children danced up and down, graceful shadows in the MG's headlights.

"Leonard, you're indeed a wise young man," Alex said, and turned to face the older woman. "I don't think we've been properly introduced. I'm Alex Barrons, and this is my friend Maggie Davidson."

"I'm Frances Poteat, and I'm mightily glad you came by tonight, Mr. Barrons."

The smallest boy, dressed in cutoff pants and a striped shirt, began to hop on and off the pavement.

"Well, let's hope we can get you back on the road." Alex pointed in the direction of the MG. "Leonard, I'm going to need you to keep everybody back while I get this truck jacked up."

Heady with power, Leonard corralled his cousins. "Hey now, quit that jumping and get on back from there."

Alex wrestled a tire from under the truck, smudging black across his shirt in the process.

Frances Poteat walked toward me, her feet moving in a step-together-step fashion as she maneuvered the bumpy shoulder of the road. She stood beside me, patting first her face and then her bosom with a voluminous white handkerchief, trying futilely to mute the effect of the hot night air. "Aren't you kin to the Parkers that Tessie Warwick works for?"

"Yes, ma'am, I'm Mrs. Parker's granddaughter."

"Tessie told me about you. You the one that's got the power?"

"Well, I pray for folks anyway. How do you know Tessie?" I looked to change the subject.

"Oh, we go way back. Her mama and I are both charter members of the Full Gospel AME Zion Church."

"This sure is a little car." Leonard and his cousins stood around the MG. In the distance, the headlights of a car moved toward us.

"You children, come away from that road," Mrs. Poteat warned. The car passed us, the sound of the engine lingering for a moment longer than the car. It moved the still air around us and provided a welcome moment of breeze. Over behind the MG, the two smallest children began to chase lightning bugs, cupping their hands to catch them and then opening their hands, where the bugs would sit glowing off and on like radioactive emeralds until they flew away into the night air.

The truck creaked as Alex pumped the jack handle. The tire inched off the ground.

Leonard left the MG and walked over to peer under the truck.

"Stay back," Alex said. "It's not very stable. Maggie, I need you to come over here and stand behind me. Otherwise these lug nuts will get lost in the grass."

I moved behind him and extended my hand. Alex gave me the lug nuts one by one as he took them off the wheel. "Did anybody ever tell you that you're the prettiest garage mechanic in the world?"

"Alex Barrons, concentrate on your job."

He rolled the new tire over and lifted it onto the axle. One by one I handed him back the lug nuts.

"Really, I may go let the air out of my own tires just to get your help," he said happily. The children giggled.

I lowered my voice. "I seem to remember calling you a fast-talking college boy tonight. I rest my case."

"Aw shucks, ma'am, I'm just trying to pay a girl a compliment. Move back now. I'm going to let it down." He motioned me back with his hand.

I joined Mrs. Poteat and the children.

"All done," I said.

The smallest of the children, a little girl with braids coming out in every direction, took a hop toward the truck. Mrs. Poteat reached out and pulled her back.

Without any warning, Leonard dashed forward as Alex released the jack. "You did it! You did it!" he shouted, and then his bare foot caught on a rotting limb that sat near the edge of the road. He stumbled. His arms flapped up and down, as useless to stop his fall as a bird's broken wing. Mrs. Poteat and I screamed. As in a bad dream, the truck wavered for a second like it might somehow defy gravity and stay suspended in midair. In one motion, Alex turned toward our cries and dove for Leonard, catching the boy and shoving him away from the truck. The force caused Alex to stumble against the truck, so that it struck his head as it bounced. His shoulders jerked forward and he crumpled to the ground.

The truck gave one last shudder before it settled next to Alex's limp body.

"He's dead. He's dead. I done killed him, Granny," Leonard cried. Mrs. Poteat hobbled toward Leonard and Alex, her handkerchief pressed to her mouth, her eyes wide.

"Alex." I ran to him and took his hand, trying to feel his pulse. I leaned over, my heart pounding in my ears, and pulled my scarf off my head. I felt his breath on my face just as my hand found the spot where the blood beat through his wrist.

"Thank you, God. Thank you."

Behind me, Leonard wailed.

"It's all right, Leonard. He's breathing." I cradled Alex to me, stuffing my scarf in the pocket of my dress. *Lord, dear Lord, help him now. Check his head, you need to check his head.* My thoughts and prayers crowded together.

Leonard's cries became muffled as his granny wrapped him to her. "Thank you, sweet Jesus, thank you," she cried. We huddled on the ground, the four of us, like we'd just uttered the line "All fall down" in Ring Around the Rosy. Mrs. Poteat fanned her handkerchief first at Alex and then at Leonard.

On the back of Alex's head, I felt a bump about the size of a hen's egg. When I shifted him gently to see if he was bleeding, he began to moan.

Inside my own head, the racket was as loud and mixed up as when Abraham and Isaac got into the henhouse. How could I pray? What should I pray?

"Dear Lord, help Alex. Send your healing touch—"

What would I do if God didn't answer that prayer? I couldn't think with Alex's head laying there in my lap.

Mrs. Poteat's voice broke through the cacophony. "Sweet Jesus, help this boy's head." She raised her arms to the sky, waving her handkerchief high as she called down the power of the Almighty.

"Lord, please help him. Help me know what to do." I stroked Alex's head as I looked for other injuries. "Lord, please." I didn't feel any heat in my arm, and no light suddenly appeared. There was only Alex's dark hair, wet in one spot with blood. My fingers felt slick, and I held my hand up, looking at the blood and then back up at those around me.

Leonard sniffed. The other three children stood to our side like a trio of singers who had suddenly gotten an attack of stage fright.

Lord, send something. Send someone.

Mrs. Poteat quit praying as she leaned over me. "Reckon we better take him to the hospital?"

Again, her steady voice, with its logical question, helped me focus my own thoughts.

"No, there's only the one knot. It isn't far to the house. I think I ought to get him home. I can call the doctor from there. Leonard, I need you to go and look in the boot of the car for a blanket. The keys are right over there in my pocketbook."

Leonard sniffed again but didn't move.

"Now, come on, baby. Go do like Miss Davidson asked you." Mrs. Poteat nudged him with her hand.

Leonard wiped at his eyes as he made his way over to the MG. The other three children went behind him, leaning over to peek in the boot while it was open.

Alex moaned again. "It'll be okay," I said, and I knew it was so.

But my prayer had seemed wrong, cockeyed, like when Mrs. Lucy Gardner, who claimed to be some distant relation to Ava, told you in choir practice that you were singing from your throat instead of your diaphragm. Diaphragm singing was the only way, and Mrs. Lucy ought to know; after all, she had studied music at Holmes Bible College. Throat singing was forced, thin singing. Later when Mama asked me about that night I told her, "It felt like I was praying from my throat and not my diaphragm, or like I'd forgotten something I'd known forever, like how to ride a bicycle. Every time I got up and started to pedal, instead of rolling along, I was scrambling to keep my hind end off the ground."

Between my throat prayer and Mrs. Poteat's beseeching, somehow the two of us and the four children got Alex into the truck bed. Each child struggled to contain a wayward limb; I hoisted him by his belt like a sack of potatoes, counting on Mrs. Poteat to guide his head and shoulders onto the old blanket Leonard had brought from the boot of the MG.

A truck passed by full of voices that were there with us and then gone into the dark of the highway. The children surrounded

Alex and myself, watching him carefully. Mrs. Poteat tried to ease the truck onto the road, but we jostled back and forth as each tire rolled onto the pavement.

She stopped the truck and leaned out her window. "Y'all okay?"

"It's fine. We're okay," I answered, and the children echoed, "Okay, Granny."

Headlights shone on us.

A voice called from a pickup now blocking our path. "Hey, ever thing all right?"

"Everything's fine, sir," Mrs. Poteat called.

The doors opened and two men stepped from the truck. They blocked the light as they walked toward us. One wore a cap on his head and the other had his hands stuck deep in his pockets. The motors of the trucks droned in unison and drowned out the crickets and the frogs.

"Well, we was just wondering what y'all are doing out here this late of an evening," the one with his hands in his pockets said. By this time the two of them were even with the truck, and the man with the cap leaned into the cab of the truck and turned the key. Beneath us, the gentle shimmy of the engine's idle died. The other truck's engine idled on alone. Beside me the children seemed to shrink into the side of the truck, the littlest one half hiding behind me.

The man with his hands stuck in his pockets leaned over the side of the truck bed and I recognized him as a boy I knew from over near Salemburg.

"Beg your pardon, we need to be on our way," I said. "We've got someone injured."

"What?" He shaded his eyes with his hands like that would help him see. "Who is that?" His partner now leaned away from Mrs. Poteat and the cab of the truck.

"Some white girl," he said.

"I know that," the Salemburg boy said, and turned his back on his friend. "What are you doing out here with this bunch of coloreds this time of night?"

"It's Maggie," I said, "Maggie Davidson. And we don't have time to mess with you. Alex is hurt and we've got to get him back home."

"Shoot, I should have knowed it be you." The Salemburg boy leaned further over into the truck bed. The hands of the little girl sitting beside me dug into my ribs. "I'd heard you'd been running around with some Communist type from up North."

"Don't know why you'd be in a hurry," his friend called. "No great loss if he dies."

"Look, I don't have time for your small minds and your silly games." I talked louder than I needed to. "We've got to be going, and now."

Neither of them moved. I thought the children had forgotten how to breathe, it was so quiet in the bed of the truck.

Dear Jesus, do something.

Mrs. Poteat spoke. "We was just trying to help out Miss Maggie and her friend. No one means any trouble, but the Lord done spoke to Miss Maggie's heart and we got to get her back on home now. You all was raised Christian, I'm sure. You know, don't nobody want to mess with the will of the Lord."

The two took a step back, and at that moment, a pair of headlights appeared down around the curve of the road.

"Well, will of the Lord or not, mixing with coloreds and New York ideas is going to find Miss Maggie some trouble one day," the boy from Salemburg called back over his shoulder as the two made their way back to their truck.

Before they were in the cab, Mrs. Poteat had the truck cranked again. She moved in behind the car that came by us and stayed with it a ways until the two and their truck were only a bad dream faded into the night.

I alternated between stroking Alex's head and patting the children's hands to reassure them. The metal of the truck bed felt cool beneath me; still, the heat encased us even as the wind blew my hair around. Mama would fuss when she saw I didn't have on my scarf. We stopped at a crossroads. Mrs. Poteat stuck her head out the window. "Right or left here, sugar? I can't remember."

"Left," I said.

"Left, Granny," the children echoed.

I stroked Alex's face. I could say what I wanted to about spaceships and rich daddies and us not belonging together, but I loved this man. I loved him with his sleeves rolled up. I loved him swinging children from a truck. I loved him writing in his notebook, stopping me to ask another question or read back a sentence. I loved him, and knowing that made me almost as afraid as I had been in that eternity between when the truck fell and when I felt Alex's breath on my face.

At the house, we put him on my bed. Mama, Granny, and I rotated between taking care of Alex until Dr. Kincaid arrived and comforting Mrs. Poteat and her grandchildren.

Finally, Mama walked them out to the truck with her arm around Leonard. "Dr. Kincaid is the absolute best doctor in the world and he will have Alexander fixed up in no time," I heard her say through the screen. Then the truck started and good-byes were said.

Dr. Kincaid arrived. After a brief examination in which Alex participated by naming the number of fingers the doctor held up, he turned to the three of us.

"I wouldn't move him around a lot tonight. He'll have a bad headache tomorrow. Other than that, I think he'll be okay. He's lucky he didn't take the full weight of that truck. Any nausea or double vision and you call me."

Mama escorted Dr. Kincaid to the door. We heard the sounds of his feet on the porch and then Mama snapping the lock on the front door. She came and stood beside me, with Granny on the other side; the three of us shadowed Alex's face. He opened his eyes.

"I'm okay?"

"You're fine," Granny said with such power in her voice that Alex closed his eyes and didn't stir again even when Granny sent me from the room so that she and Mama could get him into one of my granddaddy's old T-shirts.

"All clear," Mama called. I walked back into the room just as Granny settled into the rocking chair beside the bed.

"Granny, I'll stay here. You go on to bed."

"Think I'm too old, do you? Well, I'm not. I'll call you if I need you."

"Maggie," Alex mumbled, and stretched his fingers out toward me. I patted his hand.

Granny pointed to the door. "I'm not too old and you're not too young, so just march on off to bed, Maggie," Granny said as she turned back to the bed. "Alex, I'm right here if you need me." But it was too late; he'd already closed his eyes and gone off to sleep.

"Why don't we say a short prayer?" Granny asked. "Maggie, will you pray?"

I thought back to the evening and Alex's head in my lap. "Granny, would you pray?"

Granny looked for a long moment like she could look right into my heart. Then instead of answering, she started, "Lord—" Mama and I bowed our heads. "Lord, you've sent us this boy for a reason. Watch over him tonight. We thank you it's no worse than it is and we pray that you'll see fit to mend him. Amen," Granny said. Barely pausing for breath, she added, "Now shoo, you two, off to bed."

Mama took me by the elbow and sighed, "Good night, Mama. Call us if you need us."

I was so exhausted that I didn't even think to mention the two men on the road. Despite all the goings-on, I woke at five, threw on a cotton blouse and jeans, woke Granny, and sent her on her way. About an hour later, as the pink light of morning spread into the room, Alex stirred. He opened one eye.

"I've died and gone to heaven." He grimaced as he attempted to raise his head.

"Lie down." I pushed gently at his shoulder. "Dr. Kincaid said you needed rest."

"He did?"

"Yes, he did. The truck smacked you pretty hard." I stood beside the bed.

Alex tried to sit up. "Leonard, what about Leonard?"

I gently pushed him back down. "He's fine. Shaken up a bit, but okay because of you." He closed his eyes.

I sat on the bed and kissed him lightly on the cheek. "You were very brave. A lot of people wouldn't have even stopped to help, let alone jumped to save Leonard." I traced the rose pattern on the quilt beneath me. Alex grimaced, and I stroked his forehead.

"Does this mean I get to lie here all day with you sitting beside me and stroking my head and saying nice things to me?" he asked, opening one eye.

"I guess it does."

"Then Dr. Kincaid was wrong. I'll need at least a week to recover. Especially if you're going to sit on the edge of the bed."

I was suddenly aware of his khakis folded neatly on my desk. I felt my face flush and stood up. I'd become so familiar with Alex. And what scared me was the close proximity only made me want closer.

"No." He patted the bed. "Sit back down, I promise I won't do anything that will compromise your honor."

"If you keep this up, I'm going to call Granny in here to sit with you."

"I'm sick and you speak to me so." He patted the bed again.

I sat on the very edge of the bed. "I can see this is going to be a problem."

"You're right. I'm going to be the problem that you'll never get out of your life."

CHAPTER

13

Alex received the news of his Fulbright scholarship one day in late July.

Mama, Granny, Tessie, and I sat in a circle under the pecan trees shelling peas. The breeze came in waves like the ocean, cooling us and then slipping away. The smile on Alex's face when he came around the corner of the house made me cling to the arms of the metal porch chair as if it was a life raft in the middle of the Atlantic Ocean.

He told us all about his Fulbright and how he would get to study in England at Oxford University for a year.

The end of a pea shell pricked my finger. His enthusiasm caught me up; I felt happy for him despite the churning in my stomach. Mama rushed to hug him while Tessie nodded her approval and bent to get more peas from the washtub.

Granny smiled. "I'm going to miss having you around. I thought we were pretty close to saving you."

Everyone joined in Alex's laughter.

Later at dinner, Mama announced, "This is just so wonderful. I always dreamed of studying the Bible at college. And in England no less. I almost went to Holmes Bible College myself."

Granny thunked down a bowl of steaming field peas. "I don't know as I knew you when you were planning that."

Mama held up her hand. "Now, Mama, what about camp meeting the summer I was fourteen?"

"I remember that, all right. That was the summer you announced in one of the evening services that you were going to the Congo and minister to the heathens."

Mama sighed. "I don't know why I didn't get to go to the Congo."

Granny replied, "The Lord arranged for you to minister to the heathen right here the day you met Butch Davidson. Seems like the devil owed me a debt and paid me off with a son-in-law."

"Mama, really."

I cut off the sure-as-night-follows-day discussion on my daddy's shortcomings. "When will you leave?" I couldn't look at Alex as I asked; instead I prodded my chicken with my fork.

"If I leave in about two weeks, by the time I drive home, that will give me about a week to get ready. I'll have to push it, but I'd rather spend the time here than at home."

"And we want to keep you as long as we can," Mama chimed in enthusiastically. I smiled but focused my attention on a lady playing a piano in the picture on the wall. Clad in a hoop skirt, her fingers forever frozen on the piano keys, she smiled as if she'd just received the news that her beloved was returning home from the war. I willed the stinging tears out of my eyes.

After supper, Mama took command of the dishes and shooed Alex and me out to the porch. We sat on the metal glider still warm from the summer sun. If you pushed your hand against the cutout squares of the glider's seat, it imprinted your flesh like sugar cookie dough.

Alex took my hand. "Maggie, the only part of this that makes me sad is leaving you. Leaving all of you, really. It's like leaving the family that was taken from me when my mother died. A year seems like an eternity. I can't imagine my life without you in it."

"And I can't imagine me in your life. Alex, people in your life work different. I'd be like some girl from the carnival." I looked across the yard at my granny's hydrangea. Wouldn't it be nice if a stem of it stirred into my bathwater cured me of this?

"So these past few weeks don't mean anything to you?" Alex asked.

"Of course they've meant something. I'm not the one leaving. But I've got just enough of my granny in me to know that you can't put a duck in the henhouse and make a chicken. Life doesn't work that way."

"Maggie—"

I turned back and faced him.

"Do you have enough of your mama in you to dream?" He leaned toward me.

"Look where dreaming has got my mama," I said as I longed for a hydrangea bathwater cure. What I couldn't decide was what I wanted to be cured of, the hurt or the love.

He kissed me.

"There's got to be a way to combine your mama's dreaming and your granny's common sense. Think about it," Alex said.

"I don't know. Is there a way to combine your daddy's preordained, tied-up-in-a-bow, blinder-wearing faith and your study-it-to-death and march-for-social-action-in-the-streets university theology?" I patted him on the leg.

"Maggie, you are being obstinate," Alex said.

"I'm being practical. You'll get over there in England and you'll meet someone who suits you. You'll see that I was just a way to get back at your daddy, a surefire way to get him to sit up and take notice. Maybe think on whether he really wants you to work in the family business. Then you'll need to figure out a way to break it to me easy." I paused. "I'm just trying to skip the part that's so messy."

"Maggie, I'm amazed that you can have faith in God, a God that appears at His or Her leisure, and yet you cannot believe that sitting here in front of you is a man who loves you. This is crazy."

"I never claimed otherwise. But just the other day, you told me that your daddy has definite ideas. And I think I know what his idea of me would be. It would be like one of those movies Mama loves to watch. Your daddy'd probably offer me money to go away and never be heard of again." I tried to smile and instead a tear escaped down my cheek. Alex pulled out his handkerchief and wiped it away.

"You know that's not so. I love you."

"Alex, sometimes that's not enough. My mama loved my daddy, but it wasn't enough." I couldn't tell Alex that I already missed him so much that I was surprised I continued to breathe.

He leaned over and kissed me again, a kiss sweet with the short time we had together. I leaned my head into his chest. I could not think and yet all I could do was think. What I felt could not be real. I knew that if he left, this chest would never be a safe harbor for me again. And I knew he could not stay. The Fulbright was his Golden Fleece. Alex had to go. That must have been the case with my daddy. My mama let him go because if he'd stayed he would have shriveled up to nothing right before our eyes. Of course, my daddy never offered to stay.

Alex sat up and took both my hands in his. "Maggie, marry me."

What amazing words, spoken so clearly in the waning light of the day. I wanted to kiss him and hug him and shout out a yes. Instead I smiled. "You don't mean that."

"Yes I do, Maggie. I love you."

"Alex, you love the idea of me. You love having a faith to hold on to when, try as you might to ignore them, those doubts come creeping in. You haven't figured out yet how to conquer them, so you need me."

"And what if I do? But you're not right. I love you for being all the things I could never be—I'll admit that, but I do love you for you." Alex dropped my hands and brushed my face with his hand as if he could wipe away my answer like a stray eyelash. "Why wait?" he asked. "Why not now?"

"Because you're on a quest, a quest to prove yourself to your daddy." I patted his hands.

"But that's okay, you can go with me," he said, and kissed me again.

"No, I can't. I have a quest of my own," I said as the shadows began to deepen around us.

Looking at me with wide eyes, Alex said, "What are you talking about?"

"I'm talking about finishing my education and figuring out how to live with or without this gift. Not to mention trying to see what the Lord intends for me to do—what my calling is."

As the sun began to set, the light from the kitchen lit up more of the outside, and my mama's face was outlined in the window above the sink. My quest: being content enough with home that I didn't need to run away, but being sure I could walk away if that's what I needed to do. My calling: I did not know.

"But think, after a year in England, you could finish your studies and that would give you time to see what the gift means," he said.

"Alex, I'm not talking about my studies. They're only preparation. And I'm not talking about the gift; the gift is the gift. It comes and it goes in God's time. What I'm talking about is my calling. A calling is something that wells up inside of you and takes a hold of you. My granny got a call to farm this land as clear as Preacher Liles got the call to preach. There's no mistaking a call, and if you turn your back on it, you might as well cut off a piece of your heart. When you see people walking through their lives like they got that 'tropical sleeping sickness,' then you know they didn't listen. There's no one more alive than somebody who's in their calling."

"Well, I'm called to marry you," Alex said, and kissed my cheek.

"Alex, please." I closed my eyes and opened them to see him looking at me with the tiniest bit of exasperation playing around his face like a moth fluttering around a light. "Listen, I'll make you a deal," I said. "You go to England. If at the end of your year you come back and still think you love me, then we'll talk about it."

He sat quiet for a minute, thinking on this. “Deal. But you have to do one thing for me or I’m not going to go,” he said.

“What is that?” I asked.

“I want to go to White Lake for the day,” he said, and grinned at me.

“Alex Barrons, you’ve lost your marbles.” I closed my eyes to emphasize my point.

“Come on, Maggie. You’ve always said you wanted to go. It’s White Lake, not Sodom and Gomorrah.”

I opened my eyes and put my finger to my lips. “Shh. Granny and Mama will hear you.”

“Well, I don’t see why that worries you. Your mama would want to come along.” Alex cupped his hands and pretended to shout. “Who wants to go to White Lake?”

I pulled at his hands, laughing as I did. “Okay, Mr. Big Mouth, I’ll go.”

As we began to plot our holiday, Mama finished the dishes and turned out the kitchen light.

We left the next Saturday morning after an early breakfast of biscuits and fatback. As far as anyone at home knew, we were on our way to the seminary in Wake Forest to visit Alex’s friend and enjoy the lunch that Mama packed for us to eat at a roadside park along the way. Like two spies, we alone knew our secret destination. Alex looked handsome in his pressed cotton pants and starched white shirt. The cap sleeves of my navy dress fluttered when I leaned toward the car door. My cotton shirt and Bermuda shorts, fashioned from an old pair of blue jeans, were stowed away in the MG’s boot.

The confused voices in my head remained at a high pitch, each trying to out-shout the other. One led me to believe I was Jezebel, the other Joan of Arc, willing to stand up for right and good. Various mutations of these voices hammered at my brain. They continued building to a crescendo while I changed my clothes in the ladies' room at the Esso station and quieted only momentarily when I saw the lake.

Before we found a quiet spot of our own, we passed several groups where the boys and girls played in the water together. The water clung to the girls, dressed in stylish swimsuits like movie stars, and glistened off their skin like diamonds.

We drove on until we found a spot secluded by overgrowth.

"This looks like it," Alex said, and cut the engine off.

He took my hand and we walked to the edge of the lake. The clear water stretched in front of us. The reflection of the sunlight on the lake blinded me for a minute and I raised my hand to shield my eyes.

"You okay?" Alex asked.

"Fine," I said, and dropped his hand so that I could tug at my shorts. In my clandestine attempt to make them over, I'd cut quickly into the cloth. Once I made that first cut, there was no going back. When I stood next to Alex on the sand, the ragged edges seemed so much shorter than I remembered.

"I'll get the blanket," Alex said, and walked back to the car.

He took the blanket from the trunk and stretched it out across the sand as I waded into the clear water. The sand became liquid, squishing between my toes and swirling off the bottom to obscure my feet from view. I stepped further out, bolstered by the firm lake bottom beneath my feet; it was there one minute and gave way the next, causing me to push my hands out for balance like a tightrope walker about to meet the net below.

Alex sat down on the blanket. "Hey, come on over here and sit beside me before you fall in."

"Ha! Fall in. I was just playing." I went over and squeezed his outstretched hand but didn't sit down. Instead I walked to the edge of the woods where the honeysuckle grew thick and fragrant. The sweet smell ran all through the air around me, pushing back the scent of the hot sun baking the sand around the lake's edge. Sprinkled throughout the green vines like a light frost in early winter were yellow and white flowers. I reached in and pulled a trumpet-shaped flower from the bushy vine.

"What's that?" Alex asked.

I turned to him. "It's honeysuckle. Don't you smell it?" In one motion, I pushed the flower toward him and wrinkled my nose as if this would somehow encourage him to smell.

"The sweet smell—I thought it was you," he said.

"Oh my, the girls in England won't know what hit them." I broke the cap from the bottom of the flower's yellow tube and pulled out the stem with its blanket of nectar. Being polite, I offered it to Alex. "Want some?"

"You're going to eat the flower?"

"No, silly, only the honey that grows inside." I licked the nectar with my tongue. The taste took me back to days before that first vision. It took me back to days of riding broomstick horses with my cousins and getting piggyback rides from my daddy. Washing over me, these things threatened to send me running for home.

"Honey?" Alex asked, and brought me back to White Lake.

"Nectar. It's sweet, like honey." I dropped the broken flower to the ground and pulled another from the bush.

"Hey, bring that over here."

I pulled several more from the bush and carried them over to the blanket where Alex sat Indian-style. I sat down beside him, broke open another stem, and offered it to him.

With one eye closed as he prepared for the worst, he took the drooping flower from me and tasted it. Opening his eye and trying again, he finished licking the nectar from the stem. "Not much to taste," he said.

"Well, I can't help it if you had some sort of stilted childhood and missed the finer things in life," I said as I popped another stem open.

He laughed and flicked his tongue at my nose. "Missed a drop." Then he kissed me with the intensity of the sun. The memories, so real a few minutes earlier, faded into the kiss. He put his arms around me and whispered my name like a drowning man going under for the last time.

I pushed away. "Lunchtime," I said with a voice that was part June Cleaver and part Donna Reed.

Jumping from the blanket, I bustled to the car, armed with enough energy to hold back all the water behind the Hoover Dam. My hands shook like I had the DT's as I pulled the carefully packed basket and the jug of tea from the car.

"Here, let me take that for you." Alex came up and took the basket before I could protest.

Fried chicken, biscuits, potato salad, brownies, plates, and forks I unpacked and placed on the blanket between us, building some sort of demilitarized zone like they did in Korea. It ran right down the seal of Princeton University in the middle of the blanket.

"Sure looks good," Alex said, taking the aluminum foil off the chicken.

"Are you going to bless it?" I asked.

"Why don't you?" Alex bowed his head.

I looked out across the lake. "Lord, we thank you for this food. We truly are your children. Watch over us. Amen."

While we ate, Alex respected the paper-plate barricade, reaching across once to wipe a bit of potato salad from my chin.

"What do you suppose they're doing at home?" I asked, feeling a ripple in my stomach at the thought of our deception.

"I don't know. Probably talking to my friend in Wake Forest to find out when we'll be home. We've been gone about, what, four and a half hours, so they'll have called the State Patrol as soon as they get off the phone with him."

I threw a piece of brownie across the DMZ at him.

After lunch, Alex stood and took off his shirt. "Ready to go in?"

I averted my eyes. "You can't go in yet, it hasn't been thirty minutes. You'll get cramps and then I'll have to rescue you."

He bent down and turned my face to his. "Live dangerously."

"Alex."

"I promise, I'll just swim back and forth along the shoreline. I won't even be over my head. If you have to save me, you can just walk out and grab me."

"Suit yourself. I'm waiting." I gave up on trying not to look at him. How could looking at his bare chest at White Lake be more sinful than looking at the Elliot boys' chests as we barned tobacco? In some small part of myself, I knew that the chests of the Elliot boys had never made me feel the way I did watching Alex walk toward the water.

He had just stepped in the water when three distinct giggles echoed across the lake. The sounds of splashing were followed by more giggles that drifted our way like the light gray clouds at the beginning of a thunderstorm. Paddling along with their hands, three girls came into view. They were lying on floats like Cleopatras drifting on the Nile. They wore two-piece swimsuits that reeked of the exotic, complete with earrings and necklaces that made you wonder if they were getting ready to swim or to go somewhere besides around and around in the middle of White Lake.

With the whole lake stretching in every direction, they drifted toward Alex as if pulled by a current. At the same time, they didn't seem to see him until they were right up next to him. Alex stopped swimming and stood up as the first float pushed into his chest.

"Excuse me," a pretty blond girl said, holding her hand to her chest as if Alex had come out of nowhere and startled her.

I could feel myself beginning to go to ash in the flame of jealousy.

"No problem," Alex said. The others steered their floats around him in a circle, but he dove underneath and swam out of the center.

"You're quite a swimmer," one of the others said, making little circles in the water with her finger.

"If you think I'm quite a swimmer, you must be a wader," Alex replied, flashing them an "Aw, shucks, ma'am" look. I kept hoping he would swim away and not look back, but he hesitated.

"Well, we're here about every day if you need to practice your strokes," said the one whose bosoms swelled out of her suit like overripe melons, bursting at the seams.

The third girl had a high-pitched giggle. I felt certain she had a name like Gidget or Trixie.

Alex turned and grinned at me. "Well, I appreciate that, but, you see, I'm just up here for the day—my girlfriend and I."

"Oh, what a shame," the blonde said, squinting in my direction.

"Yeah, a real shame," her two friends echoed.

It's a shame all right, I thought. *A shame those floats didn't develop a fast leak.* The three floated off in the direction they had come, their departure marked by an occasional giggle.

"Come on in," Alex called.

"I don't think so," I said.

"Then I'm coming out." He walked from the water, grabbed his towel from the sand, and dried off. When he stretched out on the blanket beside me, I pretended to be deeply involved in the copy of *Exodus* that I was reading. When I continued to stare at the page I was on despite his presence, he shook his head and flicked water onto me.

"Stop that!" I closed my book and pursed my lips before I continued. "My, you attract admirers wherever you go," I said.

"They just can't resist my Ivy League charm."

"I hate to burst your bubble, but I don't think it had a thing to do with your Ivy League charm."

"You wouldn't be jealous, would you?" he asked.

"Hardly," I said, and I leaned across the seal of the great university and kissed him square on the lips.

"Do people really just lie on blankets in the sun for hours on end and do nothing else?" I asked Alex sometime later.

He nodded his head yes and stretched like a lizard on a rock.

"That's a pretty silly way to spend your day." Then, imitating the blonde, I said, "A shame, just a real shame."

Alex laughed and kissed me.

The sun got warmer and the sand shifted beneath us, but we

hardly noticed. By the time we started for home, the sun's last rays had faded.

On our way home, Alex pulled onto a dirt road. We bumped past two tobacco barns and into a spot where the whole sky seemed to open before us. We counted stars. I nestled against his chest, and my sense of time melted away into the sky.

Riding back to the house, Alex talked of how much he would miss me. He held tight to my hand and then spoke of Oxford with the same longing in his voice.

The voices in my head were not so steady. They didn't teach me about this in Sunday school. No one had warned me about how your senses leave you, about the melting sensation. We'd talked about the pleasures of the flesh all right, but only how they happened to heathens. No one told me that my body would betray me, and that it would feel so good. I had perfect-attendance pins for all of my first twelve years of life. Granny had brought me to church when I was just a few weeks old and put me in the aisle on a cotton quilt, but still I must have missed the Sunday that covered this. I wasn't so worried about saving myself for a husband. I wasn't really planning on having a husband, but then I hadn't planned on my body's betrayal, either. Alex talked on, seemingly unconcerned. Maybe Presbyterians weren't so concerned about the sins of the flesh. I guess all that doctrine of predestination absolved them. Alex seemed full of joy as he squeezed my hand, dropping it only to shift gears at stop signs.

The lights were on at the house. As we pulled up in the noisy MG, Aunt Vernie and Tessie stood on the porch, peering out at us like lighthouse sentries in the midst of a storm.

"What's Aunt Vernie doing here?" I asked, startled.

I pulled my hand from Alex's and grabbed the door handle. Alex steered the MG into the drive.

"It's okay, Maggie. It's okay," Alex said as I opened the door. But it didn't feel okay; it felt as if I was stepping into the darkest jungle of Africa, where creatures I couldn't imagine waited to prey on me.

"What's wrong?" I was on the porch before Alex could cut off the engine of the car.

Tessie started to speak, but Aunt Vernie was quicker.

"It's your mama. She's bad off. Might not make it through the night." The hysteria of her voice covered us all like dew on grass—dampening us completely.

"What happened?" I grabbed Tessie's hand and looked in her dark eyes for some understanding. "An accident?"

Behind us the car engine sputtered and died.

"No, baby, no. She's sick," Tessie said, and patted my hands like I was senile.

"Apoplexy," Aunt Vernie said, trembling. "Personally, I saw it coming. Lilah has always been—"

"Where is she?" Alex interrupted as he joined us on the porch. In the light, the shadows creased his face and made him look older.

"—high strung." Aunt Vernie ignored Alex.

Opening the door, Tessie shooed us in as if we were wayward children. "She's down at Clinton."

Alex paused inside the front room. "How could this be? She seemed fine this morning."

"It was sudden-like. One minute she was singing along with one of them records, and the next minute she was on the floor, fainted dead away," Tessie said, taking my hand as we made our way into the sitting room. That rough brown hand was the only thing that kept me from falling off the face of the earth. As I teetered on the edge, Tessie, full of understanding, held tight.

Uncle Jasper perched on the sitting-room couch, watching a rerun of *Bonanza*. His striped pajamas peeked out from under his gabardine slacks. Uncle Jasper sold insurance, and that made Aunt Vernie a little uppity, on account of her husband doing public work of the professional sort. Besides her large frame, both her frugal nature and her uppity-up airs were what stood out about Aunt Vernie.

"Anyway, Jasper has a good head for making arrangements and all, and I know your granny's going to need all the help she can get." Aunt Vernie gathered up her pocketbook, the strap cradled in the crook of her arm and her other hand protecting the clasp like we were all waiting to set ourselves upon her and find out what she had inside.

Tessie ignored Aunt Vernie. "Maggie, you go on up there and pray for your mama." On the television, the Cartwrights were shooting it out with a band of desperadoes.

"Jasper, go warm up the car. We've got to carry Maggie up to the hospital." Uncle Jasper always warmed the car engine for fifteen minutes, be it fall, winter, spring, or summer.

Before Uncle Jasper could move a muscle, Alex said, "I'll take her."

Aunt Vernie sputtered, but Alex already had my hand firmly in his and he was leading me out to the car. He tried to talk to me on the way to the hospital, but I couldn't make out the words. His voice sounded like a radio not quite tuned in to the signal. The voices in my head were louder and clearer than his. *I told you so,* they screamed.

The hospital loomed ahead of us, still and quiet like a giant mausoleum. Inside, the night staff moved ghostlike through the halls. As we made our way through the silent corridors, our footsteps echoed around us. *She's gone. She's gone,* my heart taunted.

CHAPTER

14

Alex pushed the door of Mama's room open, revealing a group of people large enough to fill the choir loft on Sunday: Preacher Liles, Mr. and Mrs. G. T. Spell, Mr. and Mrs. Lovingood, Aunt Willowdean and James, and Mr. and Mrs. Elliot among others. In the fluorescent light, they looked a little pale and less themselves. Preacher Liles wiped the sweat from his forehead with the sleeve of his double-knit jacket while several of the other men wore the overalls they'd been wearing when summoned from the field. Everyone turned. I could feel the color rising in my face. Why were they staring?

Alex tried to keep hold of my hand, but I pulled away, looking for Granny as I made my way over to my mama. Granny stood on the far side of the bed and beckoned me to her. It occurred to me that the crowd around the bed wasn't staring so much as they were looking to me for a healing prayer.

When the group shifted, I saw Mama for the first time, her hair splayed out around her on the pillow like a golden red flame.

Granny spoke first. "Maggie."

Mama's eyes fluttered open, but she didn't speak.

"Mama." I hugged her, trying to hold the life in her with my arms. Gone was the radiance that made her pale skin vital, its creamy glow dulled by her body's treachery. *Dear God, where is my mama?*

Granny put her arm around me. She alone was not waiting for me to pray. She alone was waiting for me to be me. That was the glory of Granny's faith—it didn't rest on the actions of men, but was rooted in a God so powerful, none of us could get in His way.

I took Mama's hand. Her mouth was drawn up on one side and one arm lay limply on top of the bedsheet. My mama was full of life and movement and dancing. My mama was not the woman who lay in front of me, the sheet rising and falling with each shallow breath.

"How are you?"

Mama's hand moved slightly in mine. "I'm fine. Just a little dizzy. And my hand doesn't want to work right. I just had one of those fading-away spells, only this one lasted longer than usual."

"What fading-away spells?" I pulled the sheet with my free hand, nervously arranging it to suit me.

"I've been having them for about a month now. I thought they were age." Mama tried to smile.

"Well, what does the doctor say about them?" My voice sounded eerily calm.

Granny patted me on the back. "The doctor says your mama's fine for now, but he wants her to go to Duke for some tests."

Mama smiled at me. "Maggie, would you pray for me, honey?"

I hesitated, and the crowd drew a breath, clearly planning to hold it, like a temper-struck child, until I prayed.

I bowed my head.

"Dear Jesus, Dear God—mother and father to us all—we come to you in such need."

I stopped and with my free hand grabbed the iron bed rail for support. Around me I could hear the prayers of the others. Who was I to pray? Who was I to so selfishly want my mama healed, while so many suffered? The germ-killing smell of bleach washed over me, and I gripped the iron rail tighter. As they missed my words, the others' prayers began to slow down. Granny shifted slightly behind me and took my hand from the bedstead, encouraging me to lean on her. Pulling in a deep breath, I continued. "Knowing that you can make the springs run where deserts abound . . ."

There was a lot of peeking going on. People watched me. I opened my eyes. There were no lights, no voice, nothing. Just the heaving of Mrs. G. T. Spell's bosom as her lungs fought the weight of her body for breath. I felt the earth shift beneath me again. I trembled.

God's silence defined me.

Alex stood across the room, drawing me with his presence like a sailboat to a safe harbor. I stopped. How could I pray anymore? The other voices drifted into a silence so full that a pin might have pricked it and sent us all flying around the room like balloons expelling air.

Granny squeezed my hand and continued. "Lily is sick, Lord. She needs your touch in a special way. Please give her your hand. Amen."

Everyone echoed the amen and we lifted our heads. Mama lay as she was before the prayer, trying to make her lopsided mouth turn into a smile. "Godstmeisnotime," she said.

"What?" I leaned closer.

"God's time is not our time." I felt her breath on my ear as she spoke slowly, taking her time to try to pronounce each word.

Mr. Lovingood cleared his throat. "Well, we'd best be leaving so Lilah here can get some rest."

Preacher Liles grasped my hand. "Don't you worry, honey. God's going to take care of this thang."

With no spectacle imminent and Mama settled for the night, the others followed the Lovingoods' example. Aunt Willowdean stopped and patted Mama's hand. "I'm sure Peter will get over here tomorrow." Just then I thought Mama's drawn mouth twitched ever so slightly.

After everyone had left, Alex offered to stay with Mama while Granny and I walked out to get a Coke.

"So what do the doctors know?" I asked Granny as soon as Mama's door swung closed.

"They think there's some sort of leak or block or something in her brain. Like maybe she had a stroke. Dr. Kincaid wants her to go on to Duke. He doesn't know what can be done, but he's afraid she's going to have a major stroke if we don't do something. He's got her on blood thinners already."

"Aunt Vernie said she was touch-and-go, that she might not last the night." Our footsteps echoed in the hall around us.

"Aunt Vernie's the only one touched." Granny said, turning red and scowling at the wall. "Still, I'll rest easier when they know what it is."

We returned to find Mama asleep and Alex with his head in his hands. I patted his shoulder and went to Mama's bedside. *Dear God, please let her live. Please heal her.*

Alex came up behind me and put his hands on my shoulders, but I felt a shiver of guilt and shrugged away.

"Granny, I'll stay tonight. Alex can take you home and let you get cleaned up before we go to Duke tomorrow."

"No, you go on. I'm staying right here tonight," Granny said.

Alex tried to reach me, but I couldn't speak on the way home.

As quickly as it began, my experiment with being a normal young woman ended. In the flutter of a bird's wing, in the beat of a heart that pumped blood to the wrong spot, Alex stood outside a wall built by me around my mama's illness.

The next day, Alex paced our front porch like an expectant father, but I could not see him and I would not see him. I could not trust that my body wouldn't betray me again and cause me to say things that I didn't mean, make commitments to Alex that I couldn't make. My mama needed me now. I had not been there when she needed me—I'd been just like my daddy.

As I got ready to go relieve Granny, I couldn't help but peek at Alex, positioning myself to see through a crack in the picture-window curtains.

"Maggie, are you peeking out that window at Mr. Barrons?"

I jumped as Tessie came up behind me.

"Oh, go on, Tessie. I was just checking to see if a cloud was coming up." I pretended to wipe my face, trying to hide a deep blush. I'd been thinking how nice it would be to lay my head on Alex's shoulder.

"Uh-huh, I didn't just fall off the turnip truck, you know." Tessie raised her eyebrows at me.

"Well, I don't see a cloud in sight." I turned and walked back to my bedroom.

Later, Alex stood by the car when I came out of the house to go to the hospital. His hair was sticking out on one side and his shirt looked like it had tossed and turned all night and wrinkled itself with worry.

"Maggie, Maggie, you've got to talk to me," Alex said.

"No, I don't," I said, not trusting myself to look at him as I walked.

Alex got between me and the car. "Maggie, don't shut me out this way. Why are you doing this?"

I stopped and looked at the ground. "It's all very simple. If I'd done what I was supposed to do, none of this would have ever happened." The earth beneath me stood as solid as it always did; it was only me who was shifting violently to and fro.

"That's not true."

"Yes, it is." I looked up.

"That is exactly the opposite of what you've been telling me for the last six weeks," he said.

"No, it's not." I wanted to pop his face for trying to take my misery from me.

"Think about it. What you're telling me is that you controlled God. That because you and I went somewhere you felt you shouldn't go and because of what we did that night, God decided to strike down your mama."

"I can't think about it. I'm too busy feeling it. And I said no such thing. That's not it at all. I wasn't there for my mama," I said.

"Why is it that grace is something God provides for everyone else but not for you?" He turned his hands up. "Maggie Davidson, lone exception to the love of God."

"Alex, we are not in theology class. Why don't you go to New

York and study that statue of the Virgin Mary that weeps blood? I can't see you."

"I'm not interested in studying you, I'm interested in loving you. Not just you, I love the whole place. Haven't you said yourself that I love your mama and your granny? And how about Mr. Neb and Tessie? I love them, too. Because you know what? Once you're open to love, it multiplies inside of you. And it takes you to places you've never been before." Alex paused. "Maggie, you've been inside of love your whole life, it surrounds you. Take it from someone who hasn't been that fortunate, when you find it—nothing ever looks the same again."

Alex held out his hand. "I don't want to leave, but I can't wait to see my father. You know why? Because he won't look the same. Because I love you, my father will never look the same again."

I put my hands up in front of me. "All I know is my mama is laying in there sick. And I can't seem to help her."

"Let me help. I can be with you. I can call my father and have the finest doctors here within hours." Alex dropped his hand and shifted from one foot to the other like he'd done that day I'd come upon him and Annie Ruth in the Salemburg Grill.

"No, Alex." My stubbornness only added to the wall that I'd built, pushing me further and further from his love. I walked around to get in the car.

He followed me around the car.

"Maggie, I'm not giving up."

"Alex, there is nothing to give up. We can't do this. You can give up or not, but I can't change this." I started the car, looking away so he couldn't see the tears in my eyes.

"We can work it out," he said. "I love you."

I drove with tears streaming down my face. Maybe I shouldn't be so quick to tell him I'd never see him again. I tried to think what it would be like not to ever see him again, but all I could do was think how people in an earthquake must feel when everything that had been firm in their life shook beneath their feet and threatened to open up and swallow them.

The reporter caught me at the hospital. He'd positioned himself at the front door with his photographer by his side. I think that if the Lord had only sent a plague of reporters on the Pharaoh, Moses and the Israelites could have walked free without so much as even a peep from anyone in Egypt.

"Hey!" he shouted at me as I walked past. "Hey!"

"I have no comment," I said, trying to slip through the hospital door before they could stop me.

"Hey, little lady, not so fast. You don't even know what I'm going to ask." He and the photographer came through the door behind me.

"I don't care what you ask, I'm not going to talk to you." I walked quickly toward the visitors' desk.

He moved around me. "I think you might want to talk about this. You see, I hear that you've been holding out on us. You're seeing God and She's a lady. Now, I got to tell you, me and Harold here were discussing this in the car on the way over here, and we decided that if we saw God and She was a lady, she'd look like Marilyn Monroe. What about you? Why don't you tell us what She looks like?"

The flashbulb exploded a burst of light in my face. "I don't know what you're talking about." I tried to blink out the black spots and keep walking.

"Don't try and deny it. That boyfriend of yours has told a lot of people. Come on, one statement and the whole United States will know."

I shut my eyes. Alex. How could Alex have told?

My knees went weak, and before I could tell myself not to, I slid right down onto the floor. I did have the presence of mind to tuck my skirt under me as I went. Before I'd hit the ground, the receptionist was hovering over me and screaming, "Code Red, Code Red."

I watched through slitted eyes as the reporter and his sidekick were banished from the lobby. The receptionist alternated between fanning me and yelling for help until a nurse and an orderly arrived. After determining that I had no life-threatening condition, they helped me into a wheelchair with the precision of a drill team at the Friday-night football game.

Granny took one look at me when they wheeled me into Mama's room and said, "Well, I think I'd better get them to bring another bed in here."

Mama was asleep, still as wane as the night before. Granny laid down the book she was reading and started to get up.

"No, I'm fine." I turned to the orderly behind the chair. "I'm fine, really. Just went woozy for a minute."

"Well, they want me to take you down to one of the examining rooms," he said.

"I don't want to go to an examining room." I turned to Granny. "It was that reporter—he was bothering me."

"Oh, well," Granny said, understanding a bit better what I was doing in a wheelchair. "There's no need for her to go, she can stay right here with me."

"All right, but if anything happens, I'm going to tell them you made me leave."

"Young man, I'll take full responsibility. Now go on and tend to someone who really needs it," Granny said, looking down her nose.

As soon as the door closed behind him, a tear slid down my cheek.

"What in the world?" Granny asked.

"Alex told, he told," I managed to say while my insides whirled around.

"Told what?" Granny asked.

"That She's a woman. The reporter knows, I guess everyone knows. I can't go through it again, Granny. I can't. People prodding at me with constant questions and following me. I just can't do it."

"Lord have mercy, child, you know he did no such of a thing."

"I know he did. Why would he betray me? I've never done anything to him." I put my face in my hands.

"Well, honey, you never know why people act like they do." She walked over and put her hand on my shoulder. "But you can take it and you will take it, and we'll be here for you every step."

"But look at her, Granny, she's so weak right now. And you've got so much on you. How will you ever do it all?"

"People will disappoint you and betray you. They can't do anything else, but God never will. Honey, were you thinking we get to fall in love with a god? Not hardly. We are humans and we fall in love with humans and they make mistakes. There is a forgiveness that we're responsible for every step of the way. God is in that."

At Duke that afternoon, Dr. Kincaid told Granny and I, "We're going to be doing a procedure called cerebral angiography. We'll inject a material that's opaque to X rays into the blood vessels entering the head. This makes the vessels within the skull visible to the X ray."

I wondered as he talked if the X rays would show anything of Mama's inner workings, provide any clues to what had made her such a Parker heretic all these years.

Dr. Kincaid continued. "I'll be back to you as soon as I know anything."

Time moved with the beat of a funeral durge. I paced while Granny needlepointed a cushion for the sitting-room couch. Around us people flowed in never-ceasing streams, each carried along by a loved one's illness, a job to be done, or news of an illness or accident to be heard and digested, their lives so different and yet the same, ending up in this spot where the illusion of control disappeared as quickly as the shimmering mirage of water on a hot blacktop road. Once the reporters found us, the hospital moved us to a special waiting room sealed off from prying eyes.

In the university medical library, *The International List of Diseases and Causes of Death* listed, matter-of-factly, some eleven hundred distinct ways of departing to the great beyond, one heading of which was the crippling effects of stroke. Dr. Kincaid took a more gentle tone when he returned to us. He came after Mama had been X-rayed and pricked so often that she said later that she thought they were checking to see how long it would be before she bled a different color.

Granny and I sat with him in the hall down from Mama's room, where she lay in a deep, dreamless sleep, courtesy of Valium.

"I'm afraid the tests haven't given us much further insight." Dr. Kincaid pulled on his bow tie. "It appears that there's some small clot that's done a bit of damage. With blood thinners to help dissolve it, I think we'll be all right this time. I'm going to send her back to the hospital in Clinton so you can be near her while she recuperates. As to whether this could happen again, I have no idea. In strokes, three out of four times, they're caused when one or more of the vessels are blocked by thrombosis—a clot that forms either in the brain or in another area of the body and is carried to the brain by the bloodstream. That's what happened with Lilah. Fortunately for Lilah, her clot was small and the tissue damaged will regenerate or its function will be taken over by another part of the brain, I think." It was as large an "I think" as I ever recalled hearing.

In short, Mama's bloodstream, that life-giving messenger of the body, had gone wacky and tried to do her in.

"How will we know whether she's going to be okay?" I asked.

"That's what we can't say right now," Dr. Kincaid said. "Your mama might live to be one hundred or she might suffer a stroke tomorrow that would leave her paralyzed or worse."

Or worse, or worse, or worse. His words echoed through me like our footsteps in the dark hospital halls the night before.

"We are in a wait-and-see situation," he said.

"Seems like more wait than there is see to it," Granny said.

Three days after Mama took sick, I made my way in the gray morning light to the tobacco barn. Blessedly there had been a train wreck in Roseboro and a murder in Clinton—one man had murdered another, and it was reported that they were funny and lived together just like a married couple. So the reporters had gone for now, trying to be the first to get the gory details. Alex usually arrived in the afternoon to pace the porch.

In the barn, I knelt and put my elbows on the caned bottom of the old chair. Pressing my hands together until they hurt, I prayed.

"Please, God, please. Make my mama well. Heal her. Forgive me for my sins and my selfishness."

A fly buzzed around my head.

Emptiness and anxiousness were as real to me as the caned pattern of the chair that my elbows rested on. What was I doing here? I saw my mama's face and heard her voice singing with Doris Day's, "Whatever will be will be." There had to be a way to change what would be.

"Lord, I need a healing for my mama. I don't care what people think. I don't care what people know. Whatever You need from me, You just say. If You never show me Your face again, if I never look on Your glory until I see heaven, that's okay. Forgive me, Lord. Touch my mama."

There was nothing. Tears of frustration mingled with the gnats and the flies. Their buzzing and my sobs were the only noise in the barn.

I wanted light. I wanted voices. I wanted all the things people had asked me for for the last year and a half. In God's silence, I could find no reassurance.

I wept. My heart felt like one of those oranges that Miss Patsy squeezed in her machine down at the Salemburg Grill. I tried to find comfort in the Scriptures memorized for Bible drills.

Trust in the Lord with all your heart and lean not to your own understanding. In all your ways acknowledge Him and He will direct your path.

My path had become hopelessly snarled with brambles, and even with God's guidance, I felt I would not find my way without tearing the skin of my faith.

I saw Alex at the hospital in Clinton later that day. He called to me across the parking lot.

I walked over to the MG. "How could you? How could you tell about Her?" I asked.

He looked puzzled. "Tell what?"

"You know tell what. I may look like a country bumpkin, but I'm not stupid." I crossed my arms and bit my lip.

"Maggie, what are you talking about?" Alex's white shirt and khaki pants, so neatly pressed now, seemed to melt a bit in the early afternoon humidity.

"Haven't you seen the papers?"

"No, I've been trying to get ready to leave and trying to see you." He touched my shoulder.

"Well, according to the reporter who set himself on me, thanks to my boyfriend, the world knows all about Her."

Alex opened his mouth to speak and then closed it. He shook his head. "I've never talked to a reporter. I didn't talk to anyone." He closed his mouth and his eyes told me that the words were wrong. His breath came in rasps, as if he'd just run a race. "I didn't tell a reporter, I didn't. I told Rex Morgan over at the seminary, but he would never tell."

"Well, he did." I didn't want to believe that Alex had told, but at the same time, believing it was another reason I couldn't see him. Another reason to confirm my suspicion that even though he acted different from my father, he wasn't really different after all.

"Maggie, I'm so sorry. I can't believe he'd tell. It wasn't like you're thinking. I was just telling him how much I loved you and all the incredible things about you. It just slipped out, but he isn't the kind of guy who'd tell. I don't understand." Alex paused. "What are we going to do?"

"Alex, there is no we. I shared the deepest secret of my heart and you told. I've got to go, Mama needs me."

"In time, don't you think it will all be okay in time?" Alex asked.

"I don't think I've got any more time." I bit my lip harder.

"Maggie, I would never do anything to hurt you. We can work it out," he said. "I love you."

I turned away from him, biting my lip so hard that I tasted blood.

The door to my mama's room was open.

Mama sat in bed, looking at a photo spread of Doris Day's new home. I kissed her, barely noting the scent of lavender sachet floating like an unseen aura around the new rosebud-appliquéd bed jacket that Aunt Vernie had bought her at Leder's Department Store.

A bouquet of red and white variegated carnations sat on her bedside table as well as a vase of red roses so perfectly formed that they might have been made of wax.

"You just missed Alexander," she said. "He brought you these flowers." She motioned to the roses.

"No, actually I saw him." I examined the red lines in the carnations.

"Did you speak to him?" Despite the draw of her mouth, her tone sounded very grannylike.

"For a minute," I said, rolling my eyes like I was sixteen.

"Magdalena, that young man deserves your attention. He deserves more than a minute."

"Mama, I have talked with him until I'm flat talked out. I can't be happy with him. He's not who I thought he was. There is nothing more to say." I couldn't tell her about the newspapers and add one more burden to her body.

"I don't think you've given him a chance, Magdalena. Whatever happened, he deserves a chance. He loves you and I think you love him. You're acting like a spoiled child," she said.

"So now are you going to take up acting like Uncle Peter, telling me every move I'll make?"

Mama's head moved back as if I'd slapped her. Tears welled in the corners of her eyes.

I was instantly contrite. "Mama, I'm sorry."

"I won't try to tell you what to do. But, Magdalena, you can't give up on love because of me. Of all that I wish for you in this world, I wish for you to truly know love. I may not be here to see it, but I want that for you."

I knelt beside her. "Mama, don't talk that way. Of course you're going to be here. You're on those blood thinners now, and there's something new happening all the time up at Duke. You're going to be fine. Mama, I thought I loved him, but I don't. I'm not meant to be married. It was a passing fling, a summer romance. Alex hasn't made it out of the heat of July yet, but he will and then he'll see."

I didn't tell her that her illness and his betrayal had brought a blast of January to my heart. I put my arms around her, and the thought of losing her melted my resistance. "If it will make you feel better, I'll talk to Alex."

She kissed my cheek, the pucker of her lips stilted because of her slightly drawn mouth. "It'll be better, you'll see."

I left about an hour later, planning to stop in at the library before I headed for home.

As I walked to the car, I could see a square of white on my windshield. As I got closer, I could see my name printed in craggy script across the top. The end of the tape stuck to my fingers as I pulled the note from the glass. I glanced around to see who was nearby as I pulled the note open, but around me were only Falcons, pickup trucks, station wagons, and one lone Edsel that would never reach its full potential.

I Love You, Maggie Davidson.
And one day you'll believe.

The note was like a postcard from my soul. *Believe*—belief was not a knowing thing as my mama had told me so often. Belief was not an understanding thing, necessarily. Belief was faith. *Now faith is the substance of things hoped for, the evidence of things not seen.*

I never saw Alex. Unbeknownst to Mama and me, he left for home that afternoon.

CHAPTER 15

"I'm going to quit school and look after Mama," I declared to the chickens one day near the beginning of the fall term. Clucking and pecking at the seed that fell beside the feeder as I filled it, they agreed. The same could not be said, however, for Granny, who squawked and flapped her hands in disgust.

I mentioned my plan to her as we cleaned out the chest freezer to make room for fall peas.

"Beg your pardon, young lady, but Tessie and I can do just fine. I believe we raised you and your mama. I believe we did. So don't think we can't handle your mama now."

She plopped down some frozen peas for emphasis.

"Well, I've got to do something. I can't stand by and do nothing." I plopped down a bag with equal determination. The bag burst at the seams and frozen peas scattered across the floor like beads from some five-and-dime necklace.

I burst into tears, a reaction that was as big a surprise to me and Granny as if the peas that lay at our feet had become pearls.

Granny took me by the shoulders. Her hands were cold through the striped cotton of my blouse. "It's peas, Maggie, peas." And then softer, "Child, listen and listen carefully. You've got to quit trying to place fault with this thing. You're not to blame; your mama's not to blame. If God were going to visit punishment on people for evil actions, do you really believe your mama would be first in line? To be sure, the Lord is used to her flightiness by now. Besides"—she began to sweep the peas from the floor—"you moping around here feeling sorry for yourself is not going to help a one of us. People will talk about this till the next thing comes along. It'll pass, but you can't let it eat you alive before it does."

The doctor's test had shown us the possibilities of Mama's illness: sudden paralysis or death. What the doctor couldn't test Mama for was the fact that invalid was a lifestyle that did not suit her. She shed it over the next few weeks like a snake losing its skin, pretending that her visit to the hospital was a holiday and that the draw to her mouth was a minor inconvenience that would soon right itself like an acrobat catching her balance on the tightrope. But Granny, Tessie, and I knew better, our unspoken pact sealed with understanding that one of us would always be with her, that we would check if she took too long in the bathtub, that we would encourage her home therapy exercises, and that we would pray for the blood to keep circulating unimpeded through her body.

I pled my case for dropping out of school to my mama and got the same results I'd gotten with Granny. Granny and Mama's steadfast faith in God and in me only served to push me further into my black hole. The black hole had started when I saw Aunt Vernie and Tessie standing on the porch the night my mama got sick, and it kept taking in more and more of me all the time. I felt like one of those people in a vampire movie who had been bit. I was just going through the motions.

Sometimes when I woke up in the morning and caught the briefest whiff of the lavender on my sheets, I'd almost think that everything would be okay. Then the cold tile of the bathroom floor brought me back, and I tumbled headfirst into the hole when what I meant to do was wash the sleep from my eyes.

If I tried to step around it, the hole shifted and I tumbled in, unable to grab any of the familiar things of life to hang on to. The presence of God's absence in my life was "deep and wide," like the words of the song we sang as children.

Not so for Granny and Mama. Mama became more determined than ever to bake and can, dragging her arm, limp at times, determined by sheer force of will to can and bake every combination that came into her head. No one stood a chance in the Home Demonstration Club contests that year. Mama overwhelmed them and left them gasping for breath. No one had any idea of what we went through to get those blue ribbons. We had strawberry huckleberry jelly and peach apple jam. Each combination seemed to Mama more inspired than the last.

She dragged Tessie along on this culinary journey as well, pushing her to the limit with mixtures that Tessie considered well beyond the bounds of acceptable repasts. When pushed over the edge by some particularly awful combination, Tessie would praise God that Mama had only had a slight stroke.

"The Lord as my witness, if He'd have knocked you in the head any harder, Miss Lilah, I'd be afraid to see what we'd be doing. As it is, I'm about ashamed to admit what we're canning. Every day when I go home, I tell them not even to ask."

"Now, Tessie, we are finally canning with some pizzazz around here," Mama would say, and smile like a French chef gone mad, her mouth drooping slightly on one side.

The determined reporter from Raleigh continued to try to find news where there was none. His article came out complete with the headline HEALER CANNOT HELP HER OWN MOTHER, and a quote from Miss Patsy: "Things haven't been the same with Maggie since her mama got sick." I stayed home with Mama several Sundays after that. Crowds at the church, which swelled slightly out of curiosity when the God-as-a-woman issue hit the paper, now thinned. That was a relief to me; I just wanted to look after my schoolwork and my mama and be left alone.

Seizing the opportunity to increase commerce, the Lawton mayor rid himself of the first healer. It had been widely rumored that on more than one occasion the saintly reviver relied on the liquor bottle for his dose of the Spirit. So Mr. Neely Lipscomb quickly joined up with Brother Oscar and, using their flair for promotion, they advertised the new Miracle Tabernacle—miracles for those feeble in the brain, the body, the soul, and the pocketbook. They pasted fresh new sheets of words on the interstate billboards, and they found a local radio station that would carry the proceedings. Many went, leaving the Canaan cinder-block chapel and its new brick counterpart to exhale with relief. The grass in the churchyard fought its way back to the surface, and the ruts in the parking lot stayed flat for weeks at the time after Clyde Elliot's boys smoothed them with their tractor.

I tried to smooth over my life as well, glad for some breathing space. Alex's letters piled high on the desk in my room; the mound grew quickly at first—it would slow later as the months went by. The blue airmail envelopes spilled over onto my schoolwork. While I refused to open them, despite urging from every member of the household, including Mr. Neb, I could not bring myself to throw them away. I often thought of Alex and of that day, but it always ended with a vision of my mama's drawn mouth and the reporter skulking around the hospital with the evil so thick around him, it might have been a swarm of honeybees. Sometimes I'd think that it could all be washed away with my mama's healing, but then I remembered Alex's betrayal. The pain of missing him stayed with me daily, missing who I thought he was. It was not a searing pain like a white-hot coal, more a constant discomfort of heat with the ember fanned to flame every now and then by memories. I'd see something and think, *I'm going to tell Alex about this,* and then remember I couldn't. I'd stop at Turlington's store and buy me a Coke and remember how it felt to lean against that MG and laugh and talk of God.

In mid-September, I had a Bunsen burner in chemistry lab that wouldn't burn and then burned too much, which meant I had to stay late to do my lab work over. I arrived home just in time for supper. I yelled hello as I rushed in the door, put my books down on the coffee table, and headed to the bathroom to wash my hands.

"Your granny's on her way in from the Elliots'," Mama called from the kitchen. "You're late this evening. Everything okay?"

"Yes, it's fine. I think it's safe to say I'll never come up with the formula for the atom bomb by accident," I called back as I dried my hands and sniffed in the familiar lavender scent of my mother's bath powder.

"What?" Mama asked.

I walked through the sitting room and into the kitchen, where the smell of biscuits baking reached out and picked me up from my long day. "Nothing. I couldn't get the Bunsen burner to do right. It—"

Sitting in the middle of my plate was a blue envelope with an Oxford postmark. I picked it up by the corner as if it were on fire and turned to take it to my room.

"Magdalena, don't put it away. Why don't you read one? Aren't you even a little curious?" Mama asked.

I turned back. Mama stood with the dish towel in her hand, her face covered with all the encouragement her spirit allowed. I felt very tired. "Mama, haven't you heard that curiosity killed the cat?"

"Oh, but what a wonderful life she led!" Mama said. The corner of her mouth drooped slightly, and I walked back across the kitchen and kissed her on the cheek.

"Thanks for trying, Mama," I said.

"One day, Maggie, you're going to understand that pilgrimages are more about sore feet than they are matters of the soul. You're letting your sore feet get in the way."

Thereafter, Mama placed the letters on my plate daily. From there they made their pilgrimage to the pile on my desk, sent off on their journey with a loud sigh from my mama. Not that I wasn't curious. Once I almost steamed one open when Mama was napping and Granny was gone, but then I thought of Pandora and her box and I poured the boiling water down the sink.

In late September a letter arrived with a New Bethel postmark. A sheet of thin white writing paper fell into my lap as I opened the envelope.

September 25, 1960

Dear Maggie,

I am writing to ask you if you will meet me at the Salemburg Grill on Saturday at 11:30. John and I are going to South Carolina to get married. Will you stand up with me? Max Hudson is going to stand up for John. Daddy will not give his permission for us to marry, so this is how it has to be. Please let me know in tomorrow's mail.

Your friend,
Norma

Ever since he had discovered that Norma and John had gone to Meryl's Sugar Shack, a dance pavilion over toward the coast, Uncle Peter had been determined to marry Norma off to a farmer in his church. Even now, Uncle Peter ruled his children's lives so completely that they were shadows of adults. Only James would stand up to his father on occasion. The boys continued the work of the farm; they had all married colorless women who bore children bright with joy but who in the constant rubbing of life with Uncle Peter became washed out before your very eyes.

Norma was the surprise at the bottom of the Cracker Jack package. She refused to marry the beau picked for her by her father after the dance pavilion disaster. Instead she took a job at Woolworth's in Raleigh, using her work to pry herself from the Parker farm in Johnston County.

For some time, we had heard rumblings of Norma's "problems." Under cover of shut-in visitation, Norma had actually been visiting with Cary Grant and Doris Day. Mama defended her every chance she could, telling Granny that Cary and Doris were indeed shut-in at the movies. Norma's betrothed, whom she refused to be trothed to, promptly married a McCloud girl from over in Pender

County. He said he needed help on the farm and couldn't wait forever. Uncle Peter fumed.

So did Mama. She scolded Uncle Peter when he came by that next week. "So this is what you would have for your daughter? That she would be one more piece of equipment needed to run a farm?"

Uncle Peter responded with a comment about the babbling of the heathens. Mama cut her eyes at him and stuck her finger in his face. In doing so she looked very much like my granny. Even in my glee at Uncle Peter's tongue-lashing, I was so very conscious of Mama's arm, which struggled to keep up with her wrath.

"You can't raise a child by principles alone. There has to be some love in there somewhere, and they have to know it." Her finger wagged on, inches from Uncle Peter's nose. "Principles will desert them, but that piece of your love never will."

In some way, I suppose Norma and I were both disappointments to our parents. Mama wished I were a little more interested in Doris and Cary. Uncle Peter wished for Norma to renounce the world.

I sent Norma a letter back the next day. Her situation had the aroma of fresh-baked pecan pie that drew you to it without a second thought. I'd never been to Dillon, South Carolina, but I'd heard about it. You could be married there without benefit of blood tests or any other rigmarole contrived by the state and anxious parents to keep two star-crossed lovers apart.

On Saturday morning, I finished my chores early. It was no problem to leave the house. Given the narrow bounds of my life, Granny, Tessie, and Mama would have pushed me out if they could. I did tell them about the elopement. I could not bear another secret. Granny began to prepare a list of things that would need to be done to have a shower for the newlyweds, while Mama insured that I loaded the Brownie with film to take lots of pictures.

"Who's Sorry Now?" was playing on the jukebox at the Salemburg Grill when I arrived. The front counter was so full and Miss

Patsy so busy, I didn't even speak on my way in. The intendeds were in a booth about midway back. Norma sipped an orangeade through a white and red paper straw. When she saw me, she put down her glass and waved.

Norma looked as beautiful as I'd ever seen her. Until that Saturday the closest any of Uncle Peter's children came to a glow was the shiny nose Norma developed on a hot summer day. But that day Norma's face had taken on a vitality that I'd never seen before. She wore an ivory crepe dress with a gored skirt and a lined jacket, ivory gloves, and a small ivory felt hat trimmed with a wired ivory bow that stood at attention like a military escort under a piece of ivory netting. Sitting across from her in the booth, John wore a dark blue suit and looked more like a sturdy farmer than a knight in shining armor.

"Norma, you look beautiful. That dress is lovely," I said.

She stood and twirled around to model her outfit.

"John's sister helped me. I saved my money from Woolworth's, and we sewed when no one else was there. Everybody thought I was at the movies."

I hugged her and smiled, thinking about Uncle Peter railing against Doris Day and Cary Grant.

"Well, it is just beautiful. I wish Mama could see you. They all wish you the best." Norma sat back down in the booth.

"Maggie, I'm glad you're here. It's nice to have family with us. Not that I'd want my daddy even if he would come." Her hand shredded a napkin while she spoke, betraying the false confidence of her voice.

I stuck my hand out to John.

"Well, now I suppose we're going to be cousins."

He leaned over, ignored my hand, and gave me a hug. A throat cleared behind me and I turned to find a lanky fellow grinning at me.

"Oh, sorry," Norma said. "This is Max. Max, this is my cousin Maggie."

Max stuck his hands down in his pockets to give them something to do. He didn't seem all that eager to touch me. "Nice to meet you. I seen that picture of you in *Life* magazine. I could tell right off you were Norma's kin."

"Nice to meet you, too." I turned back to Norma. How did he think we favored each other?

Miss Patsy leaned over the counter as I walked by. "Maggie." She motioned me over. "What in the world is going on?"

"Oh, Miss Patsy, we're going to a wedding. And we're late." I smiled and quickly joined the others outside in the sunshine.

Norma and John stood beside Max's daddy's new Thunderbird while I snapped a picture, holding my breath while I pushed the button. Norma and John looked as full of new as that Thunderbird. I envied them.

Why couldn't I be a normal girl who worried about trousseaus and matching shades of lipstick? A girl who hung on to her boyfriend, who accepted the realities of life? Had my vision of God opened up heaven to me and closed the world? And now without that vision, what was left?

Norma bubbled on and on about their prospects as we drove out of Salemburg toward the highway, Max and me in the front, the newlyweds-to-be snuggled in the backseat.

"Now, are we gonna swing by the house and pick up Norma's daddy?" Everyone laughed at Max's joke, and by pure reflex, he reached out and jabbed me in the arm. After that he relaxed. I suppose he realized electric current wasn't going to jolt through him simply by touching his hand to my shoulder.

The South of the Border wedding chapel ran with the precision of a well-oiled machine, a wedding machine that produced happy couples the same way Lawrence Welk's champagne music machine popped out bubbles. But first there were papers to be signed and witnessed and the fee to be paid.

Norma turned to John as he signed forms. "Oh, honey, wouldn't some flowers be wonderful?"

Flowers cost extra at the South of the Border Chapel.

"Norma, we've got to look at more than today. You're not getting rich at the five-and-dime. I'm gonna have to scratch out what I can from Daddy and the back forty. If you wanted flowers, you should have said so. Mama's got a whole bed of them."

He continued to fill out the form. A shadow of disappointment crossed Norma's face.

"Don't pull that long face. I got more important things to worry about than flowers."

Norma's stroll through the Garden of Love had experienced its first toe stumping. She smiled at me, behind John's back, biting her lip in the process. Without a word, I walked to the glass refrigerator in the front room.

"Please, I'd like those ivory roses with the pink streamers."

"My favorite." The chaplain's wife clapped her hands. Then she put the money I gave her in a metal cash box, treating the money as tenderly as she did the flowers.

I returned to the chapel vestibule with my gift. John looked up as Norma squealed. "Best wishes," I said, handing her the bouquet.

John snorted, signing the last blank with a flourish.

The only thing left was the ceremony, a kiss, and a few more signatures. They placed us just so on little tape X's on the floor.

The chaplain's wife came up behind me and threw her arm up in the air in the best drum-major style. Her daughter, seated at the old pump organ, began a rousing rendition of "Whither Thou Goest I Will Go," with her Adam's apple bobbing in time to the music.

The wedding commenced.

I imagined Alex at his wedding. Something grand and stately like when Elizabeth married Philip and then became a queen. Nothing like the South of the Border chapel where the X taped to the floor peeled beneath my toe. The tears rolled down my face; the chaplain's wife hugged me and exclaimed, "It's the same for me. I never see one that I don't cry." As if she feared disappointing me, she promptly demonstrated her commitment to this standard.

After the ceremony, Max and I followed Norma and John to the door, the strains of the wedding march playing behind us. Norma gave me her bouquet while she adjusted the veil of her hat. Max had hidden away bags of rice in the car and searched his pockets for the Thunderbird's keys. As we reached the door, he pulled them from his pocket and took my elbow to guide me through the door. We stepped out into the sunshine and looked up just as the photographer clicked our picture.

The reporter whom Granny had run off the property stepped forward. "Tying the knot, are you? I figured you for the old-maid type." He scratched his head and jotted something on the pad in front of him.

"It's not my wedding. And please don't print that picture." I turned to Max. "This is really aggravating."

"Ma'am, how do you think I'll sell any papers without some good pictures in them?" the reporter asked.

Max stepped toward the two men. "Why don't y'all just give me that film?"

Despite Max's easygoing manner, the air between the men crackled with the intensity of the words.

"Sure." The photographer acted like he was going to open the camera. Instead he pushed into Max, knocking him off balance. The photographer and the reporter took the opportunity and ran for the car. They were on their way out of the parking lot before Max and John could reach them.

Norma chewed her bottom lip. "Oh, dear Lord, I hope they don't print that."

I patted her shoulder and handed her back her flowers. "Don't worry. Your daddy can't stop you now."

A cloud passed over the sun.

The picture made Monday afternoon's newspaper. The caption read, "Healer Weds as Mother Worsens." Some of the major papers reprinted it, in the section reserved for the antics of college students and movie stars, but not the retraction that followed the next week. By then I was old news.

Granny tried to hide the paper with the picture and its awful caption. She placed it under a stack of papers with the results of the soil testing. Shortly after Mama had become ill, copies of *Today's Health* began to arrive, only to be hidden on Granny's desk, never to see the light of day again while we were around. On occasion I would catch her reading one, which she would stow away with the air of a preacher caught looking at a girlie magazine. The newspaper with the wedding picture met the same fate.

Mama snatched the paper from under the stack on the desk. "Mama, if I believed everything I read in the paper, I'd have been dead a long time ago."

That was the nature of our topsy-turvy house. Granny, whose mission in life had been to try to keep my mama's head out of the clouds, now spent her time trying to shield Mama from reality. Mama, on the other hand, normally lost in the cosmos, now battled to know the details of her own reality. Tessie seemed to be the balance in the new order—cheering my mama when she needed it and comforting my granny. My contribution was to try hard to stay out of the black hole and distinguish myself at Pineland with high grades.

The film from the Brownie was developed, and Norma and John came to the house the next Sunday to see the pictures. Mama and Granny held a floating shower in their honor with a true October extravagance, an orchid corsage for Norma. Uncle Peter forbade Aunt Willowdean to come. Even though Norma proclaimed it okay, I think she and the orchid wilted a little when the last minutes ticked away with no sign of Aunt Willowdean's Rambler in the yard.

Uncle Peter arrived the Tuesday after the shower in the late afternoon, waving the newspaper above his head like a battle flag. Fearing the dandelion spread of insurrection in his family, he could not help but try to contain it at what he thought was the source.

"Mama, how could you allow this to go on under your roof?"

"I don't know what you're talking about," Granny said, and turned back to the counter, where she sliced a country ham.

"You know very well what I'm talking about," Uncle Peter

said. "Norma and this marriage that Maggie pushed her into. The Lord says, 'Children, obey your parents.' "

Granny waved the knife above her head. "The Lord says a whole lot, including 'To everything there is a season.' Norma is almost twenty-one years old. It isn't your season to decide what she does anymore."

The newspaper fluttered to Uncle Peter's side. "Well, I guess not, with her cousin trying to make sure she does anything she can just to spite me. We certainly see what a fine example her cousin set for her, running around town with that Communist intellectual who tells the world all about Maggie's blasphemous vision of God like it's the latest baseball score. Thank the Lord that he left. And then there's your daughter." He pointed the newspaper at Mama. "She picked a fine one."

"Peter, I'm not going to talk about this. Not one more minute. You go on back over to Johnston County, and when you can talk decent, then I'll be more than happy to talk."

When Uncle Peter could talk decent, that would be a month of Sundays.

"You know, Mama," Uncle Peter said, "you'd better watch that pedestal you've put Lily on since she's been sick. Somebody might just get up and knock her off it. As for Maggie, mark my words: From what I hear, Neely Lipscomb isn't finished with her yet. You think that reporter keeps showing up here by accident? When Neely Lipscomb is slighted, he's got a long memory. She needs to understand he's not happy with the lack of cooperation he got around here. Life isn't all poetry and movie stars like Lilah's told her."

Uncle Peter turned, waving the newspaper in our direction as if he were blessing us with it as he left.

CHAPTER

16

No matter how much Aunt Willowdean went on and on about Sundays being their busiest day, we knew that the real reason she did not invite Norma and John for Sunday dinner, or even speak to them, was because Uncle Peter would not allow her to. When Uncle Peter discovered that Norma and John were going to be our guests for Sunday dinner, he refused to come or let anyone else in his family share the table with the leaders of the family insurrection. As with the wedding shower, he left Aunt Willowdean to make excuses, her voice trailing off on the phone as if she had completely used up all the oxygen in the room around her.

In the tradition of newlyweds, Norma and John alternated Sunday dinners between our house and the Herrings', moving back and forth like a pendulum, spending equal time in both places.

In late October, when the summer couldn't quite seem to breathe its last, Norma, John, and I would ride to the Dairy Queen after Sunday dinner. I tried to get Mama to ride along with us, but she refused.

"I'd be more than any young people need to bear." She smoothed her dress as she spoke.

"Mama, you sound like Aunt Vernie." I tried to keep the fear out of my voice.

Granny christened each Sunday voyage a frivolous endeavor

with her declaration, in our wake, that there was perfectly good ice cream to be made by the freezer-full if we wanted to stay on the back porch.

Before many Sunday dinners passed, Norma seemed to have lost some of her bride's blush. In her Garden of Love, there were now in-laws, bills, and a young husband who had been told it was indeed his young wife's job in life to make sure he got the right mix of plant food, water, and sunshine, but never to prune him. Young husbands were not meant to be pruned, and so they frequently came to overshadow the entire garden. But Norma smiled bravely through it all, her pallor growing closer to its original color as each Sunday dinner passed. John seemed oblivious to these events; he simply followed the directions put in the soil of his being many years earlier.

Early November arrived.

"Anyone home?" Aunt Willowdean stood on the step and knocked gently on the side door.

"Come on in," Granny called from the kitchen. "Maggie, see who that is."

"It's Aunt Willowdean." I hopped up from the couch, where I read my English lit, and opened the screen door for Aunt Willowdean, who had a pot in her hands.

"Willowdean." Granny dried her hands and moved to join us. "This is a surprise."

Aunt Willowdean looked at the floor. "We've been overrun with collards this year and I didn't know as to how you were doing, so I brought these on." She hesitated. "I'm on my way to a Ladies' Auxiliary meeting in Fayetteville."

And as at the long-ago cornhusking, I felt sorry for Aunt Willowdean. She was more of a cripple than my mama would ever be.

Granny took the Dutch oven from her hands. "Thank you, Willowdean. Let me put them in a bowl and then you can take your pot on back home with you."

Mama came in, holding a copy of *Silver Screen* in her good hand. "Willowdean, what a surprise. Don't you look grand?"

Actually, Aunt Willowdean looked like a pilgrim. She wore a severe dark blue dress with a white collar. Her matching hat rested flat down on her head. With no perky angles or flashy net, the hat resembled its owner. Her blue oxfords and heavy stockings grounded her further. Even so, there was an edge to the way she moved.

Aunt Willowdean frowned at my mama's enthusiasm. "Not really. How are you feeling, Lilah?"

"Fine, just fine. Once I work this stiffness out of my arm, I'll be as fit as a fiddle." No one contradicted her. "Sit down, Willowdean. Did I hear you say you were on your way to an auxiliary meeting?"

"Yes, that's right." Aunt Willowdean perched on the front of a chair, working her gloves round and round in her hands.

Mama smiled. "It's hard to believe Thanksgiving is almost here."

Aunt Willowdean looked as if she'd been slapped. "Yes, it is hard to believe that. My, there will be a lot of work to do between now and then."

Granny put Aunt Willowdean's clean pot on the kitchen table and came into the sitting area. "Well, Willowdean, be sure and let the boys know that I'm planning to have everyone for dinner like I always do."

"We couldn't do that. Why, you've got Lilah to worry about. I had thought I'd have the boys . . ." Aunt Willowdean's voice trailed off.

Granny spoke. "Willowdean, I've had this family every Thanksgiving for the last forty years. I'm not about to let Peter's pouting stop that. I don't mean to put you in the middle, but you let Peter know that the whole family will be here, including Norma and John."

"How is Norma?" Aunt Willowdean twisted her glove so hard I thought it would rip. This was the question that she'd come to ask.

"Oh, Willowdean." Mama lit up. "She's doing well." Then to

reassure Aunt Willowdean, she added, "But she needs her mother. Why are you letting Peter's foolishness stand in your way? Call her. Go see her. Don't let Peter take your baby from you." Granny made no move to speak. I thought they were a ventriloquist act; Mama said what Granny thought.

Aunt Willowdean jumped from her perch. "I didn't see the time. If I don't go, I'll be late to my meeting. Good to see you." She was out the door and down the steps as if her blue oxfords had sprouted wings.

"Aunt Willowdean, your pot." I grabbed the Dutch oven from the table and ran for the door.

The engine in the Rambler kicked to life as I rounded the corner of the house.

"Aunt Willowdean." I waved the pot lid frantically.

She rolled down her window, took the pot, and put it on the seat beside her. "Thank you, Maggie. I'm just not myself these days." She grabbed my hand. "Tell Norma I asked about her."

I nodded, but before I could speak, she let go of my hand, rolled up her window, and backed into the road with tears flowing down her face.

Granny left shortly afterward to check on some more soil tests Mr. Clyde was doing.

Mama and I both read, she *Silver Screen,* and I, a translation of Plato. I became stuck on the sentence "If the head and body are to be well, you must begin by curing the soul."

After a few minutes, I put down my book. "You really are mad at Uncle Peter, aren't you?" I asked Mama.

She thought for a moment, closing the magazine in her hands and tapping it on the chair arm. "I am angry at Uncle Peter. He can't see past the nose on his face. But more than that, Maggie . . ." She hesitated. "You know I don't like to speak poorly about your father, but we could not depend on him. Steadiness isn't in him. Your granny and granddaddy were steady to a fault, and so I naturally thought what I didn't need was steady. I was so young that I didn't realize how much that steadiness would mean to me and then to a child. Turns out I was wrong. Now, don't think that your granny hasn't let me know I was wrong. But the thing that your granny did all that time ago, she let me know how she felt. We were living in town with nothing and your daddy took off on one of his adventures. Your granddaddy, in his pious way, had instructed your granny that we were no longer a part of this family. I imagine partly because of that and partly because she was mad herself, your granny stayed away. I was not welcome in my own home.

"Your daddy cleaned out most of the money before he left, and so I determined that if we were going to eat, I was going to have to get a job. And then the flu struck. I was so sick. I couldn't even get out of the bed, and there you were toddling around. Your granny came—I still to this day don't know how she knew. I thought at first she was an angel." Mama laughed. "That's how sick I was. And without even as much as an I-told-you-so, she and Tessie bundled you and me into the car. I don't remember much about the next few days, but I do remember every time I woke up, your granny was there. We were hers and she loved us. I don't know how she and Daddy settled it. I think you might have melted his heart a bit. We'll never know; he died not long after that.

"If you're ever to have a glimpse of the power of God's love, Magdalena, you've got to have somebody in your life that loves you no matter what. Greater minds than mine have thought that. Albert Schweitzer, as brilliant a man as he is, he knows that Jesus' message was love and only love." Mama paused. "And you know, there is nothing that you could do that will stop me from loving you." She looked at me straight on, leaving the particulars unsaid.

"People get all worked up and preach about the road to perdition and what it's paved with. Alcohol, tobacco, rock and roll, and the pleasures of the flesh are the easy ones. When a preacher preaches against those, he's skimming the cream from the top of milk. Who wants to deal with things like hate and being so busy with the work of the church that you ignore the work of God? Love—and only love—don't forget that."

She leaned back in her chair. "And you can quote me on that anytime you'd like."

Though it would be years before she had Norma home again, Aunt Willowdean did start, right after that visit, going to Raleigh, shopping at Woolworth's, and eating lunch at the Woolworth lunch counter with Norma. Sometimes afterward, for a treat, they would pop a balloon and try to get an ice cream sundae for a penny. If Uncle Peter knew, he never acknowledged it.

CHAPTER 17

That fall the leaves withered brown on the trees. Never turning brilliant red or orange, they simply gave up and fell to the ground in the week before Thanksgiving. The cold blanketed Canaan on Thanksgiving morning.

"I hate linen. These wrinkles never come out." I tugged the white tablecloth flat and slapped the iron on it. The warm fabric bunched underneath my hand, refusing to give up its wrinkles. The smell of sweet potatoes baking wrapped around me as I ironed.

Tessie turned from where she stood doing Mama's bidding in the kitchen.

"Maggie, if you would slow down that iron, them wrinkles would take care of themselves."

"Tessie, if I had all day, I could stand here and talk the wrinkles out."

Mama stood back and admired the chocolate cake she'd just finished. The recipe had come from *McCall's* special dessert section on a card that you cut on the dotted lines to put in your recipe box if you had such a thing. Mama's recipe box was a cigar box that I'd wrapped in a wallpaper sample many years earlier at Vacation Bible School. I'd always hated the way that the crooked letters I wrote on it, *Mama's Recipes,* ruined the look of it. The instant I put the marker on it, I wished I'd left it plain. But there was no way to go back and undo my mistake even though Mama told me again and again that she loved it just the way it was.

With Granny, Mama, and Tessie working in it, the kitchen took on the look of a bus depot, with various dishes arriving and departing the counter with split-second precision.

I sprinkled starch onto the tablecloth and the iron hissed as I pushed it across the fabric. I wondered what Alex was doing now. I supposed not even celebrating Thanksgiving. There was no Thanksgiving on this day in England. England seemed as far away as the moon. I shivered and pressed the iron harder, willing out wrinkles and ending up with creased cloth instead.

Norma and John arrived first. Then came the boys, Eli, Adam, and James, all with their wives and children. Toddlers and babies seemed to spring from the couch cushions. The house vibrated with squeals of those too young to understand that they were Uncle Peter's issue. Aunt Vernie and Uncle Jasper came in.

Then, as the sun began to slip away, Uncle Peter and Aunt Willowdean arrived. Aunt Willowdean had not been able to convince Uncle Peter to come. It had taken a note from Granny. She never said what she wrote, only that she wanted us all together on Thanksgiving. I'm sure it contained a reference to her will. One was never certain in which order Uncle Peter loved God, money, and himself, but clearly that Thanksgiving the back forty won. Uncle Peter walked into the kitchen like he knew the secret word that would loose Groucho's duck on us.

Granny took no notice of the chill that passed between Uncle Peter and John Herring. She pushed everyone to the table. Norma defiantly grabbed John's hand, but her knuckles turned white, and it seemed more like the gesture of someone needing to be saved from drowning in the swimming hole than a sign of affection.

Aunt Willowdean, with a backward glance at Uncle Peter, stepped forward and hugged Norma. It was a very brief and clean hug, as if Aunt Willowdean was afraid Uncle Peter would scold her if she left anything of herself behind.

Mama pulled John out of the line of fire. "John, could you help me with this heavy roaster?"

"Pretty dress, Norma." James's wife spoke up, ignoring a cold glance from Uncle Peter. The rest of the boys and their wives moved in circles outside Norma and John's orbit. They were pulled by Uncle Peter's gravity, forever in *his* orbit.

Mama insisted on showing pictures of the wedding. Earlier when she and Granny had argued over it, Mama said, "For heaven's sake, Mama, it's not like it was some shotgun affair. Peter is going to have to accept the reality."

Granny replied, "Pretty silly to think you can stand in front of a bull waving a red flag and not get gored."

"Oh, Mama, Peter eats up his own soul, not mine."

Granny blessed the dinner while everyone stood around the table. Despite her admonishment to Mama, Granny made a point of thanking God for all babies born that year, for all marriages, especially Norma and John's, and for all of life itself. "God, grant us the wisdom to endure our foolish deeds. Amen."

The older children fixed their plates and went to the back room, where we had laid out a table for them.

Over dinner, Aunt Vernie and Aunt Willowdean threw out neutral subjects like they were clay pigeons, each one shot down after five or ten minutes of conversation, leaving the alternating aunt to throw another subject up in hopes of holding off any real discussion. Aunt Willowdean and Norma carried on some sort of rhythmic ritual, twisting napkins, as they had been twisting their gloves and anything else not moving, into knots.

Then the talk turned to hunting just in time to save the aunts, who had nearly exhausted their vanilla material. It's hard to say how the talk of politics started. Somewhere over that chocolate cake from *McCall's* magazine or the pecan pie, the subject slipped from Uncle Peter's lips and soon circled the table like a wild boar that neither of the aunts could contain. They wore startled expressions, their mouths opened in O's that the breath moved out of silent as death.

"A Catholic as president. It's the beginning of the end. The plagues all over again." Uncle Peter cut the tip off his piece of pie as he spoke, then pointed his fork, challenging anyone to disagree.

Mama took up the challenge. "Don't be silly, Peter. The man is full of life and energy. He's going to make a fine president."

"Mark my words. It will be like having the pope running the country," Uncle Peter said.

"Peter, you're selling Mr. Kennedy short," Mama said.

"I just know a wolf in sheep's clothing when I see one," Uncle Peter responded, pointing his fork in Mama's direction.

"As usual, you're looking for the worst," Mama said. "I believe Jesus called it the splinter in someone else's eye. There's a big log in your own."

"No. As usual, Lilah, your heathen persuasion shines through."

"I'm adopting a wait-and-see attitude myself," Uncle Jasper interjected. Then he added, "I mean about the politics, not . . ." His voice trailed off.

"I'm telling you, Kennedy won't be happy until he has the whole country genuflecting before those fancy crosses and going to school with nappy-headed coloreds."

"Well, there's a good example of Christ shining through. Brotherly love and all that. What the Bible is all about." Mama's voice held steady in spite of the pointed fork.

Uncle Peter's eyes bulged like a stomped-on bullfrog. "Lilah, you don't know what it's all about and you'll never know. But let me help you. You sit here and suck the life out of all that Daddy worked so hard to have. But as for Christian love and concern, instead of worrying about my daughter and who she marries, maybe you should worry about something else. Maybe you need to be worried about what Maggie and that Communist from up North were doing, him leaving here in such a hurry and all."

I flushed at the mention of Alex, but no one noticed as Uncle Peter's torrent of words continued unchecked.

"And maybe what you need to be worried about, Lilah, is that Maggie's going to take up where her daddy left off, because he sure left quite a mess. I'll tell you, Lilah, what you need to be worried about. You need to be worried about going down to Robeson County and finding the half-breed that Maggie here can call her sister, the mess that Butch Davidson left. That's what you need to be all worried about."

The words filled up the room, shaping us all with the space they left us. No one moved. Even one of Adam's children, who came into the room to ask for more gravy, stood, plate in midair, waiting.

I thought I saw my mama flinch and then move her good arm, as if to push Uncle Peter's words from the air around her.

"What sister would you mean?" There was the slightest catch to Mama's voice.

I heard her clearly though my head had gone light, and my breath came in shallow rasps.

"Why don't you ask Neely Lipscomb?" Uncle Peter said. "He's the one that told me. Neely's not letting go until he's shook every drop of blood out of you."

"I will ask. I will most certainly ask him," Mama said, and closed her eyes.

Granny looked down her nose at Uncle Peter. "Peter, you'll regret this overzealous self-righteousness that you have."

Uncle Peter excused himself and left the table. The cold air touched my legs as he opened the door and walked out onto the porch. Whatever he'd done, he'd done for himself and not for my mama or me.

"If that don't take the rag off the bush," Aunt Vernie said, forgetting her uppity-up airs.

I reached out to touch my mama, who sat with her eyes closed.

Aunt Willowdean glanced toward the door and wrapped her napkin around her finger.

"Oh my, I believe I've eaten myself right on into another size." Norma's shredded napkin lay beside her plate.

Mama still did not open her eyes.

Norma and Aunt Willowdean started to clear the table.

"Mama, why don't you go lay down?" I asked. She quivered ever so slightly. Gently, I touched her shiny, golden red hair, fearing that if I pressed too hard, she might burst open.

She shook her head. "No, I'm fine. Just need a minute, that's all."

Granny pooh-poohed any offers of help with the dishes, and so everyone began to gather their children. In a few minutes, they disappeared—stacked dishes and a bruised heart the only evidence they'd been there. Norma and John lingered. Norma hugged my mama to her, the way she might have hugged her own mama if circumstances were different.

"Aunt Lilah, you take care." She twirled her gloves. "I feel like this is my fault."

Mama roused herself momentarily from her trance. "Oh, Norma. Honey, this started long before you were born. It's no more your fault than the sun rising in the east tomorrow morning."

With everyone gone, Mama moved to the phone, picked it up, and cradled it beneath her chin while she dialed with her good hand. After she identified herself and the "hellohowareyous" were complete, she continued.

"I was hoping I might speak with the mayor."

She tapped the fingers of her good hand on the desk as she spoke. "Yes, I see. No idea when he'll be back. Well, if it's not late this evening, would you have him call me?" She provided our number and hung up.

Each of us let Uncle Peter's pronouncement settle into our world. Mama put a Rosemary Clooney record on the turntable and stared off into space as she listened. Granny read her Bible, thumbing to spots that fell open in a familiar way. She gave no indication of the extraordinary evening except to glance from time to time at Mama.

I insisted on washing and drying the dishes myself. The rhythm of washing and drying calmed me and soothed my jumbled insides. What had my daddy done? When was Neely Lipscomb going to be satisfied?

The last pot, an old pressure cooker without the top, was the one that Granny cooked mashed potatoes in, and I had to push the steel wool against the pieces of potato left on the sides. I scrubbed at each lump, imagining Uncle Peter's and Neely Lipscomb's faces there and then gone, washed down the drain and out of our lives.

Later in bed, I heard my mama's sobs, ragged and raw, and my granny's words—soft and smooth. I reached under my pillow and touched Alex's note and other papers hidden there. And though I thought it useless, I prayed.

Friday and Saturday passed with no word from Neely Lipscomb. The Saturday after Thanksgiving I stood in the kitchen washing the last of the supper dishes. It was my favorite plate, trimmed in tiny lavender violets and scalloped with gold. As I put the dish gingerly in the drainer, a wail came from the porch.

"What in the world?" Mama said, looking up from an article on Elvis Presley.

"I'll see about it," I said. The side of the chair caught my knee as I hurried through the front room to the door. I clutched my knee with one hand and used the other to pop the silver hook on the screen door. Behind me I could hear Granny and Mama stirring as the wail continued.

As I stepped onto the porch, I could see something half hidden behind the glider. I hobbled around to the side of the porch. In one instant, my hand dropped from my knee as I found the source of the noise, red-faced with its eyes squeezed shut like a kitten at birth.

"Come quick," I yelled, and the others pushed open the screen door, trying to make it through at the same time like the Keystone Cops. By the time they got themselves unknotted and made it to me, the baby rested in my arms.

CHAPTER 18

We all talked at once, everyone calling out various ways to stop her crying. Mama spotted a bottle that had rolled under one of the boxwoods. It looked nasty. The nipple showed signs of dirt that went deeper than what it had picked up lying under the boxwood. The baby, wrapped in a flannel blanket that had once been pink, squirmed in my arms. A note, written on a piece of torn paper bag shaped like Florida, was pinned to the blanket.

This baby is yurs.

The colorless blanket didn't fit the occupant, a dark-skinned girl with a shock of dark hair, dressed in a grimy undershirt and soggy diaper, who proclaimed her hunger the entire time it took to clean the bottle and nipple to Mama and Granny's standards. They sent me to the Open Air Market to find some more bottles and to get some Eagle Brand milk that we could mix with Karo syrup and water for the baby. I got the milk, but the Open Air Market didn't carry baby bottles. Woolworth's in Clinton closed at six, so that forced me to stop by and borrow a baby bottle from Mrs. Hobbs, whose milk had dried up long about baby number eight.

I arrived home to find Mama and Granny having a heated discussion in the sitting room. The baby nestled under a blanket in a dresser drawer to the left of Mama's chair, an empty bottle on the end table to her right.

I reported the results of my trip to town and then Granny and Mama resumed their discussion.

"Jacqueline is out of the question," Granny said.

"Well, Esther makes her sound like an old woman. Jayne with a *y* has a nice ring to it, or possibly Aphrodite."

The baby slept knees to chest in one of my daddy's undershirts that Mama had found in her cedar chest. The sweet aroma of cedar filled the air around the drawer. Oblivious to the gravity of the discussion going on around her, the baby slept noiselessly, her fist at her mouth.

Granny closed her copy of *Progressive Farmer.* "That is one of the dumbest names you have ever come up with. I wouldn't name a dog that, much less a young'un."

"Of course not. If you have your way, the child will be marked forever with a name like Ethel or Agnes. Some throwaway name with no character."

Granny paused long enough to make a list of things that would need to be done the next day for our new arrival. I could tell she was pleased to be fighting once again with my mama. It was as if I'd left a house turned upside down by my mama's illness, went to the Open Air Market, and returned to a house somehow righted. The way Mama and Granny acted, so casual, it was like every day a baby arrived on our front porch. Like the mailman couldn't fit her in the box at the road, so he put her on the porch for us instead.

I sat on the couch by Mama. "Has anyone given one thought to how we're going to find out who this baby belongs to? Do we even know for sure she's my sister?"

Both of them looked at me as if I had asked should Debbie Reynolds have given Eddie Fisher a divorce.

Mama flipped her *True Detective* on the table. "Well, Magdalena, I've called the mayor. I'm sure he will be only too delighted to help us find the answer to that question."

The fact is we never needed Neely Lipscomb to tell us anything about the baby. Early the next morning I went out to hang the assorted baby clothes and bedding that we'd gathered from wardrobes and chests of drawers around the house.

Granny had left after breakfast to consult with Mr. Clyde about some problem with one of the tractors. She would be back around noon. Soon it would be time for me to plow under some of this year's tobacco fields, getting ready for the winter.

In back of the house, a girl slept curled up by the scaffolding that held the oil drum off the ground. She startled about the time I set my basket on the ground and looked at me with the eyes of a dog that someone had beaten, blank and downcast. I picked a wet pillowcase out of the basket, shook it out, and clipped it to the line. It was easy to see where the baby got her coloring.

"Ground makes a mighty rough bed, doesn't it?"

No answer. I tried again.

"My granny would have made you a bed in the potato house if you'd let us know you were out here." The smell of Clorox came up from the laundry basket as I took out another pillowcase.

Her eyes searched the ground. Out of the screen door came the baby's cry for breakfast. The girl's face thawed for a moment, a flicker, before going back to its original silence. She pulled her right elbow close in to her waist and held her forearm against her breast. I noticed a circle of milk working its way across the fabric of her frayed cotton dress despite her arm's best attempt at stopping it.

Something in my own breast ached for her.

"That your baby in the house?"

She pushed her hair, dark and stringy, off her face, but made no move to answer my question.

"Are you going to take the baby back? If you need help feeding her, you could've just asked. We'd have helped you out."

Her hand continued to push back the strands of hair woven together by oil and dirt. I reached in for another clothespin to snap over the pillowcase. The spring squeaked in protest as I pinched the pin apart, and I realized that she had no intention of speaking to me. She stood and crossed her hands around her middle, gathering the faded blue material of her shapeless dress to her thin body. Her eyes watched me as I finished hanging out the clothes. The wet white sheets felt cool beneath my fingers. I wasn't careful about where I put the pins, which would bring a lecture from Granny or Tessie if they noticed.

I motioned and the mute girl followed me across the yard and into the house. Her bare feet noiseless behind me, she blinked as we came into the house.

Mama sat in the chair by the heater grate, cooing to the baby, who nursed from the bottle as if there wouldn't be any more milk. Mama had turned so that the arm of the chair propped her weak arm and protected the baby. Tessie was in the kitchen peeling potatoes for the noon meal.

The baby's mother (who I named Mona Lisa—part after the record Mama had and part after the picture I had seen in books at school) stood rooted to a spot inside the kitchen door. Her circled dress identified her like a sign.

Mama looked up. "Magdalena, come see how much milk this baby can drink." She caught sight of the girl and smiled. I attempted to show good manners by offering introductions, introducing our new guest to Mama and Tessie as the baby's mother. Mona Lisa stood there looking at the floor; she never opened her mouth or even nodded her head. Before I even finished the introductions, Tessie was uncovering the breakfast leftovers, fatback, biscuits, and scrambled eggs.

"There's some breakfast if you'd care for any," I said.

"Please, help yourself." Mama smiled.

Mona fell on the leftovers with the same gusto the baby had for thc milk. Above her head Mama and I exchanged eyebrow signals, trying to decide what to say next. This was a sign for me that the house was not completely righted after all. In normal health, Mama would have never been at a loss for words. Tessie turned back to peeling the potatoes, singing softly, "I'm on the battlefield for my Lord, for my Lord. Yes, I'm on the battlefield for my Lord."

Mama's face lightened as she made her way across the sitting room toward the kitchen.

"Does your baby have a name?"

Mona Lisa continued eating eggs and watching us. Her eyes wary, she held her fork like a weapon, prepared to strike should we try to get the food from her.

Mama acted as if she were actually having a conversation with something other than the air. "She looks so young. I've got several suggestions if you haven't been able to come up with anything satisfactory. A name really comes from your soul."

The girl continued to chew. Mama shifted the baby to her shoulder. She trapped the baby there with her good arm and jiggled the wriggling form up and down. "Names are very important, you know. All words are, but a name can determine the course of your life."

The baby burped and Mama and I simultaneously exclaimed, "Oh." Someone might have thought we were the ones with air in our stomachs. "Can you imagine how different his life would have been if Julius Caesar had been named Joe or Milton?"

This question appeared not to be one that had puzzled the girl before and it didn't interfere with her chewing now. I mentally sized her up against the dresses in my closet. Fashioned after my granny, I stood tall and sturdy. This girl with her petite looks stood a better chance of fitting into my mama's dresses.

I left to go plow under the tobacco. By the time Granny and I both got back home around noon, Mama had talked herself into keeping the girl and the baby. Mama gave the girl one of her dresses and dispatched her to the tub shortly after our arrival so that she and Granny could discuss the situation.

At the very least the girl must stay until we could get her to speak to us and find her a proper place to work and live, Mama told Granny. Granny argued for the sake of arguing, not because her heart was in it. Mama knew that before they even started. They pretty much exhausted the arguments for and against; still, Granny felt the need to get in the last word. "Well, we'll have to put her to work on the farm. She can't do public work if she can't talk."

The girl seemed to take all this as a natural turn of events, going right to work after a one-sided discussion with Granny.

We cleared Uncle Peter's room out for Mona and the baby. But we had not reckoned with some need in Mama. She kept the baby, whom she named Rosemary, with no protest from the child's mama, in her room at night. She said it was to be a temporary arrangement until the mama rested up.

Not everyone rejoiced over Mona's arrival. Uncle Peter came one Monday after he'd heard about our guest from one of his congregation at Sunday-evening service. He found Granny on the back porch getting ready to sweep.

Uncle Peter carried himself with the air of an impatient schoolteacher. He cocked his head to one side and paced back and forth across the enclosed porch. "Mama, you don't know what you're doing. Don't know who this girl is. Just let her come right on in here. She probably has Butch hid around here, waiting for the chance to kill you in your sleep and steal everything you have. You know how Indians are, worse than gypsies."

The sunlight bathed Granny with a yellow glow as she moved across the back porch. She picked up the broom as if Uncle Peter wasn't even speaking to her and started to brush the cobwebs out of the corner by the door.

"As God is my witness, Mama, you'll be sorry for this. You have no business doing this. I'd expect this out of Lilah, but not you. I did my best to keep it out of the papers, and this is the thanks I get. You trot her in and put her up in the house my great-granddaddy built with his own hands. I'm telling you, it's crazy. For all you know, she's got Butch waiting in the bushes to kill you. You don't even know what she is. . . ."

Granny turned and pointed the handle of the broom at Uncle Peter, looking down her nose at him as she did. "Settle on down,

Peter. You're repeating yourself. You were mighty anxious for us to know that girl not that many days ago. And you're starting to wear my patience real thin. You want to know who that girl is, I'll tell you who she is—she is one of the least of these my brethren. I suppose you remember that, 'Inasmuch as you have done it unto one of the least of these my brethren, you have done it unto me.' My take at it is that puts her right up there with Christ."

Uncle Peter's jaw dropped open. "Mama, that's blasphemy. . . ."

Granny shook the broom handle for emphasis. "I've got a farm to run, mouths to feed, and a sickness on top of it all. The last thing I need is for you to be over here telling me what to do."

That settled the issue for the moment.

CHAPTER 19

We developed a regular routine that revolved around Mona Lisa working with Tessie and Mama at the house while Granny and I worked the farm. The extra hands were needed as I finished some courses that I'd delayed when Mama was first ill. Mutely, Mona Lisa went about her work. She, like her namesake, felt an emotion that one could never quite read from her face.

One evening as we watched Mona Lisa walk across the yard, Mama said, "It's a good thing they came when they did. Rosemary would have never learned to talk otherwise." But I wondered, *Did Mona talk and coo to Rosemary before they came to us?* Mona seemed so worn and so willing to throw over her baby to us.

A few months after her arrival, we discovered that Mona Lisa's real name was Janie Locklear. Norma shared this information with us. She'd heard it from Aunt Willowdean, who'd heard it from Uncle Peter, who'd come upon it by way of his conversation with Neely Lipscomb. But by the time we found it out, the first half of her new name had stuck with her and she was always Mona to us. I think she had turned her back on being a Locklear, a family where it appeared that the boys marked their passage into manhood by doing time in one jailhouse or another. To my knowledge, none of the Locklears ever sent after her or inquired about her even when they found out where she was.

Mona often walked the road to the Open Air Market. Though I offered many times to carry her in the car, she refused, appearing to exorcise some demon as she walked with great care and deliberation in her step, as if the road were a minefield and one false step would blow her to kingdom come. On occasion when a car or a tractor strayed into her space, she'd stop still. When the interloper moved on, she'd continue on the slim path she imagined beneath her feet.

She attended Canaan Free Will Church with us. Some of the faithful questioned her arrival and her marital status. Those faithful unlucky enough to question my granny on these two subjects met with long cold stares. The more fortunate quizzed my mama on the subject, and despite her presence in the church aisle, she treated them to a tale of the miraculous that was somewhere in between Noah and the Ark and babies in the cabbage patch.

I don't know that my mama ever told it the same way twice, which led to much confusion when the concerned compared notes after the service. There were some in the congregation who never acknowledged Mona's existence, as if they were so pained by her and my daddy's behavior as to be struck dumb. Though some walked the other way when they saw her coming up the aisle and some talked about asking her to leave, no one ever openly challenged her place at the church with us.

Rosemary was growing every day. After an initial bout with an ear infection, she bloomed into a rosy-cheeked baby who smiled and scooted herself across the floor using her arms and leaving one leg tucked under her like some exotic sea creature sliding along the ocean floor.

Meantime, Mona served as a model for all Mama's makeover techniques. Under Mama's guidance, the outside of Mona was transformed. Her hair was clean and shiny, styled in a more becoming fashion by Mama. The gaunt look left her face and occasionally the veil of sadness lifted from her eyes and she smiled. She hardly looked eighteen.

Immediately after Mona's arrival, Mama went to work producing two dresses and a Sunday hat that suited Mona exactly. The compliments at church so impressed Mama that she went into fashion production with the same zeal that she had originally approached canning right after her stroke. As Mona had no training in sewing, particularly finish work, and Mama had limited use of her hand, I became the seamstress, which I did with little good attitude and lots of pricked fingers.

Mama ordered the latest Simplicity patterns, thinking of alterations even as she looked at the ads in the back of *Ladies' Home Journal*. Soon we were combining the pinned tissue of Simplicity patterns with the magic of Lilah to create unearthly clothing that Mama pronounced fit for a queen.

Rosemary was not spared the fashion onslaught. As she began her first tentative steps of toddlerhood, only Caroline and John-John Kennedy rivaled her in fashion. Rosemary's game now involved edging around the room holding on to couch and chair, inching painfully toward a wayward Simplicity pattern piece. On occasion no one would intercept her mission, and we would hear the sharp tearing sound of the thin brown pattern piece, followed by the slightest sigh of satisfaction from Rosemary.

Lavender lace, blue grosgrain ribbon, and scraps of wool and crepe fabric littered the house on any given evening. Instead of complaining, Granny gathered the bits and pieces from the floor like they were the season's latest crop. "We're going to have the fanciest quilt Sampson County has ever seen," was all she ever said.

We watched the outside cocoon of Mona change to a butterfly, the mystery of Mona locked inside even after the butterfly emerged. None of us knew how the inside transformation was going. Sometimes I thought all Mama's fussing over her was like pouring buckets and buckets of good feelings into a tub with a hole in the bottom. Everything leaked back out. I suppose Mama figured over time we could mend that hole somehow so Mona could keep some of that love inside her.

One night Mama pulled out her Pango Peach lipstick and experimented with Mona's face. After she had smeared the color carefully onto Mona's lips, Mama sat back, obviously impressed by her handiwork. "Men will sit up and take notice when they see this face."

The lipstick clattered to the floor as Mona jumped up and pushed Mama's hand away. We heard the bathroom door slam and then silence. I kept thinking we would hear her cries, but I was wrong. When Mona returned some minutes later from the bathroom, her lips rubbed red, no Pango Peach remained on them. Her eyes glistened with the only tears I'd seen her cry.

Mama signed her apology. Never again did she put Pango Peach lipstick on Mona, nor did she mention men so lightly. From the beginning, Mona and Mama had formed a quick bond and spoken in a sign language that they developed between themselves. For months after her arrival, Mona did not talk to us. Mama and Mona often seemed to share something that neither Granny nor I were a part of, the club of women who had loved Butch Davidson to no good end. Mama was the voice and Mona the hands of this group.

Both of them had loved a man, loved him enough to have a baby. I struggled to understand. Besides the birth of farm animals, I had been present when my granny helped Mrs. Hobbs have her fourth baby. It was a hot July day and it seemed Mrs. Hobbs struggled for hours. It was to my constant amazement that thereafter she would produce a baby almost yearly like a holiday.

I did understand that my daddy had the dashing good looks of Clark Gable, but he had the heart of Khrushchev. He was not bound by responsibility, except to himself.

He would come home to Canaan with stories of hoboing—stay around town somewhere until Mama was sneaking off to meet him like a teenager—then another woman would catch his eye or another husband would catch him, and off he'd go for years at a time.

"A man is a two-faced, worrisome thing who'll leave you to sing the blues in the night." My mama's Rosemary Clooney record sang her pain. "Blues in the Night" was written for Mama. Yet Mona's ar-

rival seemed to remind her of some long-lost secret she knew. And instead of hating her, Mama treated her like the sister I'd never had.

How could it be? How could it be that my mama could tolerate the sight of this woman? Not only tolerate her, but moreover, cradle her baby and comfort her soul? Did Mama not see my daddy's betrayal? Or had she denied his true nature for so long that she just didn't care?

And Mona, did she ever long to punch my mama in the nose? Did she want to snatch her baby and run screaming from our house? Did she ever think fondly of my daddy? Or was he a memory that she'd like to forget, but was constantly reminded of by Rosemary's uplifted hands and her insistent voice entreating, "Up, up."

Rosemary was our common thread—the innocent whom we all could love—woven through our cores and back out again. She was everywhere in our lives, and evidence of her (a rattle or a teething biscuit or a discarded bib) was strewn throughout the house. Frequently she played on a quilt on the floor of the sitting room. That's where she was one February afternoon when the mailman stopped in.

Mona sat on the couch hemming a nightgown and watching over Rosemary on the floor. Mona's stitches were becoming smaller and smaller as she practiced. One of her feet was tucked under her, and she wore two pairs of socks, a habit she had started when the weather grew cold. Every now and then, she leaned over to give Rosemary back a toy she'd batted away, a plastic apple that chimed. Rosemary spoke bursts of gibberish from time to time that she directed at Mona or, occasionally, at Mama or me.

Granny was at the church attending a Ladies' Auxiliary meeting and Tessie was gone for the day. Mama and I were working at the kitchen table when Mr. C. A. Barefoot, the mail carrier, handed a brown package through the screen door and went on his way, refusing Mama's invitation for a cup of coffee or a glass of tea.

"New Orleans. I don't know a soul in New Orleans," Mama said. She opened the package and shook it, letting the contents fall into the middle of kitchen table, where we had stretched out a dress pattern for Rosemary. I stood beside Mama with a pair of scissors, waiting for her to decide that the pattern was placed in the exact right spot on the blue wool so that it lay on the straight of the grain.

A picture fell onto the cloth. It was a baby on a man's knee being held toward the camera. The camera had focused on the baby, so the man's face was fuzzy. It was a picture of my daddy and me.

"Wonder what your daddy was doing in New Orleans?" Mama asked. "And why would he send me this picture?"

When she unfolded the letter, a newspaper clipping fluttered to the table. Mama read the letter and then she moved it further away and read it again, as if getting some distance from the words would change them.

"What is it, Mama?" I asked, and pulled a chair out from the table for her to sit on. She folded down into the chair and handed me the sheet of notebook paper.

> *To Whom It May Concern:*
>
> *After Mr. Butch Parker's untimely passing, I found this address among his effects. I've enclosed a picture, which I came across while looking through his things. I thought you might like to see it and that it might help you to be sure I have the right family. I've also cut you out a newspaper article about his unfortunate death. All Mr. Parker's belongings are packed. I'll be happy to forward them to you if you would be so kind as to send $42 that Mr. Parker owed me in back room and board.*
>
> *Yours in sorrow,*
> *B. J. Lattimer*

I scanned the clipping. The newspaper might as well have been written on the day my daddy was born as the day he died. NORTH CAROLINA MAN SHOT DEAD was the headline. Butch Davidson lost his life in the Mardi Gras Bar, shot dead by a sailor whose ship arrived in port a week early due to favorable conditions. Favorable conditions did not extend to my daddy, who had taken up with the sailor's girlfriend.

I read the clipping and the letter out loud. The letter smelled of cedar, fresh and sweet like the inside of Mama's hope chest, where she had stored away her wedding dress. I read once where King Solomon's temple required eighty-thousand men to chop and shape the cedar that he used to build it.

I sat down in a chair beside my mama. Mona paused slightly while I read aloud and then proceeded with her stitches. She pushed the needle in with great care and then popped it back through the fabric; the thread followed it silently through the cloth. Mama began to cry, small tears that rolled down her face and hesitated on her chin before falling onto the navy fabric below. Mona put down her flannel project and came to stand behind Mama. I patted Mama's arm, while Mona pulled a tissue from her pocket and wiped Mama's tears, first at her chin and then on her cheek. Rosemary began to cry.

"What's wrong, Rosemary?" I asked, and got up to go and check on her.

She pushed a pudgy hand under the couch and cried harder. Her apple had rolled out of reach. I got the apple, and then I took her in my arms. We were truly fatherless now.

"I'm going to put her down for a nap," I said. Smelling of Ivory Snow and that vague mix of scents that we called a baby smell, Rosemary pushed back in my arms. As we walked into Mama's bedroom, she tried to pop free, having no idea that success would hurt so badly. Her face opened up full and red; her screams came unabated while I changed her diaper.

"Here," I said, and I handed her a rubber duck, which she tossed over the side of the table. Realizing it was gone, she screamed louder.

"One more snap," I crooned, "just one more and you're all done." I pulled her squirming body from the changing table and swaddled her to me. She quit screaming and breathed with an occasional halfhearted sniff left over from the insult of the diaper change.

I sat in the rocker and sang to her, "Hush, little baby, don't say a word; Daddy's going to buy you a mockingbird. If that mockingbird won't sing, Daddy's going to buy you a diamond ring."

I looked at the dark curls and the nose that looked like God had taken it right off my daddy's face, whittled it down, and stuck it onto Rosemary, and I wondered what life held for her. She would have no memory of her daddy, or of this cold February afternoon when I rocked her into the land of the sandman.

Would she ever wonder if her daddy loved her? We would tell her he did. Would she ever imagine what he was like? And if she asked us, what would we do? Would we create a mythical daddy for her? Give her a character map that showed a daddy who would have always known what to say when things weren't right, like Robert Young on *Father Knows Best,* one who stood for law and order, like Ben Cartwright, but was loving and wise in a country way like Andy Taylor on *The Andy Griffith Show*? One who was lost to her, just as mine had been lost to me.

Having played out all the fight she had on the changing table, Rosemary dropped into sleep before I finished my song, her tiny fingers wrapped around one of my fingers. I put her in the crib beside Mama's bed and gently peeled her fingers from mine so as not to wake her.

When I returned to the sitting room, I found Mama resting on the couch with a washcloth draped over her forehead. Mona was scrubbing the kitchen floor. Her hands had begun to bleed from the effort, but still she continued on.

"Is there anything I can bring you?" I asked Mama.

"No, I just needed to rest for a second. Did the baby go down okay?"

"Yes, fine," I said. "She was sleepy." I sat down on the floor beside the couch and rested my hand on Mama's arm.

Granny came in the side door. "Lord have mercy, what's going on here?" She pulled her hat off and stood looking first at Mona scrubbing the kitchen floor the way you'd scratch a bad case of poison ivy, and then at Mama, reposing with the white washcloth sitting like a lump of dough on her forehead.

I pointed to the table. "It's my daddy. He's dead."

"Are you sure?" Granny walked to the table and put her hat down. She picked up the article and the letter. She read them, took off her coat and hung it on the coatrack in the front room, and came back to read the letter again.

"I guess they buried him down there. Just as well, Butch always did favor the warmer weather." Granny walked over and touched Mama's arm. "Lily, you okay?"

Mama reached up and moved the washcloth. "Fine, I've just got one of those big headaches. Of all the things I thought Butch Davidson would do, dying wasn't one of them." Her eyes grew teary.

"Maggie, what about you?" Granny bent over and looked me straight in the eye.

"I'm all right." My eyes held even with hers.

Mama sat up, holding the washcloth up toward heaven like some kind of sacrifice. "Your daddy is better off. He suffered so with his love of alcohol."

"Unfortunately," Granny said, straightening up and looking down her nose at no one in particular, "he wasn't the only one what suffered."

"Please, let's don't talk about it," I said, standing up.

Granny put her hand on my shoulder. "He did leave behind"—she looked in Mona's direction—"two daughters that are blessings." Then without another word, she went to her desk and signed a check to B. J. Lattimer for forty-two dollars, wrote a short note to accompany it, and sealed it in an envelope that she addressed with her spidery scrawl.

Later, alone in my room, I cried. I let the anger flood me. I wondered what was wrong with me that he left, only to return when he needed something and then leave again when I could not give it. Was I not good enough for him? Could he find nowhere in his Khrushchev heart for a little girl?

Was he so convinced of my mama's strength that he indulged his weakness? Maybe he'd seen that muscle beneath that we had all only recently glimpsed.

I couldn't say. I knew so little of him. What his favorite TV show was, whether he liked his coffee black or with cream and sugar, if he truly loved me.

Maybe he was the worthless waste that my granny portrayed him as. The only map of my daddy that I had was divided into two regions. The half created by my granny was arid and dry, but the map was split down the middle, and on my mama's half was a lush tropical forest of the man she had once loved. I got lost in all the back-and-forths.

I longed for a daddy like Mr. Clyde Elliot, a steady man with no sharp dividing lines in his map—not for a mythical daddy like Robert Young, Ben Cartwright, or Andy Taylor.

Several weeks later, Tessie arrived for work carrying a baby the color of heavily creamed coffee with beautiful wiry hair standing around its head like a crown.

Tessie's niece had died a week earlier, and except for the funeral, we had not seen Tessie that week. She and Neb had only one child, a son who moved to Chicago when he was twenty. Tessie's sister had died young, and so Tessie and Neb had raised her three children, two boys and a girl, as their own. The funeral had been hard on Tessie, and Neb as well, though he bore his hurt in the same silent way that the earth bears us up.

The day Tessie returned to us, Mona reached for the baby almost before Tessie had her in the door.

Mona smiled as she held the baby, and I wondered at the change in her in only a few months.

"My niece, she tangled with the wrong woman's man," Tessie said as she hung her coat on the coatrack in the hall. "Had this child. Then the woman, they say, she worked the roots on my niece. Poor girl, she gets crazy and throws herself right in the pond. Cain't swim a lick. Left this poor motherless child." She explained this to Mona as if we hadn't already told it all to her. Talking helped Tessie, as it did us all; repeating the awful somehow reduced its power over us.

"Tessie, you know that God's power is stronger than the devil or any hex someone claims to work." I admired the baby as I spoke. Mona pulled her closer in, the baby squirmed, and with that instinct that little can overcome, Mona bounced her gently, humming her a wordless lullaby.

Tessie nodded her head as she arranged a blanket and pillows on the couch. "I know that, I know that, but I tell that girl, I say, 'You better put some sulfur and table salt in your shoes to keep from getting hexed.' But would she do it? No, ma'am, and now she don't have no need of them shoes. She's walking the streets of gold."

Tessie tried to take the baby to settle her on the blanket so she could begin cooking the noon meal, but Mona wouldn't give her up. She sat in the rocking chair with the baby, assuring Tessie through signs with Mama interpreting that all was well. (And it would be until Rosemary woke and realized that there was an infidel among us.)

Granny came through on her way out to the fields. "Tessie, I think you know good and well that the Lord does not need salt or sulfur to protect us from the devil."

Tessie busied herself in the kitchen. The set of her mouth told us she did not think for one minute that the Lord couldn't use a little help warding off an evil spirit.

Mama sat down at the table and immediately began to draw up a list of names. With Mama's encouragement, Tessie named the baby India. India benefited from my mama's burst of fashion zeal. By now, the ever-silent Mona had perfected her stitching and use of the sewing machine. Secretly relieved to be out of the tailor business, I did feel the sting of jealousy that Mona's fingers flew where mine had only plodded.

"It's time to start on our Easter outfits," Mama declared one evening in early March. So magazines and newspapers were consulted, fabric selected, patterns purchased and altered. Each decision represented life-changing potential to Mama. Like willing subjects of a mad scientist, Mona, Rosemary, Granny, and I asked few questions. We were a very agreeable lot, though I did draw the line at a bright pink–flowered print Mama first chose for my Easter dress.

It was during one of these sewing extravaganzas with Granny, Mona, and Mama that the phone rang. I picked it up and the voice on the other end said, "Send that Indian back with her own kind. And them half-breed babies, too. You'll be sorry if you don't."

As I said, "Beg your pardon," Mona looked up from the floor, where she sat cross-legged, pinning together the halves of a crepe sheath.

The phone clicked on the other end.

"What in the world?" Mama said, leaving her pattern book on the couch and coming to stand beside me. "Maggie, who is it?"

I put the receiver down. "Nobody."

Mama raised her eyebrows at me. "The color ran right out of your face."

"Just a wrong number, that's all. I couldn't understand what they said, so they got mad, cursed, and hung up."

In the other room, Rosemary cried out in her sleep. Mama started toward the bedroom, but Mona signed to her. She draped the crepe fabric across a chair and went into the bedroom to check on her baby.

"It was some redneck on the phone trying to act tough about Mona and the babies," I said as soon as I heard the bedroom door shut. "He recommended in his own ignorant way that we send them back 'where they come from.' "

Granny put down the sock she was mending. "People act any way they want to on the telephone. They think just because you can't see them, they can say any durn thing that comes in their head."

"I'm sure it's all talk," I said as Mama moved back to the couch and Mona returned from quieting the baby.

This term at Pineland would be my last. If I continued, it would be at Women's College in Greensboro or ECTC, East Carolina Teacher's College in Greenville. Underneath my pillow, there was an article from Granny's *Reader's Digest* and a note from Alex. Often at night, I slept with my hand slipped under the pillow. As if it was a ball of knotted yarn, I hoped somewhere in that article to find a thread that would unravel the secret of my black hole and my mama's illness.

That Easter I pulled Alex's note and the *Reader's Digest* article out from under my pillow. I prayed as I did every night, feeling my words come from my mouth and then lay around me on the bed, as Tessie said, like biscuits that stooped to rise and got caught in the squat.

The article, "The Facts About Faith Healing," talked about people with the gift, most who weren't named because they "for the most part shun publicity." An engineer from Baltimore talked about his gift. He seemed so matter-of-fact; he never mentioned looking people in the eye when you knew you couldn't do them any good. He didn't mention people looking right past you and never seeing you at all. He was different. He'd healed his sister after she was sick, not like me, who healed everybody in the world and then not my own mother. "What remains highly arguable," the article read, "is whether these personalities draw on some power within themselves or some power outside—or a combination of both."

A power within themselves. That was a joke. If I had the power within myself, I would have healed my mama long ago. I would have stopped her pain and given her mind back its power over her arm, which now struck out on its own whenever it took a mind to. Instead I made good grades and sewed dresses and tasted jams that no one could have guessed the ingredients of.

I unfolded the piece of notebook paper that Alex had taped to my car's windshield the previous August. On it were the two lines so familiar to me:

I Love You, Maggie Davidson.
And one day you'll believe.

His letters stopped coming in June. This sudden shift was like riding a horse that balked at the water and then threw me over headfirst. I tumbled further into the black hole, no longer tethered to hope by the knowledge that he thought of me. In June, the month when he was to return, Alex left for good. I folded the note and put it away down in the dresser drawer underneath my jeans. The summer stretched before me, full of hard work and long nights.

The August heat shimmered off the pavement in front of the Salemburg Grill like ripples of lake water catching the sunlight. I parked the truck in front of the Grill beside the only car there, a white Ford that belonged to Ben Elliot.

I came on a mission that Saturday afternoon; Mama craved orangeade with lots of crushed ice. One lopsided smile was all it took to find me swinging open the front door and standing in front of Miss Patsy at the counter.

Monroe nodded his head at me from behind the grill, where he sang along with Pat Boone on the jukebox while he flipped a hamburger.

The orange booths were empty except for Ben Elliot and Annie Ruth Lovingood, who sat so close together that I doubt you could have got a sheet of paper between them. I waved before I stepped to the counter. Ben waved back, but Annie Ruth looked down. Ben touched Annie Ruth's shoulder with his hand and said something. She looked up and waved her hand at me, then flopped it down quickly, as if the gold charm bracelet she was wearing weighed a hundred pounds.

"Hey, Miss Patsy, how are you?" I said, turning to the counter.

"Can't complain." Miss Patsy gave her standard answer and I waited for the second part.

"Wouldn't do me no good if I did." She chuckled.

"I know that's the truth. Everybody at home's craving orangeade. I'll need four, please, ma'am."

"Hey, Maggie, good to see you." Ben and Annie Ruth came walking up. Ben stopped to speak, but Annie Ruth continued on out to the sidewalk like a sleepwalker.

Miss Patsy frowned at Ben. "You're not leaving, are you? Jack isn't even done cooking your hamburgers."

"Annie Ruth's not feeling so well. I'll just pay you for them and come back by later."

"Now, honey, don't you worry about it. I'm not gonna let you pay me for cold hamburgers."

"Miss Patsy, we ordered the hamburgers and I'm going to pay you for them." He put a couple of dollar bills on the counter.

"Not as long as I'm breathing." Miss Patsy pushed the money back around the counter at him. "Jack hasn't had him any lunch yet. He'll eat them."

Meantime, Annie Ruth stood out by Ben's car, clutching at her stomach with her right hand.

Ben took the money and put it back in his pocket. "You're sure about that?"

"I'm positive, and tell your mama I missed her at circle meeting the other night."

"I'll do that. Well, I better go on and get Annie Ruth home. I don't know what hit her so fast like that." The glass in the door rattled as Ben closed it behind him.

"I can't remember the last time I saw Annie Ruth. I forgot that she and Ben Elliot were going together." I tapped the counter with my finger as I watched Ben help Annie Ruth into the car.

"She took up with him not long after that Alex left here," Miss Patsy said as she started to cleave the oranges.

"Granny said there was some kind of virus going around; Annie Ruth must have got it," I said.

"Only bug she's got is the shame bug." Miss Patsy stopped cutting and shook her knife for emphasis. "It's shameful what she did. I mean, I've been known to tell a tale or two, really out of service to the community. Course, that reporter did quote me when your mama got sick and I felt bad about that. But there's a limit."

I leaned on the counter. "Annie Ruth told something?"

"Oh, honey, you mean you don't know?" Miss Patsy busied herself with the oranges.

"Know what?"

"Lord, child, I hate to be the one that tells you." Miss Patsy tried to look saddened by the thought.

"Miss Patsy, you're making no sense. What is it?"

"Why, Annie Ruth Lovingood is the one that was listening on the party line when that college boyfriend of yours told his friend"—here Miss Patsy paused—"about your, well, you know, that stuff about God."

I couldn't tell if Miss Patsy didn't want to embarrass me by bringing up what the paper printed or if she was afraid lightning would come and strike her if she mentioned that God was a woman.

"She eavesdropped on Alex?"

"Who do you think told that reporter?"

"Annie Ruth told?"

"You wouldn't expect I did, would you?"

All that time I'd thought Alex had told someone else, but really it was Annie Ruth's jealousy that did the telling. Miss Patsy stared at me.

"Oh no, I wouldn't think you told." I sat down on an orange vinyl stool. I stood up. "I've got to go."

"Sug, you haven't even gotten the orangeades you ordered."

"Right. I'll wait." I sat down on the stool and pushed the counter with my hand, sending myself and the stool spinning with my feet flying out and then tucking them in so I could spin again.

Miss Patsy found a box top to put the orangeades in, stuffing paper around them so they wouldn't spill before I got them home.

Placing the drinks on the counter, she said, "I swan, if I knew you were going to be that happy about it, I'd have told you a long time ago."

I delivered the orangeades and went straight back to my room, where I gathered the letters on my desk and dropped them in an open Piggly Wiggly bag.

I made my way to the tobacco barn refuge, carrying the Piggly Wiggly bag as gingerly as if it were dynamite. I spread the blanket that Alex and I had used for our sunbath at White Lake on the floor of the barn. The winter sun lit even the barn's dark corners. From the sack I pulled a stack of unopened letters, slit the first envelope, and began to read.

My Dearest Maggie,

I love you so much. And I know that you are deeply hurt. It doesn't have to be this way. Marry me. Together we could look after your mother. I could find a teaching post somewhere and we would be happy.

You've taught me so much of the things of heaven. Things that had to be experienced. In exchange I feel I brought you pain. And while you brought me closer to God, I've pushed you further away. This wouldn't be what the God you've taught me about would want. For I'm convinced that God is more concerned with the agonies of earth than the ecstasies of heaven.

Please find it in your heart to forgive me. I never meant to betray you. I have no idea what happened. Rex says he didn't tell anyone and I told no one else. I should have never even told Rex, but I was like a schoolboy with his first crush. I just couldn't stop talking about you. I know you feel betrayed, but I never wanted to hurt you.

If you cannot forgive me, I understand. But, please, whatever you do, you must *find it in your heart to forgive yourself. You are a beautiful, lovely woman and*

God would not take Herself from you as punishment, instead you separate yourself from Her.

I will write more later. I love you, Maggie Davidson. One day you'll believe.

Alex

I wept, and I felt the pain of a love so deep, it stops your heart and starts it all over again. I believed that Alex Barrons loved me, and I understood that that love had not separated me from God. It had been in the letters on my desk all that time, but I could never open them.

And so I cried. I cried for lost possibilities and for missed chances. Then one by one, I opened the letters and read them. The letters told me of Alex's year at Oxford ("The library housekeeping staff dusts over me now I'm there so much"); of his struggle with his father from across the sea ("He's convinced stockbrokering is in my blood"); of his family ("My brother joins the fray on my father's side, I suppose he wants me to be as miserable as he is"); of his thoughts ("I know I shouldn't need anyone to stand up to Father, but if I knew you were there, it would make all the difference"); and of his love for me ("Nothing you do could ever stop me from loving you").

When I finished reading, I folded the blanket and returned to the house. I placed the letters in a cedar box that had belonged to my granddaddy. Searching through my jeans, I found Alex's note that I'd hidden there and placed it on top of the letters. I sprinkled the dried petals of the yellow roses he'd given me on our first date on top of them all and closed the lid.

I sat down at my desk. What did you write after ten months of letters? How do you say I've let my sore feet get in the way?

Dear Alex,

Welcome home. I've just finished reading your letters. (That's right—just finished.) I'm sorry it took me so long to come to my senses. I guess I was afraid. I've missed your friendship this last year. When you left, I hurt so bad it took me a while to sort out what was ache for Mama and unanswered prayers and what was missing you. I thought you had betrayed me, but I was wrong. And now I hope against hope that this letter is not too late.

I love you.

Love,
Maggie

I waited for the ceremonial placement on my plate of the letter with the New York postmark, but no letter arrived. Any feelings of despair that I had, I turned down like an annoying hi-fi that you didn't want to listen to. No one at the house knew I'd written the letter, so no one knew that I waited for a reply.

A few weeks later I began my first term at ECTC. The busyness of the new place kept me from feeling much; I was too busy doing. I would stay in the dorm during the week and come home on weekends to help with the farm. Rosemary and India grew every week, it seemed, and everyone welcomed me home each time like I was the prodigal son in for a two-day stay.

One Friday in November, Granny went to an agricultural seminar in Raleigh and stayed overnight in Lillington with a first cousin of hers.

I'd come home in the early afternoon to find Mama sitting on the floor helping Rosemary and India beat cooking pots with spoons. The din stopped momentarily for Rosemary to plant slobbery kisses on me. Not to be left out, India wobbled over and did the same. Then they toddled back to the circle, and the three began a racket guaranteed to wake the dead long before Judgment Day did.

"What wonderful music," Mama said, encouraging her two young cohorts to bang their spoons harder, as she beat time in the air with her good hand. If you looked at her from one side, you wouldn't have known there was anything wrong.

The phone rang. "Shh," I said, and put my fingers to my lips as I lifted the receiver. "Hello."

The babies giggled and Mama grabbed them up, kissing their cheeks and causing them to giggle harder.

"Hello," I said again. I heard breathing and then the click of the receiver on the other end being put down. I hung up.

Mama sat with a toddler on each knee. "Who was it?"

"Wrong number, I guess." I went to bring in my suitcase from the car.

That evening the supper table resembled the opening day at the tobacco market in Clinton—people up and down, children bidding louder and louder for attention. I held Rosemary while we ate, having wrestled her from Mama. Tessie tended India. With Granny gone, Tessie insisted on staying later. She sent Mr. Neb on home in the early evening. I told her we'd be fine alone, but that went in the same ear that the hex issue did. As we finished supper, the dogs began to bark.

"Did you hear a car?" Mama asked.

"No, somebody must have walked by on the road," I said, glancing out the window into the dark night.

Tessie put away food and I washed dishes while Mama played pat-a-cake with Rosemary and India. Mona went to check on the chickens, which was her habit of an evening. As I scrubbed the remnants of chicken from a plate, a scream came out of the benign darkness of the front yard, filling it with unknown terror.

By the time Tessie and I arrived on the porch, Mona stood in the yard as wan as the first day I saw her. A cross blazed beside her, illuminating the area around the porch. On the other side of Mona stood a white-robed figure with a gun. Behind him, a group of robed figures twitched in anticipation.

Except for their height and their shoes, nothing distinguished one robed figure from another. Their shoes held clues to the figures beneath. There were brogans and steel-toed work shoes like you would wear to work in the weaving room at the mill. Here and there a pair of wing tips marked the men who used their brains more than their backs to make a living. The figure next to Mona wore a pair of black wing tips that were wide and short.

Rumors of the KKK were always with us like the shadowed underside of the snake. Still, it didn't seem possible that they stood in front of us now. Another time their pointy hoods and flowing bedsheets might have seemed funny—another time.

At the back of the group a bottle glinted in the hands of a brogan-wearing figure and then disappeared into the folds of the white robe. The man next to Mona waved his gun for emphasis. When he spoke, a ripple moved through the group like a giant centipede.

"Listen up, you bunch of nigger-lovers, the next time we come back, there won't be any need for crosses in the yard. The house'll be gone. Nobody's gonna tell us who we got to eat with and send our young'uns to school with."

I heard my own voice, thin and high. "What are you talking about? You've got no quarrel with us."

The figure pointed toward the house. "We know you're mixing the races in there. Such as you is what gives people unnatural ideas about things. You've been warned already, but you ain't listened. Do you hear me now?" The pointed hoods cast eerie shadows on the ground as they nodded their agreement.

"I'll thank you to move away from that young woman," Mama said. "You and your big talk are not helping anyone." She moved to the front of the porch as she spoke, her soft spirit giving way to show a ripple of muscle I'd only recently seen. It helped that the light from the cross glinted off the barrel of a shotgun she held pointed in the direction of the robed group. I could see her weak hand tremble with the effort. "We are not afraid. Y'all are the ones so frightened by a few women that you must hide under masks and pointy hoods," she said.

The man stood silent. Mama continued. "We are defenseless women." I thought she moved the shotgun slightly on the word *de-*

fenseless just to emphasize her point. "We ask nothing from you but to be left alone. Two sweet half-breed babies and a young girl will not be the demise of this community. Your hatred will."

Then drawing herself up a little further, she added, "Go home and pray God will forgive your cowardly and ungentleman-like actions."

The pine needles crackled beneath their feet as the men disappeared one by one into the night. Soon only the bottle bearer and the lone figure beside Mona remained. Without warning, the man with the bottle darted forward and threw it at the cross's base. Mama cocked the rifle. The bottle broke. The liquid inside exploded. Flames leapt into the night air, and the smell of whiskey surrounded us. The man darted into the woods where the others had gone. That left the lone figure beside Mona who raised himself tall at his cohort's display of courage. He blustered at us for a moment, but Mama held steady.

"Don't think I won't use this gun. He who lives by the sword better be ready to die by it."

Dropping his gun to his side, the man walked away into the trees, the crunch of pine straw sounding in his wake.

Behind me, Mama said, "Thank you, Jesus."

I went to Mona, who stood with the light of the burning cross dancing across her face. She trembled, and clutched her arms across her breasts the same as the first day I saw her. All my questions left me. I put my arms around her. "It's okay."

For a moment, her hand came up and touched my hair as if she wanted to reassure me that it was. My tears flowed like cleansing rain, washing the hate from the dark corner of my soul, where I had harbored it like some lost treasure. This girl-woman hadn't taken my daddy from me.

"I'll get some water," I said finally, and the two of us fetched buckets of water, throwing it onto the burning wood. The smell of the damp wood mixed with the whiskey, and I wondered if you could smell evil. We watched the fire hiss and splutter and the smoke roll into the night sky until at last nothing remained except charred black wood and the voices of Mama, Tessie, and the babies singing, "One little, two little, three little Indians."

Mama, Mona, Rosemary, and I all took India and Tessie home. We didn't want to leave anyone home alone in case the white-hooded men decided to come back. Only when we returned home did Mama admit to a case of wobbly-knees. Only then did she ask if I'd recognized the voice of the man in the yard as the voice of Neely Lipscomb.

CHAPTER

20

It happened the day after our hooded visitors slunk from the yard.

"Hey, y'all, quiet down or you'll wake up India," I said to Mama and Rosemary.

"Shh." Mama pressed her finger to her lips. Rosemary giggled. Weaving in and out of the sunlight in the sitting room, they danced and sang in an exaggerated whisper, "All around the mulberry bush, the monkey chased the weasel, the weasel—"

Mama quit singing in the middle of the line and crumpled to the ground. She seemed to disappear, leaving only the heap of her dress, the fabric billowing out and piling up on top of itself like a scoop of vanilla ice cream. The sudden fall plopped Rosemary down with her chubby legs outstretched, a cry of protest breaking from her lips.

From where I sat at the kitchen table, I thought at first it was Mama's high drama, meant for Rosemary's entertainment, but then Rosemary's indignant cries brought no movement from Mama. If Mama was playing possum, she was doing a fine job. Rosemary grabbed at the necklace of late-blooming dandelions that Mama had chained together for her, breaking it and causing her to howl with the loss. Still Mama did not move.

"Mama," I called, rising from the table. "Mama." I ran for the sitting room. "Tessie, it's Mama."

I knelt beside her and tapped her face, hoping she would stir. Her cheek felt cold. An indignant Rosemary tried to climb onto my lap, with her hard-soled Buster Browns digging into my leg as she pushed up. "Hold on, baby." I sat her sideways beside me. Unlike Mama, who had yet to move, she wiggled with life and frustration.

I turned back to Mama and shook her. "Mama, wake up." She lay as still as deep water. "Tessie," I called again.

Tessie, who had been in the bedroom checking on a napping India, came up behind me, looked at Mama, and ran for the kitchen. "I'll get the salts. That'll bring her round."

Mona stepped in from outside, where she'd hung a load of clothes on the line. Seeing us there, she covered her mouth with her hand. Later when I thought about it, it seemed an odd gesture given that no words ever escaped her mouth. Then in one swift motion she swooped Rosemary from the floor.

I put Mama's head in my lap and felt the faintest breath on the fingers I held to her mouth.

Thank you, God. She's alive.

"Here they are." In her hurry, Tessie shoved the smelling salts under my nose. My head jerked back as I fought off the vial, pushing it toward Mama's nose. She made the smallest of movements. Mona watched us intently while Rosemary squirmed in her arms.

"Please, dear Jesus, please. Help Lilah." Tessie fanned herself with the front of her apron as she prayed.

Mama stirred again, which caused Tessie to fan harder and pray louder.

"Tessie, call Dr. Kincaid." I tried to think, but loss crowded my thoughts.

Mona disappeared and returned with a cool cloth for Mama and some plastic pop beads for Rosemary. She sat, intent on pulling the brightly colored red, orange, and yellow beads apart, while Mona and I lifted my mama to the couch. Mama stirred again.

This was the day I dreaded; the day I prayed would never come. The day the blood quit flowing through her brain and dammed itself in one spot.

Dear God, please let her live. I know this is selfish, but I can't give her up yet. She needs Your healing touch. Let her blood flow. Give her life. Please, Lord, please. I prayed while Mona stroked Mama's cheek and placed the cool cloth on her forehead. The only response to my prayer was Mama's continued breathing. Tears of frustration trickled down my cheek, flowing from my uselessness.

Dr. Kincaid found us that way: Rosemary popping beads, me offering mute prayers and wiping tears, Mona stroking Mama's forehead, and Tessie fanning herself with her apron and praying aloud.

He examined Mama tenderly, confirming my worst fears when he announced, "I'm going to call the ambulance to take her to Duke."

It didn't seem real. I kept thinking I would wake up and be surrounded by the smell of lavender sachet. Instead uncertainty enveloped us, almost gagging us with its sharp scent, like the wood smoke and whiskey had the night before.

"I'll call ahead for the neurologist to meet us," he said, and tugged his ever-present bow tie as if it were cutting off his breath. I tried to see on his face whether there was hope, but I could read nothing there.

At Duke, Dr. Kincaid walked swiftly beside the gurney as they wheeled Mama away.

"No, honey, no. You can't be going back there." An old nurse stepped in my way. The sight of her, gray hair flying out from under her nursing cap, and her wrinkled face, stopped me. The picture of Charon ferrying people across the River Styx came to me as I stared at her grizzled, hard face. I had no gold coin to give her, and so she left me to wander along the bank, aimlessly around and around.

"The waiting room's right through those doors. The doctor'll call you when he's ready to consult with you." She snapped the clip on the chart she carried and walked away, turning every so often to make certain that I didn't attempt a crossing on my own.

The waiting room looked like we were making ready for dinner on the grounds except nobody remembered to bring their food. Clusters of people spoke in quiet tones; an older man dozed, his head bobbing to his chest. A young boy dressed in overalls walked circles around a row of chairs, putting one foot in front of the other like he was walking the circus tightrope.

I found an empty chair between a family whose son had cut himself with an ax and a mother holding her limp baby in her arms.

The ax family moved like an amoeba we'd seen in a sophomore biology film. Expanding and contracting, every now and then it lost a member to the Coke machine or the bathroom. The group circled back around them, like protoplasm, upon their return. An older woman seemed the nucleus. She announced at regular intervals for all of us to hear, "I tolt him and tolt him that ax was nothing to be foolin' around with."

The chrome arms of the chair gleamed bright at me; the green vinyl seat stuck to my legs despite my nylons. While waiting for the ambulance, Tessie had insisted I slip on a dress.

"I'm not going to Sunday school," I'd snapped at her.

"No, but there's no need for you to look common when you get up there to Duke." And then coming and taking my mama's hand, she'd gently nudged me toward the bedroom. "Go on, honey. I'll hold your mama's hand."

In the chair beside me the fevered baby stirred, her brown curls shifting about her head.

"It's okay. It'll be our turn soon." The mama crooned to her, holding her as tight as a miser would a penny, but as gentle as that first butterfly you ever catch.

I prayed. *Lord, send healing to my mama.*

The ax family moved off. They were replaced by a man come to see about his son who'd been in a motorcycle accident. He'd spoken very loudly on the pay phone to someone named Myrna, ordering her to cancel his appointments. Then he hung up with a vengeance before coming over to the row of green chairs.

He sat down, looking toward the hall where Nurse Charon stood guard. He'd tried to talk to her, but she merely shook her head and pointed a long, bony finger at the waiting room. Next to me now, he examined his fingernails, looking for a hidden mystery to his hands that he had never seen before. He rubbed his face. Up and down, up and down, thinking, I guess, that if he rubbed long enough, the room would disappear. He would be back where his life was before the phone rang and his world spun away from him like a top that hits a crack in the floor and veers off in some crazy direction, following some unimagined path.

"Been here long?"

His question startled me. "Me?"

"Yes. You been here long?" he asked again.

I uncurled my leg. "About two hours."

"They told you anything?"

"No, not a word," I said.

He rubbed his face again and turned to face me. There was a shiny diamond pin in his lapel. "I'll go nuts if I'm here for two hours with no word."

"Is your son bad?" I asked.

"Yes. They say he probably won't make it." He covered his eyes. "Got the motorcycle for his eighteenth birthday. You know kids, they think they're invincible."

I nodded as if I knew all about this.

When he moved his hands from his face, there were tears in his eyes. "His mother didn't want him to have it. She's gone to Winston-Salem to visit her mother. I don't know what will happen when she finds out. She's so fragile anyway."

"Maybe he's better than you think," I said, looking at his face, which collapsed under the weight of fear and regret.

"I've got the money for the best. I can take him wherever he needs to go. I've got contacts." He emphasized the word *contacts* as if it were the sun at the center of the universe. "But they say he can't be moved, moving him will kill him for sure. They won't say anything else."

The rich man in hell.

"Damn doctors. What do they know? They don't know a thing about working hard to make money. Not like I've had to work in the insurance business. Puts you gone a lot from home." He stopped to think on this. "I'd give all those contacts to help him now." He fingered the diamond pin and then added, "You don't realize what something means to you until it gets taken away."

We sat for a few minutes, the only sound the tapping of his leg against the chair. He stopped in midtap. "Say, what are you here for, anyway?"

"My mama. She's had a stroke. She's been real sick, but I thought she was getting better."

A blond nurse came to the door. The man beside me rose halfway from his chair before she said, "Peggy Ballard?"

The room sighed as the young mother next to me gathered her bags and her baby and started off.

The man sat back and rubbed his face again. "Maybe your mama will be all right."

"I'm praying for that." I looked at my hands in front of me; they seemed as useless to me now as the ax family's oracle.

"Will you pray for me?" he asked.

"For you?"

"For my son." He paused and then plunged on ahead with a shiver as if he'd jumped into a pond in the middle of winter. "I can't pray anymore. I suppose God's given up on me. I've gotten busy with my family and my job and the Rotary Club. I'm so lost I don't even know where to start. To tell you the truth, I don't feel a thing sitting in that pew on Sunday. There's not much difference to me between the Rotary Club and church."

"God never gives up on anybody. We give up on God." The words were out and I listened to them as if they weren't my own. A feeling ran through me as if they had taken me back into one of those blue-curtained rooms and given me a blood transfusion. Still, I wasn't interested in praying.

"Your son, what's his name?" I asked out of politeness.

"Michael, his name is Michael. I love him more than life, but I guess I'm not very good at showing it." His pain distorted his face and his shoulders drooped.

I wondered if my daddy had ever confided his love of me to

anyone. In New Orleans as the blood oozed out around him, had my daddy thought of me? Did Michael, who lay somewhere in another place cut off from us by Nurse Charon, know that his daddy loved him?

He shook his head and extended his hand. "I'm sorry I haven't introduced myself. I'm Roger Benefield. And you are?"

"Maggie. Maggie Davidson," I said, and I wondered what it would be like to have one more chance to talk to my daddy, one more chance to say I love you and one more chance for him to say the same. I knew that I had to pray.

I took the hand of the man beside me. "Lord, we ask that you place your healing hand on Michael. Grant him and his daddy peace. Let them experience your healing love through each other. Show us the way and send us your power. Amen."

Tears welled in the man's eyes. "Lord, bless Maggie here and her mama. Answer her prayer. Amen."

The short prayer seemed a benediction on my darkness. Warmth flowed through me. I was a prisoner come into the light from a cellar. I blinked and brought my hand to shield my eyes. The light encircled me. I felt its firmness, supporting me and flooding the dark of my soul with a hymn. She was there then, and with Her, another. He and She merged and the light intensified until they were one—the great I AM, the loving Mother and the gentle Father, the Spirit of goodness and kindness to be found somewhere in us all. A love that is above anything we can comprehend. It stepped out of the ax family and the baby's mother and Mr. Benefield sitting next to me. And without voice, I heard the words, "My child."

I knew whatever happened to my mama, I'd found peace again.

Tears ran down my cheeks. Something white waved before me. Mr. Benefield offered his handkerchief. "It's okay," he said, and patted my shoulder.

"I tell you what's the truth. They'll let any half-wit in the state have a driver's license."

"Granny." I stood, drying my tears quickly. Beside me, Mr. Benefield rose from his chair.

"Any word?" Granny waved her hand in our direction, indicating for us to sit. And then she sat beside me.

"None," I said, and introduced Granny to Mr. Benefield.

Nurse Charon stood in the doorway. "Roger Benefield."

He stood. "Finally."

"God bless you," I said. *Please, God, let him talk to his son one more time. Let him say I love you.*

He walked beyond the waiting-room door to where a doctor met him in the hall. They talked, gesturing back and forth. Right before he walked back to us, Mr. Benefield pumped the doctor's hand.

"It's a miracle. He's going to make it. He's going to make it." Mr. Benefield grasped first my hand and then Granny's. "I can see him as soon as he wakes up." He wiped at his eyes with his handkerchief and then began to pace up and down in front of the chairs. Before long, he made his way to the phone, and we could hear him talking again to Myrna at the insurance agency.

Dr. Kincaid arrived about ten minutes later. Nurse Charon summoned Granny and me to the hallway. With Dr. Kincaid came a young Ben Casey look-alike.

Using his stethoscope as a prop, Ben Casey launched into a detailed description of my mama's condition.

Granny cut him short. "In plain English, how is she?"

Ben Casey draped his stethoscope over his shoulder and folded his arms. "She's resting comfortably. I'm afraid there is greater paralysis in the arm and her speech is slurred. We'll have to wait a few days to see what can be done. There's definitely a cerebral hemorrhage, and the best way to treat that is through medication."

"Is she stable enough to travel?" Granny asked, and I wondered if I was going to have to carry her on over to Dix Hill in Raleigh and just let them put her in one of those padded rooms. Where could my mama go?

"Yes, I suppose." The doctor wrinkled his nose. "But I don't recommend it. We've no way to know when her system is going to shut down completely. Or when a piece of that blockage could break off and then we'd lose her."

"I've been reading about this Dr. Ralph at Columbia Hospital," Granny said. "He's doing some mighty amazing things with a certain kind of hemorrhage surgery. People get back movement they've lost and such as that."

The doctor shook his head. "I'm not sure that your daughter is the best candidate for that procedure."

Whether my mama was the best candidate or not had little to do with my granny's resolve.

"She may not be," Granny said. "But that's why you've got your calling and I've got mine. She's going to have whatever chance I can give her. If she's stable enough to travel, then we'll risk it."

The doctor shrugged. "I'm not going to guarantee she'll make it to New York."

Granny leaned forward as if whispering a secret. "When it comes to that, you can't even guarantee I could make it across the street out in front of this hospital. All we can do is go on. I'm not going to sit and watch her die."

"Well, ma'am—" the doctor's tone was full of his uppity-up attitude—"I wash my hands of this matter and leave you to Dr. Kincaid's care. One of the junior residents under my supervision will be your daughter's attending physician for as long as she remains here at Duke."

He stalked off, his white jacket flowing behind him like Superman's cape.

Finally they let us see her. Little green lines ran diamond patterns through the glass in the door. Mama lay on the other side with tubes coming out of her. We walked in, and I pushed the door closed behind us.

Granny patted Mama's hand. "It's going to be okay." And then again, "Lily, it's going to be okay." Mama never stirred.

We returned to the waiting room, where Granny placed a call on the pay phone. Her head shook in rapid motion as she talked. By the time she hung up and came back to the row of green vinyl chairs, the head-shake was a small one, as if she'd developed the palsy and couldn't stop.

"That woman, his secretary, insists Dr. Ralph only does surgery from referrals. He won't take your mama."

Granny walked over to the desk and spoke to the nurse. She turned from Granny and picked up a silver microphone.

"Paging Dr. Kincaid to the surgical waiting room."

Granny returned and paced back and forth in front of me until a few minutes later when Dr. Kincaid walked in.

Granny stopped pacing. "I've called this Dr. Ralph and I didn't seem to get anywhere," she reported.

Dr. Kincaid shook his head. "Now, Mrs. Parker, I told you to try and let me handle this."

"And have you?" Granny wanted to know.

"I'm working on it. This isn't like running down to the Piggly Wiggly for some milk." Dr. Kincaid's voice was full of his long day. When Mr. Benefield bounded up and stuck his hand at him, Dr. Kincaid tugged at his bow tie before he shook it.

Mr. Benefield pumped Dr. Kincaid's hand. "Roger Benefield. I couldn't help overhearing Mrs. Parker's distress. I told Maggie here earlier, I'm in insurance. I may know somebody that can help. No promises, but I'll try."

And that is how Mr. Sanford R. Jolly of the American Health Plan came to call Dr. Marshall Ralph at Columbia Hospital in New York, and that is how Dr. Marshall Ralph agreed to try his new surgery on my mama. And that is how we found ourselves on an airplane, Granny and I climbing the steps from the runway and Mama being carried aboard, smiling lopsidedly because of her paralysis. We descended to New York and were met by an ambulance, courtesy of Mr. Roger Benefield and the American Health Plan.

The ambulance wound its way through the mass of streets and buildings planted as neatly apart in the pavement as rows of tobacco in the field. Mama strained to see. You might have thought she was in New York to see the window displays instead of fighting for her life.

"Lily, lie down before you bust a goozle. They'll be plenty of time to see this later." Granny pressed Mama back on her stretcher.

Mama sighed. "Oh, Mama, sometimes we just can't worry about tomorrow." Her words slurred together like she'd been drinking.

All around us there was constant movement—people everywhere, some dressed in clothes that would have gotten you a one-way trip to Dix Hill, with the other feeble-minded, if you'd worn them back in Canaan. There were more buildings and concrete than you could have imagined, all jammed up together as if people didn't realize the whole rest of the United States was out there, and they needed to put together every building they ever thought of in two square blocks.

"Mama, have him drive by Macy's, please," Mama said.

"What?" Granny said.

"She wants to drive by Macy's," I said.

"Good Lord in the morning, yes, and while we're there, let's all pick us out a new frock to wear." Granny wrapped her hands tight around her pocketbook. "Lily, you've lost your mind."

"Please," Mama whispered so that Granny had to bend close to hear.

"By all means," Granny said, shaking her head. She turned to the front of the ambulance. "Son, if you don't mind, we'd like to go by Macy's, please."

"You kidding me, lady." The driver looked up in his rearview mirror.

"No, son, I'm not. Don't make me get ugly with you," Granny said.

The driver made a face in the mirror, but before long Granny and I sat on either side of Mama, holding her so she could see the incredible Christmas decorations set inside the dioramas of the store windows.

"Beautiful," Mama said, "beautiful."

Once past Macy's, the ambulance picked up speed, faster and faster, almost sideswiping a yellow taxicab whose driver shook his fist and shouted at us. Jostled by the sudden swerve, Granny fell against the window, knocking her black felt hat to a precarious angle. She righted herself, righted her hat, and leaned around to get a good look at the driver.

"We're not in a hurry here, son, unless you keep driving like that, in which case by the time we get to the hospital, they'll have to find a room for every durn one of us. My daughter does not need to be jostled around."

"Hey, lady, I'm just doing my job," the driver shot back.

"Well, I must say you're not doing so well at it, and unless you'd like me to come up there and drive for you, you better find a way to get that lead foot of yours off the gas pedal."

The driver snorted but slowed.

The hospital bustled with the same intensity that the city had. Within a day, they'd wheeled Mama off to surgery in a flash of green gowns and blue masks. The operation went well, and Granny pronounced Dr. Marshall Ralph as sensible a man as she'd ever met.

People were drawn to us for a reason Granny considered the silliest thing—the way we talked. It wasn't uncommon to have other patients and their families come up and make the request, "Say something." To which Granny would reply, "Something," and turn and walk off, muttering, "Simple-minded, just like that Fridley boy that got knocked on the head when he was little."

When we were finally allowed to see her, Mama lay with the tubes so familiar a sight now, they might have been a hat she wore to church on Sunday.

I prayed and I prayed. *Please God, please God, send a healing. Let her see every building in New York, let her laugh without drool finding its way down her chin.*

With Mr. Benefield's prayer, peace had come at last. What lay ahead I could not say, I could only pray, knowing at last my words were not weighted by my own darkness.

CHAPTER 21

First her toes wiggled and then her hand squeezed Granny's and then Mama popped her eyes open and said, "I dreamed I was married to Clark Gable." Of course, we didn't know that's what she said. At the time her garbled words could have easily been a recitation of Shakespeare, a recipe for Chocolate Cake Surprise, or a confession of murder, and we wouldn't have known any different.

What we knew was the draw of her mouth seemed slighter. And that our mama, Lily, Lilah, who had the soul of a poet tethered to earth by the strings of *Photoplay* magazine, was back among us.

Granny went home to look after the farm and I stayed in an efficiency room at the Big Apple Hotel, right across the street from the hospital. I spent my days reading to Mama and helping with her physical therapy. The green tile of the hospital became as familiar to me as my bedroom floor. She and I would remain for four weeks at Columbia, and then we would spend another four weeks at Duke, where we could be closer to home.

I walked beside Mama, encouraging her, coaxing her, and reading aloud the previous six months' worth of *True Detective, Modern Screen,* and *Photoplay.* There was nothing that happened in the world of Hollywood in the last half of 1961 that I did not learn about that December and January.

I painted her toenails and fingernails. My tendency to paint the cuticle was a source of exasperation to Mama until one of the nurse's aides, Vicki, took pity on us and assumed manicure duty in her off-hours. Her only reward was our gratitude and the chance to listen to our accents, full of Sampson County. Mama, of course, called her Victoria, her given name, which Mama wormed out of her within five minutes of meeting her.

I washed the fuzz that grew on Mama's head and then combined the little hair that grew in during those eight weeks. Many days of growth were needed to cover the U-shaped scar on the back of her head. I became a purveyor of scarves. Each day I purchased ten or so and deposited them on Mama's bed, where she picked slowly through them like a harem girl doing the dance of the Seven Veils.

I would sit beside her on the bed, giving my opinion if asked. Sometimes she would squeal and then put her head on my shoulder when she found one that particularly offended her taste.

"You can't be serious," she said. "I know I raised you better than that." She did her best to imitate Granny, but her face and arm wouldn't cooperate.

"Well," I defended myself, "there's only so many scarves, even in New York. I've either got to start bringing in some of the runts or move on to another accessory."

The second week we were in New York I'd looked up Alex's number in the phone book. The phone book was bigger than three years' worth of the Sears catalog. Sitting in the phone booth in the back of the coffee shop up the street from the hospital, I ran my finger down the pages of Barrons until I found one that matched the return address on the last letter Alex had sent me.

A knock on the door of the booth startled me and I slammed the book. I half expected to look up and see Granny standing there instead of the man peering in the door, who wore a shirt with an oval patch that read *Bob.*

"Hey, lady, are you awake in there? I need to use the phone."

I pulled open the door, feeling as if I'd been caught stealing penny candy from the five-and-dime.

"Excuse me," I said as I made my way past Bob.

I was at the third booth from the door when he yelled, "Hey, lady, you forgot your purse."

It took another week for me to go back and dial the number, letting the voice on the other end say "Barrons residence" before I hung up. I held on to the phone after I hung up, trying to make myself call again and ask for Alex. All this time and there had been no letter from him. I was too late. Too late I realized what a ninny I was, and too late I'd tried to make amends.

At night I spent my time involved in a test of wills with the steam radiator that heated my room at the Big Apple Hotel. The switch worked like the spinner on a board game. If you flicked it with your finger, it moved around and around, but where it stopped had no bearing on the amount of steam produced by the radiator. The manager assured Granny he would fix it, but a few days after she left, I simply gave up and opened a window to keep from being cured like a ham in the smokehouse.

Sounds floated into the window at night: cars honking, babies crying, men laughing, and women singing in languages I couldn't understand. The city was like Rosemary when she couldn't settle down for bed. It had to kick out here or twist over there, squeeze out one more burp to ease its stomach, and some nights it sat up for one last cry of sirens before it could melt down into a peaceful sleep. It was hard to imagine that people slept with all the light and noise around them.

At the hospital, a few people recognized me from my picture in *Life* magazine. When they asked I told them there was a mistake, a misprint. Fortunately, their interest in that Maggie Davidson lasted about as long as their interest in the hula hoop.

Mama was different. Even from her hospital bed, it seemed that Mama drew people to her. In the first days after the operation, when she lay like some modern mummy and could not respond to them, hospital personnel found their way to her bedside to speak her name or tuck in a bedsheet. The nurses on duty scolded to no avail. One in utter desperation gave up and posted a NO VISITORS sign. Then she underlined the word *no* with black Magic Marker.

It did no good. After Mama was in a room of her own, I'd go downstairs to get lunch or supper, and when I returned, the room would be full of hospital personnel. Mama, the queen, held her own court, sitting in bed with her scarf crown on her head. By coming to New York, Mama had finally found a place big enough for her to be herself.

Sometimes Vicki would insist that I get out while she did Mama's nails and I would walk, my coat wrapped tight around me against the cold wind that swept down the street, chilling everything in its path. The churches I saw were amazing. Inside St. Patrick's Cathedral there were lit candles everywhere, as if it were a birthday party, but people made their wishes when they lit the candles, not when they blew the candles out.

And then one day I came upon a church with a sign, 23RD STREET DUTCH REFORM. It was a magnificent stucco building with a black wrought-iron fence that stood a halfhearted guard against the ravages of the city. There was an air of neglect about it. The building with its fading pink stucco reminded me of a tulip tree with blooms killed by a late frost. The incredible pink beauty the tree once held is veiled in the muted brown blossoms.

I walked up the stairs and pushed the heavy wooden door open. Dusty beams of light filtered through exquisite stained-glass windows and lit the sanctuary. Pews of beautiful mahogany with faded purple cushions opened out on both sides of the center aisle.

I looked up to see Jesus sitting there with outstretched hands welcoming children—fair and dark skinned—some with lambs in their arms. His face glowed with the light of the sun. I sat on the back pew. Did the artist who created the window see Jesus that way? If that artist had lived in deepest Africa and never seen the pictures I had of Jesus, would they still have put the glass together so or would they have found glass the color of the pews to make the face and the outstretched hands of the Savior?

And then Jesus was gone, but not the children. Their glass faces glowed and the light coming in through the colored glass around them bathed the pews in front of me. In that moment, I was part of more than my small spot on that faded purple cushion.

And there in the midst of the children I saw a building, a brick structure that looked like the teachers' dormitory over at Pineland. It confused me, and I closed my eyes. I didn't need a dormitory. But women and babies were everywhere—they appeared on the green lawn in front of the dormitory, swinging on a tire from a tall oak in the side yard, and coming in from the garden, tomatoes piled up in the crooks of their arms. Following behind their mamas were toddlers eating tomatoes like apples, with the red juice running from the corners of their mouths down their chins. A home for unwed mothers and orphan babies. It all opened up before me and surrounded me with its quiet message. I shook my head. "There's no land," I said, and waved my hand as if to shoo a persistent fly. But it filled my mind as completely as those ads they flashed in movie theaters to make you want to go to the candy counter and fill up on Cokes, popcorn, and such.

The image disappeared, but not before the Voice said, "My sheep."

And then a very earthly voice said, "Is beautiful, no?"

I jumped up from the pew, turning my back on the window.

Behind me a dark-skinned man in suit and tie stood looking at the stained-glass window.

I pulled my coat on tighter, pushing my purse further up my arm. "Yes, it is." I glanced back at the round window filled with the children and the very serene, very handsome Jesus.

The man in the aisle coughed and I turned toward him. He gestured at my tightly clutched arms. "I scared you. I'm sorry."

"No, that's all right. I didn't see anybody when I came in." I moved into the aisle to see if he would block my way, but he didn't.

"I've just come in. I was out visiting a new mother in our congregation. I am Jesus Ramerez, pastor of this mission." He extended his hand and I shook it.

"I'm Maggie Davidson. I'm afraid I don't know much about

the Dutch Reform Church." My heart began to return to its normal rhythm.

"Oh no, Miss Davidson, our sign must have fallen down again. We are not Dutch Reform. They moved to the suburbs and built another church. I am the pastor of the Baptist mission that bought this church. As you can see, we have little funds to keep up the building, but we try. The windows are my favorite." He gestured at the Jesus window. "I see you like them, too."

"Yes, they are beautiful." I looked at my watch. "I must have been here longer than I realized. I'd better go."

"Then take our windows in your heart and be at peace." He walked me to the door.

I turned and shook his hand again. "Thank you," I said.

Dusk had begun to settle while I was inside. I hurried back to the hospital to find Mama all decked out in Pango Peach lipstick and discussing Natalie Wood's love life with Vicki.

Christmas came with a box from home full of goodies. I sent one home as well, each gift I purchased for Granny, Mona, Rosemary, India, and Tessie approved with a nod from Mama. I found a little tree for Mama's room, and our visitors brought ornaments and goodies in a stream that never seemed to end.

There was one young resident, Tim, who came by daily without fail. Lean and tall, he ambled through the hall and into Mama's room as if he were a tourist on the twenty-five-cent tour.

He stuck his head around the wooden door one morning about two weeks after her surgery. "How's the patient?"

"She's making progress, thank you. We've been working on the muscles in her hand." As I spoke, Mama smiled, a still slightly lopsided effort.

"How about the patient's daughter?"

I held up the squeeze ball. "My biggest problem is the muscle between my ears. I'm supposed to be helping her with this exercise, and I can't seem to get it right."

He walked further into the room. "You mean the strengthening one," he said. "Here, let me show you." He took Mama's hand in his to demonstrate the exercise.

Mama nodded her thanks. She spoke with deliberation. "Not bad for a Yankee."

"Oh, Mama, I wouldn't go that far." I smiled at Tim.

"You two magnolia belles better watch your step. I'll get Nurse Methuselah transferred up here," Tim said, and shook the squeeze ball at us.

"We can handle her." Mama struggled to pronounce each syllable. Despite her handicap, Mama soon had Tim revealing his life.

"Tim, where are you from?" Mama asked him, rounding her lips like she was Eliza Doolittle learning elocution in *My Fair Lady.*

"I'm from Maryland. Came to New York looking for a better life." Tim's smile faded a bit.

"And you found it." Mama smiled.

"I guess you could say so," Tim said.

"Was the old life so awful?" Mama asked as she reached to adjust her scarf.

"Mama, please, I think that operation addled you," I said. I punched her pillows up and rearranged them behind her head.

"Oh, I don't mind," Tim said. "For me the old life was awful. My dad died and left my mom with four of us to raise. She did her best. I was the only boy. She named me Timothy Matthew Charles Randolph Lassiter."

It was my turn to forget my manners. "That name itself must have been a burden."

He laughed. "A practical woman, my mother named me after all my uncles. She hoped one of them would get rich and remember me in his will."

"That was clever. Did it work?" Mama asked as I tugged on the last pillow.

"Not so well. I got fifty dollars and a watch that doesn't keep good time. That's all it did for me." He slapped his knees. "And that's quite enough about me. Get busy with that squeeze ball or it's Nurse Methuselah for you." Tim stood up. "Ladies, I'm off to my rounds."

Two days later he asked if I wanted to go get a cup of coffee.

"Well, yes," I said, a slight flush creeping up the edge of my neck.

The hospital cafeteria was decorated with the same green that filled the entire hospital.

"You start to wonder if you're inside some grape and don't know it," I said as I made my way through a sea of green chairs.

"What?" Tim asked, raising his voice above the clatter of the trays.

"All this green. It's wearing after a while." I pointed to the walls and the chairs.

He laughed. "Just be glad the coffee's not green. I'll get us some, if you'll pick the table."

I made my way to a table in the corner. A few minutes later, Tim arrived with two coffees on a tray with little packets of sugar and cream strewn all around the cups.

"Your mother is doing well," he said.

"Yes, very well. Of course, you know we've got three to six months before we know the lasting effects." The coffee steamed up around my face as a couple of interns passed by and patted Tim on the back.

"Everything will work out, just wait and see." Tim stirred a packet of sugar in his coffee. "Do you like movies?"

"What?"

"Do you like movies?" he repeated.

"I suppose," I said, "they're okay." Did he mean did I like movies or did he mean did I like movies with him?

"I see you've got those *Photoplay* magazines." He eyed me with suspicion.

"Oh, those." Now his question made sense. "They're Mama's. She's the one that's a bit star-struck. I've always liked a good book."

"And a good book would be?" he asked.

One thing you could say, he was persistent. *"War and Peace,*

Exodus, To Kill a Mockingbird." Mama and I had read *Dr. Zhivago* that year, but we'd had to put a slipcover on it so Granny wouldn't see the title.

"Well, we couldn't go out for a book, but we could go out to a movie. What do you think?"

"I'm not sure I could leave Mama." My hands went to my stomach, which suddenly felt as if I'd eaten all the Christmas nuts by myself.

Tim drummed his fingers on the table. "Now listen, your mother is fine. Being cared for at one of the premier hospitals in the country. I could arrange for double-duty nurses if that would make you feel better."

"Well, maybe," I said. I hadn't been on a date since my mama got sick.

"And then we could pick a lousy movie and not enjoy it at all, if you think that would help." He pushed his eyebrows together and forced a frown.

"Is that how they taught you to sweet-talk a girl in Maryland?"

He smiled and loaded the remains of our coffee and trash onto the tray. "Good. My rotation ends tomorrow morning. I'm going home and sleep. I'll pick you up tomorrow night about six. We could grab a quick bite before we head to the theater."

I nodded my approval as we rose to leave. "What do your three sisters think about having a doctor in the family?"

"Mostly they're unimpressed. They put up with an awful lot of my shenanigans when we were little. You know, I was the only man in the house. More than a few girls have told me I'm spoiled."

"Are you?" I asked as I tried to calculate how many more-than-a-few was—ten, twenty, more?

"I don't think of it as spoiled. I think of it as knowing what I want. And I get what I want." Our feet clacked on the tile as the clatter of trays faded behind us.

We saw the movie *Breakfast at Tiffany's,* with Audrey Hepburn sailing across the screen as Holly Golightly. I wondered if she had a cushion of air underneath her. As always in the movies, true love prevailed, even for Audrey's Southern belle trying to find her way in the big city.

After it ended, I wouldn't let Tim walk me home until I'd gone by the hospital to see that Mama was okay. Walking the darkened halls, I remembered walking through the hospital in Clinton with Alex the night Mama got sick. That terrifying feeling of falling and of having someone you love be so close, but being unable to touch them for fear you would shatter, leaving bits of yourself everywhere.

"Maggie," Tim said. "Are you okay?"

"I'm fine," I said, and shook my head. "Just a little tired."

As we approached Mama's door, the new night nurse crossed her arms and stood in the middle of the hall. "You can't go in there. She's settled. I'm quite capable of looking after the patients on my floor."

Tim stepped between us. "Of course you are, Sue."

"Well . . ." She gestured toward me, her face muscles softening slightly. "What does she need to go in there for?"

Tim reached out and put his hand on Sue's arm. "You know how it is. She's had a bad scare. It's her mother. She'll just be a second and I'll take full responsibility for the patient."

"Okay." Sue moved aside slightly and I pushed the wooden door slowly open. The light from the hall illuminated the tile floor and the end of Mama's bed. I stepped in and paused, pushing the door closed so that the light was not so strong, and gave my eyes a moment to adjust. I thought I could see the slight movement of her chest as she breathed; the noise of the machines covered any sound she might make.

I bent over her. Her head was wrapped in a white bandage, and for a moment she seemed like my daughter. I patted her back ever so slightly, needing to touch her, to reassure myself that my trip to the movies hadn't diminished her in any way. Then I turned and walked quietly to the hall where Tim waited.

"I told you she would be fine," he whispered.

"And now I know," I said.

"You do remind me so much of my sisters. Needless worry." He took my elbow and propelled me toward the elevator, giving Sue a smile as we passed the nurse's desk.

"I'll worry needlessly if I like," I said, pulling my elbow back toward me.

"Well, if I'm around, you won't have to worry." He pushed the elevator button.

"Tim, don't be silly. You'll be here in New York and I'll be in North Carolina."

"You'd be surprised how quickly that can all change," he said, and took my hand as we got in the elevator.

"I don't think so," I said, slightly annoyed at his I-know-more-than-you-do tone.

"Women, they never know their own minds," Tim said as the elevator doors closed, shutting out the light from the hall.

The days passed quickly after that. Sometimes Mama progressed well, and other times she faltered. On the bad days, I was like a new mama with a colicky infant, paralyzed by the fear that this might go on forever. Then I realized it would pass and I let Mama have her bad days, understanding that it was my job to try to distract her from them.

Tim and Mama plotted to push me out of the hospital nest every few days into the world of New York. I'd buy postcards and write notes on Mama's progress and my visits to the Empire State Building and the Metropolitan Museum of Art and such as that. Tim and I saw *The Parent Trap* and *Splendor in the Grass* and more movies than I saw in a year when I was in Canaan.

Mama looked better every time I came back. I had no idea until much later that she conspired with the nursing staff every time I left to make certain her scarf and makeup were freshly arranged when I returned.

Her speech improved daily, and she slipped Tim's name into any reasonable discussion and some that weren't. Watching the

"Blonde Bomber" fight her way through the Roller Derby on TV, getting her hospital bed rolled up to eat breakfast, working on speech therapy, Mama brought the conversation around to Tim sooner or later.

"Mama, you're addled. Tim and I are friends. He's just being nice, that's all!"

I didn't dare tell her that he kissed me the last few times we'd been to the movies. I tried not to think about it. His kisses seemed like the rest of him, sure and quick. I couldn't help but think of Alex and the tenderness of his kiss. If only I'd realized that summer how much Alex's kisses had matched his personality. If only Mama had no use for "if onlys." Still I couldn't help but wonder what would have been if I'd understood instead of know who Alex was.

Tim's kisses, among other things, made me uneasy. I'd come in from shopping and heard him screaming at Vicki because she'd given a patient the wrong medication. Later when I asked her about it, Vicki said, "I gave Mrs. Austin what was written on the chart, but then someone changed the chart after I got in trouble."

"That's not right," I said.

"He's a doctor. I'm not," Vicki said, and she went back to counting the pills on the medicine cart.

Granny called every weekend and we wrote in between times. Her letters were full of news and updates on the latest of Rosemary's antics. She preceded these stories with the words "Tessie wants me to tell you this."

I was the official Lilah letter-reader and scribe, replying to everyone who wrote to Mama. And much to our great surprise Mona wrote. I suppose I'd never thought about her being able to write, what with her not talking. I don't know who I thought wrote that note we'd found with the baby on the porch, but somehow I never put it together in my mind.

The first letter came tucked inside one of Granny's letters, written in the penmanship of a fourth grader on a piece of paper from one of my old school tablets.

Dear Mizriz Davidson,

Rosemary and me we sure do miss you. Tessie and Mizriz Parker are helping us but Rosemary just keeps walking to yur room and looking for you.

We pray for you.
Mona

"Well, how about that?" Mama took the letter and studied it. "These are her first words, Magdalena."

"Well, what about the ones on the note with Rosemary? She'd have to have written them," I said. I looked over Mama's shoulder at the letters that leaned this way and that, some threatening to fall off their lines entirely.

"Those don't count. She didn't know us then. Those words were just to the people that lived in the white farmhouse. These are our words." Mama waved the note in the air. "Our words."

She couldn't have been any more proud if Mona had been elected president of the Home Demonstration Club.

The next weekend when Granny called, I asked about the letter. "Did Mona say anything when she gave it to you?"

"Not a word. Just walked up and laid it on my desk while I was writing a letter. I asked her if she wanted me to send it and she nodded and that was it. I guess she found one of your old writing tablets somewhere. She's a hardworking thing, I'll give her that. She's—"

I missed the next few words as Mama motioned to me. "What did she say? Ask her about Rosemary."

"Well, Mama wants to talk now," I said, and handed the phone over.

Two more letters came after that, sparse on words and with letters as wobbly as Mr. Roy Worrell after a night of drinking. Mama and I referred to them as first, second, and third Mona, epistles that we both studied for clues to Mona's life.

Our last week in New York, Mama's improvement was steady.

I thanked God for it. Like a woman hanging on a cliff, I'd found a toehold that day at Duke when I prayed with Mr. Benefield and I rejoiced in it. Since that day I began inching my way back up the cliff, until it melted before me, and I was at the top, resting and looking out with wonder at the fall I could have taken, further and further down the cliff and into the black hole of my guilt.

I had taken the window in the Spanish mission to heart. I began to think of the dorm for mamas and babies less as a vision and more as my calling. It was in my dreams, in the middle of Mama's *Photoplay,* and sometimes it even replaced my face over the sink in the bathroom mirror at the Big Apple Hotel.

The last Wednesday, I'd gone on one final scarf expedition, pulling two new ones right off the display mannequins at Macy's. Mama's goal appeared to involve having more scarves than anyone at the Duke Rehabilitation Center had ever seen. We'd long since passed the point of any reasonable number. One day many of the scarves would find their way to quilts just as the scraps from our season of Lilah couture did.

The sales clerk fawned over a woman whose yearly purchases must have been equal to her girth, making me wait for fifteen minutes. Pressed for time to get last-minute things done before I went to dinner with Tim, I rushed into the hospital and turned the corner for the elevators like an Olympic sprinter. Too late, I realized Tim stood right around the corner. When I saw him, I tried to slow down, but couldn't keep myself from colliding with him. Our bodies bumped and our heads knocked together, then we bounced apart like clowns in a circus act, grabbing at each other as we tried to stay upright on the slick hospital tile.

At last my feet quit sliding, and I put one hand to my head to survey the damage. The brown Macy's bag slipped from my grasp. I grabbed for the bag, but it hit the floor and the scarves billowed out across the floor like fallen banners of a medieval knight on the losing end of a joust.

"Maggie." Tim caught me to him. I suppose he was afraid I was going to go woozy on him because he shouted at me. "Are you okay?"

I couldn't speak. The lights in the hall were causing my eyes to play tricks on me.

"Maggie." He shook me.

I nodded and gripped his arm tighter. Behind Tim stood Alex.

CHAPTER 22

I felt my head. Surely the bump I'd received had produced this hallucination. Only days earlier I'd been thinking of his kisses and now I imagined him in front of me. Then my hallucination spoke.

"Maggie, is that you?"

My feet put down roots right through that green-tiled floor. The air around me became thick, and I fought to push it in and out of my lungs. Tim turned from me, relaxing his grip, and spoke to the apparition.

"It appears she's not talking."

Several floor nurses stopped in midstep, ready to dispense any required help of the medicinal variety. Their white caps stood at attention on their heads like a line of sailors at the ready.

I shook my head.

Tim turned back to me. "Maggie, say something."

"Something," I said. "Alex?"

Tim released his grip.

"Yes." Alex stepped forward, moving around Tim with a little dip as if he were square dancing at the VFW on Saturday night.

The crisis past, the row of white caps moved on. Above us the fluorescent light flickered, and we looked for a moment like characters in a silent movie, mouths open and raised eyebrows all around.

Alex reached out and hugged me—an action that was constricted, as if we were trying on new clothes that didn't fit.

"But how did you know about Mama?" I asked.

"What about your mama?" Alex held my arm, his touch as forgotten as the cool rains of April in the midst of August.

My heart slowed. "Mama's had surgery. Isn't that why you're here?"

"I had no idea. My fiancée's father had some minor surgery. I'm here to visit him." He dropped my arm. "Tell me about your mother. What's happened?"

Fiancée, he had a fiancée. My letter had been too late.

"Maggie?" Alex stepped toward me.

"I'm sorry. I just needed to catch my breath." My feet started to break free of the floor. I felt the air become thin enough to breathe again. Tim handed me the bag, the scarves safely wrapped back inside.

"Where are my manners?" I said. "Tim Lassiter, this is Alex Barrons. Alex, this is Tim."

The two shook hands like boxers before a match while I explained my mama's condition.

"Mama's up in four-twenty. Stop by anytime." I tried to make my voice natural and easy, but somehow it came out like I'd just run a mile.

Tim took me by the elbow.

"Nice to meet you, Tim. Maggie, tell your mama I'll be by shortly," Alex said as he patted my free arm.

Tim tightened his grip on my elbow. "Let's get going."

He pushed me gently toward the elevator. He seemed afraid that, without his push, I would remain in the hospital foyer forever like a potted plant stuck along the wall between the elevators. With his insistent hand prodding me on, my feet moved. They got the message and kept stepping one in front of the other until Tim turned me around in the elevator, ready to march out when the doors opened.

"Nice guy," Tim commented as the doors closed and the elevator began to hum.

I realized he was staring at me.

"Yes, he is," I said, and reached up to mash the fourth-floor button, which was already lit.

"He's certainly not from your part of the country. How'd you meet him?" Tim asked.

"He worked on a project down near us a couple of summers ago." I stared at the lighted two above the elevator doors.

"The civil rights movement?" Tim said. The three lit up above the doors.

"No, a religious project. He was a student at Princeton Seminary." It seemed odd that Tim knew nothing of this part of my life, but then how did you go about telling someone that on occasion God appeared in front of you as plain as the Empire State Building stood watch over Manhattan? And furthermore, how do you casually mention that sometimes people experienced a healing touch because of that?

The four lit up and the elevator doors opened. Tim, with his hand on my elbow, pushed me toward Mama's room.

I offered her the bag of scarves. The paper rattled and the bag shook as I handed it to her.

"Magdalena, you look like someone licked your candy." She sat back and raised her face to get a better view of me.

"I'm fine." I sank into the chair at her bedside, picturing Alex as he drove the MG. I put my hand to my cheek as I felt the humid air of those summer nights brushing my face.

"Maggie, aren't you going to tell your mother who you saw?" Tim asked.

I looked up and realized that they both were staring at me now, my mama holding in her good hand the bag of scarves, pushed away from her as if they had the odor of something dead, and Tim standing beside the chair looking down at me.

I could have imagined a scene out of *Splendor in the Grass* when I saw Alex again. Deanie saying to Bud, "Are you happy?" and Bud saying to Deanie, "I don't think about happiness much anymore." Natalie Wood and Warren Beatty wistfully watching each other as they part, the noble words of Wordsworth coming out of the speakers.

> *"Though none can bring back the hour*
> *Of splendor in the grass, of glory in the flower.*
> *We will grieve not, rather find*
> *Strength in what remains behind."*

Instead of that, I'd been standing in the hospital hall clutching a bag of Macy's scarves and stuttering.

"Alex," I said, trying to use the tone of voice of one ordering pot roast. "Alex is here."

Mama dropped the bag onto the bed. "Oh my. Is he really?" She looked toward the door. "You did invite him up?" She looked back at me.

"Yes. Yes, I did," I said. I pulled a scarf from the bag, shook it out, and let it float across the bed in waves of blue and green. "He's here to visit his fiancée's father."

Mama sat back against the pillow, thinking on this for a minute. "How about that?" She fingered the scarf in front of her as if it were a Braille tablet and she could read what I'd written there with my touch. Her look was the same look that Granny wore when we first brought Mama home from the hospital two years earlier—she searched my face for a tremor, a sign that I would freeze up completely and be unable to get my body to follow my mind.

Tim fiddled with the chart at the end of the bed. "He came up right after Maggie rounded the corner and knocked me over."

"He said he'd stop by"—I reached to adjust Mama's pillow—"but we'll see."

"Imagine the pediatric nurses are wondering where I am." Tim started toward the door and turned back. "We're still on for dinner tonight, right?"

"Of course," I said, wishing it wasn't so.

I picked up a copy of *Silver Screen* and began to read to Mama. She continued to finger the scarf, and right in the middle of Brigitte Bardot's statement on free love, she spoke.

"Magdalena, what do you suppose it means?"

"Mama, I think she's pretty clear on the subject," I said.

"Not her, Magdalena. Alexander. What do you suppose it means him being here?" She twirled the scarf above her head, and it floated gently down around her shoulders.

"It means, Mama, that his almost father-in-law is having surgery," I said.

"But it is amazing. The two of you—"

"Mama, I'm not going to talk about it. I'm fine, he's fine, and Brigitte Bardot has more to say." Mama looked like she had more to say as well, but before she could, I snapped the magazine in front of my face and continued to read.

A short while later there was a knock at the door.

Mama said, "Come in."

The door opened. Alex stood before us, stopping only long enough to glance around the room before he headed for the bed to embrace Mama.

"Mrs. Davidson, how are you?" he asked with a lightness in his voice that suggested they were meeting for an orangeade at the Salemburg Grill.

"A minor setback." Mama pointed to her scarf. "I'll be up and causing trouble in no time."

"I have no doubt about that," Alex laughed.

Mama gestured to the chair. "When Maggie told me you were here, I pinched myself. You must sit. I have to have a full update on what you've been doing. Are you still in school? Are you living here in New York?" Mama's questions tumbled out like new puppies out for a romp.

"Yes, ma'am. I'm lecturing at Columbia University in the philosophy department and doing postdoctoral work at Union Theological Seminary," Alex said.

"And your trip to England?"

Alex described his Oxford experience, pausing now and then to answer a question.

While he talked I studied him, watching him and trying to see where he'd changed. Maybe he was leaner, I thought. He now had a new degree and a fiancée. *Fiancée:* There were seven letters that could change your life forever.

Did those ancient scribes who developed the alphabet realize what each letter had packed into it? Take seven of those letters and they could transfigure your life.

How about *sick*? Those four letters, *s, i, c,* and *k,* they could transform your existence, even end your life. Letters placed side by side in words like *guilt* and *sin*—spontaneously combusted like a science experiment and consumed lives—altered the world.

Could the power of those letter combinations be overcome? Or could they only be muted by words like *love* and *grace,* four and five letters respectively?

"Maggie, did you hear me?"

Alex and Mama were looking at me.

Alex spoke again. "I asked about your husband. Is he back in Sampson County?"

I blinked. "My husband?"

"Yes," he said.

"I don't have a husband." Mama seconded my statement with a nod of her head.

"I'm sorry," Alex said. "Did he die?"

"No, he didn't die," I answered, becoming more and more peeved that he was acting so dense.

"Oh," Alex said, and looked away.

"No, you don't understand." My voice rose as I talked. "He didn't die because he never existed."

Alex turned to face me. "I saw your wedding picture. My father showed me the clipping from the newspaper when I got home."

"Oh," Mama and I said together, like we were members of the Ladies' Chorus.

Mama spoke gently. "No, no. Alexander, what your father showed you was some reporter's overzealous effort to create a story. Magdalena was attending her cousin's wedding in that picture. The newspapers retracted the caption the next day."

"I see," Alex said. "So you're not married?"

"She's got several possibilities, but she's not serious with anyone," Mama volunteered.

"Mama, please. Alex didn't ask for an update on my personal affairs," I said.

Alex grinned. "I'm sure anything your mother wants to tell me, I'll be happy to hear."

Mama opened her mouth to speak.

"Stay out of this," I snapped at her. Alex and Mama both studied me with wide eyes. I could just see Mama going on about how I'd pined for Alex. Her doing that while he had some fiancée picking out her trousseau, I wouldn't stand for it.

"I mean it," I said, sounding like a bank robber threatening to shoot anyone who made a false move.

"Alexander, why don't you tell us about your fiancée?" Mama asked.

"Not much to tell, really. Tod, we call her. Her full name is Elizabeth Todhunter Martin. She's an old classmate from high school. I ran into her at a party when I got home last June. And, well, one thing led to another and here we are," Alex hurried on. "We've just become engaged in the last month."

"Well, congratulations," Mama said, and I nodded my mute agreement. "And it's her father that is in the hospital?"

"Yes. He's a stockbroker like my father. He had some back surgery."

"You must bring Tod by to see me. I've never known a stockbroker's daughter," Mama said.

"By all means," I added, "bring her by."

But I was not thinking of stockbrokers, I was thinking of a two-line note tucked in among my granddaddy's cedar box at home. I was thinking of my unanswered letter. And then it occurred to me that Alex must have thought that I was married when I sent that letter admitting my love for him. I flushed at the thought.

The phone rang. It was Granny, double-checking our arrival time at the Raleigh-Durham Airport.

"You won't believe who is here," Mama said, and proceeded to go through a guessing game with Granny.

"No."

"No."

"Well, Mama, you don't have to be so ill about it. It's Alexander. That's right, Alexander Barrons. Well, I don't know. I'll ask him."

Mama covered the receiver. "Alexander, have you been saved or are you still a Presbyterian?"

Alex laughed. "Tell Mrs. Parker hello."

"Mama, he hedged. Said to tell you hello. I think he's not only not a Presbyterian anymore, he's gone completely the other way, a Hindu or Buddhist or something. Put Rosemary on the phone. Just for a second, Mama. I haven't seen her for so long."

Mama covered the receiver again. "She's gone to get her." Then back to the phone.

"Hello, Rosemary. Rosemary, it's Aunt Lilah. Rosemary, what does the dog say? Well, that's exactly right, of course he says that."

Alex looked at me.

Mama made a face. "All right, Mama, all right. Yes, she's fine. Standing right here. Yes, I'll tell her." Mama hung up the phone. "Your grandmother wants you to be sure to get a receipt from the cabdriver tomorrow. Alexander, you haven't met our Rosemary, have you?"

"No, ma'am, I haven't."

Before Mama could launch her elucidation on Rosemary, the door swung open and Tim stepped into the room.

"How are my two magnolias this evening?" He nodded to Alex as he spoke to us.

"Fine. Just fine," Mama said. "You've met Alexander?"

"Earlier in the hall." Tim nodded to Alex again, at once acknowledging and dismissing him in the same breath. "Maggie, you ready?"

"I'd forgotten the time. Mama, will you be okay? Everything ready for tomorrow?" I asked, not wanting to leave yet. I kissed her on the forehead.

"I'm all set. They're springing me out of this joint tomorrow," Mama said to Alex.

Tim walked to the side of Mama's bed not occupied by Alex. "We're going to have to go over to Carbones and then the movies. What do you say we bring you back some Milk Duds? I can bring them in past the nurses."

"Oh my, Timothy," Mama said. "Thank you for the offer, but I believe I'll pass."

Alex stood. "I'd better be going."

Mama touched his arm. "Oh please, do stay a minute more."

"Good to see you, Alex. Take care." What else was there to say? I touched his arm. Tim had me by the elbow again and propelled me across the room and through the door. He pulled it closed behind us, obscuring the hospital room and the two people in it.

CHAPTER 23

The smells of garlic and tomato sauce mixed with the large supper crowd at Carbones. Candles in red globes flickered on tables as trays of heaping pasta came from the kitchen in waves as unceasing as the Atlantic Ocean.

"Maria, you look lovely tonight."

Our waitress blushed and giggled at Tim's compliment.

"Oh, Mr. Lassiter, you're the big talker." Maria looked at me. "Isn't he?"

I studied the menu. "Yes, he is." And I'd heard about all the talk I was interested in.

Tim held his menu in front of his face. "Don't let on, but I'll come back after I ditch her and we'll run away together."

Maria giggled again.

I folded my menu and smiled. Tim had not spoken to me on the way from the hospital. After we'd left my mama's room, I'd pulled my elbow from his hand and told him, "I'm quite capable of moving myself from one place to the other without you using my elbow for a rein." Too late, I tried to soften my tone with a smile, but Tim ignored me until we reached the restaurant.

I gave my menu to Maria. "I'll have spaghetti, please."

Sitting in the midst of all those people, I felt more alone than if I'd been standing in the middle of a plowed field in Sampson

County. My mama had spent the last year and some odd months as the focus of my life. Now she stood on the verge of walking out of the center under her own power and with a lightness in her spirit that I couldn't have believed that long-ago August night.

I realized then that the black hole had offered one comfort. In the black hole, feelings were mute. There was simply a roar in your heart like there was in your head right before you went into a faint. Having come this far, I now faced a choice—nothingness or pain. Alex's arrival had made me understand that the pain could not be walked around. I had tried to ignore the pain in my heart for months. Each passing day that didn't yield a letter on my plate had been cause to pretend that I didn't even know the name Alex Barrons. But now I saw the nature of pain was such that it would come up behind you and drag you down if you had not walked through the fire one day at a time, minute by minute, hour by hour until you reached the boundary and crossed over into understanding.

When our food arrived, Tim spoke. "If I didn't know better, I'd say the mysterious Alex means a lot to you."

The plate of spaghetti in front of me seemed endless. For every bite I took, the noodles grew by two. I felt a gulf between myself and the dark-eyed man who faced me across the table. What my feelings were for Alex had no place at this table.

"Maybe once," I said as I watched the light from the candle dance across the glass around it.

Tim grabbed my arm. "You know how I feel about you."

I looked into his eyes, but the feeling that I saw there made me shiver despite the warm room around us.

"Don't you?" His voice raised slightly. Even in the midst of the lively restaurant, the couple at the next table glanced our way and stopped talking.

I pulled back, but Tim didn't let go. "I don't know, Tim. I'm sure you like me and I like you—"

"Like you? I'm crazy about you," Tim hissed, the anger inside him threatening to boil over and burn us both. "Haven't you heard what I've been saying to you?"

Obviously, Tim hadn't heard what I was saying to him, but in the face of his anger, I didn't try to talk him out of his affection. The pressure on my arm increased.

"Tim, it's been a long day. I feel like I've topped out three fields of tobacco and then set out a summer's garden for the fun of it. You've been kind enough to show me a bit of New York, but you wouldn't say I know my way around New York any more than someone could say that I know you."

"Maggie, what's to know? I've already been looking at hospitals in North Carolina. I could set up a practice there." He let go of my arm.

"Tim, I've got a lot ahead of me. I'm not even finished with school. I've tried very hard to make you see that." I felt tired.

"But I do see, Maggie. Something that you don't. You don't have to finish school. Don't you know what I could do for you? When I finish my residency, the sky's the limit."

I didn't want the sky.

Tim shook his head and spoke in measured tones like I was deaf. "Your mother is going to be fine. You don't have to be Florence Nightingale anymore."

"Tim, this isn't about my mama. This is about me." And for the first time that seemed right. And despite what Tim thought I knew, I knew I couldn't stand one more hour of him trying to browbeat me into agreeing with him. "I'm all done in and I've got more packing to do. I'm sorry, I think we better skip the movie tonight."

He stared across the table at me. "Fine. We can talk about this later."

I ignored him and excused myself to the bathroom, where I breathed in and out, resolved to be rid of Tim's expectations, which weighed on me as heavily as if I'd eaten half a red velvet cake.

We walked back to the Big Apple Hotel in silence. Tim tried to kiss me long and slow, but it ended when I turned aside. "I'm not going to beg, you know," he said, and stomped down the sidewalk, his stiff body outlined by the streetlights.

I leaned against the brick wall of the hotel. The bricks felt cool and distant. I longed for the porch glider with its soothing rhythm. This foreign Mecca I'd come to four weeks earlier offered me no comfort now. Alex's sudden appearance had washed the new and fun from my surroundings. Just as salted meat made you thirsty, his appearance made me long for home.

I climbed the stairs and found my room. One more day, one more day, and I would be home. Home, where I could begin to cry, where I could begin to heal, where I could begin to find peace. Having checked and rechecked my list of things to do, I slept fitfully and dreamed of Alex and Rosemary.

The next morning I dressed carefully in a blue wool suit that never got much use in Canaan. I surveyed the room that I'd called home for the last four weeks and looked under the bed one more time to be sure I'd gotten everything. I picked up my travel case and headed downstairs, said my good-byes, settled my bill, and was told, "Y'all come back now," a half dozen times by the well-intentioned staff of the Big Apple Hotel.

At the door of the Big Apple, Alex appeared. He wore a navy cashmere overcoat that made him seem older.

"Maggie." He held out his hands and waited for me to take them, but I hung on to my travel case with both hands.

"Good morning, Alex."

He lowered his hands. "Maggie, could we go and talk a minute? Maybe get a cup of coffee?" he asked.

"Okay, but I've only got a few minutes." I stopped, uncertain of where to turn.

"That'll be fine." He smiled and used his hand to head me away from the hospital. "I think I saw a shop up at this first corner." With an air of authority and good breeding, he reached for my travel case. "Let me take that."

"I've got it," I said, pulling the case from his reach.

We walked a few steps. "Don't you have class or something?" I hesitated.

"Got one of the other guys to cover it," Alex replied.

We walked on. If I'd ever imagined being in New York with Alex, I'd never imagined it like this. I wrapped my scarf tighter around my neck. Mona had crocheted it for me and sent it in the Christmas box. The corduroy car coat I wore was hard-pressed to keep out the wind that blew down on us.

We ordered coffee at the counter and then found a booth. Behind us sat two men, drinking coffee and studying their newspapers as if the print contained the secret to life. The seats were yellow vinyl, and the yellow tabletop was decorated with a white-petaled plastic daisy stuck precariously in a vase. My skin itched where the wool of my suit rubbed it.

Alex wasted no time coming to the point. "Maggie, the last year and a half melted away when I saw you yesterday." He took my hand. "I talked with your mother and I know how hard things have been on you."

I pulled my hand back. "You know Mama. An afternoon sprinkle becomes Hurricane Hazel by the time she's through with it."

"That may be so, but I know she loves you," Alex said. "I know that I loved you more than I can say. I didn't give up until I saw that newspaper picture."

I heard the past tense very clearly. I felt like I'd been awarded Miss Congeniality in the Miss America contest. I tried to smile accordingly.

Alex continued. "I wanted you to know that. I couldn't let you go away thinking that I wouldn't have come back if I'd known you were free. If I could go back and undo anything, I would."

"Hush," I said. "Nothing can be undone. It wasn't what you did. I'm the one that didn't write you for almost a year. If I'd answered your letters sooner, who knows?"

"But you never answered my letters," Alex said, and patted my hand as if I were his forgetful old aunt.

"I know now it was too late when I sent it, but I still meant everything I wrote you. After I found out about Annie Ruth and the reporter, I had to write."

"Wait." Alex held up his hand. "First of all, I never got a letter, but let's come back to that. What in the world are you talking about with Annie Ruth?" He put his hands back around his coffee cup.

"She's the one that told the others. You know the Lovingoods had a party line—she listened in on your call," I said.

"Wow, that is such a relief." Alex stretched his legs out toward me. "I feel so much better."

I looked down my nose.

"Well, I did tell it, but only to a professional colleague who would have never told otherwise. . . ." His voice trailed off.

I laughed. "It's okay."

"But about the letter," Alex said. "I never got one. I suppose some chap in Oxford read it after I left."

"No, not in England," I said. "Here, I sent it to you here after you got home."

"That's strange," he said.

"Well, I wondered why you didn't write back. Of course, I didn't blame you. With me never answering your letters for so long. Anyway, while I've got you here, let me say how awfully sorry I am." Tears came to my eyes. "It took a long time for me to forgive myself. I couldn't think of you in that dark place where I was."

"Is that what you wrote in the letter?" Alex asked.

"Yes, that and that I loved you." Tears continued down my face.

One of the men in the booth behind us glanced up from his paper, saw my tears, and quickly looked back down.

Alex slid his handkerchief across the table. "And I loved you. It's okay. I understand. It hurt me then, but I understand now. Are you better?"

I wiped my eyes. "Yes. Every step my mama takes makes it better; every word she speaks without bumping it into the next makes it seem like spring. I've got a year more or less to go with my schooling, and then who knows. I've got things I'm thinking about that I've never thought of before."

"Oh, really?" Alex smiled. "Like what?"

"I suppose Mama told you about Rosemary and Mona?"

"She did," he said.

"That baby's done a lot for Mama. But I wonder how many Monas there are in the world. And nobody to do for them. I've thought about some kind of place for girls like Mona. Something like that I could do and still help Granny run the farm." I'd never yet told anyone, including Mama, about this place, this calling, and here I was telling it to Alex.

"That's admirable, but I've seen the way that Tim character looks at you. I wouldn't be surprised if there were wedding bells in your future." Alex leaned back, watching my reaction to his pronouncement.

I felt my face redden. "I'm not discussing that Tim character with you. And I don't believe I've felt the need to comment on the elegant and lovely Tod, so I'll thank you to extend me the same courtesy." I threw his handkerchief back across the table at him.

He laughed. "Okay, okay. I forgot who I'm dealing with here." Then he took my hand. "There's one more thing I wanted to say. I wanted to say thank you for sharing your faith with me. I was quite the cynic to start with, but you never allowed that to sway you. I owe you a lot."

"It wasn't me, Alex, but thank you just the same. And thank you for helping me become more than a sideshow at the circus. But you know, you never sent me a copy of your thesis." I put my hands around the warm coffee cup and held tight.

Alex coughed. "I didn't put you in it."

"Really?"

"No." Alex hesitated and stirred his coffee, looking first out on the street and then at me, with his face so wide open that it almost hurt me to look at him. "There was too much of you in me. I was afraid a dry theoretical tome could never do you justice. And after the whole thing with the newspaper, I felt responsible, and I didn't want to do anything else to hurt you." He quit stirring and put the spoon down on his saucer. "Besides, I was afraid if I did put you in, they'd give you the doctorate instead of me." Alex smiled. "Do you see Her anymore?"

"Not for a long time, and then a few times recently. I'm at peace about it now. 'Every good and perfect gift comes from above.' " I stopped; this felt too much like the summer days of 1960. "Speaking of good and perfect, I wish you and Tod all the best. She sounds wonderful, and I'm sure you'll be very happy." At that moment I knew my mama and my granny had done right by my raising. I could blame no one for my predicament but myself. I was so jealous of Tod I could barely speak her name and yet I carried on.

I reached over and squeezed Alex's hand and we finished our coffee. Two old friends meeting by chance and sharing a few minutes. I thought my face would crack open if we sat there much longer.

Outside the shop, Alex turned. "I'll walk you to the hospital, and then I promised Tod I'd meet her for some wedding nonsense."

"No need. I'll find my way. I'm quite the independent type, you know."

Alex gave me a quick kiss on the cheek. "Yes, I remember. Take care, Maggie." And he walked away from me, turning to wave once, and then disappearing into the sidewalk crowd.

For the second time in the last day, I found a cool brick wall and leaned against it while I cried tears I would never have to cry again. All the unsaid things with Alex spilled out of me in water instead of words. At the hospital, I washed my face in the public restroom downstairs.

I passed Tim in the hall. He leaned against the wall and talked to a student nurse. Never looking my way, he put his hand on her back and rubbed it as if he were polishing a prize medal. He seemed pointed in his need to act as if the continent separated us and he was standing somewhere in California. I thought I might have dreamed him except that he put his hand on the student nurse's elbow and steered her off down the hall and out of my sight.

I found Mama ready to be on her way. It seemed that the entire staff walked us to the hospital foyer while Vicki pushed Mama in the wheelchair and I walked beside her. Tears formed little gullies in Vicki's face powder and there were red blotches on her face and neck. Besides the wheelchair's handles, she clutched a silver comb in one hand and a silver brush in the other that Mama had given her. They stuck out on either side like clipped wings. Despite Vicki's veil of tears, she managed to stop the wheelchair directly in front of the cabdriver.

He tipped his hat. "With all this rigmarole, I thought youse was going to be Princess Grace."

The plane became airborne with a pressure that hurt your ears, and then the bright sun skimmed straight across the clouds and into the cabin of the plane. Looking across the heavens, I prayed for Mama and for the hole in my heart, and I felt that peace was just over the horizon. For beyond the pain, I knew there was a place with the brightness of that morning sun.

Mama took my hand. "Magdalena, we're going home."

CHAPTER 24

Mama's homecoming produced a joy in Mona, I suppose, that could not be contained. Her first words, spoken to my mama, were a simple declaration, "You're home."

Mona's smile took up her whole face. I thought that she had finally broken through that Da Vinci painting and come into her own.

That day, those two words stopped the world. Even Rosemary paused long enough to wrinkle her brow in Mona's direction before continuing to sing "Li Li" and grab for Mama. Rosemary's and India's giggles filled the air.

On the other hand, Mama's return to health came to us slowly, easing up on us and taking us in just as the first rays of the sun suddenly bring forth that great orange ball. As she grew stronger, Mama also grew more beautiful, even with the wrinkles of time beginning to show around her eyes. When the doctor at Duke termed her released, each of us took it in a personal way.

About two weeks after our return home, I went to the tobacco barn refuge. Sitting in the old chair, I lifted my face to the winter sun streaming in through the slats and prayed. *Dear God, help me to accept what I cannot change. Give me a heart bigger than my love for Alex, but not so big that I let my sore feet get in my way again. Amen.* I prayed over and over again, letting the pain come in waves and wash over me while the muted winter sun warmed me.

I pictured a grand church in New York filled with white deep-throated orchids and big satin bows on the pews where Alex's dad and the parents of Elizabeth Todhunter Martin sat. The bride arrived on a June day in a horse-drawn carriage like those around Central Park—only hers had a team of matching horses bedecked with ribbons and flowers like some sort of four-legged flower girls.

It was done.

So there wasn't any use wallowing in it and tormenting myself over it. I let it go, as Granny would say, turned it over to God with my prayer repeated again and again. I'd held it back for a long time, kept it for my own private hurt. And when I finally let go, there was a peace like I hadn't felt in a long time. Not that I wasn't ever sad. Sometimes I'd remember a line from one of Alex's letters and it would bring tears, but after some months, the tears dried.

Sitting there watching a granddaddy longlegs make his way across the barn floor, I realized that a part of who I was I owed to Alex just as he owed a part of himself to me. That was the best I was going to get. That and receiving a calling—a calling to the house by the creek.

There were people who went their whole lives and never got blessed to see things as clearly as I did. And there were people who saw a lot more than I had. But this I knew, that the Almighty was out there, defying us to define Him, surrounding Herself in mystery, and that the greatest joy of this earth was to glimpse the holy in others and in ourselves. To glimpse the extraordinary in the ordinary, to go beyond the flesh that holds us together, and then to end up right back there in it.

I returned to ECTC and worked very hard to catch up on lost time. When a professor grew long-winded, I'd dream of the day when I could build a house for girls like Mona. She continued to amaze us. For the most part, she used her words as Mrs. Letty Surles, the egg lady, spent her money: very carefully. Then something would strike her and she would talk up a blue blaze, chattering on like speech had been hers since time immemorial. Her thrill at everyday things had a way of making me feel that I was the luckiest person on earth. Her sheer delight in the smallest of things reminded me that she took nothing for granted, not her next meal, not her bed at night, not even indoor plumbing. And after our trip to the county fair that March, not even her own safety.

The March night hinted at the spring to come. Standing at the end of the midway, we were waiting for Mama and Rosemary to finish a grape Sno-Kone. Sawdust covered the hard-packed earth just as it had covered the aisle of Brother Oscar's Traveling Tabernacle. The night glittered around us with the colored bulbs of the Ferris wheel and other rides that threatened to shake your insides out.

A man with three front teeth motioned to us from his booth. "Hey, girlies, step right over here and knock over these pins. Knock over three and you win you a fishy to take home. Come on now, you know that little girl wants her a fishy."

A row of goldfish bowls lined the front of his booth, with an orange fish swimming circles in each one.

Rosemary didn't pay the least bit of attention to those goldfish. She was trying to drink the last purple juice from the bottom of her white paper cone. Mama put her hand on it to try and slow her down, but Rosemary pulled away and tipped the soggy cone higher.

My ears still rang from the Tilt-a-Whirl. Mona had never ridden one, so while Mama tended Rosemary, Mona and I swung round and round. We clung to the blue metal bar and were flung this way and that until it felt as if we might fly out into the night past all the blinking bulbs and right across Sampson County like a UFO. Mona, who'd been silent for so long, let out every noise she'd saved during her mute months. When we clanged down the metal steps on the side of the ride, drunk from the motion, I told her, "Mona, I bet Granny heard that all the way at the house."

Mama nodded. "I know now who Rosemary gets her set of lungs from."

The man crooked his finger at us. "Come on, girlies. That baby wants a fishy." I shook my head at him.

It was at that exact moment that Pagan Harris walked by. Actually, Pagan Harris didn't walk, she strolled. She slung her hips with a controlled erotic fury that mesmerized the men who followed in her wake. Like a pack of puppies, they pushed and nipped at one another, jostling for the spot where they could drink from the sweet milk of Pagan's attentions.

Pagan was six feet tall, with about the longest legs known to man. Perfect attributes, I suppose, for a hoochy-koochy dancer. She strolled by us, her spike heels not even leaving an imprint in the sawdust of the midway. She was right even with us when Rosemary sucked the last grape juice from the paper cup.

"More, more," Rosemary screeched. She held her empty cone up to Mama.

Pagan hesitated for a moment, looking down at Rosemary as if Rosemary had startled her from sleep. The group of men behind Pagan squirmed to be on the move again. But she didn't budge; she closed her eyes and appeared to go into a trance like Talullah, the fortune-teller.

Rosemary looked first at Pagan and then at Mama. Unsure what to do, Rosemary began to inch toward Mama.

"It's okay, honey," Mama said, and I wasn't sure if she was talking to Rosemary or to Pagan.

Pagan swayed slightly, jingling with the sound of the bracelets that lined her arms. Then, without a word, she opened her eyes and continued on her way, gliding down the midway with the substance of a cigarette's smoke.

"Good Godlimitey!" One of the men broke from the pack and came toward us.

"Janie," he said. He looked like a young man, but with four days of stubble on his face, and his jet-black hair all matted down under a ball cap, it was hard to say exactly how old he was. He reached an arm out. "Janie."

Mona took in a big breath. Her hand touched my back, and she stiffened, half-crouched behind me as if this were a game of hide-and-seek.

"I'm sorry," I said. "You're mistaken."

My denial only made him more insistent. "No, missy, I'm not." The man staggered a bit and shook his finger at me. "I'd know Janie anywhere. Janie upped and left us. She and that baby was too good for us. Couldn't be living over with all us trashy half-breeds. No sir, she needed to go somewhere special."

"I don't know what you're talking about," I said. "That's not Janie." I reached my arm around to Mona to reassure her as best I could.

The man lurched toward the midway. "Pagan's not interested in me"—he pointed down the midway—"but I can have Janie. Come on, darling. Come to Tom." He stumbled as he turned back to me and tried to step around me. "I knew if we come over this way that sooner or later we'd find her."

"Get on out of here, Tom. I ain't going nowhere with you," Mona said, and clung to my arm.

Mona's voice seemed to spur him on.

"Yes sirree, darling, you are." He was up next to me now—the liquored smell of his breath on my face.

"No, she's not," I said. I pushed him, not hard, only enough to let him know he wasn't coming around me. "I told you, she's not Janie."

Surprised by my resistance, he sat down hard in the sawdust. "Damn it, woman. Don't tell me she ain't Janie. She just called me Tom. She remembers old Tom. She ain't forgot how good I was to her."

"Mona, get the baby," Mama said. Before Mama had finished the sentence, Mona had gathered Rosemary in her arms. Rosemary continued to cry as Mama nudged them back down the midway toward the car.

"Go on," I said. "Go on, I'll meet you at the car."

By this time, the man on the ground had begun to try to stand up, fussing at me as he struggled. When he got to his knees and started to shake his fist at me, I checked to see where Mama and the others were.

As I turned back around, my head popped back with the full-force of his hand coming across it. I stepped back and put up my hand. My face stung with the heat of his palm.

He towered over me now. "I told you to stay out of my business. My business is with Janie."

I put my hands up, but before I could speak, there were two men on either side of him hooking their arms around his.

"Hey now, you leave this girlie here alone." The goldfish man held on to one of Tom's arms and a supervisor from the rides held the other.

"You're drunk and no fitting body to be bothering them ladies," said the ride supervisor, a broad-shouldered foreign-looking fellow who towered over Tom.

"Ma'am, you want me to call the sheriff?"

Mona watched us from the edge of the carnival with her hands clenched at her side. I hesitated. "No, that's all right. I just want him to leave us alone."

"We can take care of that, then." With one hand the supervisor held Tom, and with the other he shooed me on my way. "Go on, ma'am. If you'll go on, we'll get this fellow somewhere he can sober up and get him some manners."

"Thank you," I said. "Thank you so much." I turned, shaking from a danger far enough past to think about. I began to make my way toward Mona as my hand slipped from my cheek. It burned like I'd been in the sun all day. With my every step, people melted away into the lights of the night.

"I'm sorry," Mona said as she studied the ground around her.

"Nothing you could do. Let's go home," I said, and took her arm.

Mama sat in the backseat of the car with Rosemary standing on the seat beside her. As soon as Mama saw us, she opened her door.

"Are you okay?" she asked.

"I'm fine." I opened the car's front door. "What some men will do when they get liquored up," I said as I got in the driver's seat. Mama studied my face in the carnival light but didn't say anything about it. Mona didn't talk anymore the whole way home.

Instead, Mama and I sang "Three Blind Mice" with Rosemary until she tired and drifted off to sleep in Mona's arms.

The next day I went to sit and do some reading for sociology class by the creek. Rosemary and India were at an age where climbing into my lap and playing with the pages of any book I tried to read was an adventure of the greatest magnitude, so solitude for reading was a welcome respite.

We'd been talking in sociology about "families of origin." That made me think of my daddy some. What part of me was he responsible for? Maybe it was something good like my sense of humor or my high grades. Daddy had never made it through school, so it was hard to know. Or maybe it was only my long legs or my deep-set eyes, the same eyes I saw in Rosemary's face.

I sat propped against an oak tree and watched black ants make their way to and from their hill, carrying bits of a grasshopper that had died in the grass. If I put a stick down to try to divert them, they just walked up and down it, until they found a good stepping-off point from where they could make their way over to the hill with their treasure clasped between a set of legs.

What about last night's drunk? What was his family of origin like? Or Pagan Harris's? Or my daddy's, for that matter? We never knew his people.

Out across the newly plowed field I saw a figure that walked steadily in my direction. For a second, I shivered, thinking that somehow I'd conjured up my daddy or the drunk from the carnival. I closed my eyes and opened them as the apparition took human form; I recognized the dark hair and slight figure of Mona. She came silently across the field, then sat down beside me under the tree.

I closed the book. "Everything okay?"

"Just fine. The babies were getting on my nerves, so I asked your mama if I could walk on down to the Open Air Market. I thought you might be over here. You reading?"

She studied the cover of the book when I turned it around. "It's sociology, the study of humans and society—you know, families and groups of people, tribes and things."

"Humph," she said, eyeing the textbook as if it might reach out and grab her.

"Did you know that man?" I asked like I didn't know the answer.

"Sure did," she said. She touched my face. "He left you a mark. He's like that. Pick on a woman."

"He must have been mean to you."

"Yes, he surely was," she said, but offered nothing else.

I didn't press her about Tom. We sat quietly without speaking for a few minutes, and then it came to me to ask her about my daddy. Was my daddy as painful a subject as Tom?

"Mona, what was it like with you and my daddy? Do you think that he loved you and Rosemary?"

She blinked a few times and looked out over the field. "I think your mama loves us."

"But my daddy, what about my daddy?"

She looked me in the eye and then she looked away. "You stood in for me last night. You took what was meant for me, so I'll tell you a thing that you don't know much about. Ever since I sprouted these titties, they's always been boys or men around. The kind that won't leave you alone till they get what they come after. I didn't have a mama and a granny to protect me like you do. My daddy left for weeks at a time, and my mama died when I was a little thing. So no one cared one way or the other. One of the boys that lived down the road was the worst—Tom, his name was. That was him last night.

"Really, your daddy did me a kindness—he kept Tom away from me. And when he hadn't drunk hisself out of his right mind, Butch could be all right."

Overhead a crow cawed and lit on a branch in the tree above us. Mona squinted and shaded her eyes as she looked up. "I don't know about loving Rosemary. He sure did make over her when she was born. He left one day about a week later, going to go somewhere and look for work. Over near Rockingham, he said. Never saw him again. Didn't take long for Tom and the others to figure out he was gone. That's when a man come and told me about Lucy. That's what I called her then. Anyway, he come and told me that Lucy had a sister and that you was rich and we could get us some money from you."

She stopped a moment and put her hand on my arm. "They's nothing else I could think to do. I couldn't let all that with those men start up again. So I came on. I thought I'd get us some money and we'd be all right. But when I saw your house, I thought to myself, Janie, your baby deserves to grow up in a house like that. So I left her there."

I remembered the squirming bundle I'd found on the porch, the patch of dark hair so stark against the dirty pink blanket. Mona had lived a lot of life's good and bad, butted right up next to each other.

"Why'd you come back?" I asked her.

"I wasn't going to. I was going to try to find my aunt that lived in Fayetteville, but I didn't get far. Something told me to go back. I tried to push on, get to the bus station so I could get to Fayetteville, but it was like something just held me back. I didn't have no idea what I was going to say, but then it turned out I didn't have to. Your mama said it all for me."

We laughed.

"I'd think about the words, but I just couldn't get myself to say them. It was like somehow I figured if I talked, I'd wake up from the dream.

"And now to my mind, I'm not Janie anymore, I'm Mona, and Rosemary, why, she will never even think to remember when she was Lucy. Trouble is others do think about it. I was a ninny to think that the only place them men could get me is when I'm dreaming."

Before I could reassure her that she was safe with us, she put her hands on my shoulders like she was laying on hands for prayer. "As for your daddy, he loved me as good as he could."

One Sunday after service, Mr. G. T. Spell asked if he might speak to me. Mr. G.T. had prayed side by side with me and Granny on Sunday mornings past, over more sickly folks than a normal person might see in half their life. As chairman of the deacons, he'd walked the fine line between keeping the church happy and keeping the sideshow mentality of the Sunday-morning crowds penned in enough not to swallow us all.

When I looked at his face, I knew why he was there: the land. Three acres of land that he wished for me to have. The land by the creek that I loved so much.

He edged his hand around the rim of his hat. "Maggie, the Lord's laid it on my heart to give you the land. To be truthful, I planted some of it with corn late last year, but ever stalk wilted over and died. It was like a warning. The Lord had been pressing me about giving you that land, but I wanted corn for the animals." He stopped and fanned for a minute, his hat stirring the air between us. "Showed me real quick who's going to provide for those animals. It's been coming on awhile. I surely tried to ignore it, I did, but the Spirit got ahold of me last night and I wrestled with it all night long. I don't understand it, but Lord knows, it's not ours to understand the moving of the Spirit."

He insisted on taking me over to look. "I know you've seen it a hundred times, but if you'll just go on over there with us, you'll know right what to do with it." It was as if we were in a game of hot potato and the land was the potato that Mr. Spell had to be rid of that Sunday morning or get burned.

Mrs. Spell heaved slightly as she wedged into the front of the two-tone Electra. "Lord, Maggie, G.T. has been up pacing the floor all night long. 'Bout wore me out. I finally told him, 'If letting go of a little piece of land is going to let us get some peace, then, G.T., you'd better get right with God and do it.' That's what I told him. My nerves were shot. Him back and forth and back and forth across the floor all night long. When he wasn't pacing, he was laying in the bed fidgeting like he had ants in his pants."

So off we drove, Mr. Spell, Mrs. Spell, and the three Spell children still of an age to be living at home.

The land I'd gone to so many years was the place I'd pictured in my dreams: the house, oak trees, spring, and all. Mr. Spell nodded when I said I could use it.

"That is sure a relief to me." He wiped his forehead against the early humidity of March.

It was different that April—no voice in my head, no shiver up my spine. Even when the dorm mother, Mrs. Avery, met me at the front door of the dorm one Thursday afternoon, I felt no awareness of doom.

"Maggie, could you step into the parlor?" she asked with a formal air.

I tried to think what I could have done wrong. What was the problem? I hoped it was something as benign as a request to judge the dorm talent show, or possibly one of the girls on the hall had been liviliered by her boyfriend and we were planning to throw her in the fountain with her new charm dangling from her necklace.

Deserted in the afternoon, the front parlor looked spare and remote. Later in the evening, couples would occupy each Queen Anne sofa, their heads bent together as they shared the secrets that cement the two into one. The old upright piano that was used in sing-alongs sat in one corner like a black monument to livelier times.

"Have a seat." Mrs. Avery's navy dress rustled slightly as she indicated a red brocade settee. Only then did I begin to feel something amiss. Something not at all connected to Mrs. Avery or ECTC.

"What is it?" I held my books tightly to me. Before she could respond, I asked, "Is it my mama?"

"No, no. But you must sit down." She waited until I was seated to continue. "I'm afraid there's been an accident. I couldn't quite understand who it was, your sister or your cousin." Mrs. Avery appeared perplexed at this inefficiency on her part. "Sakes alive, I can't remember. But your mama wants you home as quick as you can get there."

My hand found a spot worn smooth in the red brocade. "Would you remember the name? It has to be Mona or Rosemary."

"Mona, that was it. Mona." Mrs. Avery answered like a student who suddenly recalls the answer while standing in front of the whole class. She smoothed the skirt of her dress. "Anyway, I'll take care of excusing your absence with the dean. You get your things together." Martha Truelove walked into the parlor. "Martha has agreed to drive you home."

Martha was a professional worrier who practiced her look of Christian concern with those of like mind over at the Baptist Student Union. She gave me that look now, a mixture of pity and imagined omniscience.

"No, I'm fine. Whatever it is, I can get home." I crossed my legs at the ankle and kept my hands on my books so that they wouldn't shake and cause me to have Martha forced on me like the last pick for dodgeball in grade school.

Martha's look of Christian concern crossed over to one of disappointment. I held my books tighter still. What could have happened to Mona? I saw Tom in my mind, reaching out his hand at the county fair. No, maybe it was all some frightful mistake. A telephone conversation gone haywire—that was it. The lines had been crossed down at the phone company, so Mrs. Avery heard wrong.

"Did my mama say anything else? Anything at all?" I asked. What I wanted to ask her was, Are you sure it was my mama? Do you know her voice? Truly, it was Martha's mother, you just got it confused.

Mrs. Avery looked at the rug. "No, not really, sugar." She shifted in her chair like her girdle was too tight and she was trying to get air.

The road home stretched further and further, as if the hand of God or the North Carolina Department of Transportation had conspired to lengthen it before me. The wheels thumped Mona's name in tandem with the prayer I offered up.

When I pulled into the yard, I knew Mona was dead. Already attached to the wrought-iron front-porch support was a bundle of white mums and white ribbon more telling than if the Angel of Death sat on the front-porch glider, sipping a glass of tea before going to his next appointment.

The small army of people on the front porch parted as I approached. I ran through them and into the house. Mama sat still as a statue on the sitting-room couch while Granny talked in the kitchen with Mr. Matthews, the undertaker.

"Magdalena," was all Mama said before she burst into tears. I held back the hundred questions pounding a wild rhythm in my head and put my arms around her. Granny came in from the kitchen and patted Mama's back.

"Lily, you're going to end up back over at Duke. You've got to quit carrying on or I'm going to have to get Dr. Kincaid to give you some nerve medicine."

Mr. Matthews came over to pat on Mama and me, a professional pat developed from years of being the last whistlestop before heaven or hell. He patted everyone's family the same. For no matter what you were in life, a saint, a drunk, or something in between, by the time Mr. Matthews came around, nothing could be altered. You had written your history in the sands of day-to-day life, thinking it could be wiped over, only to find that it could never be erased. Only grace smoothed that sand again and made it new.

Later Will Atkinson told me all about it. Later I heard the horror, but for now there was only Mama, Granny, Tessie, India, and

Rosemary. The Elliots and Mr. Neb managed the details of life as we mourned our lost sister.

Mr. Matthews laid Mona out in a red velveteen dress that she and Mama had made for the Home Demonstration Club Christmas banquet. The red reminded me of the settee in the dorm's front parlor. No sign of her last-minute brush with madness remained, only the sweet peaceful face of a woman whom life took the words from for so long, only to return them and then take her from us.

Rosemary searched the house in vain, thinking at first that Mona was playing some sort of peekaboo game with her. Mama, Granny, and I took turns rocking Rosemary's soft toddler form at night when she cried, "Mama, Mama."

We buried Mona in the Parker section of the Canaan Free Will Church cemetery. Uncle Peter tried to object, but all his trouble got him was a red face and a bad case of indigestion.

The Home Demonstration Club members and the Ladies' Auxiliary turned out in full force despite the rainy April day. With each gust of wind, they pulled their coats tighter around them. Funny after almost two years you couldn't remember who had ignored Mona in the church aisle those first few months. Whoever had had been won over by the sweet nature of Mona and the gentle erosion of their indignation. Time had moved like a creek through the clay of their self-righteousness, washing it out, and widening their souls to include a mute woman and her half-breed baby.

The spring rain baptized us and mingled with our tears, spilling down onto the fast-fading flowers that covered the casket. I pushed my toe into the mat that shielded us from the red clay and held my mama's hand as we sat in the folding chairs by the open grave. Preacher Liles read Psalm 23.

> *"Yea, though I walk through the valley of the shadow of death,*
> *I will fear no evil: for thou art with me;*
> *thy rod and thy staff, they comfort me.*

Thou preparest a table before me in the presence of mine enemies:
thou anointest my head with oil; my cup runneth over.
Surely goodness and mercy shall follow me all the days of my life:
and I will dwell in the house of the Lord for ever."

He pulled at his lapels with each passage that he spoke as if he'd just put on his jacket and needed to adjust it.

"I know you weren't right ready to let her go, but God had a different plan." He looked at Mama and at Granny and me sitting there and at Rosemary, who moved like a centipede across our laps, bunching herself up and then stretching out into the next lap.

"God's time is not our time."

The story that the Clinton newspaper printed called the men acquaintances. They weren't really acquaintances because they didn't know Mona, they knew Janie. As I read the newspaper story, I remembered the story Mona had told me under the oak tree. It had been Janie's story really, for Janie had died and Mona had been born the day I found her under the oil drum and Mama adopted her. Too soon it had all ended; too soon she was gone. We had not been able to protect her.

I found Will Atkinson fertilizing a strawberry field. He climbed off the tractor when I got out of the car, flinching when he recognized me, like I had raised my hand to slap him.

"I want to know what happened. I've heard everybody else's version, but I want you to tell me."

Will pulled on his shirt collar. "Maggie, you don't want to know."

"Will Atkinson, don't you tell me what I want to know." I folded my arms.

Will pulled at his collar again.

"I'm not letting this go, Will." I settled against the fender of the car, pushing my feet out as if I fully intended to stay awhile. The fender reflected our images standing there, Will in his work pants and me in my blue jeans.

Somewhere inside the bowels of the car there was a short hiss. I didn't move.

After a long moment, Will began his story.

"I came up south from Ivanhoe toward the Open Air Market. I saw this truck beside the road. I couldn't recall seeing it before. The thing is I should have stopped and got out, but I didn't. It was parked right there by that one patch of woods between the Elliots' and the Open Air Market up from Boogey Mack Hill. You know where I'm talking about."

Will paused for me to nod and then continued.

"Anyway, I went up and got me a Pepsi and a Zero bar at the Open Air Market. I decided I'd come on back by and see if that truck was still there. Figured I'd let Clyde and his boys know about it if it was. I drove past and turned around. I was coming back by the truck when she come out from in front of it. She was a sight—her dress was torn and her hair all every which way. There was blood on her face. I put on the brakes, tried to turn the wheel. The truck sorta skittered catty-cornered, and she was clear." He turned his head and coughed dust from his day's work in the field. "Next thing you know, she's laying there in the road.

"I hopped out of the truck, and I heard somebody yelling, 'You're mine, Janie. Damn it, come back here.' Then before I could do another thing—a couple of boys, they say they're from over in Robeson County—they come out of the woods. They took one look at her in the road and me beside her and they jumped in that truck and hightailed it outta there. It come to me to go after them, but the girl needed help. Sheriff caught them boys anyway, so I guess it doesn't matter.

"She moaned and I told her don't move, that I'd get Miss Lilah and Miss Naomi. She said, 'Tom can't get me anymore. Tell Lilah to take care of Rosemary. I love her.' And then she closed her eyes, and as God is my witness, I think she smiled and breathed the most content sigh I've ever heard. Right out there on the road."

Will shuffled from one foot to the other. "I don't think I'll ever forget the look on her face when she came round that truck. Pure madness. It'll haunt me till my dying day. How somebody could be that crazy one minute and that peaceful the next—it threw me for a loop."

"Well, of course she was crazy. They were chasing her," I said. I looked at Will, who stared off in the distance. "What is it, Will?"

He took off his cap and wiped the sweat from his forehead. "Maggie, as I stand before you today, she threw herself in front of my truck. Just as hard as she could. It looked like she was trying her darnedest to get where it would hit her straight on." Will stopped and looked at me as he wiped his eyes. "What she do that for?"

"I don't know, Will. You did the best you could. That's all we can do."

I patted his shoulder and walked over to the car door and tried to imagine a life where the pain was so great that it couldn't be shut off.

All three of the men from Robeson County were let go, including Tom. There would be no earthly justice for Mona. Her legacy on earth would be the house by the spring, and Rosemary.

Granny took Mona's dying words to heart and began the process of Rosemary's adoption for Mama. When Granny met with a stumbling block because we lacked birth certificates and weren't blood kin, she spoke to Neely Lipscomb and he smoothed the way. The two of them formed an uneasy alliance much like Russia and the United States in World War II. Roosevelt and Stalin, Parker and Lipscomb, powers of might and war.

In fact, to say the word *Armageddon* in the same breath as "Granny" and "Neely Lipscomb" would be fitting. The Four Horsemen of the Apocalypse would have turned tail and run had they been in our front room that Wednesday afternoon when I came in from a trip to the Clinton Feed and Seed. In the darkened front room that day, Conquest, War, Famine, and Death would have seemed as inconsequential as those plastic army men you could buy down at the five-and-dime.

I came up on the porch through the gloom of a June thunderstorm. The charcoal clouds poured rain that bounced like five-cent firecrackers off the top of the white Cadillac sitting in front of our house.

Voices, agitated as the dead at the Second Coming, came from inside. I tried to place the voice other than my granny's as I put my umbrella down beside the front-porch glider.

Through the screen, I recognized Mr. Neely Lipscomb with his Porter Wagoner hair combed back and puffed up.

"I understand what you're saying, Mrs. Parker, but surely you understand my position. These things have nothing to do with me."

Mr. Lipscomb sat on the couch with his arm stretched out across its back like he and my granny were discussing crop rotation. His ears had not gotten the message to relax, and they were laid back on his head like a mule does his when he's getting ready to bite.

"That, Mr. Lipscomb, is an out-and-out story, and you know it." Granny looked down her nose at him.

"Maggie." Mr. Lipscomb crossed his legs by resting one foot on his knee. He held on to his white buck as if it were a lucky charm.

"Good afternoon," I said—though it didn't look like a very good afternoon at all.

Granny never even looked my way. "Don't make me come after you."

I tried to imagine what she meant. And the mayor's answer was stranger still.

"Come after me if you like. It'll never go anywhere." Mr. Lipscomb took his hat from the couch beside him and stood up. He tried to remain indifferent looking, but his ears were still laid back on his head.

"It'll go far enough," Granny said, and stood with such a look in her eyes that I thought I might have to get between them.

"I'm not discussing this anymore in front of your granddaughter. If I agree to finish this, to get this baby mess straightened out, I don't ever expect to hear about it again." The mayor crossed to the door and stood there, gathering as much of his office's grandeur as he could. "I want your word on it."

"Well, if my word's as good as yours, there's not much point to that. But all I ever asked is that you see this baby gets to where she rightfully belongs. And that you help me make sure no one but the good Lord can take her away from us. And to tell you the truth, I passed asking a long time ago and went on to telling." Granny straightened, her face as strong and radiant as any archangel.

Backed down by her presence, Neely Lipscomb moved toward me, but Granny was there with her hand on my arm before he got two steps toward me. The sweet almond smell of her Jergens lotion surrounded us.

Neely Lipscomb stopped and then turned back to the door. "I'll call you as soon as I hear something." He jammed his hat on his head and let the screen door close behind him with a bang.

I turned to Granny. "What in the world, Granny? Why is he helping us?"

"It's simple. It was his own neck on the line," Granny said, and picked up a copy of *The Southern Planter.* With her steadiness, you would have imagined that she'd just invited the mayor for Sunday dinner.

"I don't understand that," I said, and brushed the spot on the couch that the mayor had occupied before I sat down.

"Well, while you and your mama were in New York, Neb and I found out, from some of those ne'er-do-wells down at that juke joint on old 51, that India's daddy and Mr. Neely Lipscomb were one and the same. Neb never did think that India's mama drowning like that was any accident, but there was no way to prove different. And even if we could, Neb and I agreed that Neely'd never pay for it in a court of law." Granny opened her magazine. "What with her being colored and him being white. Sad to say, but that's the truth."

"So that's why he came marching in the yard with that bunch of cowards." It made sense to me now. "Trying to keep that baby as far away from us as he could."

"Yes, that's right. So I figured the good Lord would fix it in the end, but in the meantime, I'd find a way for that Negro girl's death to mean something one day. And when Mona died the way she did and Rosemary needed a home where there wasn't a doubt she'd stay, that seemed like as good a time as any to help Neely Lipscomb do a little good."

"Granny, you never cease to amaze me." I marveled at her resolve.

She opened her magazine and began to read. "Don't count this old girl out yet."

"No, ma'am, I wouldn't dream of it."

And so it was that each of us vowed to make Mona's life count for something.

CHAPTER 25

I finished my degree in the next year, commuting to ECTC during the week and coming home on weekends to help Granny with the farm.

I came home after exams in early December. I'd had to add an extra semester because of the time I'd spent with Mama in the hospital. Rosemary now reigned supreme in the house on Canaan Church Road. Somehow Granny had seen fit to make sure that my raising gave me character, but Rosemary was quite a different story. With her angel's face surrounded by dark curls, it was hard to begrudge her all the pacifying that she got even from Granny.

Christmas Eve I visited Mona's grave as I often did in the months that followed her death. In the damp morning air, I placed a poinsettia in front of her tombstone. I sat, leaned up against the cool stone, and talked to her.

"We're going to start on the house next spring. People have been giving money at the church, and last week an anonymous donor gave one thousand dollars. Granny and Mama wouldn't tell me who it was, but I suspected that it was Granny prodding Neely Lipscomb's guilty conscience.

"I've been using graph paper to lay out the rooms. I think you'd like it. Mama's already picking out fabric for curtains and all. We won't even pour a foundation for three or four months, but you know that won't stop Mama."

I straightened the bow on the poinsettia I'd brought. The green foil that wrapped around the poinsettia's pot caught the sunlight and made me blink. "Rosemary's getting so big. Mama made her this beautiful red velvet dress with a pinafore to wear over it. I helped her smock the pinafore. I sure wished you were here for that. Every time that needle pricked my finger, I thought how you were so much better at that than me. Even with a thimble I managed to prick myself, don't ask me how."

I ran my thumb over the sore spot on my index finger. In the stillness of the cemetery, I thought of how Mona had changed our lives. "You know, Mona, some days I think you were our angel sent to us, God's abundance breaking forth into this world of sorrow. Not at first, mind you; at first I didn't think much of you. I tolerated you all right for my mama, but I didn't see the holiness that was right there in front of my eyes. Maybe because you reminded me of the brokenness of my daddy. And then you helped me to glimpse the mystery, the bond you shared with my mama, the baby you brought who saw all things new—all those things helped me experience becoming one with *the beyond being and knowing* again." I sat in the morning sun grateful for Mona's time with us, missing her with a sadness that was as real as the pricked spot I rubbed on my finger. I wiped tears from my eyes.

"It's funny how I let my worries over my daddy come between me and so much. I was so busy worrying over not being like him or loving anybody like him that I couldn't see the people standing right next to me. You, some, and Alex—I wished you'd have known Alex. By the time I'd come to believe in his love, I missed it. Somebody once said we're always striving for some far-off thing and trampling beautiful fragrant violets as we go. Anyway, I wished you'd known him." I stretched out my leg and sat for a moment, still as the stone behind my back.

"We've had the worst time with Rosemary pulling the tinsel off the tree. She thinks it's a game now. She drops the pieces behind her like she's Gretel, marking her path in the woods. The house is filled with her silvery paths.

"And Norma's getting bigger and bigger. John says he thinks she's having twins. Imagine Norma a mama." I wondered if helping to raise Rosemary was the closest I'd come to being a mama. "Uncle Peter's church split over gifts of the Spirit, really over speaking in tongues. Uncle Peter's in with the crowd that got the church building. Been a lot of stress on him and Aunt Willowdean. James's wife told us that the last snow Aunt Willowdean went out and made snow angels in the yard with some of her grandchildren. Mama said she wished the church had split a long time ago if that meant Aunt Willowdean was going to have a little fun.

"I don't know who'll have the most fun this Christmas—Rosemary, or Granny, Mama, and me. Granny got Rosemary one of those Sno-Kone machines. It's made to look like a snowman. You put ice in the top and turn the crank and it crushes the ice. Ice comes flying out the snowman's stomach. It came with flavor juice and those little paper cones like you get at the state fair. I told Granny Rosemary was too young for it. But you know Granny. You might as well spit in the wind. Never thought I'd see the day that she'd make over a baby so. Mama got Rosemary a baby doll, and I got her her own table and chairs to sit on. So she can color pictures and have tea parties when she gets a little older. Tonight when she hangs up her stocking, I wish you'd be there to help her. It's one of Granddaddy's old socks. Since we don't have a mantel, she'll just put it on the chair.

"I've got to go now. Mama's making these Christmas tree cookies. She's using a cookie press and she wants me to help her." I stood and put my hand on the granite stone; its edge felt rough and cold. "I'll give Rosemary an extra kiss for you."

That Christmas morning we rose early, creeping into Rosemary's room.

"Rosemary," Mama called softly, "Rosemary, rise and shine."

Rosemary rolled over and stretched, scratching her toddler's round belly through the snaps of her pajamas. She pushed her dark curls from her eyes and stretched again, stopping when she became aware of the three of us standing there.

"Santa," Mama said, and clapped her hands. "Remember? Santa came last night."

Rosemary rubbed her eyes and then turned on her stomach, backed off the bed, and padded into the sitting room. Her plastic pajama-feet bottoms scuffed the floor.

"Look, Rosemary, it's a snowman." Granny practically tore open the box herself. Rosemary peered inside as Granny pulled the snowman from the box. Granny happily turned the crank on his back. "Look at that, Rosemary!"

Rosemary ignored the snowman and reached in the box to pull out the paper cones, dropping them on the floor when she caught sight of the new baby doll.

She clasped the baby to her. "Baby, my baby," she said, then poked its eyes, which opened and shut as she turned the baby up and down. In short order, she carried her baby doll with her arm wrapped around its neck and climbed on and off her new chair. When she was safely on, she would sit for a minute, the conquering warrior, and then climb down to do it all again.

"Are you feeding the baby?" Mama asked, and offered her the play bottle that came with the baby doll.

"No," Rosemary said, pushing the bottle back at Mama with her chubby hand. She climbed down off the chair and scuffed across the floor, pulling one of the white cone papers from the Sno-Kone machine box and putting it to the baby's lips.

"Mmm, yummy," she said, smacking her lips as if she'd forgotten her dentures.

We laughed. "She's sharp as a tack, that one is," Granny said. She fingered the cable sweater Mama had knitted for her.

"Granny, that color blue sure looks nice on you," I said.

"Pshaw," she answered, but I noticed her later looking at her reflection in the hall mirror.

"Apple." Rosemary spied her Christmas stocking full of fruits and nuts and dropped the baby long enough to go pull a red apple from the top. Instead of biting it, she rolled it across the floor.

"Smart or no, I think you've hit your limit, little girl," Granny said, swooping the fruit up and putting it out of Rosemary's reach.

Rosemary scowled.

"You'd better go get your baby," Mama said. "Poor thing's on the floor."

I peeled a tangerine and let the smell, sweet and bright orange, bring back many Christmases to me.

"Some, peas. Some, peas." Rosemary stood in front of me with her chubby hand extended.

"What nice manners you have," I said, and loosened a section to hand to her. She took it and held it as gingerly as if it were a raw egg. After a second, she walked to her new table, laid the tangerine slice down, and then climbed into the chair, sitting up straight and tall before she ate the fruit.

"Well, I'd better start breakfast or they'll be a lot of aching stomachs around here," Granny said.

Soon the salty smell of country ham and redeye gravy filled the air. Rosemary climbed in and out of Mama's lap with her baby doll while Mama tried to read the directions to the new Instamatic that Granny bought her. I set the table using the special Christmas napkins that Mama had made from a remnant she'd found at the five-and-dime. She'd sewn green rickrack around the edges of the red fabric.

"Eggs are hot," Granny called.

Rosemary sat at her table. "Eggs, eggs, eggs," she sang.

I pulled her high chair up to the kitchen table. "Come on, Granny says it's ready."

She shook her head and patted the table in front of her.

"No, ma'am, we're all going to eat at the big table." I patted the stool. "You're all set. Quick, before the eggs get cold."

She sat looking at me. "No."

Mama got up from the couch. "Rosemary, come get in the

high chair and let Lilah take your picture." Mama posed with one hand behind her head for Rosemary.

"No," Rosemary said.

"Tell you what." I grabbed up one of her new chairs and moved it beside her stool. "Let's move your baby over here and let her eat beside you."

There was a howl of protest from the pajamaed toddler. She only howled louder as I picked her baby up and placed her in the little chair. Surely God had planned for two-year-olds to be small enough that you could move them from place to place without necessarily having their permission. I plopped Rosemary into the high chair.

"Smile for me," Mama called, and a flash of light popped around us.

Rosemary stopped crying, eyeing Mama suspiciously.

"I hate to take off this coat," Mama said, twirling one more time in the London Fog coat I'd bought her before she laid it carefully across the couch and came into the kitchen.

Granny blessed the food. "Lord, thank you again for the gift of your Son, and for this glorious Christmas morning."

Rosemary clanked her fork against her plate. I opened one eye to find her peeking back at me. She giggled.

"Bless all those saints who've gone before us. We thank you for the plenty you've given us. Help us to be mindful of it. Amen."

Rosemary giggled again and Mama joined in. "You silly girl."

"Look, your baby loves her new chair." I pretended to feed the baby doll grits. Then I buttered a biscuit and put some strawberry preserves on it for Rosemary. Before long she wore red jelly spread around her mouth like a clown's made-up smile.

"I wonder if we have enough dessert. I might better make a batch of brownies this morning," Mama said. In the early afternoon, the Parkers and the various combinations made when they had struck up with members of the outside world would arrive with babies and children still caught up in the heat of Christmas.

"What we don't have, they don't need," Granny said. Rosemary squirmed in her high chair, eager to get down and get back to her own table.

After breakfast, I put on my jeans and an ECTC sweatshirt to go and feed the chickens. They gathered around me, unaware of the day's significance, clucking loudly as if to scold me for waiting so late to feed them.

Bucket in hand, I latched the gate behind me. The yard and fields were brown with winter. I imagined if I could see down to the church and the cemetery how red the poinsettia would look on Mona's grave. It would stand out from the pale gray of her headstone, its green foil calling us to remember, reminding me of what a blessing it was to clean the grits from the chubby cheeks of a toddler even as her pudgy fingers pushed me away.

Off in the distance I heard a car. It was too early for company. I thought that maybe Norma and John had decided to surprise us. Norma was in her last months and sleep came so hard then anyway.

I put the bucket down and headed to the house, brushing bits of chicken feed from my jeans. A cloud of dust began to form at the edge of the road. In short order, a car appeared. Not Norma and John's Chevrolet, but a low green car. The car that my mama had once called the car of a true adventurer.

The car bumped slowly along the road and into the yard. A solitary figure emerged from the car. What was he doing here? And where was Tod?

I brushed harder at the kernels on my jeans and then pushed my hand up to try to tuck stray strands of hair into my ponytail.

The driver moved toward me with steps that seemed deliberate and sure.

"Maggie."

By the time he said my name, I could reach up and touch his face. All this time, and here he stood.

"Merry Christmas, Alex."

Alex took my hands. I kept trying to understand, fitting pieces in and out of the story as if I were working a jigsaw puzzle. *He was just passing through*—no. *He'd left Tod in Fayetteville, she'd be here any minute*—no. *He'd decided to do postgraduate work at Duke*—no.

"Merry Christmas to you. Magdalena Davidson, I love you like I've never loved anyone. Will you marry me?" He just spit out the words as if he was afraid that if he didn't run them all together, he'd never get to say them.

He touched my mouth. "Before you speak, I want you to know I won't take no for an answer. I'll camp out in this front yard. I'll wait you out this time."

I shook my head, but before I could say anything, he continued. "Maggie, I've thought about it and there's no reason we can't be together. I've written your mama and she says you're not seeing anyone else. I don't know what a guy's got to do to get you to consider him, but I'm ready to figure that out. I've been talking to a guy in Chapel Hill about a teaching position. I could commute three days a week and make enough for us to live on. I do have a small trust from my mother's family, enough to give us a nice start."

I started to speak. He reached up and put his finger on my lips.

"And before you say anything—while I've been thinking, I've also been feeling. The love I feel for you brings depth and meaning to my life. Whether we are together or not, I've told my father I'm not going to be a part of the firm. I'm going to do something that makes me part of President Kennedy's New Frontier, teaching or working in some way that makes a difference. My calling isn't like yours; it didn't come to me in a vision. It crept up on me and now it won't let go of me. And you know what you say about people who aren't living their callings . . ." He made a face. "They're just walking in their sleep."

I pulled my hands away from his and put them on my hips like I had seen Granny do since Eve bit the apple. "Alex, are you going to let me talk or am I supposed to stand here in the yard like I'm some prop in a play you're putting on?"

He frowned. "Well, I just wanted to get it all out. I mean, Maggie, what's a guy got to do? I'm serious, I'll camp out in the front yard."

"You'll do no such thing." I took his hands in mine. "Because my answer is yes. But not because you'd sit out here and moon for me. Because I love you, Alexander Barrons. I don't have any speeches to prove it, I just know it like you know when it's time for a berry to come off the vine. How it gets ready and why it is is a mystery to me. But this last year I've understood in a new way how short life can be and how every moment counts."

His put his arms around me, secure and warm. My face rested against his shoulder, and I breathed the scent of him. It was a scent that drew me in, not one that sent me skittering like a deer catching the whiff of danger.

"What about Tod?" I asked.

"I tried for a year. I kept thinking of reasons to postpone the wedding and she accepted every one of them. She's a wonderful girl, and I finally decided she deserved somebody that loved her like I never could. My father had me lined up to start in the firm after the first of the year, but after the hospital I just couldn't. After I saw you in New York, my head and heart were in two different places. I couldn't get you out of my heart."

He drew me to him again and kissed me.

"Are you sure?" I asked. "We're pretty quiet compared to New York."

"Quiet, never. Different, yes, but a different that I love."

"And I imagine your daddy's not going to be interested in leaving you the family firm." I pushed back from his chest.

"I found out that my father is the one who kept your letter from me. He and I have come to terms with the fact that I'm going to live my own life. Besides, you know the old Scripture, 'Blessed are those who do not inherit the family firm, for they shall have their own life full of joy.' "

I laughed. "I believe you and Granny went to the same Scripture-quoting school."

He kissed me again. "I've never seen anyone more determined to try and talk somebody out of loving her than you are."

"What my mama hasn't taught me, my granny has, just being practical."

"There's nothing practical about love," Alex said.

"No, there's not," I agreed, and kissed him.

Then Granny, Mama, and Rosemary surrounded us.

Mama clapped her hands together. "Our anonymous donor has arrived."

"You," I said, stepping back and seeing Alex again with fresh eyes.

"Well"—he flushed—"your mother and I talked several times."

Then everyone talked at once until finally Granny declared, "There's no need to stand out here with the door wide open like we were raised in a barn. Let's go in the house, for goodness' sakes."

Abraham, hobbled with age, came up, and Rosemary chased off after him with the look on her face that usually preceded a tail-pulling. I ran after her as Mama and Granny escorted Alex into the house.

I scooped Rosemary into my arms and she squealed. I kissed her tummy and she giggled. Mama said something to the group heading into the house, and they all laughed. Mama's soprano, Granny's alto, and Alex's baritone laugh blended together with Rosemary's giggle. Alex's baritone added a dimension that we'd missed.

And in the midst of their laughter, I heard a still, small Voice.

ABOUT THE AUTHOR

Brenda Jernigan's short fiction has been published in *The Crescent Review, The North Carolina Literary Review,* and elsewhere. She has received numerous awards, including the Rupert Hughes Award for Distinguished Writing. Ms. Jernigan lives in Raleigh, North Carolina, with her two children.